Walter Tevis

THE KING IS DEAD

Walter Tevis is the author of *The Hustler, The Man Who Fell to Earth, Mockingbird, The Steps of the Sun, The Queen's Gambit, The Color of Money,* and the short story collection *Far from Home. The Man Who Fell to Earth* was the basis for a major motion picture and the inspiration for a streaming series on Showtime. *The Hustler* and *The Color of Money* were also adapted for film, and *The Queen's Gambit* was the basis for a Netflix series. Tevis died in 1984.

Praise for Walter Tevis

"Tevis makes you care about his quirky characters. . . . [He] wrote like a dream, and he told some wonderful stories." —*Los Angeles Times*

"There is a rocking, hypnotic peacefulness in the way [Tevis] puts words together." —*The Daily Beast*

"Tevis has a gift for vivid characterization and propulsive narratives. . . . His style is direct and efficient, never calling attention to itself; yet it grows in power through the course of a novel by its very naturalness." —Tobias Wolff

"[Tevis's] work is unique, with that element of infinite rereadability Nabokov held as the hallmark of great literature. Like his characters . . . Tevis's work will endure." —*Fantasy & Science Fiction*

"With intense grace, Tevis finds the art to describe art." —*The Village Voice*

"Tevis's characters, no matter how fantastic or far-fetched, whether they are gamblers or aliens, always feel true. At times, reality has even bent toward his fictions, rather than the other way around. . . . His fiction feels as true as ever." —The Ringer

Also by Walter Tevis

THE KING
IS DEAD

THE KING
IS DEAD

Stories

Walter Tevis

Introduction by Kevin Brockmeier

VINTAGE BOOKS

A Division of Penguin Random House LLC
New York

A VINTAGE BOOKS ORIGINAL 2023

The Cataloging-in-Publication Data
is available at the Library of Congress.

Vintage Books Trade Paperback ISBN: 978-0-593-46752-7
eBook ISBN: 978-0-593-46753-4

vintagebooks.com

Printed in the United States of America
10 9 8 7 6 5 4 3 2 1

CONTENTS

PUBLISHER'S NOTE

Dear Reader,

This collection marks the first time all of Walter Tevis's stories have appeared together in a single print volume. While Tevis is known in part for his novels that went on to inspire numerous film and television adaptations, he was also a prolific writer of short stories. In the pages of these stories, Tevis grapples with many of the themes and motifs that also appear in *The Hustler*, *The Queen's Gambit*, and *The Man Who Fell to Earth*.

While these stories are outstanding works of literature, they are also firmly of the time and place in which they were written. They may contain outdated cultural representations and language. We present these stories as originally published. We hope that you enjoy discovering, or rediscovering, them.

Sincerely,
The Publisher

THE KING IS DEAD: INTRODUCTION

Kevin Brockmeier

The easiest way to tell the difference between a mainstream author, a cult author, and one of the many unsung shadow figures of literature is to stand in front of an audience of readers and say their name. Mention a mainstream author—an E. M. Forster, a Joan Didion, or a Gabriel García Márquez—and the faces you gaze out on will show a gloss of tranquil education: they took that test long ago and they've already passed it. Mention a shadow figure—a Sandra Petrignani or a Michal Ajvaz—and a different kind of serenity will greet you, the serenity not of recognition but of dispassion, like the stillness of a lake onto which a petal has fallen: maybe the water will absorb the petal, maybe the water will allow it to go floating by, but either way it will leave barely a dimple behind it. Mention a cult author—a Russell Hoban or a Dino Buzzati, a Susanna Clarke or a Clarice Lispector—and out of a hundred faces, five or ten will immediately light up, as if, by invoking exactly the right name, you have tripped a lock, and the door has opened, and the glowing room has been revealed.

Walter Tevis is a cult author. For as long as I've been reading him, whenever I have mentioned his name, it has opened those glowing rooms to me—never more than a few of them, but always that same few. This has remained the case as his books have slipped into and out of print, as awareness of them has swelled and receded, and as various production companies have optioned and occasionally realized their stories for screens large and small. I could not have been happier when, following the recent success of *The Queen's Gambit* miniseries, the Tevis novel on which it was based reached the bestseller lists nearly forty years after it was written, but I suspect that most of the readers who sought it out did so to reexperience the TV show rather than to encounter the novel in its original form, as an independent work of art. At any rate, the attention the series garnered did not seem to alter his cult status.

In fact, you would struggle to name another author whose work has been at once so honored and so overshadowed by its screen adaptations. As of 2023, four of Tevis's six novels have been translated to film or television, with a fifth, *Mockingbird*, reportedly on the way. Some of those adaptations have kept faith with his books, while others have jettisoned much of what originally made his fiction distinct—the emotional tones, the character shadings, the narrative architecture—in favor of their own designs. All but one of them, though, have been dynamically and artfully executed, blessed with directors who brought them to life with obvious passion and skill. (The exception? The unsold 1987 feature-length TV pilot for *The Man Who Fell to Earth*, which could also, I suppose, though in a much different way, be said to have executed its material dynamically, but is worth seeking out if you've ever wanted to observe an entire cast full of actors wondering nothing so much as what they should do with their hands.) It is a testament to the imaginative power of Tevis's fiction that nearly all the films and television series it has engendered stand as icons—and not only that, but icons of their own very different cinematic ages. I can't help thinking, though, that in a more just world, the aching, elegant, intimate, catalyzing books that inspired *The Hustler* and *The Color of Money*, *The Man Who Fell to Earth* and *The Queen's Gambit*, would be as well known page by page as their offspring are image by image.

Instead, Tevis remains a cult author. His devotees, though few, continue to find one another. When we do, the conversation often turns to that evergreen question—which novel is his best. The only one I've never heard anyone champion is *The Color of Money*, not for any faults it might possess but because it's a sequel to *The Hustler*, and if you admire Fast Eddie Felson and Minnesota Fats, you're likelier to envision them in the poolrooms of the 1950s, all dry browns and yellows, than the tournament halls of the 1980s, all cool blues and whites. My own candidate? That would be *The Man Who Fell to Earth*, which is not only the Tevis book I love best but, when it comes down to it, my single favorite science fiction novel by anybody. Usually, when I press it into the hands of people who don't already know it—or know it only from its David Bowie (or, more recently, its Chiwetel Ejiofor) iteration—I tell them it's the novel Graham Greene might have written if he had turned his hand to science fiction: a swift, graceful, surpassingly absorbing parable soaked in frailty and loneliness about an alien who discovers his humanity and thereby loses his soul. I may or may not go on to confess something more personal:

that *The Man Who Fell to Earth* is a sort of totem book for me, one of two novels, along with Italo Calvino's *The Baron in the Trees*, that are absolutely essential to me, in part because they strike what I think of as the ideal balance between brevity and depth, escape and immersion, and fantasy and nuanced human feeling, but also because I regard them as emblems of my own character. Calvino's book represents me as I feel to myself when I am standing in the brightness of the world; Tevis's, as I feel when I am standing in its darkness; each the obverse of the other and so both equally necessary.

I've heard other readers with a taste for science fiction in its more dystopian or refractory modes make the case for *Mockingbird* or *The Steps of the Sun*, while readers more partial to realism—and specifically the sugar rushes and stratagems of competition—have argued that his real masterpiece is *The Hustler* or *The Queen's Gambit*. Each and every one of these books is lively and gripping, dexterous, brisk without seeming slight; thrilling, in a word, if not precisely thrillers. And each and every one of them possesses a bruised and complex wisdom regarding addiction, failure, and redemption—Tevis's three great themes. This is why those of us who admire his books find it is so invigorating to spar over them: which is the most accomplished is a question with no wrong answer. (*The Man Who Fell to Earth* is the rightest, though.)

Tevis himself planted a flag for his short stories, particularly the seven-story sequence of perverse, tormented, daringly revealing Freudian science fiction fables you will find at the end of this book. In a 1980 interview for *The Courier-Journal*, conducted shortly before his collection *Far from Home* was published, he referred to these late stories as "the most important thing in my work in a long, long time. It is what I consider to be a new kind of science fiction; it's used almost entirely for a kind of psychoanalytic mythmaking. It's about my Oedipus complex and my narcissism and a lot of things of that sort. I feel the stories are very, very good. I feel that they are some of the best things I have ever written. They are close to home in that they are meant to deal with the feelings that I find in myself most powerfully and most affecting and most unresolved."

Not long after, in a radio interview he recorded for KPFA in Berkeley, California, he amplified this claim: "A lot of what opened up for me in writing these stories is my realization that I can use this psychological material in a science fiction context and it works extremely well for me. I feel very comfortable doing it that way. Whereas, if I were to write confessionally or autobiographically, it would be a mess."

I find this a slightly misleading assertion, since whatever strange or fantastic trappings they might deploy—purgatory or time dilation, paraphysics or metempsychosis—these late stories, beginning with "Rent Control" and ending with "Sitting in Limbo," *are* confessional, *are* autobiographical. It's nearly impossible not to perceive the intimacies of Tevis's own experience in them, "a kind of self-dredging," as James Sallis observed in *Fantasy & Science Fiction*, "that doesn't always imply salvage, and that can prove as wrenching to the reader as to writer." Otherwise, though, I agree with Tevis's assessment: the final short stories he wrote, so perilous and so cutting, stand with the very best of his work. Most memorable among them has to be his disturbing psychodynamic resurrection diptych "A Visit from Mother" and "Daddy," stories which, all these years later, still register as shockingly transgressive. "All these years later," I say, and I'm not sure why, since I'm not convinced, not at all, that our moment is more liberated or less hidebound than his was. It's noteworthy that these two stories, along with "Sitting in Limbo," which reads as a sort of coda to the pair, adopting the same character set and the same obsessions but shuffling all the players a seat to the left, are the only stories Tevis ever wrote that were not also published in a magazine. They're disturbing enough—and authentically disturbing, not fashionably disturbing—that I suspect they would have just as much difficulty finding an accepting editor today.

When he was working in his speculative mode, Tevis stood with one foot in the golden age of science fiction, one foot in the new wave. For this reason, it was a delight to me when I discovered that Theodore Sturgeon, a writer I'm not alone in regarding as the finest of the golden age, admired these particular stories every bit as much as I do. In a review for the May 1981 issue of *The Twilight Zone Magazine*, he wrote that "'A Visit from Mother' and 'Daddy'—which, together, make one longer story—are truly shattering; never have I seen so powerful a description of the admixture of love and guilt, hatred and pathos evoked by one's feelings for parents. The author of *Mockingbird* and *The Man Who Fell to Earth* affects me more than most people I have personally met."

(J. G. Ballard, in my estimation the finest writer of the new wave, seems not to have read Tevis, or at least not to have spoken about his work publicly. He did, however, say that he considered the Nicolas Roeg/David Bowie adaptation of *The Man Who Fell to Earth* "a brave failure, the accent on 'brave' and not the 'failure'" and the conduct of its hero "modishly psychotic." Tevis himself had mixed feelings about the movie. "I give it a C-plus," he once offered, though he believed that Bowie was flawlessly cast. "He's a very fine man. I liked him a lot. Thank

God. Because on the American edition of the book, which came out with the movie, David Bowie's name on the cover is about twice as big as mine, and it looks like he wrote it. If I had hated his guts, it would have been terribly hard to take.")

Many of the stories in *The King Is Dead* are stamped with difficulties that Tevis knew firsthand: with gambling and illness, tranquilizers and alcohol, with the fossil records of childhood neglect, with misspent love and withheld affection—all the substitutes, as he had it, people find for living their lives. Others are lighter in spirit and unfold with either a frank and surprising sweetness or a comically sharp mousetrap wickedness. The stories he wrote came in roughly four varieties, which arrived in overlapping waves, largely during the late 1950s and the late 1970s. There were the stories of gamesmanship, mostly but not always about pool hustling, material which in his hands could be as taut and suspenseful as combat and espionage. The diamonds among them are "The King Is Dead," which is the most resolute of the two chess stories in this book, and "The Hustler," which reads as (and is) a preparatory gesture for the novel of the same title. In the earliest of these stories, the tension derives from watching characters who teeter right on the knife's edge of victory fall just short of it. Later in Tevis's writing life, though, there was a shift away from an interest in the crises of defeat toward an interest in the crises of success. Where once the drama in his stories of gamesmanship was all about seeing the heroes lose, suddenly the drama does not prevent the heroes from winning.

Alongside his pool hustling stories came his early science fiction stories, often about feats of speculative engineering—and not merely speculative, but in some cases, as Isaac Asimov told Tevis, "impossible," violating as they do the basic laws of thermodynamics. Simple "what-if" stories such as these have fallen out of style in science fiction, but Tevis's exhibit a boyish, conjectural, lab-coat-and-beaker quality that is superbly entertaining, all turnabout and charm, like the best episodes of *The Twilight Zone* or *The Outer Limits*. The most beguiling of them are perhaps "The Ifth of Oofth," "The Big Bounce," and "The Other End of the Line." In his *Courier-Journal* interview, he says of these early science fiction stories that they make use of his "chess-playing mentality. I'm a very good chess player and the stories make ideas click along kinda neatly and come out neatly at the end." One such story, "Operation Gold Brick," contains an image that offers a nice little this-side/that-side depiction of Tevis's aesthetic impulses: "The birds and trees and suchlike had, of course, been obliterated; but they had been beginning to pall on the visitors anyway; and now the area had something of the look of a neo-Surrealist landscape, or a Japanese garden." From obliteration, in the world of Tevis's fiction, comes not chaos but differing forms of order: neo-Surrealist landscapes and Japanese gardens. And these, roughly speaking, are the two tendencies of his bibliography. On one side are his neo-Surrealist landscape books, *Mockingbird* and *The Steps of the Sun*, which bring a dreamlike strangeness into being, and on the other are his Japanese garden books, *The Queen's Gambit*, *The Hustler*, and *The Color of Money*, which bring a dreamlike spruceness into being. This division is challenged by *The Man Who Fell to Earth* because it does both.

Sequining the early period of Tevis's career are a half dozen tales of courtship and marriage, what he called "magazine stories," published in venues such as *Redbook* and *Cosmopolitan*. The most transporting of them, to my mind, are also the most cinematic: the patient white-knuckler "A Short Ride in the

Dark" and the affable, lightly comic "Gentle Is the Gunman"—mannerly versions of, respectively, the careening car scene and the Old West showdown scene, like the mildest possible glosses on *The French Connection* and *Gunfight at the O.K. Corral.* (Also noteworthy is "The Man from Budapest," which was adapted into a pretty good episode of *The Loretta Young Show.*) To the end of his career, Tevis maintained his affection for these stories, and though his subsequent work would pursue darker avenues, you will not perceive him clearly if you fail to notice the way he continues to nurture his characters even when he bedevils them.

Finally, two decades after most of the others, his late science fiction stories arrived, the most extraordinary of which are not only the dyad I mentioned earlier, "A Visit from Mother" and "Daddy," but also "Echo" and "Rent Control" and "The Apotheosis of Myra," which is to say nearly all of them. Tevis wrote these stories during the most creatively fruitful period of his life, following years of work with his therapist, Herry O. Teltscher, to whom he dedicates "A Visit from Mother"; following a vow to give up drinking and remain sober; following a divorce and a remarriage and a move from Kentucky to Manhattan (where—arbitrary trivia—he and his wife lived downstairs from the supermodel Christie Brinkley). There is a mad buoyancy to these stories, the badge of a writer who has tapped into a vein of material to which he knows he can keep returning. And keep returning to it is just what he does, yet somehow the effect is of augmentation rather than depletion, vitality rather than fatigue. This recursive quality is unusual in science fiction. Not so, however, in the more experimental territories of postmodernism, where the same instinct has been stretched, flexed, and knotted into art by some of the great

obsessives of literature—Thomas Bernhard and Gerald Mur-
nane, Adam Ehrlich Sachs and Éric Chevillard—writers who
are able to establish echoes and transform them into litanies,
using reoccurrence and slight modification both to shade and
to brighten their work. So, too, within limits, does Tevis. In his
late stories, he will lay down patterns in one narrative and then,
in another, bring various small changes to them, exploring similar events and similar characters, similar settings and similar
emotional dynamics, even striking a series of closing notes that
are almost alike enough to be interchangeable: "'Ooooooh!' it
said happily. 'Ooooooh!'" and then, "And he heard her say it
too. 'Oh, yes. Oh, yes,'" and finally, "'Oh, yes,' she said, her voice
trembling, bending her young body to pull down her slip with
her slim fingers. 'Oh, yes.'"

These cross-story verbal allusions are no accident. Tevis was
scrupulously attentive to the rhythms of his prose, the sonics.
He was not an austere stylist—could be, in fact, remarkably
sensuous, and for a glimpse of him in that mode, you should
take a look at the celebrated final paragraphs of *Mockingbird*—
but he preferred the subdued to the elaborate, and when he
suspected that a passage was becoming too lavish, he would
pencil out its adjectives in revision. "Novels float on their language, as much as poems do, and if the language is no good, the
book is no good," he said in a 1980 interview conducted during a visit to SUNY Brockport. "You have to get noises going
in your head to do it well, but it can fall very easily into the
slipshod, into the beery and sentimental. I wrote a blank-verse
play a long time ago, with the most surprising discovery that it
was easy. Once you get into iambic pentameter, you can have
dreams in it. You could buy shirts in iambic pentameter, order
from Sears, Roebuck in iambic pentameter, and con yourself

into thinking you were writing beautifully because you had gotten hold of a rhythm that you could putz around with." He continued, "It's self-indulgent lyricism that I dislike. I find a lot of that in Ray Bradbury, who set a trend for self-indulgent, nostalgic lyricism that involves frequent use of 'October'—in fact, Bradbury has a book called *The October Country* that sounds a little bit like Thomas Wolfe heard through a plywood partition when slightly drunk."

Often it's our mirror writers who provoke the most irritation in us. We see ourselves in them, but somehow the glass has gone bad. The colors, the contours, the symmetries—they're all wrong. We know better, and we can't tolerate it. That's what I observe in the complaint Tevis strikes here against Bradbury: a man standing before an oblique mirror. It could not be more obvious to me that Bradbury's fiction, at its best, achieves the same kind of melancholy poetry that Tevis's does. In their instincts toward language, they were, if not siblings, at least cousins. Though Tevis rejects Bradbury's "nostalgic lyricism," their stance toward lyricism differs much less substantially than their stance toward nostalgia. The most profound contrast between them, I would say, lies not in their vision of the future but in their attitude toward the past: when Bradbury looked back on his childhood, he remembered a golden age, whereas when Tevis looked back on his, he remembered all his sickness, neurosis, and isolation. Still, if a Bradbury reader asked me to recommend a writer of complementary sensibilities, I might very well suggest Tevis. Both reside in that same borderland where the impulses of genre mingle freely with the impulses of literature, and both produced their most lasting work out of a wish to heal their characters—and to respect them—not by ignoring their injuries but by acknowledging them.

In Bradbury, and in a few other writers like him, I see the kind of mainstream author Tevis might have become if the table had broken differently. The table broke as it did, though, with its particular geometries of luck and attention, and he has never been sufficiently celebrated. Chances are, if you are reading this book, you are already a member of his cult, but if you are not, perhaps these stories will entice you to join it. I hope to see you in that glowing room.

THE KING
IS DEAD

THE BEST IN THE COUNTRY

After drying himself carefully, Johnny walked into the clean bedroom and sat down, naked, on the clean bed. His suitcase was open on the floor and he took from it a fresh pack of cigarettes, peeled the cellophane jacket from it with his thumbnail, flipped open the tinfoil and slid the cigarettes into his silver case, one at a time. Then he wadded the empty package into a tight little ball, took aim and threw it precisely into the middle of the green metal wastebasket which was on the other side of the room. There was something graceful—almost professional—about the way he threw the little paper ball into the wastebasket.

Now all of the time that Johnny was doing this he was thinking about Ned Bayles, whom he hadn't seen for nine years.

He lit a cigarette and leaned back against the pillow. In the next room people were drinking. Johnny could hear ice clinking in glasses and several voices. A man was complaining about having had a first-day run of bad luck at the afternoon's races and another man was telling him that he would probably make it up before the week was out and Johnny laughed, quietly, when he heard the man say it, because Johnny knew better. Johnny knew better than to bet into a mortal lock, to bet into a game that didn't figure to lose. Like horse racing. There were always lots of other games, Johnny thought, and he laughed again. The cigarette tasted good after the hot bath and Johnny felt relaxed and confident.

Now that the day's horse races were over and the racing crowd back from the track, Ned would probably be downstairs in the hotel poolroom trying to hustle up a game. Johnny could picture him, dressed like a businessman, the way he had looked nine years before in Las Vegas: a dark gray business suit, glasses, and a brief case. Lying there on the bed Johnny could even remember the way Ned had moved, the way he had walked into the little poolroom where Johnny had been practicing—where he had always practiced when he was a kid—and had set his brief case down in the chair by Johnny's table and then had stood there, watching him shoot, looking serious and interested, looking like nothing more than just another businessman. . . .

"You shoot pretty good, for a boy." The man's voice was friendly and easy.

"How's that, mister?" Johnny looked up from the table. The poolroom was almost empty except for Clem, the rack boy, over by the desk; and the stranger, a big man, stood by himself in the middle of the room, several yards from where Johnny was practicing. *Probably a salesman*, Johnny thought, *probably about forty. Thinks he can play pool.*

"I say you shoot pool pretty good, for a kid," the man said, louder this time, and very genially.

"I shoot all right." Johnny quit practicing and began chalking his cue, deliberately. "Sometimes I even beat big, full-grown men."

The stranger's face broke into a broad grin. "I bet you do, son." He laughed. "I bet you're a real shark." His tone of voice was intimate. "They told me back East that Las Vegas was full of pool sharks, and I bet you're one of 'em. A pool shark, junior size." He laughed again, and winked at Clem, who seemed interested but said nothing.

Johnny didn't feel amused. "I'm nineteen, mister," he said, "and it's hustlers—not sharks. Only people who don't play pool say sharks."

"That a fact?" The man was still smiling. "Why, when I was a kid—about your age—I used to play a lot of pool myself. They even used to call *me* a shark!" He pulled out a big handkerchief and began wiping his forehead. It was noon and the room, though almost empty, was very hot.

"You're not a kid any more, mister." Johnny smiled this time. "But I bet you still play." He kept chalking his cue, beginning to feel a little excited, but not wanting to show it. "Maybe you even play for money."

"Now hold on, son." The man laughed again. "I haven't picked up a cue in twenty years. You'd clean me out."

Johnny set the chalk down, feeling even more superior to the stranger. *They all say that*, he thought, *they all say they haven't played in twenty or thirty years. But they shoot a couple of games every week at some hotel, know a few trick shots, hustle their buddies, and think they're good. A sucker. A cinch for ten or more.*

"What's your game, mister?" he said. "What do you play?"

"Well, I used to play bank pool." The man put his handkerchief back in his hip pocket. "But that was a long time ago."

Johnny smiled again. He couldn't have picked a better game himself. "Okay, mister," he said, "I'll play you a couple of games of bank, just to see what you know. Half a chip on the side."

"Well, I've got a train to catch in a few hours." The man shrugged his shoulders. "But all right, son, I'll drop a couple of dollars your way." He picked a cue out of the rack—a light one, seventeen ounces, the kind people who don't know anything about pool use.

"Rack 'em, Clem," Johnny called.

They played for about an hour, the stranger shot pool awkwardly, and Johnny won the first four games easily. He had to hold himself back, in fact, for fear of frightening his sucker off. After the fourth game Johnny said, "Play for more money, mister? Maybe you can get even before you catch that train."

The man laughed loudly. "What do you want to do, son—crucify me?" He threw his arms out in mock agony. "All right, all right—nail me to the cross!"

"Go ahead and break," Johnny said, feeling just a little tense. . . .

After the last game the man put one of Johnny's last two dollars in his billfold with the rest and then threw the other one out on the table, casually. "Maybe you want a cup of coffee, son," he said.

Johnny said nothing, but his stomach was tight and his fingers were trembling as he watched the man, carrying nineteen dollars of his money, pick up his brief case and walk over to the door. He did not even look at the dollar on the table, nor did he make a move to pick it up.

"Hate to take your money, son," the big man said, "but you have to eat when you're on a train." He walked out the door, waving good-by and smiling still.

Clem was still sitting by the cash register. "Shot pretty good, didn't he, kid? Weeping Jesus."

"Who was he, Clem?" Johnny could feel his face getting red. "Who in hell was that dirty phony?"

"Don't you know?"

"Why am I asking?" He slammed his cue in the rack.

"Hell, he's big time, Johnny. Big time."

"What's he doing here if he's big time? Why isn't he hustling uptown at Congreve's or Nelson's if he's so big?"

"Oh, they'd know him up there, Johnny. I knew him. Probably needed just a few bucks, so he came here and got it the easy way."

"Easy. Yeah, easy." He spat on the floor. "You could of fingered him for me, Clem. You could of told me."

"Now wait a minute, Johnny." Clem shrugged his shoulders. "You know how hustling is. He's big—and smart."

"All right, all right, so you couldn't lay a finger on him. But who was he? Maybe someday I'll want to play him again."

"You're going to have a lot to learn about pool playing before you're ready to take that man on again, Johnny." Clem looked almost reverent. "You just played Ned Bayles, Johnny. He's the best bank-pool player in the country."

The best in the country. Nine years of hustling pool had taken a lot of the tenseness out of Johnny, but now remembering Bayles and that time they had played and realizing that all he had to do to be able to play him again was to take the elevator downstairs brought a little of the old tightness to his stomach. It made him feel excited to remember Ned and his crucifix gesture—"Weeping Jesus," Clem had called it—and the reverence in Clem's voice. Not that Johnny had played for years just to be able to beat Ned Bayles and get even, but it was exciting to feel that, now that he did happen to be in Ned's town, he could get a chance to even an old score.

Then he started getting ready.

Fastened to the inside of the lid of his suitcase with two metal clamps was a thin leather case, about thirty inches long. He lifted the clamps, picked up the case, and set it beside him on the bed. Then he took from the bottom of the suitcase a jar of antiperspirant, put a small amount of the cream in one hand and rubbed both hands together, briskly, until they were dry again. He put the jar carefully back into the suitcase and began taking out the clothes he would wear: a thin, pale-green short-sleeved sports shirt, gray gabardine slacks—cut full— and brown-and-white oxfords with sharply pointed toes. He felt comfortable and fresh putting them on, and as he left the room, heading for the elevator, he noticed with satisfaction the hard, bright shine of his shoes. He knew he was going to have a good night. He could feel it.

While the desk clerk was getting his envelope from the safe for him, Johnny looked over the racing crowd in the lobby. Quietly rich people, with buttons on their coat sleeves that really buttoned, loudly rich people, with buttons on their coat sleeves that might have buttoned—but didn't—and people who, both quietly and loudly, were trying to act rich, and who sometimes didn't have any buttons at all on their coat sleeves.

When he took the envelope from the clerk he was pleased to be able to count out the forty twenty-dollar bills there in the lobby, give a confidential nod to the clerk, clip the bills together with his oversized silver paper clip and slip the roll neatly into his pants pocket. Johnny enjoyed this routine very much; it was part of the way he liked to do things.

Then, looking up, he saw the sign that said Hotel Billiard Room over a door at the far end of the lobby, by the magazine rack. He walked over, slowly, carrying the leather case.

The room was full of smoke and noise. The tables, lined up on either side of the room, were crowded with men playing, most of them in their shirt sleeves, talking loudly, cursing and laughing. There was a feeling of fast money in the air, something that Johnny could sense, could almost smell, like the tobacco smoke. In the center of the room there was a rack boy's booth and cash register and standing around it was a close cluster of men who seemed just to be loafing casually—almost too casually. Racing season hustlers, men who followed the races from state to state looking for easy money. A good game, a night of playing, then two weeks of fast drinking and heavy horse betting, then another town and the same thing over again. And again—until you lost your stroke, or got too old or punchy to stand up to a pool table, or lost your nerve, or somewhere in a dark place got a knife in your chest because you had split up a bet and thrown a man when you needed the money bad enough to take the chance of losing a pool game on purpose. Johnny knew the men he saw in the middle of the room—he had played some of them back home in Las Vegas—and he knew what they were, what they had been and would be, and he knew he was different from them. Ned Bayles wasn't there in the middle of the room and Johnny knew it was because Ned was different, too, because Ned was the best in the country. Or Ned had been.

By the cash register Fish Grogan from Kansas City was talking to a little man who must have been a jockey. Johnny had played Fish at bank pool once, and had taken him bad, in Las Vegas three years ago. The Shufala kid was there, young, sporty, and redheaded, whistling through his teeth, one of the best one-pocket players on the road, talking to Glenville, the policeman, who never had to shave, whose cheeks were fat and pink, who wore little rimless glasses, smoked big brown cigars, carried a gun under his armpit, and who, they said, killed a man with his fist for chiseling on a bet once out in Utah. New York Fats, who had invented Jack-up pool and kept himself in steak and lobster during the Depression because of it, was standing by a little wiry man called Pink Shirt Cassidy who would bet you a hundred dollars that he could throw a pool ball five rails around the table and make it stop within a half inch of the center spot, and could do it. Johnny wondered if these men would recognize him. Seeing them he felt excited, telling himself, *I could get rich off you bastards. I can beat you all at your own games, and I'm not going to do it. I'm going to wait, and beat the man you're all afraid to pick up a stick against, here or anywhere.* He put out his cigarette on the floor. *I'm going to beat Ned Bayles right here in his own poolroom and on his own tables.*

Then Fish Grogan, in the middle of the room, looked over his way and saw him standing in the doorway and turned his head. Johnny smiled, but felt himself tightening up as Fish whispered something to the jockey he had been talking to and then began to push through the smoky crowd back to the far table, where a big man in a dark-brown suit was standing, watching a pool game, his back toward Johnny. Fish began talking to the man, quietly and with an unconcerned look on his thin face, but talking in a way that Johnny had seen often enough to know that Fish was putting the finger on him. Johnny lit another cigarette and said to himself, as calmly as he could, *That man in the brown suit is Ned Bayles, and Fish is telling him who I am.*

Johnny held the match a minute, but Ned didn't turn around, so he dropped it on the floor and walked through the crowd of people, down the middle of the poolroom, back to the far end table.

He stood next to Ned for a minute, then he turned his head toward him and said, "You betting on the game?"

Ned kept watching.

Johnny fiddled with his cigarette; then he threw it on the floor, stepped on it with his heel, and said, "You on the side with this game, Ned?"

Bayles looked around at him. Then he smiled. "Why no. I never bet on other people, just myself."

Johnny smiled back. "I hear you're pretty good."

"I know how."

"They say you're so good you don't always get a game. That's what people say out where I come from."

Bayles shrugged his shoulders and beamed. "You come from Las Vegas, don't you? Name of Johnny?"

"That's right. Johnny."

"People tell me they got a kid out in Las Vegas that beats most anybody at bank pool," Bayles said, his whole face smiling at him. "They say this kid shoots the eyes right out of those balls."

Johnny laughed dryly. "Could be; but everybody says you're the best in the country at bank pool." He pulled out another cigarette. "Are you the best in the country at bank pool, Ned?"

Ned's big grin broke into a laugh. It was so loud it cut through the room so that some men playing on the front table looked over at the sound of Ned's laugh. Then when he had stopped laughing he said, "I played out in Las Vegas once, maybe ten years ago; maybe they thought I was good because I was lucky."

"Maybe you were." And Ned laughed aloud again at that, banging the side of the table with his big strong-looking hands. Johnny was still holding his cigarette, and when Ned stopped laughing he lit it for him, with a small gold lighter which he took from his vest pocket. Ned was saying, "Maybe it was because I was playing a kid that time. You know how you hate to hustle a kid, Johnny, but I needed it so bad. I took a twenty from him. I didn't like doing that at all."

"You still play for money?"

Bayles motioned to the two kids who were playing straight pool on the table and they wordlessly racked up their cues. Then he said, "I'll try you a couple. How much?"

"Twenty," Johnny said, calmly, but his hands felt tight as he opened the leather case and took out his two-piece cue and began screwing the brass joint together. Bayles picked a cue out of the house rack. Then he racked the fifteen balls in the triangle at the foot of the table. Johnny was pleased to see how stiffly Bayles moved. Bayles told him he could break.

A crowd was gathering around the table. A little sweaty man was moving around, whispering, trying to get bets. Johnny wondered what the odds would be. Big, probably. It took a lot of odds to get a bet against Ned Bayles. He was glad his hands couldn't sweat as he stepped up to break the balls.

It takes more than an hour to get the proper feel of a new table, and Johnny had known he would start out losing. Bayles beat him badly the first two, banking balls off the hump and coming through with quick runs of three or four; then Johnny pulled in closer the third game, getting it down to the game ball, until Bayles smashed the ball in with a three-cushion shot that he had to play to avoid a possible scratch, and won by a single ball, eight to seven. Then Ned made a mistake toward the end of the fourth game, leaving Johnny a cinch shot when he needed only two balls to win. Johnny made the shot, played position, and went out. Then Ned won the next three in a row and Johnny could feel the crowd around the table wondering why he didn't quit. But even losing and still nervous, Johnny knew he was going to win. It wasn't even confidence—he had lost a hundred and twenty dollars in the first hour, and when a pool hustler loses money he loses the most important kind of confidence he needs. But he knew he would win; he knew he hated Bayles so much, had hated him so long, that he had to win. It was like taking the cellophane off a pack of cigarettes; you planned it, did it carefully, and it all happened.

Then when Bayles played the cue ball safe, in the middle of a game, leaving the ball frozen on the end rail, on the hump, with the four balls he needed down at the foot of the table, Johnny decided to make his strong play. He stepped up carefully to the table, called a foot rail seven ball back up in the corner pocket, and took dead aim and swung. His cue made a sharp contact off the hump, cleaning a perfect hit on the seven ball that sent it stiffening off the foot rail and sliding, then rolling, into the corner pocket. The cue ball stopped dead. The sound of the seven ball hitting the bottom of the pocket was exquisite.

"Just like it had eyes," someone said in the crowd—which now, to Johnny, seemed very far away. Then he ran the other three easy shots and picked up his twenty. He was an even hundred behind. He knew now that his stroke was working, that he would beat Bayles now.

"Play for more money, Ned?" Bayles was racking the balls.

"Just name it, Johnny."

"Hundred?"

"Fine." The crowd rustled and was still.

Then Johnny started winning. The balls began to roll for him like he knew they would. His stroke was smooth and steady; balls clipped off rails into pockets as if they knew where they were supposed to go. His confidence had come to him and it became tremendous, so that he felt his face flushed with confidence, so that whenever he did miss a shot he knew it didn't matter anyway because he would make the next one. He won his hundred back the first game, then won two more, lost one, won another, and another. His nervousness was completely gone, he felt nothing but the certainty of his winning, the crowd with him, and he kept saying to himself, *I'm beating the best in the country on his own table. He robbed me for twenty dollars once and now I'm beating him on his own table at his own game.* And it was like music, or drinking, or even like a woman, to say it: *I've got a mortal lock on Ned Bayles.* He could feel hours passing while he won, could see Ned's stroke getting stiffer, Ned making more mistakes, sitting down between shots now, ordering more drinks from the bar, but still playing. *I've beat you, you son-of-a-bitch, I've beat you and you know it,* Johnny thought, but Ned kept on playing.

Then it was suddenly two o'clock in the morning and Johnny was putting the nineteenth hundred-dollar bill in his paper clip and Ned was saying, "That roll has got so big it must be uncomfortable," and Johnny laughed and said, "It might be, but it isn't, Ned," and they both laughed. Then Ned said, "I'm tired, Johnny. How much you carrying there?"

"Nineteen hundred."

"I mean how much are you carrying. All of it."

Johnny's hand shook, just a little. "Twenty-seven hundred."

"Tell you what, Johnny, let's play one game for twenty-seven hundred, and then go to bed."

Johnny wet his lips. He hadn't thought about this. Ned was good for his money, he knew that, and he would beat him— but he just hadn't planned it this way. But there was nothing to say but, "Suits me fine," and rack the balls. The crowd was silent. Johnny tried to think about fifty-four hundred dollars while he racked up the table for Bayles' break. After he had racked the balls he put his hands in his pockets.

Ned broke safe, not leaving a shot. Johnny returned with a safe, and they jockeyed back and forth, playing safe, leaving the cue ball at one end and the fifteen object balls clustered together at the other. Then Ned did something colossally wrong. He miscued, and the cue ball dribbled down the table, caromed off an object ball and stopped near the foot rail, leaving Johnny an open, dead shot.

Ned threw up his hands and shouted, "For the love of God. Crucify me!"

Johnny said, "Here comes the first nail," and stepped up to the shot, but when he started to shoot he looked at Ned and saw that Ned didn't look any more disturbed than if he were playing for fifty cents, and Johnny felt his hands beginning to sweat in the palms, and he tried to take aim, swung, and shot and the object ball came off the cushion and hit the edge of the side pocket and bounced out, rolling slowly across the table to a stop. The ball was the twelve ball, the one with a purple stripe; it had been a dead shot, he had taken aim with thirteen years of playing experience behind him at that dead shot and had missed. For twenty-seven hundred dollars.

Ned shot and ran three balls, played him safe, and beat him, eight to two, in five minutes. When Johnny gave him the money, Ned said, "Thank you," and took the paper clip off the bills, put a twenty in it and gave it back to him. "In case you want a cup of coffee," he said, smiling.

Johnny took the twenty out, put the clip in his pocket, and threw the twenty on the table. "I don't drink coffee." Then he went upstairs and went to bed, without undressing.

In the morning Johnny found a pawnshop and got thirteen-fifty for his silver cigarette case and paper clip. A ticket back to Las Vegas cost thirty-two dollars. Then he started looking for a poolroom, knowing it would be useless to go back to the hotel after showing his best game there the night before. He found one. A little painted window with the words Smoker Pool Room—Men Only in green letters.

Inside the door he bought a package of cigarettes from a greasy man behind a counter. As he picked up the change from his half dollar he looked at the man and asked, "Any action here this time of day?"

The man jerked his thumb toward a table. On the table a kid—maybe eighteen or nineteen—was practicing, shooting like he thought he was good. "That boy'll play you for two or three dollars if you want. But be careful; he's a hustler."

"I'll be careful," Johnny said, and walked over to the table, opening the pack of cigarettes. He wondered if the boy would have as much as twenty dollars.

Johnny pulled out a cigarette and stood, watching the boy shoot, for several moments. Then he said, "You shoot pretty good." He lighted his cigarette and threw the match on the floor. "For a kid."

THE MAN FROM CHICAGO

It must have been at least two years ago that Hustler Curtiss first came into Charlie's poolroom. I can remember pretty exactly, because right from the time he first walked in the front door, with his smooth white hair, his bright-blue plaid shirt, and his straight, still way of walking, he was the kind of man you would notice. He nodded politely at Charlie, who was sitting behind the counter reading a comic book, and said, "Good afternoon, sir." It wasn't hard to tell that for a small-town poolroom like ours, this was a pretty unusual guy.

From that time on, he started coming in regular, every day at three o'clock. Other old men came in and hung around because there wasn't any place else for them to go; but you could tell it wasn't that way with Curtiss. He didn't talk and fool around like the others; he always had his eyes right on the tables. But he never seemed interested in playing the game himself.

He didn't hang around the barbershop or the courthouse, either, like all the other footloose old men did; you never saw him, ever, until three o'clock in the afternoon. It seems he had this widowed sister who lived out on Catalpa Street—which is, by the way, about the highest-class district in town—and he stayed with her. She was why he had come to our town in the first place, I guess after he'd retired. I suppose he would spend the mornings with his sister, talking about books or paintings or something: he seemed like that kind of guy. A different kind of guy; not my kind, but a kind I respect.

For instance, he never did chew tobacco like most of the other old men did; he smoked, cork-tipped cigarettes, and he carried them in a thin, silver case in his shirt pocket. It was kind of funny, the way he would pull that elegant-looking case out of an old flannel shirt and then reach into the pocket of a baggy pair of pants and pull out a little matching lighter and light up. The lighter was different from any I'd ever seen before: it was very small and it always worked.

When I said it was funny, watching him, I didn't mean that it was the kind of a thing you'd laugh at: because Curtiss didn't do things *that* way. There was something different, something natural and smooth about the way he would handle that fancy little lighter. And about the way he dressed, too. He always had on something loose and comfortable looking; but it was never cheap or worn out. I think "casual" is the word you use for it: and that's the way he looked in his clothes. You could tell the stuff he wore was good goods, like the materials you see in the windows of those little, quiet stores in the big towns with a little sign saying "from England," and no price tag.

He never tried to tell anybody anything, either; never

seemed to want to do anything but just watch the games and smoke his cigarettes. I hardly spoke twenty words to him in at least two years; but I couldn't help liking him.

Curtiss didn't seem to strike Charlie that way, though. Charlie was the kind of guy who figured that if anybody was much different from himself—and I can't think of any two guys more different than Curtiss and Charlie—there must be something peculiar about the other guy. Charlie always was a great one for kidding people, too; especially people who wouldn't kid him back. That was Charlie's way. In fact, it was Charlie who first gave Curtiss the nickname "Hustler" back when the old man had started coming in the poolroom.

He'd been coming in for maybe a couple of weeks and had been doing a lot of smiling but not much talking and some of the boys had noticed he carried a big roll with him. Not that he flashed it on us or anything like that; but most of the boys are pretty observant when it comes to bank-rolls. So anyway, this time, out of a clear blue sky, Charlie comes up to Curtiss and says, "Mind if I ask a question, old-timer?"

Curtiss smiles. "Not at all, young man."

Then Charlie says, "Where did you get that big roll I see you carrying all the time?" Now this kind of shocks me, since a question like that is not considered very good taste around a poolroom.

Curtiss looks at Charlie for a minute. Then he gets a serious look and leans a little forward in his chair. "Well, Charlie, I'll tell you," he says, "I made my bank-roll hustling pool."

Well, naturally, this stops Charlie cold. But only for a minute. Then he starts looking very wise and nodding his head, like he understands.

"Oh," he says, "I see. And where," he says, real polite—and Charlie is never polite without a good reason for it—"did you do this hustling, sir?"

Curtiss looks at Charlie real serious again and he says, "In Chicago, young man. At Wenneker's Billiard Hall. I was houseman there for ten years."

"You old phony!" Charlie yells. "You couldn't beat my grandmother!"

Well, right off I figure there's no doubt but what the old man is pulling Charlie's leg, and beating him at his own game. But what he says seems to knock Charlie and the rest of them right on out. They must be figuring the old man is expecting them to believe him—and even I have to admit he looks mighty serious about it—and that he's out of his head. You see, everybody's heard of Wenneker's. It must be the biggest and the oldest poolroom in the country. Not that any of us has ever been there; but you can't play pool very long without hearing about Wenneker's. It's the place where the toughest—but the toughest—pool hustlers hang out, and where they say the big horse men and the Syndicate boys come in and drop maybe fifty G's and never bat an eye. And for this quiet old codger in our little poolroom to say he was houseman there—the man who plays anybody who comes in for anything they want to play for—well, I start expecting to see Charlie double up any minute and start pounding on the floor and hollering.

But I got to give Charlie credit; he's still playing it straight. He keeps the innocent look on his face and he says, thoughtful, "Well, now. After forty years I'd think you'd be mighty tired of pool playing."

At this the old man looks a little sad and wistful. "Son," he says—and I can hear some guy in back gag on that one—"Son, you're absolutely right."

"But then why, sir," says Charlie—and the guy in back is by now having a spasm—"do you spend so much time in here, watching games?"

Now, up to this time, I've figured that the old man has just been kidding Charlie along; but what he says next makes me wonder a little if he hasn't been serious. He says it like he means it; like he means it so much it hurts.

"Well," he says, "the game gets a grip on you—gets in your system. And I'm a little too old to start getting it out." Then he smiles; but his eyes still look kind of wistful.

Charlie puts a real sympathetic look on his face and says, "Gets in your blood, huh?" Then he gives a quick wink to a couple of guys who are standing off to one side, listening, and he says, "Maybe it would do you good if you played a little every now and then. That is, if you could find somebody that wasn't scared to take you on, knowing what a great, all-time hustler you are and all that."

Charlie has begun to quit taking it; and he's got a sneer in his voice that you could tell a mile off. "Maybe you could talk *me* into playing you, for instance," he says, with the big, dirty grin he's got. "Just a few friendly little games for about twenty bucks apiece."

But Curtiss has still got a faraway look; and he doesn't seem to notice that Charlie has begun talking mean, because he just says, "No, son. Thank you. I'm afraid I'm too old to be much of a player any more. I had to retire quite a few years ago. You see, my heart is not too well."

So Charlie says, "Sure, I know. But come on, Hustler"—and

this is the first time Curtiss is called "Hustler"—"you can play me just a few. Why, a few twenty-dollar pool games wouldn't be any strain on an old big-time hustler like you."

"I'm sorry, son. I'd better not."

Suddenly Charlie gets a thoughtful look. "Hustler," he says, "I bet I know what's the matter with your heart."

"Really?" Curtiss says, politely.

"Yes sir, Hustler," Charlie says, "you got the kind of heart trouble that guys who talk big get. The kind that makes you chicken out when a game comes up." Then, suddenly, he steps closer and sticks his face up to Curtiss. He says, slow and soft, "You got a chicken heart, Hustler."

Then I look at Curtiss to see how he's taking it all. Curtiss is just sitting there, like he hasn't heard a thing.

He pulls out his silver case and takes out a cigarette. He gets his lighter out of his pocket and lights up, very calm and unconcerned. Like always, the lighter works on the first try.

Most people think of hustlers as young, skinny men, with pale faces, dark hair, and hawk eyes. At least, that was the idea I had, until this stranger showed up. He was short, thick around the waist, red-faced, middle-aged, and he wore glasses—the steel-rimmed kind. He had on a brown suit and a darker brown tie, and his shirt was plain white and a little wrinkled around the collar. He looked like a small-time business man—which, after all, you might say he was.

He came in one afternoon about two o'clock and started practicing on the front table, shooting just a fair stick of pool. You know, better-than-average shots; but nothing a player like Charlie couldn't beat. He had a big roll, too, and he flashed it around. Altogether, it was a good come on; and Charlie fell for it, all the way.

He watched the stranger shoot for about fifteen minutes. Then he started talking to him, friendly; and in five more minutes the two of them were playing a game, just for fun.

You could tell Charlie was throwing off. He let the man win about four games, and then asked him how about betting a little something on the side. The man said well, yes, but of course he really didn't believe in gambling on pool games, since he thought it could ruin the game, sometimes. Charlie agreed with him, and they started playing for two dollars a game. Then Charlie won a few and he suggested they double the bet so the other man could get even. The other man was doubtful for a minute, but they doubled the bet, and before long the other man was hooked for about fifty dollars and he started getting mad and saying he'd just come in to practice a little pool, peaceful-like, and here Charlie had come up and hustled him, and he didn't see how it was fair.

So Charlie looked real innocent and said he didn't mean to be hustling anybody, and that he'd just been lucky so far, to be winning like he had, and that he knew how it was, and that he'd be willing to give the other man an even break and would be glad to spot him one ball out of an eight-ball bank game, and that they'd play one for fifty dollars and that way they'd be sure to break even. So the other guy calmed down a little and said well, okay, and then Charlie racked the balls and they started playing, and you could tell Charlie was a little nervous. Even though as far as he could tell he was a good three balls better than the stranger, that fifty-dollar bet was a good ways out of his five-and-ten-dollar league. Which just goes to show what the idea of easy money'll do: even to a guy as basically small-time as Charlie.

And then, about the middle of the game, Charlie began showing how small-time he really was. He started opening up, shooting his best game and not trying to fool anybody any more. It was almost unethical, the way he did it; just dropping his hustle all of a sudden and playing shutout pool, showing his best stick, shooting his best shots, letting his best game show. It was wrong two ways: First, he should have kept stringing the other man along, since he might have been ready to drop three to four hundred dollars; and, second, it was kind of dirty to kid a fellow along like Charlie had been doing, and then to open up on him like that and make him feel like a sucker.

So Charlie beat the man, but good. For fifty dollars. That put him a hundred dollars ahead; and, if he was cocky before, you could read "strutting high" all over his face now.

And then the stranger made his big play.

He pulled out his billfold, jerked out a wad of bills, peeled a fifty off the top, threw it down on the table, and then started counting tens and twenties from the rest of the pile, and talking—only it was more like spluttering.

"By golly," he said, counting off his money. "By golly, I'm not a gambling man; but I'll be switched if I know I can't beat your brand of luck pool."

He stacked a hundred dollars in bills together on the table, and then started counting off another hundred dollars. Charlie didn't say anything; you could see he was fascinated. As a matter of fact, we all were. I just happened to notice that it was almost four o'clock, and I looked over towards the wall, and there was Hustler Curtiss, sitting in his usual chair. He was leaning back, watching the money-counting routine like it might have been on television, and he was just kind of smiling. And when he saw me looking at him he did something I had never seen him do before. He winked at me, still smiling. I didn't understand, then, what the smile and the wink meant.

The stranger had finished counting out another hundred dollars from his roll—and the roll was still pretty big—and he was glaring at Charlie and he said, "By golly, this is two weeks' commissions and expenses; but I'll lay you the whole two hundred dollars, on just one more game, that I can still beat your kind of luck."

It was perfect. Even for Charlie it was too perfect to chicken out on. I think maybe it was the talk about "commissions and expenses" that did it. Everybody knows there's no better sucker than a traveling salesman. Of course, what we didn't know then was that there's maybe twenty fast-shooting hustlers on the road that carry sample cases into poolrooms with them—and carry the money out. Only this stranger wasn't that kind—he didn't carry a sample case.

So Charlie bit. "Okay, mister," he said. "You've got you a game." Then he racked the balls.

Racking, you could see his hand was shaking, just a little. Even playing a game he thought was a mortal lock—a lead-pipe cinch—you could see the chicken in him.

The stranger won. Not by a lot—he beat Charlie eight balls to six—and not by looking good either. His game didn't seem to improve any; but, somehow, Charlie didn't get any of the easy shots and somehow the other man did. You couldn't say the stranger was playing safe—at least you couldn't *see* it—but

Charlie was always stepping up to a hard shot, and the stranger seemed to get an awful lot of the easy kind.

When Charlie lost he looked like he couldn't believe it. He didn't say anything at all, just walked up to the cash register on the counter, rang up a No Sale, and started pulling bills out of the cash drawer. He must have had a good deal on hand; because he was able to get out the hundred dollars he needed without having to go to the safe. Then he fished the hundred dollars he had won out of his pocket, came back over to the table, and started counting out the bills. He stacked them neatly together, and handed them to the other man.

Then Charlie happens to look up and he sees Curtiss sitting there, still smiling, minding his own business. Charlie looks at him a minute, real hard, and you can see he's getting mad at that smile; and if you know Charlie you know that about this time is when he's going to start looking for someone to take his losing out on, and especially somebody who won't fight him back.

So suddenly he says to Curtiss, very mean, "What are you grinning at?"

Curtiss looks surprised. You can see he's been sort of wrapped up in his thoughts, and that Charlie has jolted him out of them. "Sir?" he says, surprised.

"Sir, my butt!" Charlie says, "I said, what do you think you're grinning at?"

"Oh," Curtiss says, "I was just thinking. Thinking about some . . . games that I had seen before, somewhat like the one you've been playing." He smiles at Charlie, like he might be smiling at some little boy. "Only, of course," he says, "that was a long time ago."

"In Chicago?" You can tell by looking that Charlie is about ready to blow his top.

But Curtiss isn't noticing. He has sort of a faraway look, and he says, "That's right. At Wenneker's."

This does it. Charlie's top blows. He grabs his cue stick and slams the butt of it down on the floor, hard.

"Good old Wenneker's in Chicago!" he says, spitting out the words. "Good old Chicago where you used to hustle." He looks at Curtiss real hard, and says, slow and loud, "You give me a pain."

Curtiss raises his eyebrows, just a little. "A pain?" he says.

"That's right. You crummy old phony. You couldn't hustle my grandmother, and you know it." He spits on the floor. "Chicago!" he says, like it's a dirty word.

For at least a minute nobody says a thing. The stranger's been quiet, naturally; and I feel as if I should say something, but I don't know exactly what; and I'm standing there thinking of ways to tell Charlie off, when somebody speaks up from the crowd that has been gathered around the table and says to Charlie, "Lay off the old guy, will you? He never bothered you none." And Charlie turns around to say something back when, suddenly, Curtiss speaks up.

"Charlie," he says, "you don't believe that I know anything at all about pool playing, do you?"

Charlie looks at him. Then he spits again. "Hell no!" he says.

"I see," says Curtiss. "I really suspected as much." Then he looks at the stranger. "And you, sir, how about you? Would you say I was a good pool player?"

The stranger looks annoyed. "How should I know?" he says. "You might be Willie Mosconi, for all I know."

All of a sudden Curtiss' smile turns into a grin, and he chuckles, real soft. Then he says, "Well, gentlemen, this is a new one. Here I am trying to tell you that I'm a pool hustler, and you won't believe me. And this gentleman here"—he waves his hand towards the stranger—"has been trying very hard—and, evidently, succeeding—to show you that he *isn't* a hustler." He gazes at us all, very confidentially, looking like a king sitting up on his throne. "Now that *is* an odd one, isn't it?"

"Wait a minute," says the stranger. "Who says I'm trying to hustle anybody?"

"Why I just did, young man," Curtiss says. "Aren't you?"

The stranger starts getting a mean look on his face and he says, "Now hold on a minute, old-timer . . ."

"Don't get angry, young man," Curtiss interrupts. "You won't lose your chance of winning yourself some money." He leans back in his chair, and pulls his silver cigarette case out of his pocket. He takes a cigarette out of it and holds it, for a minute, between his fingers. Then he says, "*I'll* be glad to play you."

The stranger says, "What?"

"I said I'll play you," he says, and he leans forward again, fishing in his pocket for the little lighter. "Although my doctor wouldn't approve—not at all—and although I can't guarantee that you'll beat me; I'll tell you that I have a lot more money than Charlie has; and I'll play you longer before I quit."

Charlie is still staring. "Well, I'll be damned!" he says. Then he laughs. "Well, I'll be damned!" he says again.

Only this time he doesn't seem quite so sure of himself.

The stranger has had a mean look on his face; but now he starts looking sort of puzzled too and he says, "Now, listen, old-timer, I was doing all right here before you started butting in."

Curtiss just smiles and reaches for his billfold.

His billfold is one of the kind that opens from the side and is long—so as not to bend the money I guess—and he opens it and pulls out a very neat looking stack of bills and then he holds the stack in one hand and flips through it at the corner with the thumb of the other hand, real graceful, and he more or less answers the stranger's objections that way, since as far as I can see every one of the bills has the number "50" neatly printed on the corner, and there are a very great many of the bills. Then, to clinch his argument, he says, "How much would you like to play for?"

So the stranger looks at Charlie, who he must have known was about ready to quit anyway, and he looks at Curtiss, who looks very old and feeble, as well as very rich, and it doesn't take him long to make up his mind.

"Let's start it with fifty, old-timer," he says; and you can hear respect in his voice for the first time.

But all of a sudden Charlie begins to look indignant or, more truthfully, he *continues* to look that way—and he says, "Hey! What about my hundred bucks, mister? I got a right to win it back." This is amusing on Charlie's part; because we all know that Charlie probably was getting ready to quit anyway when Curtiss got into it.

But Curtiss smiles at him and says, "All right, Charlie, I'll give you a chance to get your money back—probably a much better chance than you would have had playing this fellow yourself."

"Now wait a minute," Charlie says, "I was beating this guy. So he won one game, so what? I was a cinch to do all right with him."

But Curtiss just says, "You were out of your class. All of the way out of your class. You're lucky I stopped you." Then he pauses for a minute; and when nobody says anything he goes on and says, "Very well, then. Here's my proposition: I'll bet you right now a hundred dollars that I win this first game."

Charlie just stands where he is, looking at the old man, and he doesn't seem to catch on. He doesn't say anything; just looks.

Then Curtiss says, "How can you lose?" His face is deadpan; but I can see kind of a twinkle in his eyes. "Certainly this man is a better player than your . . . ah . . . grandmother?"

Then Charlie seems to come out of his daze and he says, "Hell no." Real loud.

Curtiss says, "He isn't?" He raises his eyebrows. Somebody in back laughs. Charlie looks pretty stupid, and I have a hard time keeping a straight face, myself.

"NO!" Charlie says, "I mean, no I won't bet." He seems suddenly to try to look sly—like he is seeing things going on that nobody else sees. "How do I know I'm not pushing a rigged game. I don't like it."

It's really pretty plain what Charlie is beefing about. Here he's got what looks like a big, beautiful bet being offered to him, the kind of a bet no self-respecting gambler should ever turn down; and he hasn't got the nerve to cover it.

But Curtiss just keeps smiling and says, "All right, Charlie, have it your way."

Then he gets down out of the high chair—you could almost call it a throne—and goes over to the rack, and studies the cues. Then he picks him one, and starts chalking up. It almost makes me feel sick, watching him. He moves so slow and careful; you can almost hear his joints creaking; and I don't see how he's going to make it when the time comes for him to bend down over the table.

So they play: eight-and-out bank pool for fifty dollars a game. The stranger breaks the balls, banks one, and misses. He has left Curtiss a so-so kind of shot—not too hard; but not so easy, either. In a fifty-dollar game, that's a hard kind of a shot to deal with.

It doesn't take Curtiss long to figure it out; but the way he bends over the table to get into position, we think it's going to take him forever. But he gets there, way up over the table, and he calls his shot, "Cross the corner, young man," real pleasant, pumps his cue stick once, and then pokes into the cue ball. The ball goes: cross corner.

At this point, I feel like applauding. But if I am expecting any miracles I am soon to be disappointed. Curtiss misses the next one. So the game goes on; but it's a quick game; because both of these boys, it seems, know what's what with a pool table; and when it's over the stranger has won. But it's a close score; eight to six.

Then they play another, and Curtiss loses it, too. This time the score is eight to five. This game he's better, not so stiff and a little smoother; but the stranger is beginning to show his stuff, and it looks like he's got plenty. I guess the first game's score has worried him some; and, besides, Curtiss has said he knows the guy's a hustler anyway, so the guy has let himself improve a little. Now the thing that I'm wondering is: Just how good *is* this guy's best game? Has he let it all come out yet; or is he still holding back?

Next game I find out. He blasts Curtiss. The poor old guy

tries to put up a fight; but the stranger cuts him down before he gets a chance: eight to one. And the shooting the stranger is doing; nobody has ever played like that in this poolroom before.

I steal a look at Charlie's face. He looks thoughtful; I'm betting he's thinking right now about what would have happened to him if Curtiss hadn't stopped him from playing this guy.

Curtiss is paying off his third fifty dollars after this last game when he looks at the stranger, smiling, and he says, "How would you like to play a game of straight pool, young man. One hundred and twenty-five points?"

"What's wrong with what we're playing?" He stuffs the fifty in his pocket.

"Nothing," Curtiss says. "But it seems as if I'm getting tired more quickly than I thought. And, since I promised you a chance to win a good deal of money, I thought you might like trying one hundred and twenty-five points for . . . well, say, five hundred dollars?"

The stranger stares a second, then, suddenly, he grins. "You know what, old-timer?" he says. "To tell the truth I *was* getting tired of playing bank." He starts pulling money out of his pockets. Then he says to Charlie, "Rack the balls for straight pool."

Charlie comes over and racks the balls. The stranger breaks, and they start playing.

I saw Willie Mosconi shoot pool once, back when I was wearing a khaki suit and he was giving exhibitions in Army camps. He was World's Champion then, at fourteen and one, straight pool. Mosconi didn't shoot pool like anyone else I had ever seen.

I never saw playing like that again, until I saw Curtiss play that one game of straight pool, there at Charlie's pool hall. He was different from Mosconi because he was stiff and slow; but he had the same way of fitting in with the game, the same *class* of playing, the same deadly accuracy. And his eyes—I had never noticed anything peculiar about his eyes before, but now, with his stick in his hand, shooting, then chalking, then shooting again, his eyes were moving over the table, looking from ball to ball, expertly, seeming to glitter—little, black, bright eyes, glancing back and forth, looking for shots, never blinking. Then his eyes would find what they wanted, and he would bend down to the shot, stiff but no longer awkward, easy and smooth, and let fly. His speed was always the same, like Mosconi's, medium-hard, and the balls would roll with a kind of sureness that they never had before. It was beautiful to watch. You couldn't hear a sound in the room, except for the noise the balls made when Curtiss shot them into the pockets.

The game was over very quickly. For what seemed like a long while, nobody said a word. I looked at Charlie. He was still sitting just like he had been when they started playing. His lower lip was hanging a little lower than usual. He was staring at Curtiss.

Then the stranger walked over to the rack and put away his cue. When he walked back he had his billfold out. He stopped, looked at Curtiss, and said, "Well, I'll be damned." He said one word at a time, slowly, and in a low voice. Then he started pulling money out of his billfold, quietly. He didn't go through any routine, this time, of counting it out on the table.

Curtiss smiled. Then he handed his stick to Charlie, sitting behind him. "Please put it up for me, Charlie," he said. "I'm beginning to feel a little tired."

Charlie took the stick and put it in the rack.

The stranger was still looking at Curtiss. Then he said, "What's your name, mister?" and his voice sounded almost scared.

"Curtiss." He was still smiling. "Billy Curtiss."

The stranger kept staring for a minute. Then his jaw fell down. *"Billy Curtiss,"* he said—it was like a minister saying the name of the Lord—"you mean *you're* Billy Curtiss?"

"That's right," Curtiss said.

"From Chicago?"

Suddenly, Curtiss' smile changed to a grin. He nodded his head towards Charlie. "Ask him," he said.

The stranger looked at Charlie. Charlie looked at the stranger; then he looked at Hustler Curtiss.

"Well, I'll be damned," he said.

THE BIG HUSTLE

Ned Bales sat next to the Chief and watched the kid shooting at the front table. He looked good. Ned guessed he was no more than twenty-five, but from the way he shot, practicing, he looked like a master. He was wearing a cardigan jacket, chartreuse sport shirt, brown-and-white shoes. At one point, he laid his cue aside and lighted a cigarette with an extremely thin, silver lighter. He blew the smoke out of his nose and went on shooting.

Finally the kid made a very difficult shot, and Ned Bales turned to the Chief and said, "So that's the Hot Springs Babe. He looks pretty good."

The Chief laughed, his gold tooth showing. "You said it, Ned Bales. He looks almost as good as you did twenty, twenty-five years ago, when you first came to Chicago."

"A lot of young hustlers *look* good."

"That's right." The Chief laughed again. "But you, Ned Bales, you *were* good. You *were* The Best."

Ned heard the emphasis in the Chief's voice, and he knew what was going on. The Chief was backing this kid. This was the first time in fifteen years that the Chief had been willing to back anyone against Ned.

The disturbing thing was that the Chief had always over-rated him—as almost everybody had ever since they had started calling him The Best—and so, if the Chief thought this Babe kid could take him, it was going to be rough. But Ned was still called The Best and there still wasn't anybody with nerve enough to try him in an even game, even though Ned guessed there were several who could beat him.

Except for an occasional kid—like this Babe—who would try him and lose to Ned's steadiness and experience, all of Ned's games for the last ten years had been with suckers; and now Ned himself wasn't too sure of what his game would be if he had to turn it on again. One of the big troubles with having a reputation was that if they knew how to play and still played him, they were bound to be pretty good.

The Chief stood up and looked toward the Babe. "Babe," he said, "I want you to meet Ned Bales. He's The Best."

Babe shot once more, made the ball, and looked up. "Hello, Bales," he said.

"Hello, Babe," Ned said. He tried to make his voice friendly, tried not to let it show the tenseness he felt.

"Ned Bales is pretty good at straight pool," the Chief said to Babe. "You think you can take him?"

"You putting up the money, Chief?" Babe said, coldly.

"If you think maybe you can take him. I'll put up two hundred."

Babe's face was pale and smooth, but it was hard as he looked at Ned Bales. "I'll take him," he said.

The Chief grinned again. "Okay, Ned?" he asked. "You play my boy here? Straight pool, hundred twenty-five points for two hundred dollars? Or maybe you'd rather not? He's good."

Ned looked to the back of the room, where the owner of the place was brushing off some tables. "Woody," he said, "come here and rack the balls." Ned nodded to the Chief, who was still grinning, but looking really happy now.

While Woody racked the balls, Ned walked over to the green cabinet in the corner and took out his private cue, a twenty-ounce stick with an ivory point, his name engraved on the little brass ring around the middle where the two sections joined together. It had been years since Ned had needed a cue that could be taken apart for traveling as a hustler from small town to small town. But he still used the old joined cue stick. He was used to it, to its weight, balance and stroke. . . .

Ned lost the toss and Babe elected to let him break. Ned placed the cue ball, aimed carefully and shot. The break was good. He clipped the corner ball of the triangular rack one third full and brought his cue ball back up the table to freeze on the far end rail. Two balls came out of the triangle, hit two cushions, and went back, not leaving a shot. It was a perfect rulebook break. The only thing for Babe to do was to try to play safe, to repeat the same shot.

But Babe didn't. He walked over to the foot of the table and looked closely at the balls, sighting carefully. One of the corner balls had not returned to exactly the right spot, and the triangle was a little out of line.

Ned couldn't see anything that looked open for a combination shot, except maybe the twelve ball, the one next to the misplaced corner ball, but that was a rail-first shot, much too tricky and dangerous for a money game.

But Babe walked back to the head of the table and said, "Twelve ball. Side pocket."

Ned glanced quickly at the Chief. He looked a little worried.

Babe drew his stick back sharply and let fly with a clean, cutting hit. The cue ball went a neat two rails and clipped the corner ball square and firm. The twelve rolled out, across the table, and fell into the side pocket. The rest of the balls spread wide. Babe had made it. Neatly and perfectly.

Ned sat down. There wasn't anything to do now but watch.

Babe was good. He was terrific. He ran the rest of the rack, then another and another. It wasn't until the score was sixty-two to nothing that Babe got a bad roll on his cue ball, kissed off a ball with it and scratched.

Ned stepped up quietly and tried to do his best. He was able to score forty-one before he missed and left Babe a shot. Babe ran about fifty, played him safe, and then ran out, winning the game, on his next shot.

The Chief looked sympathetic as Ned gave him two hundred dollars but he didn't say anything.

As the afternoon passed by, Babe kept right on winning—not every game, but two out of three. He made brilliant shots, and his safe game was almost airtight. Ned shot well too, a calm, steady game, but by four o'clock his feet and head were aching, and he was twenty-six hundred dollars behind. A crowd had gathered around the table, and Ned could tell Babe was eating it up. When he'd make an unusually showy or difficult shot, he'd break his silence to make a remark about Ned's age, or about the "old days" of the game. There was something cocky, terribly insulting, about him. But he was beating Ned and beating him badly.

Ned wondered idly for a while why he didn't quit. He was beaten, he knew it, and the surprised, silent crowd watching knew it. But he also knew, with a terrible sense of frustration, that he couldn't stop trying to beat this cocky kid who shot pool like a wizard; until he'd lost every penny he had, all the money he'd put away in the bank, he couldn't quit. For thirty years, the other man had always quit him. Himself, he had never learned how to quit. Ned watched Babe shoot, running the game out, and he could see the thin little sneer on Babe's face as he won again.

There's only one way, Ned thought; if I keep playing this way, he's got me. There's just one way I might do it.

Ned walked over to the Chief. "How much is that, Chief?" he asked quietly.

Babe spoke before the Chief could answer. "Three thousand Bales. You've dropped three thousand." He raised his eyebrows. "Wanta quit?"

"No." Ned looked at the Chief. "Want to go it?" he said, keeping his voice level.

For the first time the Chief sounded doubtful. "What do you think, Babe? Can you go for three thousand?"

The corners of Babe's mouth twitched a little. "I can go," he said.

The Chief looked back at Ned. "I don't like it, Ned Bales," he said, "but I'll go with you. And then we quit, win or lose."

"Fair enough," Ned said.

It was the best way. His only chance was that the bet would rattle the kid. It wasn't too much of a chance; the kid had been around plenty and probably had what it took. So he, Ned Bales, would probably lose and be out six thousand dollars. In a way it might be a good thing to get beaten badly, to forget about being The Best and to quit wearing a reputation that had been awfully hard, lately, to wear. . . .

Woody racked the balls, and Babe broke. The break was perfect and there was nothing for Ned to do but play it safe. They jockeyed back and forth for a while, both of them playing safe, carefully, with precision and control.

Then it happened. It was Babe who hit a ball just barely too full, leaving Ned an open shot, a slight chance. It wasn't an easy shot, but it was the kind a good hustler can cut in and then run the score way up.

Ned chalked his cue and bent down to shoot, taking aim carefully.

Then Babe spoke. He said, softly, "Bales." His voice was slimy with insult and scorn, but with just the slightest trace of fear in it. "Bales. Don't miss that shot. If you do you'll lose. Three thousand dollars, Bales."

Ned straightened up. He looked at Babe, then he turned to the Chief. The Chief looked abashed.

Then Ned laughed. He threw back his head, leaned against the table and laughed. "Chief," Ned said, "he's trying to rattle me. This kid—this punk—is trying to rattle me."

Babe shifted his chair nervously.

"You're in the wrong league, Babe," Ned said. "I knew there was something wrong with you. You're not playing any more with the two-bit boys. You don't know who you're playing. Ask the Chief. Ask him about that yellow trick you just tried."

"That doesn't go, Babe," the Chief said. "Ned Bales don't rattle. I tried it once; I know. He's The Best."

Ned went back to the shot, aimed easily and made it. He started running. He made seventy, and then he played it safe.

When Babe came up to shoot he was trying to be calm, and Ned could see that he had him. Babe managed to run thirty-seven before he missed; but when he missed it was an easy shot, and Ned could see his hand shaking. Ned stepped up to shoot.

Something made him feel like the old Ned, the Ned Bales whose name was like a legend in poolrooms everywhere, the Ned Bales who could always run a game out when the money was up. He shot easily, smoothly, clicking off the shots in his mind and then pocketing them on the table, forgetting his tiredness, forgetting how old he was, just shooting pool, shooting like The Best.

He did it. He ran the game out, ninety-seven points without missing. When he finished, the Chief took three thousand from his pocket and handed it to him. He didn't look at Ned.

"Chief," Babe said, "let me play him another. I'll take him."

There was mild contempt in the Chief's voice. "No, you won't, Babe," he said. "You shoot good. But you don't play pool, kid. You shoot, but you don't play. You better go back to Hot Springs. You do a lot better there."

Ned put the money in a roll and stuffed it in his pocket. "Better luck next time, Chief."

"Sure, Ned Bales," the Chief said. "You come back. Someday maybe I find somebody who'll beat you."

"Maybe you will," Ned said. "Everybody's got to get beat sometime."

As Ned walked out the door he could feel the aching in his legs and feet and eyes coming back. The air outside was cool, and it was getting dark. Ned decided he'd better take a cab home. He was too tired to walk.

MISLEADING LADY

From the first sight of her it was obvious that she was not the girl for the part. For my leading lady I needed someone tall and blond with bedroom eyes; and this girl—she could hardly have been more than twenty—was about five feet two inches tall, her hair was brown, and her eyes were more suggestive of the kitchen than of anywhere else. The sort of girl who always appears as if she had just finished baking a pie. Just the type to make someone a dandy little sister. Unfortunately, I was well supplied with sisters.

Of course, I called the casting director immediately, and, of course, found him about as pliable as reinforced concrete. He went into a lengthy tale concerning the cost of operating a road show, reminding me that I was the only member of the Broadway cast retained at the original salary, and suggesting that the cost of hiring a more accomplished actress might involve a lowering of my stipend.

"Your logic," I said, "is breath-taking. But don't you think you might locate someone with more glamour?"

"At a hundred a week?" he countered. "Besides, Fred, this girl got rave reviews in Pennsylvania all last season."

"That's what I mean," I said, but he had hung up.

And so, for two grueling weeks the director and I labored, instructing this sister type to appear seductive. It was uphill labor, but we seemed to achieve a modicum of success. I had to admit, too, that she was pleasant enough to work with in a calm, homespun way.

In two weeks she seemed to have a fair grasp of her characterization, and we headed for Baltimore. Frederick Raleigh *with* Julie Abbott, in *Dishonourable Mention*.

I was, it developed, in for yet more surprises. We were quite a success in Baltimore. On the stage Julie seemed to perform a genuine metamorphosis, fitting into her part in a most amazing way. In fact, after one of our kiss scenes a truly seductive look crept into her wholesome eyes.

In Cleveland she did so well that I decided to compliment her. "Julie," I said, after her third curtain call, "you are doing nicely. In a few years you may become quite an accomplished actress."

For some reason or other she took a while replying. "Thank you, Fred," she said, a bit coolly. There was a glint in her eyes that I should have noticed more carefully. Something like the look of a fighter accepting a challenge.

And, after all, I had only intended to be nice.

Then we played Cincinnati. She had been distant with me for a few days, but it was obvious that she had a cold. It hurt her performance; and I was surprised to see that we were all slowed down by it.

Not that the show was a total loss; the applause was adequate, although not overwhelming. It was just what is called in the profession a bad night.

About twenty minutes after the show I was sitting in my dressing room, when I heard a light knock at the door.

When I said, "Come in," the door pushed open and there she stood. The grease-paint was streaked under her eyes—making them seem even larger and more wistful than usual—and some of that brown hair was falling, loose, over her forehead. She was unquestionably a mess, but, somehow or other, it was an appealing entrance.

"Fred," she said, "I think I have to talk to somebody. Do you mind if it's you?"

"Sit down," I said.

She closed the door and dropped into a canvas chair.

"What is it, Julie?" I said, surprised at the gentleness in my voice.

She tried to smile. "It's—it's pretty silly, Fred."

"Most important things are," I said. It was probably the first time I had ever made a philosophical remark in my life. Had I been wiser, at this point I should have begun watching my step.

But she lifted those big, innocent eyes up to mine, and I began to acquire a remarkable feeling in the pit of my stomach. And somehow, impossible though it may seem, that brown hair even looked attractive. Probably it was the lighting.

She drew a deep breath. "I was born here, Fred. This is my hometown. I had my first part when I was in school here."

"Senior play?"

"Yes." She bit her lip.

"Star?"

"Yes." She smiled that wan smile again. "Pretty weak competition, I guess."

"I'll bet you were marvelous." After all, I had to be nice.

She drew another deep breath. "It was a turkey. Even my own mother could see I was a flop."

"*That* bad?"

"Terrible." She tried to manage a smile, but didn't quite make it. "I froze up. I couldn't do a thing but mumble my lines. Nothing. I suppose a really famous actor like you has never done that, Fred. Gone through a whole show and felt nothing but panic."

"Julie," I said, leaning forward, "I'm afraid I've been there myself. As a matter of fact, just about everyone in this business has. There are few things less pleasant."

She grinned, shyly. "It's awful, isn't it?" she said.

"But, Julie," I said, "after all, you didn't quit. Isn't that what counts? And, you know"—I was amazed at my own words—"you are quite an actress, now."

"Thanks, Fred," she said. She began dabbing at the tear-smeared make-up under her eyes. "This is going to sound like a second-act curtain line, but do you know why I knocked myself out getting a part in a road show coming to Cincinnati?"

I had to admit, it *was* quite a line. I didn't say anything for a minute, just looked at her. Her skin was wet and shining where the tears had washed part of her make-up away. I was feeling an odd sensation in my throat. Then I said, "I suppose I do."

"And they were all out there, Fred," she said, talking faster now. "All of them. The kids I played my part with. And the teachers. They all wanted to see me make good." She turned her face away. "And I was a flop. I fell flat."

At this point I would gladly have committed hara-kiri for her, had I thought it would be helpful. But all I could do was say, "Honestly, Julie, it wasn't that bad."

She stared at the floor. "After the curtain, I didn't even go to my dressing room. I knew they'd come back looking for me. They'd congratulate me and say how good I was, and all the time they'd be wondering what I'd done to get such a big part with such a"—she turned her eyes up to me—"famous actor." She drew a breath. "To them, I'm still a flop. So I found an empty room right off one of the wings and I went in and cried like a baby. Then I came here. I thought maybe you would understand and . . ." She didn't finish. She merely began bawling—crying just like a kid.

At this point I found myself kneeling beside her. Somehow I had my arm around her shoulder and I was saying some of the most ridiculous lines I have ever heard in my career. And, what was truly amazing, I meant every word.

It was almost midnight when we located a restaurant and ordered scrambled eggs and coffee. . . .

Perhaps it was the wholesome food that she ate—Julie, as may be guessed, is addicted to the most wholesome foods imaginable—but her cold improved considerably soon thereafter. By the time we played Nashville her performances were even better than ever.

As a matter of fact, the only sloppy performance I ever saw her give was on the day we returned to New York from the road trip. Of course, she was excited at the time, since she was making out her part of our wedding license. Had she not been distracted she probably would never have put the words, "Chicago, Illinois," in the little space that said, *Place of Birth*.

When she did, and I said, "*Chicago*, darling? I thought you said you were born in Cincinnati," she merely looked at me and turned, slowly, a bright pink. She had, for once in her career, forgotten all her lines.

She looked so guilty that I found myself unable to do a thing but laugh. Which I did, heartily.

"Darling," I said. "You're quite a little actress, aren't you? You have a great future."

"No, Fred," she said, still pink, "*two* great futures." And she put her arm in mine. The left one, of course, for I was busy signing the license with the other.

THE HUSTLER

They took Sam out of the office, through the long passageway, and up to the big metal doors. The doors opened, slowly, and they stepped out.

The sunlight was exquisite; warm on Sam's face. The air was clear and still. A few birds were circling in the sky. There was a gravel path, a road, and then, grass. Sam drew a deep breath. He could see as far as the horizon.

A guard drove up in a gray station wagon. He opened the door and Sam got in, whistling softly to himself. They drove off, down the gravel path. Sam did not turn around to look at the prison walls; he kept his eyes on the grass that stretched ahead of them, and on the road through the grass.

When the guard stopped to let him off in Richmond he said, "A word of advice, Willis."

"Advice?" Sam smiled at the guard.

"That's right. You got a habit of getting in trouble, Willis. That's why they didn't parole you, made you serve full time, because of that habit."

"That's what the man told me," Sam said. "So?"

"So stay out of poolrooms. You're smart. You can earn a living."

Sam started climbing out of the station wagon. "Sure," he said. He got out, slammed the door, and the guard drove away.

It was still early and the town was nearly empty. Sam walked around, up and down different streets, for about an hour, looking at houses and stores, smiling at the people he saw, whistling or humming little tunes to himself.

In his right hand he was carrying his little round tubular leather case, carrying it by the brass handle on the side. It was about thirty inches long, the case, and about as big around as a man's forearm.

At ten o'clock he went to the bank and drew out the six hundred dollars he had deposited there under the name of George Graves. Only it was $680; it had gathered that much interest.

Then he went to a clothing store and bought a sporty tan coat, a pair of brown slacks, brown suede shoes and a bright green sport shirt. In the store's dressing room he put the new outfit on, leaving the prison-issued suit and shoes on the floor. Then he bought two extra sets of underwear and socks, paid, and left.

About a block up the street there was a clean-looking beauty parlor. He walked in and told the lady who seemed to be in charge, "I'm an actor. I have to play a part in Chicago tonight that requires red hair." He smiled at her. "Can you fix me up?"

The lady was all efficiency. "Certainly," she said. "If you'll just step back to a booth we'll pick out a shade."

A half hour later he was a redhead. In two hours he was on board a plane for Chicago, with a little less than six hundred dollars in his pocket and one piece of luggage. He still had the underwear and socks in a paper sack.

In Chicago he took a fourteen dollar a night room in the best hotel he could find. The room was big, and pleasant. It looked and smelled clean.

He sat down on the side of the bed and opened his little leather case at the top. The two-piece billiard cue inside was intact. He took it out and screwed the brass joint together, pleased that it still fit perfectly. Then he checked the butt for tightness. The weight was still firm and solid. The tip was good, its shape had held up; and the cue's balance and stroke seemed easy, familiar; almost as though he still played with it every day.

He checked himself in the mirror. They had done a perfect job on his hair; and its brightness against the green and brown of his new clothes gave him the sporty, racetrack sort of look he had always avoided before. His once ruddy complexion was very pale. Not a pool player in town should be able to recognize him: he could hardly recognize himself.

If all went well he would be out of Chicago for good in a few days; and no one would know for a long time that Big Sam Willis had even played there. Six years on a manslaughter charge could have its advantages.

In the morning he had to walk around town for a while before he found a poolroom of the kind he wanted. It was a few blocks off the Loop, small; and from the outside it seemed to be fairly clean and quiet.

Inside, there was a short order and beer counter up front. In back there were four tables; Sam could see them through the door in the partition that separated the lunch room from the poolroom proper. There was no one in the place except for the tall, blond boy behind the counter.

Sam asked the boy if he could practice.

"Sure." The boy's voice was friendly. "But it'll cost you a dollar an hour."

"Fair enough." He gave the boy a five dollar bill. "Let me know when this is used up."

The boy raised his eyebrows and took the money.

In the back room Sam selected the best twenty-ounce cue he could find in the wall rack, one with an ivory point and a tight butt, chalked the tip, and broke the rack of balls on what seemed to be the best of the four tables.

He tried to break safe, a straight pool break, where you drive the two bottom corner balls to the cushions and back into the stack where they came from, making the cue ball go two rails and return to the top of the table, killing itself on the cushion. The break didn't work, however: the rack of balls spread wide, five of them came out into the table, and the cue ball stopped in the middle. It would have left an opponent wide open for a big run. Sam shuddered.

He pocketed the fifteen balls, missing only once—a long shot that had to be cut thin into a far corner—and he felt better, making balls. He had little confidence on the hard ones, he was awkward; but he still knew the game, he knew how to break up little clusters of balls on one shot so that he could pocket them on the next. He knew how to play position with very little English on the cue, by shooting "natural" shots, and letting the speed of the cue ball do the work. He could still figure the spread, plan out his shots in advance from the positions of the balls on the table, and he knew what to shoot at first.

He kept shooting for about three hours. Several times other players came in and played for a while, but none of them payed any attention to him, and none of them stayed long.

The place was empty again and Sam was practicing cutting balls down the rail, working on his cue ball and on his speed, when he looked up and saw the boy who ran the place coming back. He was carrying a plate with a hamburger in one hand and two bottles of beer in the other.

"Hungry?" He set the sandwich down on the arm of a chair. "Or thirsty, maybe?"

Sam looked at his watch. It was 1:30. "Come to think of it," he said, "I am." He went to the chair, picked up the hamburger, and sat down.

"Have a beer," the boy said, affably. Sam took it and drank from the bottle. It tasted delicious.

"What do I owe you?" he said, and took a bite out of the hamburger.

"The burger's thirty cents," the boy said. "The beer's on the house."

"Thanks," Sam said, chewing. "How do I rate?"

"You're a good customer," the boy said. "Easy on the equipment, cash in advance, and I don't even have to rack the balls for you."

"Thanks." Sam was silent for a minute, eating.

The boy was drinking the other beer. Abruptly, he set the bottle down. "You on the hustle?" he said.

"Do I look like a hustler?"

"You practice like one."

Sam sipped his beer quietly for a minute, looking over the top of the bottle, once, at the boy. Then he said, "I might be looking around." He set the empty bottle down on the wooden chair arm. "I'll be back tomorrow; we can talk about it then. There might be something in it for you, if you help me out."

"Sure, mister," the boy said. "You pretty good?"

"I think so," Sam said. Then when the boy got up to leave he added, "Don't try to finger me for anybody. It won't do you any good."

"I won't." The boy went back up front.

Sam practiced, working mainly on his stroke and his position, for three more hours. When he finished his arm was sore and his feet were tired; but he felt better. His stroke was beginning to work for him, he was getting smooth, making balls regularly, playing good position. Once, when he was running balls continuously, racking fourteen and one, he ran forty-seven without missing.

The next morning, after a long night's rest, he was even better. He ran more than ninety balls one time, missing, finally, on a difficult rail shot.

The boy came back at one o'clock, bringing a ham sandwich this time and two beers. "Here you go," he said. "Time to make a break."

Sam thanked him, laid his cue stick on the table, and sat down.

"My name's Barney," the boy said.

"George Graves." Sam held out his hand, and the boy shook it. "Just," he smiled inwardly at the thought, "call me Red."

"You *are* good," Barney said. "I watched you a couple of times."

"I know." Sam took a drink from the beer bottle. "I'm looking for a straight pool game."

"I figured that, Mister Graves. You won't find one here, though. Up at Bennington's they play straight pool."

Sam had heard of Bennington's. They said it was a hustler's room, a big money place.

"You know who plays pool there, Barney?" he said.

"Sure. Bill Peyton, he plays there. And Shufala Kid, Louisville Fats, Johnny Vargas, Henry Keller, a little guy they call 'The Policeman'. . . ."

Henry Keller was the only familiar name: Sam had played him once, in Atlantic City, maybe fourteen years ago. But that had been even before the big days of Sam's reputation, before he had got so good that he had to trick hustlers into playing him. That was a long time ago. And then there was the red hair; he ought to be able to get by.

"Which one's got money," he asked, "and plays straight pool?"

"Well," Barney looked doubtful, "I think Louisville Fats carries a big roll. He's one of the old Prohibition boys; they say he keeps an army of hoods working for him. He plays straights. But he's good. And he doesn't like being hustled."

It looked good; but dangerous. Hustlers didn't take it very well to find out a man was using a phony name so he could get a game. Sam remembered the time someone had told Bernie James who he had been playing and Bernie had got pretty rough about it. But this time it was different; he had been out of circulation six years, and he had never played in Chicago before.

"This Fats. Does he bet big?"

"Yep, he bets big. Big as you want." Barney smiled. "But I tell you he's mighty good."

"Rack the balls," Sam said, and smiled back. "I'll show you something."

Barney racked. Sam broke them wide open and started running. He went through the rack, then another, another, and
another. Barney was counting the balls, racking them for him
each time. When he got to eighty Sam said, "Now I'll bank a
few." He banked seven, knocking them off the rails, across, and
into the pockets. When he missed the eight he said, "What do
you think?"

"You'll do," Barney said. He laughed. "Fats is good: but you
might take him."

"I'll take him," Sam said. "You lead me to him. Tomorrow
night you get somebody to work for you. We're going up to
Bennington's."

"Fair enough, Mister Graves," Barney said. He was grinning. "We'll have a beer on that."

At Bennington's you took an elevator to the floor you wanted:
billiards on the first, pocket pool on the second, snooker and
private games on the third. It was an old-fashioned set-up,
high ceilings, big, shaded incandescent lights, overstuffed
leather chairs.

Sam spent the morning on the second floor, trying to get
the feel of the tables. They were different from Barney's, with
softer cushions and tighter cloths, and it was a little hard to get
used to them: but after about two hours he felt as though he
had them pretty well, and he left. No one had paid any attention to him.

After lunch he inspected his hair in the restaurant's bathroom mirror; it was still as red as ever and hadn't yet begun to
grow out. He felt good. Just a little nervous, but good.

Barney was waiting for him at the little poolroom. They
took a cab up to Bennington's.

Louisville Fats must have weighed three hundred pounds.

His face seemed to be bloated around the eyes like the face of an Eskimo, so that he was always squinting. His arms, hanging from the short sleeves of his white silk shirt, were pink and dough-like. Sam noticed his hands; they were soft looking, white and delicate. He wore three rings, one with a diamond. He had on dark green, wide suspenders.

When Barney introduced him, Fats said, "How are you, George?" but didn't offer his hand. Sam noticed that his eyes, almost buried beneath the face, seemed to shift from side to side, so that he seemed not really to be looking at anything.

"I'm fine," Sam said. Then, after a pause, "I've heard a lot about you."

"I got a reputation?" Fats' voice was flat, disinterested. "Then I must be pretty good maybe?"

"I suppose so," Sam said, trying to watch the eyes.

"You a good pool player, George?" The eyes flickered, scanning Sam's face.

"Fair. I like playing. Straight pool."

"Oh." Fats grinned, abruptly, coldly. "That's my game too, George." He slapped Barney on the back. The boy pulled away, slightly, from him. "You pick good, Barney. He plays my game. You can finger for me, sometime, if you want."

"Sure," Barney said. He looked nervous.

"One thing." Fats was still grinning. "You play for money, George? I mean, you gamble?"

"When the bet's right."

"What you think is a right bet, George?"

"Fifty dollars."

Fats grinned even more broadly; but his eyes still kept shifting. "Now that's close, George," he said. "You play for a hundred and we play a few."

"Fair enough," Sam said, as calmly as he could.

"Let's go upstairs. It's quieter."

"Fine. I'll take my boy if you don't mind. He can rack the balls."

Fats looked at Barney. "You level with that rack, Barney? I mean, you rack the balls tight for Fats?"

"Sure," Barney said, "I wouldn't try to cross you up."

"You know better than that, Barney. Okay."

They walked up the back stairs to the third floor. There was a small, bare-walled room, well lighted, with chairs lined up against the walls. The chairs were high ones, the type used for watching pool games. There was no one else in the room.

They uncovered the table, and Barney racked the balls. Sam lost the toss and broke, making it safe, but not too safe. He undershot, purposely, and left the cue ball almost a foot away from the end rail.

They played around, shooting safe, for a while. Then Fats pulled a hard one off the edge of the rack, ran thirty-five, and played him safe. Sam jockeyed with him, figuring to lose for a while, only wanting the money to hold out until he had the table down pat, until he had the other man's game figured, until he was ready to raise the bet.

He lost three in a row before he won one. He wasn't playing his best game; but that meant little, since Fats was probably pulling his punches too, trying to take him for as much as possible. After he won his first game he let himself go a little and made a few tricky ones. Once he knifed a ball thin into the side pocket and went two cushions for a break up; but Fats didn't even seem to notice.

Neither of them tried to run more than forty at a turn. It would have looked like a game between only fair players, except that neither of them missed very often. In a tight spot they didn't try anything fancy, just shot a safe and let the other man figure it out. Sam played safe on some shots that he was sure he could make; he didn't want to show his hand. Not yet. They kept playing and, after a while, Sam started winning more often.

After about three hours he was five games ahead, and shooting better all the time. Then, when he won still another game, Sam said, "You're losing money, Fats. Maybe we should quit." He looked at Barney and winked. Barney gave him a puzzled, worried look.

"Quit? You think we should quit?" Fats took a big silk handkerchief from his side pocket and wiped his face. "How much money you won, George?" he said.

"That last makes six hundred." He felt, suddenly, a little tense. It was coming. The big push.

"Suppose we play for six hundred, George." He put the handkerchief back in his pocket. "Then we see who quits."

"Fine." He felt really nervous now, but he knew he would get over it. Nervousness didn't count. At six hundred a game he would be in clover and in San Francisco in two days. If he didn't lose.

Barney racked the balls and Sam broke. He took the break slowly, putting to use his practice of three days, and his experience of twenty-seven years. The balls broke perfectly, reracking the original triangle, and the cue ball skidded to a stop right on the end cushion.

"You shoot pretty good," Fats said, looking at the safe table that Sam had left him. But he played safe, barely tipping the cue ball off one of the balls down at the foot of the table and returning back to the end rail.

Sam tried to return the safe by repeating the same thing; but the cue ball caught the object ball too thick and he brought out a shot, a long one, for Fats. Fats stepped up, shot the ball in, played position, and ran out the rest of the rack. Then he ran out another rack and Sam sat down to watch; there was nothing he could do now. Fats ran seventy-eight points and then, seeing a difficult shot, played him safe.

He had been afraid that something like that might happen. He tried to fight his way out of the game, but couldn't seem to get into the clear long enough for a good run. Fats beat him badly—125 to 30—and he had to give back the six hundred dollars from his pocket. It hurt.

What hurt even worse was that he knew he had less than six hundred left of his own money.

"Now we see who quits." Fats stuffed the money in his hip pocket. "You want to play for another six hundred?"

"I'm still holding my stick," Sam said. He tried not to think about that "army of hoods" that Barney had told him about.

He stepped up to the table and broke. His hand shook a little; but the break was a perfect one.

In the middle of the game Fats missed an easy shot, leaving Sam a dead set-up. Sam ran fifty-three and out. He won. It was as easy as that. He was six hundred ahead again, and feeling better.

Then something unlucky happened. Downstairs they must have closed up because six men came up during the next game and sat around the table. Five of them Sam had never seen, but one of them was Henry Keller. Henry was drunk now, evidently, and he didn't seem to be paying much attention to what was going on; but Sam didn't like it. He didn't like Keller, and he didn't like having a man who knew who he was around him. It was too much like that other time. That time in Richmond when Bernie James had come after him with a bottle. That fight had cost him six years. He didn't like it. It was getting time to wind things up here, time to be cutting out. If he could win two more games quick, he would have enough to set him up hustling on the West Coast. And on the West Coast there weren't any Henry Kellers who knew that Big Sam Willis was once the best straight-pool shot in the game.

After Sam had won the game by a close score Fats looked at his fingernails and said, "George, you're a hustler. You shoot better straights than anybody in Chicago shoots. Except me."

This was the time, the time to make it quick and neat, the time to push as hard as he could. He caught his breath, held steady, and said, "You've got it wrong, Fats. I'm better than you are. I'll play you for all of it. The whole twelve hundred."

It was very quiet in the room. Then Fats said, "George, I like that kind of talk." He started chalking his cue. "We play twelve hundred."

Barney racked the balls and Fats broke them. They both played safe, very safe, back and forth, keeping the cue ball on the rail, not leaving a shot for the other man. It was nerve-wracking. Over and over.

Then he missed. Missed the edge of the rack, coming at it from an outside angle. His cue ball bounced off the rail and into the rack of balls, spreading them wide, leaving Fats at least five shots. Sam didn't sit down. He just stood and watched Fats come up and start his run. He ran the balls, broke on the fifteenth, and ran another rack. Twenty-eight points. And he was just getting started. He had his rack break set up perfectly for the next shot.

Then, as Fats began chalking up, preparing to shoot, Henry Keller stood up from his seat and pointed his finger at Sam.

He was drunk; but he spoke clearly, and loudly. "You're Big Sam Willis," he said. "You're the World's Champion." He sat back in his chair, heavily. "You got red hair, but you're Big Sam." He sat silent, half slumped in the big chair, for a moment, his eyes glassy, and red at the corners. Then he closed his eyes and said, "There's nobody beats Big Sam, Fats. Nobody *never*."

The room was quiet for what seemed to be a very long while. Sam noticed how thick the tobacco smoke had become in the air; motionless, it was like a heavy brown mist, and over the table it was like a cloud. The faces of the men in the chairs were impassive; all of them, except Henry, watching him.

Fats turned to him. For once his eyes were not shifting from side to side. He looked Sam in the face and said, in a voice that was flat and almost a whisper, "You Big Sam Willis, George?"

"That's right, Fats."

"You must be pretty smart, Sam," Fats said, "to play a trick like that. To make a sucker out of me."

"Maybe." His chest and stomach felt very tight. It was like when Bernie James had caught him at the same game, except without the red hair. Bernie hadn't said anything, though; he had just picked up a bottle.

But, then, Bernie James was dead now. Sam wondered, momentarily, if Fats had ever heard about that.

Suddenly Fats split the silence, laughing. The sound of his laughing filled the room, he threw his head back and laughed; and the men in the chairs looked at him, astonished, hearing the laughter. "Big Sam," he said, "you're a hustler. You put on a great act; and fool me good. A great act." He slapped Sam on the back. "I think the joke's on me."

It was hard to believe. But Fats could afford the money, and Sam knew that Fats knew who would be the best if it came to muscle. And there was no certainty whose side the other men were on.

Fats shot, ran a few more balls, and then missed.

When Sam stepped up to shoot he said, "Go ahead, Big Sam, and shoot your best. You don't have to act now. I'm quitting you anyway after this one."

The funny thing was that Sam had been shooting his best for the past five or six games—or thought he had—but when he stepped up to the table this time he was different. Maybe it was Fats or Keller, something made him feel as he hadn't felt for a long time. It was like being the old Big Sam, back before he had quit playing the tournaments and exhibitions, the Big Sam who could run 125 when he was hot and the money was up. His stroke was smooth, steady, accurate, like a balanced, precision instrument moving on well-oiled bearings. He shot easily, calmly, clicking the shots off in his mind and then pocketing them on the table, watching everything on the green, forgetting himself, forgetting even the money, just dropping the balls into the pockets, one after another.

He did it. He ran the game. A hundred and twenty-five points, 125 shots without missing. When he finished Fats took twelve hundred from his still-big roll and counted it out, slowly, to him. He said, "You're the best I've ever seen, Big Sam." Then he covered the table with the oilcloth cover.

After Sam had dropped Barney off he had the cab take him by his hotel and let him off at a little all-night lunch room. He ordered bacon and eggs, over light, and talked with the waitress while she fried them. The place seemed strange, gay almost; his nerves felt electric, and there was a pleasant fuzziness in his head, a dim, insistent ringing sound coming from far off. He tried to think for a moment; tried to think whether he should go to the airport now without even going back to the hotel, now that he had made out so well, had made out better, even, than he had planned to be able to do in a week. But there was the waitress and then the food; and when he put a quarter in the juke box he couldn't hear the ringing in his ears any more. This was no time for plane trips; it was a time for talk and music, time for the sense of triumph, the sense of being alive and having money again, and then time for sleep. He was in a chromium and plastic booth in the lunch room and he leaned back against the padded plastic backrest and felt an abrupt, deep, gratifying sense of fatigue, loosening his muscles and killing, finally, the tension that had ridden him like a fury for the past three days. There would be plane flights enough tomorrow. Now, he needed rest. It was a long way to San Francisco.

The bed at his hotel was impeccably made; the pale blue spread seemed drum-tight, but soft and round at the edges and corners. He didn't even take off his shoes.

When he awoke, he awoke suddenly. The skin at the back of his neck was itching, sticky with sweat from where the collar of his shirt had been pressed, tight, against it. His mouth was dry and his feet felt swollen, stuffed, in his shoes. The room was as quiet as death. Outside the window a car's tires groaned gently, rounding a corner, then were still.

He pulled the chain on the lamp by the bed and the light came on. Squinting, he stood up, and realized that his legs were aching. The room seemed too big, too bright. He stumbled into the bathroom and threw handsfull of cold water on his face and neck. Then he dried off with a towel and looked in the mirror. Startled, he let go the towel momentarily; the red hair had caught him off guard; and with the eyes now swollen, the lips pale, it was not his face at all. He finished drying quickly, ran his comb through his hair, straightened out his shirt and slacks hurriedly. The startling strangeness of his own face had crystallized the dim, half-conscious feeling that had awakened him, the feeling that something was wrong. The hotel room, himself, Chicago; they were all wrong. He should not be here, not now; he should be on the West Coast, in San Francisco.

He looked at his watch. Four o'clock. He had slept three hours. He did not feel tired, not now, although his bones ached and there was sand under his eyelids. He could sleep, if he had to, on the plane. But the important thing, now, was getting on the plane, clearing out, moving West. He had slept with his cue, in its case, on the bed. He took it and left the room.

The lobby, too, seemed too bright and too empty. But when he had paid his bill and gone out to the street the relative darkness seemed worse. He began to walk down the street hastily, looking for a cab stand. His own footsteps echoed around him as he walked. There seemed to be no cabs anywhere on the street. He began walking faster. The back of his neck was sweating again. It was a very hot night; the air felt heavy against his skin. There were no cabs.

And then, when he heard the slow, dense hum of a heavy car moving down the street in his direction, heard it from several blocks away and turned his head to see it and to see that there was no cablight on it, he knew—abruptly and lucidly, as some men at some certain times know these things—what was happening.

He began to run; but he did not know where to run. He turned a corner while he was still two blocks ahead of the car and when he could feel its lights, palpably, on the back of his neck, and tried to hide in a doorway, flattening himself out against the door. Then, when he saw the lights of the car as it began its turn around the corner he realized that the doorway was too shallow, that the lights would pick him out. Something in him wanted to scream. He pushed himself from his place, stumbled down the street, visualizing in his mind a place, some sort of a place between buildings where he could hide completely and where the car could never follow him. But the buildings were all together, with no space at all between them; and when he saw that this was so he also saw at the same instant that the carlights were flooding him. And then he heard the car stop. There was nothing more to do. He turned around and looked at the car, blinking.

Two men had got out of the back seat; there were two more in front. He could see none of their faces; but was relieved that he could not, could not see the one face that would be bloated like an Eskimo's and with eyes like slits.

The men were holding the door open for him.

"Well," he said. "Hello, boys," and climbed into the back seat. His little leather case was still in his right hand. He gripped it tightly. It was all he had.

THE STUBBORNEST MAN

He was in the kitchen, reading *David Copperfield*, his big shoulders hunched over the table, his broad, knot-jointed hands holding the book tenderly. When he heard her come in he looked up from the corner of his eye and saw that the light coming through the white curtains was very weak and that he could barely make out the outline of the barn through the open door.

Knowing what she had come to remind him of, he pushed himself back from the table to look up at her and smiled faintly, his back and his hands—especially his hands—aching even from the slight movement. She had her glasses on, steel rimmed, and she was smiling at him.

"It's past time for the cows, Fred," she said.

"I know," he said, closing the book cautiously, his big fingers awkward. "I've been a little still today. It's the time of year—the rain." He pulled himself up out of the chair, trying not to let the painfulness of the movement show on his face.

"Fred," she said, "if you want me to—"

"No." He walked to the door and took the old jacket from its hook. "This is my job."

She was looking at him over the tops of her glasses, smiling, but he could see that she had something on her mind.

"You know," she said, "you could afford a milking machine easily, now that Bill and John have finished at college."

"You sound like William," he said, letting the sudden bitterness in his voice emphasize his son's name. "Do you want television, too? And a bright green utility van? And a cocktail cabinet? We've got six cows. Six."

He turned around and looked at her again, at her small, round face, the bright, wide eyes with the deep lines round them. Her mouth was stern, thoughtful, and the thought struck him: *she's got something else on her mind. I'll hear about it when I get back from the cowshed.*

"Fred," she said, "you'd have more time to read, with a milker. And you have other machines—the tractor, the hay baler."

He opened the door when she was in the middle of saying it. When she finished he said: "During the war I milked twenty-three cows. By hand. Twice a day."

He let the door slam and almost flinched at the realization that she could answer that one. He walked on to the cowshed, cutting through the kitchen garden, through the little field with the chicken coop, now silent, and the shed. Dorothy's answer should have been simple enough; during the war he could milk twenty odd cows easily. Now, sixty years old, with arthritis stiffening his fingers, it took him an hour and a quarter to milk six.

There were low, irritated moanings from the cows as he pushed open the door, and then the soft, silken sound of heavy bodies, warm, becoming restless in their stalls. He turned the lights on and the cows began lowing in earnest, rubbing their flanks against the stalls, eager, their udders heavy.

Fred picked up the pail and the stool from against the wall and shuffled over to Cymbeline, his favorite, a middle-aged Frisian with an injured expression. He talked to her for a moment, soothing her, and then he set the stool in place and painfully eased himself on it. Then he took the rough, solid teats and lost himself in the sharp ring of the jet of milk against the pail, forgetting the ache in his knuckles and wrists, watching the milk foam up.

It took an hour and a half to finish them all and to get the milk into the churns and then to the dairy, where it would stay until after the morning's milking.

When he got back to the house, Dorothy was not listening to her wireless, as she usually did when he was out, and he knew that he had been right. She did have something on her mind. He took off his jacket inside the door and hung it on the nail. Then he walked into the parlor, eased his heavy, great-boned frame into a chair, put his feet, in their weathered black boots, on the coalbox and said to her: "All right, what is it?"

She came out from the kitchen and stood there watching him for a minute. Then she said, not smiling now: "A letter from Bill, Fred."

"From William," he said, correcting her. "What does he want?"

"He's coming home for the weekend."

"Sit down, Dorothy." He watched her walk over to the sofa and seat herself there. Then he said: "He remembers what I told him, doesn't he?" And, when she didn't answer, he said: "I told him to stay at the university and do his farming there—to stay out from under my feet."

"I expect he remembers."

She was being too firm, and he didn't like it. He could feel the old, complex fury beginning to work at him, the impotent fury he had felt so intensely that last summer when William had come home, with his degree in agriculture and his bright green utility van, fresh from his first year of teaching at the university's agricultural college, and had tried to tell him— him!—how to plan his next year's crops. William had told him that he should give up keeping chickens, that he should turn the thirty-acre into pasture for cattle, should buy a new kind of hay rake, buy a television set, build a bathroom, get an automatic electric milker.

Dorothy was still looking at him, waiting to hear what he had to say. He picked up a book. He said: "I don't want him here—and he knows that. Why doesn't he go to John's house and spend the weekend with them, if he wants to see the farm? John's his brother; they can watch the TV and talk about crop rotation and building better farms."

"You're not being fair to John," she said. "He keeps up his half of the farm, even if he has bought this TV set."

"All right. All right. But why's he coming?"

She was still smiling. "There's a girl, Fred. He wants us to meet her."

"A girl! And you know what she'll be like? Sawdust in her head and a bunch of women's magazines under her arm. I know William. She'll look like some film star."

Dorothy was looking at him over the top of her glasses again. "Is that a bad thing?" she asked. . . .

She did look like some film star, but one of the nicer kind. The girl had smooth make-up, short hair, a long throat, and an easy smile. But she'd had enough common sense to wear flat shoes to the farm, and her nails—thank the Lord—weren't painted.

William's utility van was still bright green, but it showed a little age and had some honest dust on it this time. William was being careful, and Fred was surprised at the way he was able to handle the girl's bag; the car doors; Orsino, who was barking his silly head off to see him; and the introductions. And he acted as if he'd entirely forgotten that his father had stood on about the same spot less than a year before and had told him with every Shakespearian epithet in his awe-inspiring vocabulary to go back to his cocksure college friends and stay with them.

Her name was Judith and she was, surprisingly, carrying a book. It was a good touch, and anybody but William would have told her to carry one. But William was like his mother, no diplomat. The book's dust jacket was gone and Fred couldn't make out the title.

It was late afternoon when they came, and Dorothy took over smoothly, welcoming them in to tea and going through her usual chatty little piece about Fred and herself being the "curiosities" of the district, and about Fred's father, who kept a 450-acre farm, was the finest local preacher on the circuit and wrote blank verse.

The girl let Dorothy do most of the talking, was poised, interested and didn't rattle her teacup. And then, when Dorothy spoke about the blank verse, the girl made an interested comment.

Fred leaned towards her. "Were you at the university, too?" he asked.

The girl nodded. "But I didn't know Bill then," she said. "I took my degree in English. I'm teaching now—at the girls' grammar school."

"English?" Fred said, glancing at William again. This was something he'd not hoped for. "Literature?"

"Of course," she said, looking amusedly at him over her teacup.

For a minute he was quiet, thinking about this astonishing fact, that William—William, who had revolted loudly and strongly, in his early adolescence, against Shakespeare and Dickens and all his father held dear—should have come home with this intelligent, literary girl who talked so well.

But no sooner had Fred realized how pleased he was with the girl than all his pleasure was shattered. And it was William that started it.

"Hope you don't mind, Dad," he said. "But Judith and I are going to slip over to John's later on. He wants us to see a program on his TV."

Television! He had two sons and he had brought them up no better than this, that when they met after being months apart they could bother with some silly toy like television.

"Do you like this television, miss?" He turned hopefully to the girl.

"Some programs," she said. "And it's nice when I'm feeling lazy."

He had been fooled, and he didn't like it. She was the same as the rest of the young people; like Dorothy, too, his wife: TV and milking machines.

He turned his face away and said bitterly, "I've never had much time myself for that kind of nonsense."

William broke in, with a hard edge to his voice. "I know quite a lot of things that you never had much time for."

They ate supper in virtual silence. Afterwards Dorothy and the girl talked, while Fred and William sat silent, not looking at each other. Fred kept his hands in his lap and once he caught the girl looking at them strangely.

Then it was almost dark, and Dorothy said gently: "What about the cows, Fred?" He said nothing, but, knowing he couldn't put it off any longer, got out of his chair as easily as he could and left the room.

In the cowshed he started with Cymbeline. At the first try to close his hand on the teat, he knew he wouldn't be able to do it.

He remained seated for twenty minutes, until the worried restlessness of the cows drove him from the shed.

As he was setting the pails back on the floor of the porch, the kitchen door opened and Judith came out. Seeing him, she was startled, and gave a quick glance at the empty pails at his feet.

"Oh," she said, "I was just coming out to see the cows."

He looked at her, wondering what she had on her mind. Then he said, passing by her—rudely, he knew—and opening the kitchen door, "You'll miss your television show."

Before he closed the door he heard her say, her voice calm: "We're not expected for half an hour."

In the kitchen he got the keys for the old van from the nail over the sink, went through the hall to the side door, and out to the shed. He was barely able to get the key into the ignition lock, but he did it somehow, managed the gears and steering wheel, and pulled out of the shed and on to his farm road. He had to open two gates, but once on the road he was all right, and he had no trouble driving the mile and a half to the little modern house on the other end of the farm, where his elder son, John, lived.

The store shed was a good distance from the house, and unlocked. He had no trouble getting into it and finding what he wanted. There was some difficulty in carrying it back to the van, but he managed, and in ten minutes was driving on down the road with an electric milking machine beside him on the seat. He took the long way round the farm, so that he wouldn't meet the others on his way back. . . .

He thought at first that he had forgotten and had left the light on in the cowshed himself, but just as he opened the door he heard the ringing, metallic sound of milk jetting against the side of a pail; and then, with the door open, he saw the milking stool with Judith on it, her back to him. The cow was Rosalind. He glanced quickly at Cymbeline in her stall. She seemed relaxed. The girl must have come in as soon as he left.

After a moment, she turned her head and looked at him over her shoulder. Some of her hair had fallen over her forehead and she was smiling.

"You'd better hide that," she said, looking at the milking machine that hung awkwardly from the crook of his arm. "Somebody might see you."

"But—" he said, knowing he must be staring at her.

She knew what he meant, and laughed lightly. "You're not the only farmer in the country," she said. "My father has two hundred acres in Lincolnshire." She smiled and turned back to what she was doing.

He stood there for what seemed a very long time. . . .

Finally, when she had finished with the cow and was preparing to move to another stall, he said, grinning in spite of himself: "As long as I've got this thing, we might as well use it."

They watched it work for a few minutes, and then he said: "What about the television?"

"Bill went on alone, I told him I—I would see John and Hilda tomorrow."

He stood watching her for a minute, silently, and then he asked her the important question, the one that he had asked himself when he first came in: "How did you know—"

She looked at him squarely. "I saw you with the empty pails. And with your arthritis—and your pride—"

"Did Dorothy tell you about my arthritis?" he said.

"She didn't have to."

"No," he said, looking down at his great-veined, broad hands. "No, I suppose not." He turned and started to leave. As he started to open the cowshed door, there was the sound of a car coming into the farmyard. Why had William come back so soon?

She stopped him, saying: "We've not finished the milking yet." Her voice was gentle. "And I've got something to say, too."

"All right." He stopped and turned back to her. "But don't try to give me advice, I don't take it very well."

"Okay," she said. "But let's move this vacuum cleaner to another cow."

When they had the thing fastened to Titania, Judith said: "This is what I want to say. First, you should do something about the arthritis."

"Do what about it?" She knew how to talk to him all right. No hedging.

"See a doctor. They can do things for arthritis these days."

"And then?"

She brushed the hair away from her forehead, smiling a little. "And then stop thinking of Bill as just a boy."

"How do you know how I think of him?"

"How? From the way you treat him."

"All right. Perhaps I do treat him that way. But he asks for it. He thinks he knows how to farm, and he won't work for me."

"He wanted to work in the summers."

"Look," he said, letting it come out now. "I want a son, a son to farm with me—all the year round—a son to take over for me when I die. That's what I wanted when I sent William to that agricultural college to learn farming. Perhaps he could have learned to be a better farmer than I am. Perhaps he could be taking my farm over by now." He stopped for breath, glancing at his hands.

She was quiet for a moment. When she spoke again, her voice was gentle. "Perhaps you've got a son who wants to be all those things to you."

"What do you mean?" he said.

"I mean that Bill wants to ask you if he can come here to live. He's not going to teach, except one day a week, for the next two years, while he works on his research thesis. He's going to do research on irrigation, and he wants you to let him use ten acres for that. If you'll let him work for you in return. He wants to get his hands dirty again. That's one of the things he came here about. He wants to know if you'll let him come back. Perhaps for good."

He knew he was staring at her again. He was dared by what she had said.

"Then why didn't he say something?" he asked.

"You haven't given him a chance yet. You started that fight about television."

"I started it? Perhaps I was rude to you—I suppose I was—but he had no need to make things worse."

"He hadn't?" Her voice was level again. "When you talked to me the way you did?" She smiled faintly. "Don't you think he has some pride?"

"All right," he said, "all right," trying to make his voice rough, but unable to keep down the excitement. The fourteen-acre piece behind the pasture—William could use that for his "research," whatever it was. And, for a place to live, the old cowman's cottage could be fixed up easily enough for one person. Or rather—he looked down at Judith—for two.

Titania bellowed abruptly. Judith looked startled, and then laughed. "We'd better look out or you're going to have a sore cow." She turned the milker off and disengaged it from Titania. "The last one," she said.

"Good." He put the top on the churn, which was almost full, straddled it and took hold of the handles.

"Hold on a minute," she said. "That's no way to treat that arthritis."

"Do you want me to leave the milk here?" He started to heave it off the ground, bracing his back for the strain.

"No." She stepped over and took one of the handles. "I grew up on a farm, remember. I've carried quite a few churns of milk before this."

"Well," he said, "you needn't carry this one." And then, going to the door, he called out: "William, come here a minute!" and then looked back at her, smiling.

Her eyes were wide. "You're calling Bill?"

"Why not? If he's going to work for me, it's time he started."

It took William less than a minute to get out to the cow-shed. He was wearing a white shirt, open at the neck. Fred looked at him, pleased with his young, easy strength, his big, heavy farmer's hands, his broad, honest face.

"What is it, Dad?" William said.

"We must get this into the dairy," Fred said. "Give me a hand, will you—Bill?"

THE IFTH OF OOFTH

Farnsworth had invented a new drink that night. He called it a mulled sloe gin today. Exactly as fantastic as it sounds—ramming a red-hot poker into a mugful of warm red gin, cinnamon, cloves and sugar, and then *drinking* the fool thing—but like many of Farnsworth's ideas, it managed somehow to work out. In fact, its flavor had become completely acceptable to me after the third one.

When he finally set the end of his steaming poker back on the coals for regeneration, I leaned back in my big leather chair—the one he had rigged up so that it would gently rock you to sleep if you pressed the right button—and said, "Oliver, your ingenuity is matched only by your hospitality."

Farnsworth blushed and smiled. He is a small, chubby man and blushes easily. "Thank you," he said. "I have another new one. I call it a jelled vodka fizz—you eat it with a spoon. You may want to try it later. It's—well—exceptional."

I suppressed a shudder at the thought of eating jelled vodka and said, "Interesting, very interesting," and since he didn't reply, we both stared at the fire for a while, letting the gin continue its pleasant work. Farnsworth's bachelor home was very comfortable and relaxing, and I always enjoyed my Wednesday night visits there thoroughly. I suppose most men have a deep-seated love for open fires and liquor—however fantastically prepared—and leather armchairs.

Then, after several minutes, Farnsworth bounced to his feet and said, "There's a thing I wanted to show you. Made it last week. Didn't pull it off too well, though."

"Really?" I said. I'd thought the drinks had been his weekly brainchild. They seemed quite enough.

"Yes," he said, trotting over to the door of the study. "It's downstairs in the shop. I'll get it." And he bounced out of the room, the paneled door closing as it had opened, automatically, behind him.

I turned back to the fire again, pleased that he had made something in the machine shop—the carpentry shop was in a shed in the backyard; the chemistry and optical labs in the attic—for he was at his best with his lathe and milling machines. His self-setting, variable-twist thumb bolt had been a beautiful piece of work and its patent had made him a lot of money.

He returned in a minute, carrying a very odd-looking thing with him, and set it on the table beside my chair. I examined it for a minute while Farnsworth stood over me, half smiling, his little green eyes wide, sparkling in the flickering light from the fire. I knew he was suppressing his eagerness for my comment, but I was unsure what to say.

The thing appeared simple: a cross-shaped construction of several dozen one-inch cubes, half of them of thin, transparent plastic, the other half made of thin little sheets of aluminum. Each cube was hinged to two others very cunningly and the arrangement of them all was confusing.

Finally, I said, "How many cubes?" I had tried to count them, but kept getting lost.

"Sixty-four," he said. "I think."

"You *think*?"

"Well—" He seemed embarrassed. "At least I *made* sixty-four cubes, thirty-two of each kind; but somehow I haven't been able to count them since. They seem to . . . get lost, or shift around, or something."

"Oh?" I was becoming interested. "May I pick it up?"

"Certainly," he said, and I took the affair, which was surprisingly lightweight, in my hands and began folding the cubes around on their hinges. I noticed then that some were open on one side and that certain others would fit into these if their hinging arrangements would allow them to.

I began folding them absently and said, "You could count them by marking them one at a time. With a crayon, for instance."

"As a matter of fact," he admitted, blushing again, "I tried that. Didn't seem to work out. When I finished, I found I had marked six cubes with the number one and on none of them could I find a two or three, although there were two fours, one of them written in reverse and in green." He hesitated. "I had used a red marking pencil." I saw him shudder slightly as he said it, although his voice had been casual-sounding enough. "I rubbed the numbers off with a damp cloth and didn't . . . try it again."

"Well," I said. And then, "What do you call it?"

"A pentaract."

He sat back down again in his armchair. "Of course, that

name really isn't accurate. I suppose a pentaract should really be a four-dimensional pentagon, and this is meant to be a picture of a five-dimensional cube."

"A *picture?*" It didn't look like a picture to me.

"Well, it couldn't *really* have five-dimensionality—length, width, breadth, ifth and oofth—or I don't think it could." His voice faltered a little at that. "But it's supposed to illustrate the layout of an object that did have those."

"What kind of object would that be?" I looked back at the thing in my lap and was surprised to see that I had folded a good many of the cubes together.

"Suppose," he said, "you put a lot of points in a row, touching; you have a line—a one-dimensional figure. Put four lines together at right angles and on a plane; a square—two-dimensional. Six squares at right angles and extended into real space give you a cube—three dimensions. And eight cubes extended into four physical dimensions give you a tesseract, as it's called—"

"And eight tesseracts make a pentaract," I said. "Five dimensions."

"Exactly. But naturally this is just a *picture* of a pentaract, in that sense. There probably isn't any ifth and oofth at all."

"I still don't know what you mean by a *picture,*" I said, pushing the cubes around interestedly.

"You don't?" he asked, pursing his lips. "It's rather awkward to explain, but . . . well, on the surface of a piece of paper, you can make a very realistic picture of a cube—you know, with perspective and shading and all that kind of thing—and what you'd actually be doing would be illustrating a three-dimensional object, the cube, by using only two dimensions to do it with."

"And of course," I said, "you could *fold* the paper into a cube. Then you'd have a real cube."

He nodded. "But you'd have to *use* the third dimension—by folding the flat paper *up*—to do it. So, unless I could fold my cubes up through ifth or oofth, my pentaract will have to be just a poor picture."

"Well!" I said, a bit lost. "And what do you plan to use it for?"

"Just curiosity." And then, abruptly, looking at me now, his eyes grew wide and he bumped up out of his chair. He said breathlessly, "What have you done to it?"

I looked down at my hands. I was holding a little structure of eight cubes, joined together in a small cross. "Why, nothing," I said, feeling a little foolish. "I only folded most of them together."

"That's impossible! There were only twelve open ones to begin with! All of the others were six-sided!"

Farnsworth made a grab for it, apparently beside himself; the gesture was so sudden that I drew back. It made Farnsworth miss his grab and the little object flew from my hands and hit the floor, solidly, on one of its corners. There was a slight bump as it hit, and a faint clicking noise, and the thing seemed to crumple in a peculiar way. Sitting in front of us on the floor was a little one-inch cube, and nothing else.

For at least a full minute, we stared at it. Then I stood up and looked in my chair seat, looked around the floor of the room, even got down on my knees and peered under the chair. Farnsworth was watching me, and when I finished and sat down again, he asked, "No others?"

"No other cubes," I said, "anywhere."

"I was afraid of that." He pointed an unsteady finger at the one cube in front of us. "I suppose they're all in there." Some of his agitation had begun to wear off and after a moment he said, "What was that you said about folding the paper to make a cube?"

I looked at him and managed an apologetic smile.

He didn't smile back, but he got up and said, "Well, I doubt if it can bite," and bent over and picked the cube up, hefting its weight carefully in his hand. "It seems to weigh the same as the—sixty-four did," he said, quite calmly now. Then he looked at it closely and suddenly became agitated again. "Good heavens! Look at this!" He held it up. On one side, exactly in the center, was a neat little hole, about a half-inch across.

I moved my head closer to the cube and saw that the hole was not really circular. It was like the iris diaphragm of a camera, a polygon made of many overlapping, straight pieces of metal, allowing an opening for light to enter. Nothing was visible through the hole; I could see only an undefined blackness.

"I don't understand how . . ." I began, and stopped.

"Nor I," he said. "Let's see if there's anything in here."

He put the cube up to his eye and squinted and peered for a minute. Then he carefully set it on the table, walked to his chair, sat down and folded his hands over his fat little lap.

"George," he said, "there *is* something in there." His voice now was very steady and yet strange.

"What?" I asked. What else do you say?

"A little ball," he said. "A little round ball. Quite misted over, but nonetheless a ball."

"Well!" I said.

"George, I'll get the gin."

He was back from the sideboard in what seemed an incredibly short time. He had the sloe gin in highball glasses, with ice and water. It tasted horrible.

When I finished mine, I said, "Delicious. Let's have another," and we did. After I drank that one, I felt a good deal more rational.

I set my glass down. "Farnsworth, it just occurred to me. Isn't the fourth dimension supposed to be *time*, according to Einstein?"

He had finished his second sloe gin highball, unmulled, by then. "Supposed to be, yes, according to Einstein. I call it ifth—or oofth—take your pick." He held up the cube again, much more confidently now, I noticed. "And what about the *fifth* dimension?"

"Beats me," I said, looking at the cube, which was beginning to seem vaguely sinister to me. "Beats the hell out of me."

"Beats me, too, George," he said almost gaily—an astonishing mood for old Farnsworth. He turned the cube around with his small, fat fingers. "This is probably all wrapped up in time in some strange way. Not to mention the very peculiar kind of space it appears to be involved with. Extraordinary, don't you think?"

"Extraordinary." I nodded.

"George, I think I'll take another look." And he put the cube back to his eye again. "Well," he said, after a moment of squinting, "same little ball."

"What's it doing?" I wanted to know.

"Nothing. Or perhaps spinning a bit. I'm not sure. It's quite fuzzy, you see, and misty. Dark in there, too."

"Let me see," I said, realizing that, after all, if Farnsworth could see the thing in there, so could I.

"In a minute. I wonder what sort of time I'm looking into—past or future, or what?"

"And what sort of space . . ." I was saying when, suddenly,

little Farnsworth let out a shriek, dropped the cube as if it had suddenly turned into a snake, and threw his hands over his eyes.

He sank back into his chair and cried, "My God! My God!"

"What happened?" I asked, rushing over to Farnsworth, who was squirming in his armchair, his face still hidden by his hands.

"My eye!" he moaned, almost sobbing. "It stabbed my eye! Quick, George, call me an ambulance!"

I hurried to the telephone and fumbled with the book, looking for the right number, until Farnsworth said, "Quick, George!" again and, in desperation, I dialed the operator and told her to send us an ambulance.

When I got back to Farnsworth, he had taken his hand from the unhurt eye and I could see that a trickle of blood was beginning to run down the other wrist. He had almost stopped squirming, but from his face it was obvious that the pain was still intense.

He stood up. "I need another drink," he said, and was heading unsteadily for the sideboard when he stepped on the cube, which was still lying in front of his chair, and was barely able to keep himself from falling headlong, tripping on it. The cube skidded a few feet, stopping, hole-side up, near the fire.

He said to the cube, enraged, "Damn you, I'll show you . . . !" and he reached down and swooped up the poker from the hearth. It had been lying there for mulling drinks, its end resting on the coals, and by now it was a brilliant cherry red. He took the handle with both hands and plunged the red-hot tip into the hole of the cube, pushing it down against the floor.

"I'll show you!" he yelled again, and I watched understandingly as he shoved with all his weight, pushing and twisting, forcing the poker down with angry energy. There was a faint hissing sound and little wisps of dark smoke came from the hole, around the edges of the poker.

Then there was a strange, sucking noise and the poker began to sink into the cube. It must have gone in at least eight or ten inches—impossible, of course, since it was a one-inch cube—and even Farnsworth became so alarmed at this that he yanked the poker out of the hole.

As he did, black smoke arose in a little column for a moment and then there was a popping sound and the cube fell apart, scattering itself into hundreds of squares of plastic and aluminum.

Oddly enough, there were no burn marks on the aluminum and none of the plastic seemed to have melted. There was no sign of a little, misty ball.

Farnsworth returned his right hand to his now puffy and bloody eye. He stood staring at the profusion of little squares with his good eye. His free hand was trembling.

Then there was the sound of a siren, becoming louder. He turned and looked at me balefully. "That must be the ambulance. I suppose I'd better get my toothbrush."

Farnsworth lost the eye. Within a week, though, he was pretty much his old chipper self again, looking quite dapper with a black leather patch. One interesting thing—the doctor remarked that there were powder burns of some sort on the eyelid, and that the eye itself appeared to have been destroyed by a small explosion. He assumed that it had been a case of a gun misfiring, the cartridge exploding in an open breech somehow. Farnsworth let him think that; it was as good an explanation as any.

I suggested to Farnsworth that he ought to get a green patch, to match his other eye. He laughed at the idea and said he thought it might be a bit showy. He was already starting work on another pentaract; he was going to find out just what ...

But he never finished. Nine days after the accident, there was a sudden flurry of news reports from the other side of the world, fantastic stories that made the tabloids go wild, and we began to guess what had happened. There wouldn't be any need to build the sixty-four-cube cross and try to find a way of folding it up. We knew now.

It *had* been a five-dimensional cube, all right. And one extension of it had been in time—into the future; nine days into the future—and the other extension had been into a peculiar kind of space, one that distorted sizes quite strangely.

All of this became obvious when, three days later, it happened on our side of the world and the tabloids were scooped by the phenomenon itself, which, by its nature, required no newspaper reporting.

Across the entire sky of the Western Hemisphere there appeared—so vast that it eclipsed the direct light of the sun from Fairbanks, Alaska, to Cape Horn—a tremendous human eye, with a vast, glistening, green iris. Part of the lid was there, too, and all of it was as if framed in a gigantic circle. Or not exactly a circle, but a polygon of many sides, like the iris diaphragm of a camera shutter.

Toward nightfall, the eye blinked once and probably five hundred million people screamed simultaneously. It remained there all of the night, glowing balefully in the reflected sunlight, obliterating the stars.

Probably more than half the people on Earth thought it was God. Only two knew that it was Oliver Farnsworth, peering at a misty little spinning ball in a five-dimensional box, nine days before, totally unaware that the little ball was the Earth itself, contained in a little one-inch cube that was an enclave of swollen time and shrunken space.

When I had dropped the pentaract and had somehow caused it to fold itself into two new dimensions, it had reached out through fifth-dimensional space and folded the world into itself, and had begun accelerating the time within it, in rough proportion to size, so that as each minute passed in Farnsworth's study, about one day was passing on the world within the cube.

We knew this because about a minute had passed while Farnsworth had held his eye against the cube the second time—the first time had, of course, been the appearance over Asia—and nine days later, when we saw the same event from our position on the Earth in the cube, it was twenty-six hours before the eye was "stabbed" and withdrew.

It happened early in the morning, just after the sun had left the horizon and was passing into eclipse behind the great circle that contained the eye. Someone stationed along a defense-perimeter station panicked—someone highly placed. Fifty guided missiles were launched, straight up, the most powerful on Earth. Each carried a hydrogen warhead. Even before the great shock wave from their explosion came crashing down to earth, the eye had disappeared.

Somewhere, I knew, an unimaginably vast Oliver Farnsworth was squirming and yelping, carrying out the identical chain of events that I had seen happening in the past and that yet must be happening now, along the immutable space-time continuum that Farnsworth's little cube had somehow bypassed.

The doctor had talked of powder burns. I wondered what he would think if he knew that Farnsworth had been hit in the eye with fifty infinitesimal hydrogen bombs.

For a week, there was nothing else to talk about in the world. Three billion people probably discussed, thought about and dreamed of nothing else. There had been no more dramatic happening since the creation of the earth and sun than the appearance of Farnsworth's eye.

But two people, out of those three billion, thought of something else. They thought of the unchangeable, preset space-time continuum, moving at the rate of one minute for every day that passed here on our side of the pentaract, while that vast Oliver Farnsworth and I, in the other-space, other-time, were staring at the cube that contained our world, lying on their floor.

On Wednesday, we could say, *Now he's gone to the telephone.* On Thursday, *Now he's looking through the book.* On Saturday, *By now he must be dialing the operator . . .*

And on Tuesday morning, when the sun came up, we were together and saw it rise, for we spent our nights together by then, because we did not want to be alone; and when the day had begun, we didn't say it, because we couldn't. But we thought it.

We thought of a colossal, cosmic Farnsworth saying, "I'll show you!" and shoving, pushing and twisting, forcing with all of his might, into the little round hole, a brilliantly glowing, hissing, smoking, red-hot poker.

OPERATION GOLD BRICK

Two army engineers found it while drilling a hole through one of the Appalachian Mountains, in the Primitive Reservation, on a lovely spring day in 1993. The hole was to be used for a monorail track; and although in 1993 it was very simple to run monorail lines *over* mountains, it was also quite easy to drill large, straight holes through almost anything; and the U.S. Army liked to effect the neatness of straight lines. So the engineers had set up a little converter machine on a tripod, pointed it, and proceeded to convert a singularly neat hole, twenty-two feet in diameter, in the side of the mountain. At first the mountain converted nicely, the hole tunneling along at an efficient thirteen feet per hour; and the engineers, whose names were George and Sam, were quite pleased with themselves and rubbed their hands together with pleasure; while the little machine on the tripod hummed merrily, birds sang, and wisps of brown smoke floated off from the mountain into an otherwise clear blue sky.

And then they found it. Or, rather, the converter did, by abruptly ceasing to convert. The machine continued to hum; but the little feedback-controlled counter, which normally clicked off the number of tons of material substance that had been converted into immaterial substance, stopped. The last wisps of smoke disappeared from the mountainside. The two engineers looked at one another. After a minute George picked a rock up from the ground, a large one, and threw it out in front of the lens of the machine. The rock vanished instantly. The one-tenth ton counter wheel trembled, and was still.

"Well," Sam said, after a minute. "It's still working."

George thought about this for a minute. Then he said, "I guess we'd better look at the tunnel."

So they shut the machine off, walked over to the hole in the mountainside and went in. Fortunately the sun was behind them and they had no difficulty seeing as they made their way down the glassy-smooth shaft—which needed no shoring since the converter had been set to convert part of the materials removed into a quite sturdy lining of neo-adamant. The shaft ended in a forbidding, twenty-two foot, black disk of unconverted mountain bowels. The two of them peered uneasily at this for a few minutes and then Sam said, "What's this?" and kneeled down to inspect a rectangle, gold in color, about ten inches long and four high, which appeared to be engraved in the rock at the dead end of the tunnel.

"Let me see," George said, stooping beside his co-scientist and pulling from his pocket a pocketknife, with which he proceeded to scrape around the edges of the rectangle. Some of the loose rock crumbled away, revealing that the rectangle was, actually, one surface of a solid bar of some sort.

He continued to scrape for a few minutes, removing enough rock to get a grip on the sides of the bar with his fingers, took a good hold and began to try to work the bar loose. The other engineer helped him, and they pulled, strained, wedged and pushed for about ten minutes, until finally George said, "It won't move," and they stopped, perspiring. And it hadn't moved, not a millimeter.

The two of them glared, for a moment, at the smooth surface of the golden bar, which shone, lustrous, back at them. Then Sam said, "Let's get a pick."

"A pick?"

Sam, who knew something of Army history, was patronizing. "Yes. A kind of manual-powered converter."

George was impressed. "But where?" he said.

"At U-10 Supply."

They left the uncompleted tunnel, stepped into their Minnijet, field model, officer-type helicopter and flew at a leisurely five hundred miles per hour to U-10. U-10 had been, before the 1980s Decade of Enlightenment, the University of Tennessee—the 1980s had held no illusions about what was important to the American Way of Life—and they landed their little olive-drab plastic craft in front of the library. Inside, the librarian, a young sergeant, was put into something of a tizzy at their request for a pick, and explained to them that the library shelves held only *weapons* of the past, and, as far as he knew, there was no such weapon as a *pick*. He sent them to the captain.

The captain knew what a pick was, all right; but when the

two engineers told him what it was for he called the major. The major was a tall, athletic officer with wavy hair, a very neat mustache, a firm, undaunted jaw, and clear eyes that looked squarely into the future. He smoked a pipe, of course, and was wearing a natty black field uniform with regulation crimson cummerbund and beret. His voice was friendly but there was a "no-nonsense" tone in it. "What's the deal, men?" he said out of the side of his mouth, the other side being engaged in biting, squarely, on his pipestem.

They told him about the gold bar.

"Interesting," he said. "Let's have a look-see." And he sent for a pick, a heavy-duty converter, a portable lighting system, two quarts of synthetic scotch and three privates. All of these were stowed away in a staff helicopter and then the three officers—the two engineers and the major—flew to the mountains. This being a staff helicopter, the trip took three and one-half minutes.

At the mountain, two of the privates set up the portable lighting system in the tunnel while the other studied the manual that had come with the pick. The major was first charmed, and then somewhat piqued, by the bar, after trying to prod it loose with his pipestem. The private with the pick was called, and after some difficulty with determining the proper stance and grip for swinging that instrument—the private was a recent recruit of only fourteen and naturally knew nothing whatever about manual converters of any sort—a few desultory swings were taken at the granite surrounding the bar. After a while the other two privates joined in, alternating in swinging the pick, until, finally, a rough area of about two or three square feet had been hollowed out around the bar, which was found at that time to extend only about four inches back into the mountain. Above the bar they noticed a sort of fissure, like a cicatrice, in the granite; and one of the privates remarked that it looked like the mountain either had been split open to admit the bar from the top, or that, maybe, the bar had just been there and the mountain had grown up around it.

It was impossible to cut away the rock on the other side, so the three privates got a strong grip on the bar and began to pull. Then the officers began to pull on the privates. The bar stayed where it was. They pulled harder. The bar stayed. The major took off his cummerbund and beret and began to sweat. The bar didn't move. The major began to curse, pushed the others aside, grabbed the pick handle, gave a mighty heave, and hit the bar solidly with the point. There was no sound from the impact, and the pick did not rebound, nor did the bar move. The major tried again. And again. Then they knelt and looked at the bar. It still gleamed. No scars.

The major swore for five minutes. Then he said, "Who owns this mountain?"

George spoke up, "The Army, sir. Of course."

"Good," said the major, beginning to look undaunted again. "We'll get at that son of a bitch."

"How, sir?"

"We'll convert this goddamn mountain, that's how." The major began wrapping his cummerbund back around his waist.

"The whole *mountain*?" Sam said, aghast.

"Level it." The major dusted off his beret and replaced it.

Sam spoke up querulously, "But wouldn't that be . . . ah . . . misusing our natural resources, sir?"

"Nonsense. This mountain belongs to the Army. It's not a

natural resource. As a matter of fact, it's an eyesore. I order you to vaporize it."

So they vaporized the mountain. Since the converter could not cut through the bar they set it up—the heavy-duty one—to shear off the top of the mountain. Then they moved the machine around to each of the four sides and sliced them off. Their instruments were very accurate, and when the last wisp of smoke had drifted away there stood in the middle of a plain so smooth billiards could have been played on it, sitting on a neat, rectangular column of granite, four feet high, what was now plainly seen as a shiny, gold colored brick, its sides glittering in the evening sun.

The major picked up the pick and walked slowly over to the column. There was a slight, almost unnoticeable swagger in his walk. He hefted the pick slowly, carefully, braced himself, and took aim. "All right, you son of a bitch," he said, and then gave the pick a magnificent swing.

The brick didn't move.

The major stood where he was, looking at the brick, for about three minutes. Then he said, softly, "All right. *All right!*"

He walked back to the converter—which was sitting on its tripod nearby—and began to adjust its aim and elevation and set its dials, all very carefully. When he was ready he stood behind it, his feet planted firmly, his fists clenched, his lower jaw firm and jutting, his eyes squarely ahead, focused on the brick.

"Now!" he said, and pressed the switch. There was a small hum and a tiny puff of smoke and the little column of granite disappeared. The brick was now unsupported and the major watched it, his eyes now betraying an intense gleam, waiting for it to fall to the earth. The major waited.

The brick stayed exactly where it was, four feet above the ground, completely unsupported.

It took the major a few minutes to realize that there was no use in waiting. He said nothing, however; but stepped over to the brick, looked at it a minute, and then reached casually over to it and pushed it, with his index finger. It didn't move. Then the major sat down on the ground and began to cry, very softly, as the sun sank in the west.

That, of course, was only the beginning of it. Within two weeks the little plain that had once been a mountain was covered with multicolored plastic Quonset huts through which moved so many people of such world-shaking importance that four gossip columnists had to be flown in from New York and Los Angeles to handle the overflow. Generals and admirals abounded, offering careful and profound opinions freely; slim, dark, intense young men with impeccable dark civilian suits and carrying dark attaché cases held hurried, *sotto voce* conferences; reporters did Profiles of everybody. The weather held fair, the neighborhood abounded in divers kinds of nature: birdsong and waterfall, poplar and mountain daisy, which most of the visitors found quaint and novel, and a good time was being had by all.

In the midst of this activity floated the still shiny golden brick, unperturbed, apparently as oblivious of the melee it had attracted as it was of the immutable laws governing the motion of masses: the laws of inertia and reaction, and the law of universal gravitation.

Some interesting things had been discovered about the brick. It was, for instance, completely impervious to any known form of radiant energy; it neither absorbed nor radiated heat; electron microscopes found its surface, on the atomic level, still smooth, metallic and shiny, without gaps; it apparently had no molecular—or, even, atomic—structure to speak of; it would conduct neither electricity, heat, nor anything else; and it obeyed no physical laws whatever. Thus far nine neo-adamant points, sharpened to submicroscopic pointedness and under pressures ranging up to three hundred fifty thousand tons, had failed to make any scratches in its surface; and all had eventually cracked.

The major had recovered most of his old poise and undauntedness, although his eyes now seemed to face the future with some hint of trepidation, and he was assigned to Operation Gold Brick—as the Army had cleverly named it—in an advisory capacity. In fact it was he who gave voice to a notion that had been whispered about for several days. After the ninth neo-adamant point had split against the surface of the brick it was he who marched to the orange Quonset of General Pomeroy and said, "Sir, let's try an H-bomb."

So they H-bombed it.

There was some confusion during the four days while the crater was being filled in; but after that was done and new Quonsets were built the Operation was even more pleasant and roomy, since nine more mountains had been leveled by the bomb, and about twenty others had been fused into interesting colors and shapes. The birds and trees and suchlike had, of course, been obliterated; but they had been beginning to pall on the visitors anyway; and now the area had something of the look of a neo-

Surrealist landscape, or a Japanese garden. The radiation had, of course, been absorbed by the usual means.

The brick stayed right where it was, its surface parallel to the horizon, poised, immediately after the blast, over a crater two hundred and ninety-four feet deep.

After the failure of the H-bomb the generals' pique and frustration began to turn to anger and, in some cases, fear. One pacifistic lieutenant general did in fact suggest that the brick be left alone and the monorail rerouted; but it was to the credit of the Army that his superiors rallied together and denounced his defeatism for what it was. But the generals did agree at this conference to call in a theoretical physicist, provided one could be found, in a desperate hope that some light might be thrown on the nature of their adversary.

A call was sent out to headquarters at Big-H (once Harvard University) and a two-day scramble ensued while a theory man—or "egghead" as such men were cleverly called—was sought. One was eventually found, working in a weather observatory in the Kentucky Reservation, and he was brought—a gray-haired old fellow who freely admitted that he read books and refused to drink synthetic whiskey—to the site of the brick, which he surveyed with some attention.

"Well?" said one of the generals.

"Very interesting," said the theoretical physicist, whose name was Albert, and he produced from a trunk he had brought with him a collection of peculiar-looking instruments, which he began to set up on the ground. After peering down various tripod-mounted tubes, first at the brick and then at the sun, he then said, "Amazing!"

"Yes," said one of the generals. "We know that." There was a ring of generals in brilliant tunics and of security men in black flannel suits around the physicist.

"Amazing," he said again. "This seems to be the exact set point of Propkofski's principle!" He gazed at the brick reverently.

"*Whose* principle?" said one of the security men, raising his eyebrows and fetching a little black book from his breast pocket.

"Propkofski." The physicist's eyes were aglow. The security men were raising eyebrows at one another. "The principle of terrestrial orbital space-time suspension, formulated in 1987, I believe. This is the place, gentlemen, the *exact* point, where Propkofski maintained that the mass-influx lines of the Earth's field intersected. This is the very hub, provided that Propkofski was right," and he pointed to the brick. "Yet I believe that Propkofski said something about a mountain hindering his observations."

"Yes?" said the general. "We removed the mountain."

"My!" said the old physicist, looking up from the brick for the first time. "How did you do that? With faith?"

"With a converter," the general said. "But what about that brick? How do we move it?"

"The brick? Oh." The scientist went to the floating piece of golden metal, still unmarred by the H-bomb, and examined it carefully. When he had finished checking it with a good many instruments, mechanical and electronic, he said, "I wish Newton could see this."

The security man's eyebrows went up again. "Newton?"

The old man smiled at him. "Another physicist," he said. "Dead."

"Oh," said the security man. "Sorry."

"So," said the general, impatiently. "How do we move it?"

The old man looked at him a moment. "I suggest you don't."

"Thank you," said the general, crisply. "Then how would you say it *might* be moved?"

The physicist scratched his head. "Well," he said, "I suppose the Earth might be pushed away from it, since it seems to be a kind of Archimedes' fulcrum. A pressure of about seventeen trillion tons per square centimeter might accomplish that. Of course, moving the Earth might alter the length of the year considerably. And then, again, if Propkofski's principle, which states . . ."

"Thank you," said the general. "That will be all."

After the security men had taken the physicist away for investigation the general who had interviewed him looked at another general and then at the others. He could tell they were all having the same wild surmise. Finally, he said, "Well, why not?"

"Ah . . ." said one of the others.

"The cold war's been going on for fifty years. We may never get a chance to try it out."

"Ah . . . well . . ."

One of the other, younger generals could not contain himself and abruptly spoke up. "Let's use it!" he said, his voice quivering with emotion.

And all the rest of them began to chime in, their eagerness, now that one of their number had committed himself, unrepressed. "Let's use it!" they said. "Let's use the R-bomb!"

First a pit was dug—or converted—a mile and a half deep and three miles in diameter. This was then filled with neo-adamant except for a hole in the center four by ten inches rectangular, directly under the brick. Then the R-bomb and its electronic detonator, the whole thing about the size and color of an avocado, was lowered into the hole, and then the neo-adamant walls were built up six feet above the ground to enclose the brick in what amounted to the barrel of a monstrous cannon. The states of Virginia, West Virginia, Ohio and half of Kentucky were then evacuated, and a final check was made of the figures. It was determined that the kickback from the blast would throw the Earth approximately four hundred and ten miles out of her orbit, and shorten the length of the year to three hundred and sixty-three days, a number which all of the generals found to be eminently satisfactory, in fact, a decided improvement.

The generals decided to use the old physicist's weather station, in the Kentucky Reservation, as their observation point, its elevation and its distance from the brick being quite desirable.

The station was raised on a tripod to a height of one thousand feet, and the Army had the whole structure properly reinforced and shielded. Then the equipment for observation, the TV monitoring screens and the electron telescopes, was set up and the generals moved in. The old physicist had by this time taken a loyalty oath and he was allowed to remain in the observation dome for the event since, after all, he worked there.

At zero hour minus sixty seconds the senior general carefully pressed a small red button and unwittingly echoed the words of a forgotten subordinate. "We'll blast the son of a bitch sky high," he said. Flashbulbs popped. A counter began ticking off the seconds, loudly, efficiently. All eyes were on the large TV screen, which showed the huge circle of white neo-adamant four hundred miles away. The TV picture was being beamed from a satellite eighty miles above the location of the brick; they would be able to see the actual blast before the camera was destroyed. The physicist busied himself with his own instruments, making readings of the sun's position. The seconds ticked off.

At the sixtieth tick the counter became silent. There was no sound in the little observation tower. The white circle on the screen was unchanged. Then, suddenly, the screen erupted. In a burst of flame and steam the neo-adamant circle began to crumble. Flames shot up everywhere. Mountains seen at the edge of the screen began to sizzle and ooze out of shape. It was at this moment that the states of Virginia, West Virginia and Ohio were obliterated. Then, abruptly, the picture changed. A specially controlled monitoring camera had picked up a flash of gold. The brick. It appeared to be flying through the air.

"By God," said the senior general. "We did it!"

At this moment the screen went black. There was a roar, a rumble, starting from what seemed to be the very bowels of the Earth, building to a dynamic, deep-buried scream, a screeching of wrenched rock and of the tearing of the Earth's crust; and then a sickening lurch, a nauseous dip and lunge of sideward motion, a sense of acceleration; and then a howling sound, the howling of a sudden, tremendous wind. The generals were all thrown to the floor, trembling.

Somehow the physicist had remained standing, holding the sides of the table on which his instruments were mounted. His old hands were white with the strain and were trembling, but his face was ecstatic. "Amazing!" he said. "Amazing!" His eyes were shining.

"What happened?" one of the generals said weakly, from the floor.

"Propkofski! Propkofski was right!" said the other, his voice jubilant, shaking with emotion. "That *was* the intersection of the mass-influx lines. The brick, the gold brick, was the keystone, the hub! It held the Earth up."

"What," said the general, shouting above the roar of the wind that was now like a cyclone, above the screeching of twisted rock and the wrenching of the very bowels of the Earth. "What does that *mean*?"

"It means that Propkofski must have been right!" said the other, his voice quivering. "The Earth, it seems, is falling into the sun!"

SUCKER'S GAME

Eddie pushed open the door, walked in and looked around. It took him maybe ten seconds to take it all in. It wasn't really new to him, not any one part of it. A recombination of the same things, the same dirt and noise, that were in any pool-room in any of a thousand nameless towns. Smoke, talk, dirt, signs on the walls, cuspidors and men playing pool. Even the men looked the same, almost, as they had in the last town, and the town before that.

In the front, on the front table, was the ubiquitous dollar nine-ball game, bossed by the best local hustlers, open to all comers. And five men, all of them in soiled workingmen's clothes, shooting nine-ball just well enough to think they were good, shooting for a dollar a game.

He walked over toward the wall slowly, leaned his back against it and stuck his hands in his pockets. He started watching the nine-ball game.

"Stranger in town?"

Eddie turned his head. It was one of the players from the game, leaning against the wall in between shots. A tall, thin man, red-eyed, needing a shave.

"That's right." Eddie tried to make his voice sound friendly.

"Work on the pipe line?"

"No." He had never heard of the pipe line. "Not yet, anyway."

The man pulled a bent cigarette slowly from a dirty pack in his pants pocket and started fumbling in his shirt pocket for a match. He made no move to offer Eddie a cigarette. "It's pretty good money," he said.

"That's what I heard." It was as good a reason as Eddie could think of to explain his being there. "How much?"

"Thirteen-fifty, if you handle the pipe." The man finally withdrew a kitchen match from his pocket and struck it with his fingernail. "More, if you work for the engineers." He spat on the floor at his feet. "Me, I handle pipe."

Eddie laughed. "Lost my slide rule, myself, as a matter of fact."

The other man apparently didn't understand the remark; he just said, "Yeah?" and then stepped up to the table to take his turn at shooting.

The players at the front table were typical. Crude and awkward in their shooting, all but one of them held their cue sticks high at the back, used ten- or twelve-inch bridges and followed through their shots with long, dipping swoops. They shot hard and often with high English on the cue ball, so that a great many shots jumped the table. Once one of the men sent three balls flying together off the end rail on the break shot, and somebody at a back table shouted, "Hey, it costs two dollars an hour to play on the floor!" and a couple of the old men who were sitting in chairs by the wall winked at one another.

There was one player in the bunch, however, who Eddie could tell almost immediately was a cut above the others. He was the only one in the game who had sense enough to shoot halfway easily and not to try to pocket the nine-ball in one wild, blasting attempt every time he shot. Once the man ran out six balls to the nine, and another time Eddie saw him make the payoff ball on what the others took to be a luck shot, but what was actually a fairly clever off-the-rail combination.

He was a tall, heavily built man, with a felt hat turned up all around the brim, a plaid shirt and army pants. His face was coarse and broad, his nose piglike and there was a look almost of cunning in his eyes, which were small and set closely together. Eddie instinctively disliked the man—"Turtle" was what the others called him. His nickname must have been derived from the way he moved, slowly and with apparent calculation, for his appearance was more porcine than anything else. Eddie decided that it would be enjoyable to beat him out of all he could. He also decided that a little prudence might be needed, however. Turtle did not look like the sort of man who would take being hustled lightly if he should find out that he was being taken advantage of. It would be wise to take things a little slowly.

Turtle won another game, and the man who had spoken to Eddie earlier threw his dollar bill out on the table and turned to Eddie, held out his cue and said, "Want a stick? I'm cutting out."

That was convenient. It always looked better to be invited in. "I don't know," he said. "It looks a little rough to me."

"Hell, go ahead," the other man said. "Nine-ball, anything can happen."

Anything can happen is right—Eddie thought—*especially if you know how to make it happen . . .*

He took the stick from the man hesitantly and said to the other men at the table, "Mind if I get in?"

Turtle looked at him dully. "Hell, no, friend," he said. "The water's fine."

Eddie chalked his stick. He decided from the way Turtle had looked at him he'd better be sure to lose the first two or three games. When he chalked his stick, Eddie did it inexpertly, getting too much of the blue powder on the cue's tip and making the chalk squeak unpleasantly. He held his stick awkwardly, too, in the amateurish manner he had learned after more than twenty years of hustling pool for a living.

He let himself lose the first three games, holding his game down to the safe, middle-of-the-road position—poor enough not to scare anyone out, but not so poor that he would have to improve suspiciously when the time came to start winning. In a game like this it might be perfectly possible to win enough money without ever really turning on the pressure, just by being smart and making it look like luck, winning only often enough to take in about ten dollars for each six he lost. He might be able to keep that up for hours, and on a table like this one with wide, filed-down pockets they should be able to play as many as twenty-five games an hour. And then there was always the chance of being able to raise the bet later on.

Eddie had just about decided to play it that way, the safe, sure way, for what would be about thirty or forty dollars when something happened that changed his plans completely. He had just won a game by tapping in an easy seven, eight, nine run-out when Turtle, his big face impassive, reached down in his pocket and fished out a roll—or, more exactly, a wad—of bills, with the magic number "50" poking out from almost all layers. Eddie sized the roll as carrying at least seven or eight hundred, maybe more, and he whistled inwardly. The big man was loaded. This was a setup, a fish in a barrel.

Turtle must have caught him staring at the money—he had probably flashed it intentionally, anyway—and he laughed a deep, raspy laugh and said, "Ever see money before, friend?"

Eddie laughed back. "Every now and then I see some." He smiled. "But yours sure is pretty."

There was silence for a minute; even the men in the chairs were quiet, watching them. Poolrooms were always that way; everyone seemed to be able to smell a hustle in the air.

"Why, hell, friend," Turtle said. "It might be yours. All you got to do is win it."

Ordinarily, Eddie's attitude toward other players was in every sense professional. Pool was just a business. It meant hustling nine-ball from town to town, almost like a traveling salesman. Going from one town to the next until all the towns and all the poolrooms looked the same, until all the men he played were the same—business prospects, men to be handled in this way or that, none of them particularly likable or particularly disagreeable, just men to play pool with and to win a little money from. Suckers.

But every once in a while there was a man like this one. A man with the kind of a face that made you want to hit it and the kind of build that told you you'd better not—which made him that much worse. And the man's voice, the raspy, smug, piggish challenge of what he had just said began to make the little hairs on the back of Eddie's neck feel as if they were bristling up.

The other man was still looking at him, his lips still pressed into a grin, almost a leer. "I said, all you got to do is win it, friend."

Eddie looked at him, smiling, making his voice sound casual. "As a matter of fact," he said, "I might just do that."

It had been a long time since he had put a game head-on right at the first like this. It gave him a little bit of a thrill, a pull of excitement, something like the fast hustling he had done when he was a kid, and it was almost enjoyable.

It was a little risky, too. He knew he would have to shoot a better game than he liked to now if he was going to beat this man. There wasn't any chance of not beating him, but it could be dangerous to show his class of playing in this kind of place. He had learned a long time before that people like these didn't take too well to finding a professional hustler in their midst. It was risky, but he should be able to swing it, all right. And there was good money in it.

"Put up, friend." Turtle started chalking his cue, very slowly and carefully. "Any bet you name."

Spoken like a true sucker—Eddie thought wryly.

"Suppose we play for ten dollars on the nine-ball," he said. There was a buzz along the seats by the wall, and then suddenly it got still again.

Turtle's expression didn't change. "Let's see it," he said.

"See what?" Eddie said.

"Your roll, friend." He jerked his thumb toward one of the

dirty signs on the wall and grinned evilly. The sign read: CREDIT
MAKES ENEMIES; LET'S BE FRIENDS.

Eddie smiled again, although he felt a little more angry,
almost insulted. "Do you think I'd pull credit on *you*, mister?"
he asked. "When I weigh a hundred forty pounds with my
shoes on."

"So let's see it anyway."

"Okay." Eddie shrugged and pulled his billfold out of his
hip pocket. He took out a sheaf of tens and twenties—about
two hundred dollars—and fanned them for the other's inspec-
tion. "That suit you?"

"Why, friend, I never would have guessed it. No, sir." He
threw back his head and laughed. "I feel richer already."

"Don't count on it." Eddie said it so softly that the other
man probably didn't even hear him.

Turtle looked at the other three players, the men who had
been playing at the table when Eddie had got in the game.
"How about you boys?" he said. "Still with us?"

Two of the men turned wordlessly and walked to the rack.
They put their cues away and leaned against the wall, watching.
The other man grinned. "I think you two are out of our league,"
he said. Then he followed the other men to the rack. Eddie and
Turtle had the game to themselves.

They flipped a coin for the break and Eddie won. He noticed
that the rack boy had left a very small space between two balls
on the far end of the diamond shaped rack and he was tempted
to slug the nine in on the break—a thing he could do practically
any time he had an imperfect rack to shoot at—but he resisted
the impulse and settled for undercutting the one ball with left-

hand English, so that his cue ball would lodge itself behind the stack and the one would stay out front where it couldn't be hit by the other man on the next turn.

That was the one big advantage he had. He could play safe without letting Turtle know what was going on. That, combined with calculated shots that would look lucky and with doing the wrong thing every now and then, should allow him to win about two out of three and still keep the other man thinking that he was the better player, that luck was beating him.

One thing about nine-ball was that most of the people who played it thought that it was a "luck game" or an "equalizer"—a game that gave the sloppy player a kind of equality with his betters. Since the money was always won only on the nine-ball, the last one to be shot at in rotation, the general idea was that any man could "slop" the ball into a pocket by shooting hard enough at one of the others and being a little bit lucky.

Not that Turtle was the "slop" style of player. Eddie had seen enough of his playing already to see that he knew enough to run the balls out, one at a time, when they looked easy enough to make and there weren't too many of them. But he was a long way from being able to run the game out from the opening shot—unless two or three had been made on the break—and he was miles away from the tricks that always kept the other fellow shooting at difficult shots while you got the easy ones for yourself.

But the man would still not know better than to think that luck was a decisive factor in the game, and it really was not. Not the way Eddie knew how to play it. As far as Eddie was concerned, the only decisive factor was the length of time the other man would play before he quit.

They stabbed around a while, trying to get good hits off the one ball. Finally, Eddie got an open shot, pocketed the one and ran the balls up through the five and then missed purposely, figuring it was a better than even chance that Turtle would miss before the nine was made. Then he would be able to make it himself without being forced to make a long run.

Turtle missed, as he had hoped, while shooting the seven and left Eddie what appeared to be a difficult bank shot. Eddie choked back an impulse to bank the ball a neat cross corner and, instead, played the ball three rails in the side, making it look as if he had meant to play it cross-corner.

"That's pretty lucky, friend," Turtle said.

"There's more than one way of making 'em," Eddie said, grinning. He was unused to playing like this, playing against someone he really wanted to beat for more than just the money, and he was enjoying it. He shot the other two balls in, and Turtle gave him his ten. A crowd was beginning to gather around the table.

By midnight, after three hours of playing, the crowd was three times as big and Eddie was twice as rich. He had already given the rack-man a ten, to keep the place open for the game, and he was still 230 ahead and enjoying himself thoroughly.

Eddie's enjoyment was, after a fashion, ambivalent; he was getting a kick out of playing, but Turtle had become even more belligerent as his losses had increased and the irritation had been getting almost unbearable. Which, paradoxically, made even more enjoyable the prospect of beating the other man and beating him badly. Eddie kept getting urges to let loose and shoot his best until Turtle would be forced to quit. It would almost be worth it, he thought, to show the big hoodlum what kind of "luck" it was that was causing him to lose. This, too, was unusual. Ordinarily, Eddie was quite pleased to be called lucky and to have opponents curse his "sloppy" brand of winning pool; it was sort of an unwitting tribute to his skill, but here, playing this big pig of a man, he was infuriated by it. The thought of really opening up, of letting his whole game out, of seeing what he could really do on these drop-pocket tables and against this man whom he wanted very much to beat became more and more tempting.

Then, one time, after Eddie had just made a beautifully turned out three-ball combination on the nine-ball, Turtle banged the end of his cue stick down on the floor hard and said, looking straight at Eddie, "You filthy, lucky little bastard."

The crowd around the table grew suddenly very still. The two old men, the same two who had been watching them from the very first, nudged one another with their elbows, but said nothing.

Eddie felt the blood rising in his face. He gripped his cue stick tightly and fought to keep his face calm.

"You think you shoot pretty good, don't you, Turtle?" he said, keeping his voice as level as he could.

"Good enough to beat anything but filthy luck. Nobody can beat your brand of blind-pig slop pool."

Any other time Eddie would have taken that as high praise and would have smiled inwardly at his own private joke on the other man. But now it wasn't praise; it doubled his fury.

"Turtle," he said, fighting his anger down, "how big is that big, beautiful roll you've got?"

"So who cares, lucky?"

"So *I* care. We might make a deal."

"It's five-fifty and I'm keeping it."

"Okay," Eddie said, trembling inwardly, but keeping his voice casual, "I've got just five hundred. Suppose we play freeze out. We each put up five hundred, and then we shoot 'til one man wins twenty games. He gets all the money. And I'll tell you what I'll do." He leaned forward, resting his weight on his hands against the side of the table. "I'll give you a lesson about that 'blind-pig luck'; I'll call all my shots— except the break. If I don't make the shot the way I've called it, it spots up and you shoot. And you keep yours any way you make 'em go." He paused and then said softly, "Then we'll see who's lucky."

There was nothing else Turtle could do. Eddie had him and he knew he had him, had him from all possible angles. As a matter of fact, when you looked at it the right way, it was a perfect hustle. Or almost perfect; it had one drawback; if Turtle was as rough as he looked, there might be trouble afterward, but right now Eddie didn't really care. Whatever might happen, even if the other man did get wise and beat Eddie up and take all the money, it would be worth it, just to shove this big pig's nose in the dirt. For once Eddie's business sense was completely gone; he had never wanted to do anything so much as to beat this man.

Abruptly Turtle grinned broadly. "Why, friend," he said, "I believe I've got you wrong." It was odd, and even more galling, the way he slipped suddenly into a far more pleasant tone of voice. "I believe I've misjudged you." He reached into his pants pocket and started pulling out money. "You've got you a game, friend."

Eddie got his billfold out and counted out five hundred. He barely made it; it left him thirteen dollars in small bills and whatever small change he had in his pocket. He threw his pile of tens and twenties on the table. Turtle folded the money together, stuffed it into the side pocket of the next vacant table and put three balls from the table's rack in the pocket to weight the money down. Eddie was surprised at this; it was a trick he hadn't seen since he had played in Chicago.

Starting a new bet, they flipped again for the break, and Eddie won again.

"Have to get that luck in somehow, don't you?" Turtle said, but his voice seemed to have lost its rasp. And then, when the rack man started toward them, he said, "I think maybe I'd better rack those balls myself this time." And he took the rack from him and racked them in the little diamond very tight.

Eddie stepped up to shoot. But before he bent down to the table, he paused. He felt a momentary sense of exultation, a pleasant, glowing, supremely confident sensation of impending victory. This was it; this was what he had been wanting. "Turtle," he said, smiling, "I'm going to take you to the cleaners."

Turtle smiled back. "Break the balls," he said.

The tight rack had made it impossible for Eddie to control the break shot, but he was able to spread the balls far enough so that two of them went in. Any player who knew his speed and angles could figure on making a ball on twenty-four out of any twenty-five breaks. He shot carefully and ran the balls, calling each shot in advance, up to the nine, and then slammed it in on a heart-of-the-pocket, cross-side bank. There was murmur in the crowd.

Turtle said nothing and racked. Eddie would keep on breaking and shooting until he missed; in nine-ball the winner always breaks.

The next rack Eddie got a very wide spread, stopped, thought a moment and then started calling off his shots, chalking his cue. He said, "First, I'll make the one ball in that side"—he pointed to the pocket—"then, the two in this corner, the four in that one, the five...." and so on, up through the rack. Then he started shooting and made the balls the way he had called them, playing perfect position on each one, cutting them neatly into the pockets.

When he had finished, someone in the crowd whistled, almost reverently, and Eddie looked at Turtle. The big man's face was impassive. He just racked the balls again and sat down in a chair by the wall, saying nothing.

Eddie broke and ran the balls, broke and ran, sometimes calling all of his shots at once in advance, sometimes, when the spreads were more difficult, just calling them one at a time.

When he was younger, he had always shot his best game; before he had learned to underplay it, he had been able to run as many as twenty games without missing, and here, on this easy drop-pocket table, he knew that twenty-five games wouldn't be exactly impossible, but he really didn't figure to make more than ten. He wasn't used to that kind of shooting and, besides, it would have been foolish to shoot that well.

But he shot beautifully, calling and making straight, dead shots, intricate shots, precision shots, handling his game like the master he was, getting more and more gasps from the crowd. But Turtle was silent. He racked the balls every time and then sat down to watch. Once, the man's quietness gave Eddie a momentary twinge of dread, and he looked at the man's face apprehensively. But there didn't seem to be anything frightening about him; he was just sitting, watching, with no particular expression.

It wasn't the way Eddie had expected it.

Then, finally, he missed; as every player must eventually do, he miscalculated, and a ball hit off the corner of a pocket and didn't go in. It was the middle of the fourteenth game; Eddie had thirteen wins on the string, a perfectly safe margin.

He stood back from the table, smiling, not bothering to take a seat. He didn't figure to be standing long.

Turtle got out of his chair wordlessly and ambled up to the table. He shot, made the four balls Eddie had left him and then poked one of the markers on his string with his cue rod over to one side. One game. One to thirteen.

Then Eddie racked the balls and Turtle broke.

Five minutes later Eddie sat down. Ten minutes later he started to get up and then sat down again.

It was impossible. Even with the drop pockets, it couldn't be happening. Turtle shot like a machine, like a beautiful, deadly machine. His position was flawless; the balls didn't miss; they didn't even come close to missing: he clipped them in one at a time so that they looked as if they were rolling down little invisible troughs and into the pockets.

This time the crowd was bug-eyed. Eddie could hear nothing but the steady *plunk, plunk* of balls hitting the bottoms of pockets.

It was impossible, but he did it. Twenty straight games, *click, click, click*, and then it was all over and Turtle was taking the three balls out of the pocket on the other table very slowly and then pulling out the bills one at a time and smoothing them with the palm of his hand on the table.

Eddie watched him, fascinated, for a moment, thinking. Then he spoke, and the calmness had left his voice, so that it shook a little. "Turtle," he said, "do you work on the pipe line?"

"Well, friend, no." And his face had an expression that Eddie would never have dreamed fifteen minutes ago of ever seeing there. He looked sheepish.

"Do you live here?"

Turtle grinned. His big, pig face was almost like that of a bad little boy. "Not exactly," he said, and his voice had magically lost all of its irritating, belligerent manner. "I just sort of drifted in."

Eddie's voice was plainly shaking now, and he knew it. "Just . . . on the road, you mean?"

"Yeah, you might say that, on the road." He was putting the money, smoothed out now, into his billfold. "And, friend," he said, "I hope I didn't make you too mad back there." He put the billfold into his hip pocket. "It's just part of the game."

THE BIG BOUNCE

"Let me show you something," Farnsworth said. He set his near-empty drink—a Bacardi martini—on the mantel and waddled out of the room toward the basement.

I sat in my big leather chair, feeling very peaceful with the world, watching the fire. Whatever Farnsworth would have to show tonight would be far more entertaining than watching TV—my custom on other evenings. Farnsworth, with his four labs in the house and his very tricky mind, never failed to provide my best night of the week.

When he returned, after a moment, he had with him a small box, about three inches square. He held this carefully in one hand and stood by the fireplace dramatically—or as dramatically as a very small, very fat man with pink cheeks can stand by a fireplace of the sort that seems to demand a big man with tweeds, pipe and, perhaps, a saber wound.

Anyway, he held the box dramatically and he said, "Last

week, I was playing around in the chem lab, trying to make a new kind of rubber eraser. Did quite well with the other drafting equipment, you know, especially the dimensional curve and the photosensitive ink. Well, I approached the job by trying for a material that would absorb graphite without abrading paper."

I was a little disappointed with this; it sounded pretty tame. But I said, "How did it come out?"

He screwed his pudgy face up thoughtfully. "Synthesized the material, all right, and it seems to work, but the interesting thing is that it has a certain—ah—secondary property that would make it quite awkward to use. Interesting property, though. Unique, I am inclined to believe."

This began to sound more like it. "And what property is that?" I poured myself a shot of straight rum from the bottle sitting on the table beside me. I did not like straight rum, but I preferred it to Farnsworth's imaginative cocktails.

"I'll show you, John," he said. He opened the box and I could see that it was packed with some kind of batting. He fished in this and withdrew a gray ball about the size of a golf ball and set the box on the mantel.

"And that's the—eraser?" I asked.

"Yes," he said. Then he squatted down, held the ball about a half-inch from the floor, and dropped it.

It bounced, naturally enough. Then it bounced again. And again. Only this was not natural, for on the second bounce the ball went higher in the air than on the first, and on the third bounce higher still. After a half minute, my eyes were bugging out and the little ball was bouncing four feet in the air and going higher each time.

I grabbed my glass. "What the hell!" I said.

Farnsworth caught the ball in a pudgy hand and held it. He was smiling a little sheepishly. "Interesting effect, isn't it?"

"Now wait a minute," I said, beginning to think about it. "What's the gimmick? What kind of motor do you have in that thing?"

His eyes were wide and a little hurt. "No gimmick, John. None at all. Just a very peculiar molecular structure."

"Structure!" I said. "Bouncing balls just don't pick up energy out of nowhere, I don't care how their molecules are put together. And you don't get energy out without putting energy in."

"Oh," he said, "that's the really interesting thing. Of course you're right; energy *does* go into the ball. Here, I'll show you."

He let the ball drop again and it began bouncing, higher and higher, until it was hitting the ceiling. Farnsworth reached out to catch it, but he fumbled and the thing glanced off his hand, hit the mantelpiece and zipped across the room. It banged into the far wall, ricocheted, banked off three other walls, picking up speed all the time.

When it whizzed by me like a rifle bullet, I began to get worried, but it hit against one of the heavy draperies by the window and this damped its motion enough so that it fell to the floor.

It started bouncing again immediately, but Farnsworth scrambled across the room and grabbed it. He was perspiring a little and he began instantly to transfer the ball from one hand to another and back again as if it were hot.

"Here," he said, and handed it to me.

I almost dropped it.

"It's like a ball of ice!" I said. "Have you been keeping it in the refrigerator?"

"No. As a matter of fact, it was at room temperature a few minutes ago."

"Now wait a minute," I said. "I only teach physics in high school, but I know better than that. Moving around in warm air doesn't make anything cold except by evaporation."

"Well, there's your input and output, John," he said. "The ball lost heat and took on motion. Simple conversion."

My jaw must have dropped to my waist. "Do mean that that little thing is converting heat to kinetic energy?"

"Apparently."

"But that's impossible!"

He was beginning to smile thoughtfully. The ball was not as cold now as it had been and I was holding it in my lap.

"A steam engine does it," he said, "and a steam turbine. Of course, they're not very efficient."

"They work mechanically, too, and only because water expands when it turns to steam."

"This seems to do it differently," he said, sipping thoughtfully at his dark-brown martini. "I don't know exactly how— maybe something piezo-electric about the way its molecules slide about. I ran some tests—measured its impact energy in foot pounds and compared that with the heat loss in BTUs. Seemed to be about 98 percent efficient, as close as I could tell. Apparently it converts heat into bounce very well. Interesting, isn't it?"

Interesting? I almost came flying out of my chair. My mind was beginning to spin like crazy. "If you're not pulling my leg with this thing, Farnsworth, you've got something by the tail there that's just a little bit bigger than the discovery of fire."

He blushed modestly. "I'd rather thought that myself," he admitted.

"Good Lord, look at the heat that's available!" I said, getting really excited now.

Farnsworth was still smiling, very pleased with himself. "I suppose you could put this thing in a box, with convection fins, and let it bounce around inside—"

"I'm way ahead of you," I said. "But that wouldn't work. All your kinetic energy would go right back to heat, on impact—and eventually that little ball would build up enough speed to blast its way through any box you could build."

"Then how would you work it?"

"Well," I said, choking down the rest of my rum, "you'd seal the ball in a big steel cylinder, attach the cylinder to a crankshaft and flywheel, give the thing a shake to start the ball bouncing back and forth, and let it run like a gasoline engine or something. It would get all the heat it needed from the air in a normal room. Mount the apparatus in your house and it would pump your water, operate a generator and keep you cool at the same time!"

I sat down again, shakily, and began pouring myself another drink.

Farnsworth had taken the ball from me and was carefully putting it back in its padded box. He was visibly showing excitement, too; I could see that his cheeks were ruddier and his eyes even brighter than normal. "But what if you want the cooling and don't have any work to be done?"

"Simple," I said. "You just let the machine turn a flywheel or lift weights and drop them, or something like that, outside your house. You have an air intake inside. And if, in the winter, you don't want to lose heat, you just mount the thing in an outside building, attach it to your generator and use the power to do whatever you want—heat your house, say. There's plenty of heat in the outside air even in December."

"John," said Farnsworth, "you are very ingenious. It might work."

"Of course it'll work." Pictures were beginning to light up in my head. "And don't you realize that this is the answer to the solar power problem? Why, mirrors and selenium are, at best, ten percent efficient! Think of big pumping stations on the Sahara! All that heat, all that need for power, for irrigation!" I paused a moment for effect. "Farnsworth, this can change the very shape of the earth!"

Farnsworth seemed to be lost in thought. Finally he looked at me strangely and said, "Perhaps we had better try to build a model."

I was so excited by the thing that I couldn't sleep that night. I kept dreaming of power stations, ocean liners, even automobiles, being operated by balls bouncing back and forth in cylinders.

I even worked out a spaceship in my mind, a bullet-shaped affair with a huge rubber ball on its end, gyroscopes to keep it oriented properly, the ball serving as solution to that biggest of missile-engineering problems, excess heat. You'd build a huge concrete launching field, supported all the way down to bed-rock, hop in the ship and start bouncing. Of course it would be kind of a rough ride . . .

In the morning, I called my superintendent and told him to get a substitute for the rest of the week; I was going to be busy.

Then I started working in the machine shop in Farnsworth's basement, trying to turn out a working model of a device that, by means of a crankshaft, oleo dampers and a reciprocating cylinder, would pick up some of that random kinetic energy from the bouncing ball and do something useful with it, like turning a drive shaft. I was just working out a convection-and-air-pump system for circulating hot air around the ball when Farnsworth came in.

He had a sphere of about the size of a basketball and, if he had made it to my specifications, weighing thirty-five pounds. He had a worried frown on his forehead.

"It looks good," I said. "What's the trouble?"

"There seems to be a slight hitch," he said. "I've been testing for conductivity. It seems to be quite low."

"That's what I'm working on now. It's just a mechanical problem of pumping enough warm air back to the ball. We can do it with no more than a twenty percent efficiency loss. In an engine, that's nothing."

"Maybe you're right. But this material conducts heat even less than rubber does."

"The little ball yesterday didn't seem to have any trouble," I said.

"Naturally not. It had had plenty of time to warm up before I started it. And its mass-surface area relationship was pretty low—the larger you make a sphere, of course, the more mass inside in proportion to the outside area."

"You're right, but I think we can whip it. We may have to honeycomb the ball and have the machine operate a hot-air pump; but we can work it out."

———

All that day, I worked with lathe, milling machine and hacksaw. After clamping the new big ball securely to a workbench, Farnsworth pitched in to help me. But we weren't able to finish by nightfall and Farnsworth turned his spare bedroom over to me for the night. I was too tired to go home.

And too tired to sleep soundly, too. Farnsworth lived on the edge of San Francisco, by a big truck bypass, and almost all night I wrestled with the pillow and sheets, listening half-consciously to those heavy trucks rumbling by, and in my mind, always, that little gray ball, bouncing and bouncing and bouncing . . .

At daybreak, I abruptly came fully awake with the sound of crashing echoing in my ears, a battering sound that seemed to come from the basement. I grabbed my shirt and pants, rushed out of the room, almost knocked over Farnsworth, who was struggling to get his shoes on out in the hall, and we scrambled down the two flights of stairs together.

The place was a chaos, battered and bashed equipment everywhere, and on the floor, overturned against the far wall, the table that the ball had been clamped to. The ball itself was gone.

I had not been fully asleep all night, and the sight of that mess, and what it meant, jolted me immediately awake. Something, probably a heavy truck, had started a tiny oscillation in that ball. And the ball had been heavy enough to start the table bouncing with it until, by dancing that table around the room, it had literally torn the clamp off and shaken itself free. What had happened afterward was obvious, with the ball building up velocity with every successive bounce.

But where was the ball now?

Suddenly Farnsworth cried out hoarsely, "Look!" and I followed his outstretched, pudgy finger to where, at one side of the basement, a window had been broken open—a small window, but plenty big enough for something the size of a basketball to crash through it.

There was a little weak light coming from outdoors. And then I saw the ball. It was in Farnsworth's backyard, bouncing a little sluggishly on the grass. The grass would damp it, hold it back, until we could get to it. Unless . . .

I took off up the basement steps like a streak. Just beyond the backyard, I had caught a glimpse of something that frightened me. A few yards from where I had seen the ball was the edge of the big six-lane highway, a broad ribbon of smooth, hard concrete.

I got through the house to the back porch, rushed out and was in the backyard just in time to see the ball take its first bounce onto the concrete. I watched it, fascinated, when it hit—after the soft, energy-absorbing turf, the concrete was like a springboard. Immediately the ball flew high in the air. I was running across the yard toward it, praying under my breath, *Fall on that grass next time.*

It hit before I got to it, and right on the concrete again, and this time I saw it go straight up at least fifty feet.

My mind was suddenly full of thoughts of dragging mattresses from the house, or making a net or something to stop that hurtling thirty-five pounds; but I stood where I was, unable to move, and saw it come down again on the highway. It went up a hundred feet. And down again on the concrete, about fifteen feet further down the road. In the direction of the city.

That time it was two hundred feet, and when it hit again, it made a thud that you could have heard for a quarter of a mile. I could practically see it flatten out on the road before it took off upward again, at twice the speed it had hit at.

Suddenly generating an idea, I whirled and ran back to Farnsworth's house. He was standing in the yard now, shivering from the morning air, looking at me like a little lost and badly scared child.

"Where are your car keys?" I shouted at him.

"In my pocket."

"Come on!"

I took him by the arm and half dragged him to the carport. I got the keys from him, started the car, and by mangling about seven traffic laws and three rosebushes, managed to get on the highway, facing in the direction that the ball was heading.

"Look," I said, trying to drive down the road and search for the ball at the same time. "It's risky, but if I can get the car under it and we can hop out in time, it should crash through the roof. That ought to slow it down enough for us to nab it."

"But—what about my car?" Farnsworth bleated.

"What about that first building—or first person—it hits in San Francisco?"

"Oh," he said. "Hadn't thought of that."

I slowed the car and stuck my head out the window. It was lighter now, but no sign of the ball. "If it happens to get to town—any town, for that matter—it'll be falling from about ten or twenty miles. Or forty."

"Maybe it'll go high enough first so that it'll burn. Like a meteor."

"No chance," I said. "Built-in cooling system, remember?"

Farnsworth formed his mouth into an "Oh" and exactly at that moment there was a resounding *thump* and I saw the ball hit in a field, maybe twenty yards from the edge of the road, and take off again. This time it didn't seem to double its velocity, and I figured the ground was soft enough to hold it back—but it wasn't slowing down either, not with a bounce factor of better than two to one.

Without watching for it to go up, I drove as quickly as I could off the road and over—carrying part of a wire fence with me—to where it had hit. There was no mistaking it; there was a depression about three feet deep, like a small crater.

I jumped out of the car and stared up. It took me a few seconds to spot it, over my head. One side caught by the pale and slanting morning sunlight, it was only a bright diminishing speck.

The car motor was running and I waited until the ball disappeared for a moment and then reappeared. I watched for another couple of seconds until I felt I could make a decent guess on its direction, shouted at Farnsworth to get out of the car—it had just occurred to me that there was no use risking his life, too—dove in and drove a hundred yards or so to the spot I had anticipated.

I stuck my head out the window and up. The ball was the size of an egg now. I adjusted the car's position, jumped out and ran for my life.

It hit instantly after—about sixty feet from the car. And at the same time, it occurred to me that what I was trying to do was completely impossible. Better to hope that the ball hit a pond, or bounced out to sea, or landed in a sand dune. All we could do would be to follow, and if it ever was damped down enough, grab it.

It had hit soft ground and didn't double its height that time, but it had still gone higher. It was out of sight for almost a lifelong minute.

And then—incredibly rotten luck—it came down, with an ear-shattering thwack, on the concrete highway again. I had seen it hit, and instantly afterward I saw a crack as wide as a finger open along the entire width of the road. And the ball had flown back up like a rocket.

My God, I was thinking, *now it means business. And on the next bounce . . .*

It seemed like an incredibly long time that we craned our necks, Farnsworth and I, watching for it to reappear in the sky. And when it finally did, we could hardly follow it. It whistled like a bomb and we saw the gray streak come plummeting to earth almost a quarter of a mile away from where we were standing.

But we didn't see it go back up again.

For a moment, we stared at each other silently. Then Farnsworth almost whispered, "Perhaps it's landed in a pond."

"Or in the world's biggest cowpile," I said. "Come on!"

We could have met our deaths by rock salt and buckshot that night, if the farmer who owned that field had been home. We tore up everything we came to getting across it—including cabbages and rhubarb. But we had to search for ten minutes, and even then we didn't find the ball.

What we found was a hole in the ground that could have been a small-scale meteor crater. It was a good twenty feet deep. But at the bottom, no ball.

I stared wildly at it for a full minute before I focused my eyes enough to see, at the bottom, a thousand little gray fragments.

And immediately it came to both of us at the same time. A poor conductor, the ball had used up all its available heat on that final impact. Like a golf ball that has been dipped in liquid air and dropped, it had smashed into thin splinters.

The hole had sloping sides and I scrambled down in it and picked up one of the pieces, using my handkerchief, folded— there was no telling just how cold it would be.

It was the stuff, all right. And colder than an icicle.

I climbed out. "Let's go home," I said.

Farnsworth looked at me thoughtfully. Then he sort of cocked his head to one side and asked, "What do you suppose will happen when those pieces thaw?"

I stared at him. I began to think of a thousand tiny slivers whizzing around erratically, ricocheting off buildings, in downtown San Francisco and in twenty counties, and no matter what they hit, moving and accelerating as long as there was any heat in the air to give them energy.

And then I saw a tool shed, on the other side of the pasture from us.

But Farnsworth was ahead of me, waddling along, puffing. He got the shovels out and handed one to me.

We didn't say a word, neither of us, for hours. It takes a long time to fill a hole twenty feet deep—especially when you're shoveling very, very carefully and packing down the dirt very, very hard.

FIRST LOVE

Her hair was blonde and pulled back tightly from her face. She wore a strapless gown, and her arms, shoulders, neck and face were perfectly molded. She needed nothing—save, perhaps, the shocking lightness of her pale gray eyes—to point up the classic shaping of line and structure that made her, without any doubt at all, the most beautiful girl Fred had ever seen.

And she was intelligent; it showed in her forehead, her eyes, the set of her mouth. Intelligence and grace were in the quiet ease with which she held her wine glass, the way she stood by the table in the great ballroom, surrounded but never dimmed by some of the most beautiful women in the world.

Fred could not take his eyes from her. He was overwhelmed by her. He was lost in the thought of her arms, her face, her perfect walk.

At the far end of the ballroom stood Prince Henry, alone. She lifted her eyes and saw him. Then she walked to him across the crowded floor. He held out his hands to her; she took them both in hers, gently, and smiled. The music swelled to a crescendo, and they walked out together.

All the lights came on.

"Did he marry her, Daddy?"

Fred blinked his eyes.

"Why didn't she marry the pirate, Daddy—" it was Sally again—"if she loved him so much?"

"I don't know. Ask your mother." He picked up his jacket from the empty seat on his left. His head was aching slightly, and his eyes were sore. On the other side of Sally, Alice was slipping on her shoes. The aisle was crowded with a lot of self-conscious, blinking people, leaving.

Sally was clutching an empty popcorn bag. She turned to Alice. "Mother, didn't you think that pirate was *handsome*?" She seemed to be greatly concerned about this.

Alice grinned over at Fred before she answered, gravely, "Handsome is as handsome does, dear." He did not return the grin.

"Maybe so," Sally said, with no conviction whatever. And then, "Well, *I* think the pirate was handsomer than that old Prince Henry, and she loved the pirate, and *I* think she should have married him."

Alice stood up, stretching. Then she smoothed her dress, smiled at Sally and said, "Maybe she made a mistake, dear. Lots of people make mistakes." She seemed vastly amused at something.

Fred turned his eyes to the empty screen at the front of the theater. *Lots of people make mistakes.* He began to feel an unpleasant sense of being trapped in the row with Sally and

Alice. "Let's go home," he said, more sharply than he had intended to say it. "I'm awfully tired."

They pushed their way out into the evening, got into the car and drove toward home. The sky was clear, the air warm, and the moon was almost full. The houses and trees along the road were bright and clean-shadowed in the light. The moonlight made them look as they ought to look—ideal, abstract and pure.

Sally could not seem to forget the movie. She had been silent, thinking about it, and abruptly she spoke up, with deliberation and conviction. "Well, *I* would have married the pirate, Mother. Wouldn't you?"

"I'm already married, dear," Alice said, her voice serious for Sally. "I'm happily married to a man who owns two hardware stores. Besides, being the wife of a pirate might not be very comfortable."

"Well . . ." Sally said.

"A pirate might really be very dull, Sally, when he came home from pirating in the evenings and sat around the house."

Sally did not seem to have an answer for that one, and the conversation lagged. Fred continued driving. His head still ached. . . .

After Sally had gone to bed they sat in the living room for about ten minutes—Alice, unusually silent and thoughtful, reading a magazine. Fred looking at the paper but not reading it. He was thinking of pale gray eyes, of blonde hair pulled back tightly from the face, of poise, of intelligence.

Then Alice stood up and stretched. The lamplight was behind her and, beneath the cotton dress she was wearing, the soft curves of her figure stood out. "I," she said, "am going to hit the sack." Her voice was very soft, lazy. She walked over to the bedroom door, sleepy and barefoot, carrying her shoes in one hand.

He looked away from her. "Go ahead." He rattled the newspaper. "I think I'll read for a while." He continued looking at the paper until, after a moment, he heard the bedroom door close quietly.

He sat for what seemed to be a very long time, letting his eyes wander around the room, looking at the green walls, the draperies, the neat maple furniture, the framed pictures that Alice dusted at least once a week. How long had it been since he had looked at those pictures, had even acknowledged their existence? Five years? They had been married nine. My Lord! he thought, is it nine years? The things around him in the room seemed strange. He had been in it almost every evening for nine years, had sat in this same chair, had played with Sally, talked with Alice, read his evening paper.

Nine years ago he had brought Alice into this house; and now, sitting in his own chair, in a room that was at once the most familiar and the most strange place on earth, he was alone and lost. And something in him was crying out, protesting the thing that had first cried in him when the lights had startled his dream of romance and beauty and he had found himself with Alice and Sally in a movie theater.

He walked over to the bedroom and opened the door.

The first thing he saw was the moonlight. Moonlight seemed to touch everything in the room, and on the bedspread it was like polished silver. He stood still. Somewhere outside the window an insect was chirping, quietly, insistently. Another insect answered, very remote.

Alice was breathing softly. She lay in bed, one arm out from the covers. Her eyes were shut, and there was a soft smile on her lips. Something was being done to Alice by the moonlight, something abstract and pure. And her face was beautiful.

He sat on the bed and slipped his shoes off. As he bent over to put them quietly on the floor he suddenly realized that the headache was gone, that his eyes were no longer tired, only sleepy.

There was a rustle, very soft, and Alice stirred in bed. He looked at her; she had opened her eyes. "Alice," he said, "I . . ."

"I know." When she spoke, her voice and her eyes were full of wisdom, of the real grace of Eve. "I know. I've been there too."

"Alice," he said, taking her hands, "I love you."

She smiled up at him, still half sleep. "I love you too. And I've been thinking . . ."

"Yes?"

"I've been thinking that I wouldn't want to live with a pirate. Not at all."

He looked down at her, wondering, and then he smiled. And just before she closed her eyes he saw that, in the moonlight, they were gray.

FAR FROM HOME

The first inkling the janitor had of the miracle was the smell of it. This was a small miracle in itself: the salt smell of kelp and seawater in the Arizona morning air. He had just unlocked the front entrance and walked into the building when the smell hit him. Now this man was old and normally did not trust his senses very well; but there was no mistaking this, not even in this most inland of inland towns: it was the smell of ocean—deep ocean, far out, the ocean of green water, kelp and brine.

And strangely, because the janitor was old and tired and because this was the part of early morning that seems unreal to many old men, the first thing the smell made him feel was a small, almost undetectable thrilling in his old nerves, a memory deeper than blood of a time fifty years before when he had gone once, as a boy, to San Francisco and had watched the ships in the bay and had discovered the fine old dirty smell of seawater. But this feeling lasted only an instant. It was replaced immediately with amazement—and then anger, although it would have been impossible to say with what he was angry, here in this desert town, in the dressing rooms of the large public swimming pool at morning, being reminded of his youth and of the ocean.

"What the hell's going on here . . . ?" the janitor said.

There was no one to hear this, except perhaps the small boy who had been standing outside, staring through the wire fence into the pool and clutching a brown paper sack in one grubby hand, when the janitor had come up to the building. The man had paid no attention to the boy; small boys were always around the swimming pool in summer—a nuisance. The boy, if he had heard the man, did not reply.

The janitor walked on through the concrete-floored dressing rooms, not even stopping to read the morning's crop of obscenities scribbled on the walls of the little wooden booths. He walked into the tiled anteroom, stepped across the disinfectant foot bath, and out onto the wide concrete edge of the swimming pool itself.

Some things are unmistakable. There was a whale in the pool.

And no ordinary, everyday whale. This was a monumental creature, a whale's whale, a great, blue-gray leviathan, ninety feet long and thirty feet across the back, with a tail the size of a flatcar and a head like the smooth fist of a titan. A blue whale, an old shiny, leathery monster with barnacles on his gray underbelly and his eyes filmed with age and wisdom and myopia, with brown seaweed dribbling from one corner of his mouth, marks of the suckers of squid on his face, and a rusted piece of harpoon sunk in the unconscious blubber of his back. He rested on his belly in the pool, his back way out of the water and with his monstrous gray lips together in an expression of contentment and repose. He was not asleep; but he was asleep enough not to care where he was.

And he stank—with the fine old stink of the sea, the mother of us all: the brackish, barnacled, grainy salt stink of creation and old age, the stink of the world that was and of the world to come. He was beautiful.

The janitor did not freeze when he saw him; he froze a moment afterward. First he said, aloud, his voice matter-of-fact, "There's a whale in the swimming pool. A goddamn whale." He said this to no one—or to everyone—and perhaps the boy heard him, although there was no reply from the other side of the fence.

After speaking, the janitor stood where he was for seven minutes, thinking. He thought of many things, such as what he had eaten for breakfast, what his wife had said to him when she had awakened him that morning. Somewhere, in the corner of his vision, he saw the little boy with the paper sack, and his mind thought, as minds will do at such times, *Now that boy's about six years old. That's probably his lunch in that sack. Egg salad sandwich. Banana. Or apple.* But he did not think about the whale, because there was nothing to be thought about the whale. He stared at its unbelievable bulk, resting calmly, the great head in the deep water under the diving boards, the corner of one tail fluke being lapped gently by the shallow water of the wading pool.

The whale breathed slowly, deeply, through its blow hole. The janitor breathed slowly, shallowly, staring, not blinking even in the rising sunlight, staring with no comprehension at the eighty-five-ton miracle in the swimming pool. The boy held his paper sack tightly at the top, and his eyes, too, remained fixed on the whale. The sun was rising in the sky over the desert to the east, and its light glinted in red and purple iridescence on the oily back of the whale.

And then the whale noticed the janitor. Weak-visioned, it peered at him filmily for several moments from its grotesquely small eye. And then it arched its back in a ponderous, awesome, and graceful movement, lifted its tail twenty feet in the air, and brought it down in a way that seemed strangely slow, slapping gently into the water with it. A hundred gallons of water rose out of the pool, and enough of it drenched the janitor to wake him from the state of partial paralysis into which he had fallen.

Abruptly the janitor jumped back, scrambling from the water, his eyes looking, frightened, in all directions, his lips white. There was nothing to see but the whale and the boy. "All right," he said. "All right," as if he had somehow seen through the plot, as if he knew, now, what a whale would be doing in the public swimming pool, as if no one was going to put anything over on *him*. "All right," the janitor said to the whale, and then he turned and ran.

He ran back into the center of town, back toward Main Street, back toward the bank, where he would find the Chairman of the Board of the City Parks Commission, the man who could, somehow—perhaps with a memorandum—save him. He ran back to the town where things were as they were supposed to be; ran as fast as he had ever run, even when young, to escape the only miracle he would ever see in his life and the greatest of all God's creatures. . . .

After the janitor had left, the boy remained staring at the whale for a long while, his face a mask and his heart racing with all the peculiar excitement of wonder and love—wonder for all whales, and love for the only whale that he, an Arizona boy of six desert years, had ever seen. And then, when he realized that there would be men there soon and his time with his whale would be over, he lifted the paper sack carefully close to his face, and opened its top about an inch. A commotion began in the sack, as if a small animal were in it that wanted desperately to get out.

"Stop that!" the boy said, frowning.

The kicking stopped. From the sack came a voice—a high-pitched, irascible voice. "All right, whatever-your-name-is," the voice said, "I suppose you're ready for the second one."

The boy held the sack carefully with his thumb and forefinger. He frowned at the opening in the top. "Yes," he said, "I think so . . ."

When the janitor returned with the two other men, the whale was no longer there. Neither was the small boy. But the seaweed smell and the splashed, brackish water were there still, and in the pool were several brownish streamers of seaweed, floating aimlessly in the chlorinated water, far from home.

A SHORT RIDE IN THE DARK

He got up before she did. As well as he could tell from her breathing, she was asleep. She had got out of bed several times during the night, and he wanted her to rest now if she could. It would be a long day.

She had laughed with him, during the night, after he had heard her rush to the bathroom to throw up, saying that she might be pregnant again, that John—a Captain now, overseas—had always wanted a sister. He had laughed with her; but had not been amused. Her sickness frightened him too much, increased his helplessness.

He wanted her to sleep and he did not want her to see that he was worried about the snow. He wanted to find out, himself, how bad the snow was. All night he had heard the wind, beating against their bedroom window, the wind whining and howling around the trees outside and around the edges and corners of their house, had heard it even when he slept. He knew that she had heard it too; that she was thinking what he was thinking; but they had not laughed about that. Nor had either of them spoken of it.

He found his clothes, dressed quietly, tugged on his four-buckles and went downstairs. The wind had died earlier, and it was very quiet in the kitchen, except for the ticking of the clock over the stove.

He opened the back door and then pushed open the storm door. He felt something sink in his stomach as he did this, feeling the heavy weight of the snow against the bottom of the door. He did not like it—knowing that the snow must be thick and heavy, cutting them off even more from the rest of the world. He was cut off enough already, even without the snow.

He stepped out on the porch, and then out of what he knew would be the part circle of bare floor where the outward swinging door had pushed the snow aside. Instead of stepping down into the snow his foot hit it awkwardly, hitting the drift head-on, and some of the snow spilled over and into the top of his fourbuckles, soaking, cold into his socks. That was very bad. But then it probably had drifted against the house. He walked out further, stepping out into the yard, in the direction of the barn. No more snow came down over the tops of his boots; but when he bent down and pushed his hand into it the snow came up past his wrist. He went back into the kitchen, careful to shake the snow from his overshoes before he went inside.

Back in the kitchen he heard the clock ticking and wondered, briefly, what time it was. Probably very early. He had heard no sounds, outside, from the cow or the chickens, and he could hear very well. He felt for his watch and then realized that he had left it upstairs—the special watch, with the raised numerals and the lid hinged, for the tips of the fingers.

He had dreaded this part of it as he had lain awake upstairs, thinking about the morning and about yesterday's and last night's blizzard, about the weather that had been bad enough even to keep Ben Mills' boy from coming out from town to stay with them, the way he was always supposed to when the weather was bad. He had dreaded it but he knew he had to do it. He oriented himself by the position of the kitchen door, holding the knob behind him and then turning himself just so many degrees, and walked through the dining room and into the parlor. He had to grope a little before he found the telephone; but he got it, hesitated a moment, and then picked up the receiver.

There was no humming and no *click*. The phone was dead. He had known, of course, that it would die. The line was always down when there was lightning or when the wind blew hard.

He replaced the receiver quietly, although his hands were trembling. Then he stood where he was for what seemed a very long time, listening to himself breathe, hearing the sound of his heart beating. And then he heard, upstairs, the sounds of Ellen getting up. . . . .

At breakfast, Ellen laughed at him for worrying and said, "Of course I feel fine, honey. Either I'm pregnant or it was that tunafish salad last night." But he could tell from her tone of voice that she was straining to sound cheerful, unworried.

"I doubt if you're pregnant," he said, trying to make his voice light, kidding. But it came out dry. "And I ate the tunafish salad too."

"All right, dear," she said, "You win. I probably have the dropsy. Or mange. Or, maybe, it was because I ate too much and I was worried, last night, about Jerry Mills, when he didn't show up."

"I know. I worried about him too."

He could tell she was smiling at him, from her voice. "Well we really needn't have. He's not very reliable. Probably didn't have any anti-freeze or something."

He turned his face towards her, as if looking at her—a trick that, sometimes, he had to practice. "I wasn't worried about Jerry," he said, "I was worried about you."

"Now don't be silly. You know we let Jerry come out here just because Ben Mills is as fussy about us as an old maid aunt. Besides, he'd probably run screaming if he saw a burglar."

Why did she have to act as if she didn't know what he meant? "You know that's not it," he said. "What happens if you get hurt—or sick—and with this snow on the ground?"

"Nothing happens. Don't be gloomy, Arthur. The snow isn't that bad; I won't get sick; and, besides, I've got you—even though you do look a little peaked right now. Drink your coffee."

He took a sip of it before he said it, his voice sounding husky in the big, still room. "That's right," he said, "you've got me. And all I need is a seeing-eye dog. Then you'll have me and I'll have the dog and . . . and then I might be of some use to you." And he knew he shouldn't have said it, knew that there would be a look of pain on her face—on her face, which he hadn't seen in four years—a look he did not want to put there.

He heard her push back from the table, get up, walk over to his side. And then her hand was on his arm and he heard her say, softly, "You're of use to me, Arthur," with only the love evident in her voice, and none of the sympathy. He knew the sympathy was there, in her, and he knew that she knew to keep it out of her voice.

He pulled away from her. "You're wrong, Ellen," he said. "You love me; but I'm useless now. Sure, I get the disability money and I keep you company and we tell jokes every now and then; but what do I do when something *has* to be done? What do I do if you're sick? What if this is a crisis? What if . . . ?"

"This isn't a crisis." Her voice was firm, gentle. "And Jerry'll be out after supper; or if he can't come Ben'll be here himself. And I'm not sick. Maybe just a little, tiny headache. I'll take an aspirin and a liver pill."

"All right," he said, "all right. Take your pills. I'm going out back and put the chains on the truck. You may have to drive to town this afternoon. That much, at least, I can do."

"I'll get your gloves," she said.

"I'll get them." He finished his coffee, pulled up from the table, and followed the wall to the cabinet. Pulling his heavy workgloves on, he wondered if he should tell her about the telephone. But there wasn't any point to doing it; she probably had guessed it already—she wouldn't have tried the phone herself, for he could hear the *click* from anywhere in the house—or she would find out soon enough. There would be no point in telling her and making her try to hide her worrying from him . . .

It took him the rest of the morning to wrestle the chains onto the truck tires. He worked slowly and carefully with them, entirely by feel, but he got them on tight and secure. Then he pitched some rock into the back of the truck, just in case he needed the weight. He had to knock off twice to feed the animals; and he knew it was past noon when he came into the house.

She had lunch ready. "Sit down, farmer," she said.

He pulled his gloves and coat off and eased himself down slowly. He was not strong, and the extra morning work had winded him. He could smell ham, and beans. And hot bread. Ellen had taken to serving that kind of meal—a "country meal," she called it—since they had bought the place, a few months after his pension had started. "How are you feeling, Ellen?" he said.

"Fine," she said. "Much better. I just took my liver pill."

He said the blessing and then began to eat. He did not feel very hungry, even after the work. His world seemed very dark around him and very close. He could have been deaf as well as blind; there was no noise from outside, no sound of anyone— of anything—on the road.

He tried to visualize how the road and the countryside must look, outside, covered with a vast, white quilt, houses looking like candy houses in fairy tales. But there weren't any houses between them and town—not for two miles. And already, even though it had been only four years since the wreck and the explosion, he was losing the memory of those things. He had never known he would have to memorize the look and feel of a countryside after a snow. He had driven his old car, delivering the rural mail, over those roads for fifteen years; but already he could not precisely remember how they looked, could not remember the details of the things he had seen a thousand times. He tried not to think about it, began making an attempt to eat his ham.

And then, suddenly, there was a confusion of sounds. The clang of a knife or a fork being dropped, Ellen's chair being pushed back from the table, and, simultaneously, the sound of her drawing a sudden, gasping breath. And then, silence.

And then a little, high-pitched, cry—a strange, tiny cry; but Ellen's.

"What . . . what happened?"

She did not answer for a second, breathing heavily. He leaned forward, towards her, as if by that he might, somehow, be able to see her, to see what was wrong, what had happened.

Then she said, weakly, her voice shaking, "It hurts, Arthur. My stomach. Below my stomach. My God it hurts." The last part she almost cried out to him. "I don't know . . . it hurts."

The word flashed instantly into his mind, the memory of the vomiting and the liver pill coming instantly with it. *Appendicitis.*

He bumped into and swore at the table, getting over to her. Then he found her, bent, in the chair, put his arms around her and then was feeling her forehead, astonishingly hot, bathed now with sweat. "How does it hurt?"

She almost whispered it. "Like an . . . icepick." And then, "The phone . . . ?"

"No," he said, wanting to curse, to scream for help, feeling his own intestines being twisted, poisoned, torn, with hers. "The phone's dead." He held her, impotent, raging and crying inside. Then, trying to find something to do, something a stone blind man could do, he said, "Maybe it isn't . . . what I think it is. Maybe."

"I'm afraid it is, Arthur." Her voice was stronger now. "But the pain's easing now."

Maybe it would give her a chance. Maybe it would leave her alone long enough so that she could do something. "Can you walk?"

"I don't want to try," she said. "Get my coat and carry me out to the truck. I think I could drive. Can you do that, honey?"

"Hell yes," he said. Her coat was in the front hall. He got it, helped her put it on—she seemed stiff, drawn up in her chair— and put on his own. They had their gloves in their pockets. He had not taken his fourbuckles off.

He got hold of her, under her arms with his left arm, his right arm under her back, her legs jackknifed still, and she directed him while he stumbled out the door, across the yard, and to the garage. She got the door of the truck open, and he tried to slide her behind the wheel. She cried out twice, but got in the seat. He heard her fumble in her coat pocket for the keys, get them into the lock, turn the ignition on. And then she cried out. And was silent. And then again, louder, more painfully. "Honey," she said, her breath heavy and frightened, "I can't reach the pedals. My legs move so far and then they . . . won't move any further."

Something spun in the blackness of his brain. There was no sound but their breathing. There was no world outside them, outside the close, covering blackness. And then she cried again, softly this time, and something in him—deep in him—reached out and took the spinning in his brain and stopped it. He took a careful breath. "Move over," he said. "I'll drive."

Her voice sounded frightened. "No, honey. Wait, I'll be better in a few minutes."

"And you might not," he said. He began pushing in under the wheel, helping her scoot to the other seat. "You can hold the wheel and tell me what to do. You can see."

"All right, darling," she said. "Maybe we can do it."

"We can do it," he said. And then, almost automatically, his right foot was on the accelerator, his left on the clutch, his right hand on the gearshift. And he was fighting back the memory of the last time he had driven a car, the memory of the huge red and yellow light and flame that had been the last thing on earth that he had seen with his own eyes. As if without volition his finger pressed the starter button, and something was scraping and turning heavily, slowly, inside the motor. And he was pressing on the accelerator, and the motor caught, weakly. And then died. Not even letting himself think of what might happen here, what would happen if the battery of the truck went dead—dead, like the telephone—he pressed the button again. The noise was even weaker; but when the motor caught, it began to rumble and vibrate. He listened to it, giving it gas until it began smoothing out, roaring and then humming steadily.

Then he pushed the gears into reverse and let the clutch out. But when he was backing, panic took him, suddenly, and he hit the brake hard. Maybe he had gone too far, was about to hit something. Was there a tree there?

"You're not out of the garage yet," Ellen said, her voice soft, more confident now. "About a yard more."

He had to hesitate a second or two. Then he let the clutch out again, gave the motor just enough gas to keep it from dying, and eased back until Ellen said, "Cut your wheels hard to the left," and he spun the wheel, pushing down the fear that he would hit something, telling himself that she could see, would tell him. And that, if he did hit something, nothing would happen to them; that he was going too slow for anything to happen. And her hand was on the wheel, over the back of his, guiding him.

Somehow, they made it to the fence where their little twenty-acre farm joined the road. He hit nothing, and skidded only slightly. He kept the car in low gear all the way, judging from the sound of the motor that he was going no more than five or six miles an hour. If he could keep that rate up they would be in town in twenty minutes; it was only two miles. Only two miles.

When he got back in after opening the gate she said, "Maybe someone will come along the road. You could listen, and flag them down."

"In this weather? There aren't seven houses on all nine miles of this road." He shifted the gears back into low. "Am I headed right to go through the fence?"

"Cut hard right, and then left, when I tell you."

"Can you pull the wheel?"

"I don't think so. I'll try to help. I'll push your hand, and you push the wheel."

But when he started she said, gasping, "Just a minute," and then, her voice almost in sobs, "Okay. I'm straightened up now. I can see out."

When her hand fell on his, he reached over with the other and squeezed it gently. Then he took the wheel and started the car.

He kept the car on the road for what must have been a mile, grinding along in low gear, getting back on the road from her directions, holding the wheel steady most of the time, adjusting it when she put pressure on his hand. Once, he realized, suddenly, that he was freezing cold, and he turned on the heater, flooding them with warmth from an overheated engine. He kept driving. Or not driving, but pressing the accelerator, making the car move forward.

And then she passed out.

Her hand squeezed his like a vice, like steel, yet quivering—and something caught in her throat and there was a convulsion of her body beside him and then her body went limp, her hand still clutching his over the wheel.

When he stopped the car he killed the motor. He reached over to her, holding her, running his hands over her, feeling for life. Her head was burning hot, her knees jammed into her stomach; she was twisted sideways in the seat. Her heart was beating strongly. He eased her down on the seat, her head against the back of the cushion. The seat was broad enough to hold her legs.

He could get out and walk into town. It was only a mile. Maybe less. That would take ten minutes, maybe fifteen in the heavy snow. If he didn't get lost. But he couldn't get lost; the road was lined with trees and fences. He could walk into town. Fifteen minutes, at the most. He would beat on the door of the first house, stop the first car he heard, the first person fool enough to be out in the snow. Then, minutes of confusion, a phone call, an ambulance. Did they put chains on ambulances? Ten minutes for an ambulance to get to her. Ten more, to get to the hospital. He added it up; thirty-five minutes. Beside him, on the seat, Ellen moaned softly, her breath shuddering as the air was exhaled. Thirty-five minutes.

All of this, and more, went through his mind, racing, in an instant. And, then, sharply, he began to see the road in his mind, the trees and the fences along the road, the little culvert that would be in about a quarter of a mile, the two curves, the sloping of the hills. Could see it the way he had seen it, from behind the wheel of a car, for fifteen years, as he had driven over it, delivering the mail. Could see it as it must be now, white, untracked, covered thickly, heavily with snow.

At five miles an hour he could drive a mile in twelve minutes.

He started the motor again, shoving down in himself the screaming darkness in his mind, hanging grimly to the memory of the road, reaching out from the black closet that he was trapped in, into the memory of a mile, a narrow, fairly straight mile, of good country road.

He let the clutch out. He was mumbling and he heard himself distantly. "*My God,*" he was saying. "*My God.*"

Just hold the wheel straight and pray. The car was moving, the chains biting into the snow. Something in him, in his ruined eyes, was straining, straining to see. But he was alone, locked in the black closet, and the car that was somehow beneath him and around him—around *them*—was moving slowly over the road.

He went what could have been twenty yards and then hit something. The sound was a *thump,* shaking him, jarring his spine, and the motor was dead. He reached for Ellen, she was still in the seat. He opened the car door and got out.

Immediately the darkness grabbed him and he was lost. It rushed down on him, crowded over him, blanketed him, his mind spinning, reeling. Alone. *God in heaven, alone and lost.* He felt himself falling, and was in the snow.

But he lay there only an instant until his mind began saying to him *Time is passing. Ellen is dying.* Repeating it to him.

He pushed himself back to his feet, swaying. The car must be behind him, back here. It had to be.

It was. He found it and followed it to the front. The right bumper was against a tree. He felt the wheels. Straight. And then, painfully, he got to his knees and began scraping with his hands in the snow, crawling and fumbling. And then he found it. The edge of the road, under the snow, the place where the loose, dry gravel made the shoulder. He ran his hand along it for a yard or more. His other hand felt along the side of the truck. He was only a few degrees off parallel. He could do it.

He got back in the cab, and then started the engine, racing it to build up the battery. He might be needing more of the battery. Then he backed slowly, holding the wheel straight. The wheels slipped and skidded; but he did not feel the car twist. He eased back for what must have been three or four yards, then eased the wheel to his left, a quarter turn. Was that right? Had he turned it enough? He fought back an impulse to jump out and check it again. He would find out soon enough if it was right.

He started it moving forward again, letting the wheel out and then holding it steady. The car moved forward for what must have been fifty yards. And then, miraculously, for a hundred. Should he adjust the wheel? Maybe someone was coming down the road. He stopped, putting the gears in neutral, opened the door and got out. He listened carefully. There was no sound except for the motor of the truck. Then, he walked straight from the side of the car, his hands in front of him, until he ran into a fence. That had been too far. He turned, walked back to the truck, around it, and to the other side. He felt the edge of the road as he went across it. He bent down, feeling for the edge with his hands. The truck was near it, only a foot from it; but he had held on the road! He wanted to shout out, or to laugh. He was holding the truck on the road! Just a slight inclination of the wheel, to the left, and he would be going straight.

He did it, and kept going. And then he felt the culvert, going over it; and knew, instantly, that there was a curve less than a hundred yards ahead, a mild curve, leading gently to the right. What now? Get out and run ahead, finding where the curve was? He did not have time for that.

But he kept behind the wheel. His body knew the curve, would know it. His hand, his arms, his memory. He kept going, even increasing his speed, and when the time came began turning the wheel to the right. Nothing happened. The truck kept moving. And then there was a thump, and he knew he had hit something, coming out of the curve, and the wheel twisted in his hands.

It was a fence, and he backed out of it and got back on the road. He felt for Ellen. Her heartbeat was still strong, her forehead burning. *Hold out, Ellen,* he said, aloud, *don't die. I'll drive this damn truck to town.* He jammed on the accelerator and drove what must have been across the road, into another tree. He did not get out of the cab, but cursed, backing away. Then he started forward again and, somehow, got the feel of the left wheels in the slight, snow-packed ditch at the edge of the road, and held them there for minutes, moving forward, until he lost them and ran into a fence again, overcompensating, hitting a fence on the right side of the road. He backed away, started forward again. *Hold on Ellen,* he said, *I'll get you there.*

He fought the truck and hammered it into trees and bushes and fence posts; but he kept it going. He got back on the road's edge two or three more times, making several hundred yards each time before he lost it. He fought his way around the other curve, and after he did, knew that he was getting there.

And then he hit something and felt the truck go up and onto it and knew he had hit a curb. He stopped the car, turning off the key and then he heard another car, coming towards him and he heard it stop and someone get out, saying, "What the hell, mister?" the voice tough, sarcastic. And he was saying, the words strong, rushing out, "I'm blind. My wife is dying. Take her to the hospital. . . ."

After the men had driven him there and left him in their car and then come back for him, taking him inside, they sat him down and gave him coffee and asked him what had happened. But all he could say was, "Is she all right?" but they wouldn't answer him, and he had to ask it again, "Is she all right?" but they didn't answer him. And then he heard footsteps echoing down a hall and stopping and then a voice saying, "I'm the doctor. She's all right. We took her appendix out and she's pretty sick; but she's all right."

Ben Mills drove them back. The snow was all gone; he could feel the old, familiar road under the wheels as Ben drove. Ellen had the band of tape around her—she had said that it itched terribly—but she was well now, after only a few days. And, if she was a little weak, or sick, he could help her. When he felt the car going around the first curve and then, passing it, felt the bump of the culvert, he said, "That's a pretty bad curve."

Ellen took his arm, squeezing it gently. Her voice was light, but there was a kind of vibration in it, a something that was near to being reverence. "You want to drive, Honey?"

He turned his face towards her voice, imagining, remembering the smile that would be there, the eyes looking softly up at him. "No thanks, Honey," he said, and he laughed lightly, feeling the sense—the fine, once lost sense—of his own strength. "I can make myself useful some other way."

THE MAN FROM BUDAPEST

The most appalling detail about him was his dirty fingernails. Also, his collar was wrinkled. And his hair—dark, greasy looking hair—was too long, curling slightly around his pink ears. And his little eyes, bright, alert, eager, were looking over the faculty in a way that made several of them hastily drop their glances, in embarrassment. But Miss Dodd, the Principal, did not take her eyes from him. She watched him closely, her face a mask of quiet hostility.

The Superintendent of Schools, Mr. Morton, had just brought him into the room. He was a short man, chubby, balding at the temples, dark complexioned, and with very dark, intense eyes. On his face was an open, somehow childish, smile. He wore a cheap blue suit, a black, rayon-looking tie, and black, unshined shoes. It occurred to Miss Dodd, with distaste, that under the baggy pants of his suit would be ugly, silky, maroon socks, with yellow clocks in them, and runners. One of the teachers, Gloria Shumaker, glanced at her nervously, searching out a reaction. But Anita Dodd kept her face impassive.

Mr. Morton cleared his throat, adjusted his glasses, and began his interminable "Welcome back to Jefferson High School" speech. It seemed to last for an hour, and the little, faded room was unbearably hot in the September morning sunlight. Several teachers coughed. Mr. Morton droned on. Only Miss Dodd and the new man seemed to take it with poise. She sat primly in her seat, knees together, eyes attentive; and he, the shabby little new man, stood with his hands behind his back, looking at Mr. Morton with great attention. No one had asked him to sit down, and he seemed content to stand.

Gradually, the Superintendent began to talk about one of the subjects that all speechmakers of his type had been talking about for over a year: the space program. And the need for more technical education. About Jefferson's need for a Physics Department. About how, during the summer, he and the board had decided to find a new man, a Physical Sciences Teacher, to add to the faculty. And then he cleared his throat importantly and said: "... and so it is that I am now ... proud to introduce to you Jefferson High's answer to the Sputniks, Mr. Emil Kronsteidt, formerly of Budapest. Ah ... Hungary."

The room became strangely silent. Then Mr. Kronsteidt, beaming broadly at the other twelve members of the faculty, spoke. His voice was surprisingly gentle, cultivated—although deeply accented: "Mr. Morton is much too flattering to me. I am only a small piece of an answer to a Sputnik. There are no three-stage rockets under me for propulsion. Only feet." His smile broadened, and he shook his head sadly from side to side, "And they, alas, are flat."

To this there was only an embarrassed silence from the

faculty. Gloria Shumaker, to her credit, attempted a polite laugh; but after a glance at Miss Dodd she became silent. Miss Dodd's face was much like that of a Roman empress about to give thumbs down to a bad performer in the arena. And she would: Miss Dodd ran her school properly; she knew many ways of turning down the thumb, of sending a new teacher on his way . . .

He walked briskly into his first class—Physics, 1A. The classroom buzz stopped completely when he came in; but the silence was not the antagonistic kind he had received in the faculty room yesterday. He wondered to himself, amusedly, how these same students would be receiving him a week from now.

It was a big, bright room, the walls a pastel blue, well lighted by tall windows. He tossed his briefcase smartly on the newly shellacked oak desk, picked up a stick of chalk, and spelled out his name in broad, firm letters: KRONSTEIDT. Then he walked to his desk and, with agility, pushed himself up and sat on the edge of it. He looked over the class. They looked back at him. Then he grinned. "That's no dirty word on the board. That's my name." Their faces remained expressionless. "Well," he said, running his fingers through his hair, "this class is nice. But too big for Physics. I think maybe I flunk about ten, first week or so, so we can get down to business. Okay?" The students were looking at him strangely, as he had expected. They remained silent. He leaned forward slightly. "Anyway, if you want to learn Physics, you won't flunk out. And in here, if you got brains you learn Physics. Mostly I talk. Mostly you listen. If you study hard, you do fine. But, in here, we don't play games."

One of the students, a tall, intelligent looking boy, smiled slightly. Kronsteidt grinned at him. Then, abruptly, he jumped down from the desk, reached behind him, took a felt eraser from the blackboard tray, and threw it, violently, up to the ceiling. He watched it fall with satisfaction, hands on hips. Then he looked at the class. "The eraser goes up." The smile was leaving his face now, but his eyes were both amused and serious. "And it comes back down. But what happens in between? Just for a tiny second there—a microsecond—what happens?" He looked around the class, the eraser at his feet.

No one said anything. One boy in the back row nudged the one next to him—a gesture Emil knew well. But others—most of the others—were puzzled, interested. "Okay," he said, "I do it again." He bent and picked up the eraser. Up to the ceiling. Thump. Back to the floor.

A blonde girl in the middle of the room—an overdressed girl—giggled. He looked at her. "Good," he said. "Somebody, anyway, made an observation: teachers look silly to throw erasers. A good observation." He smiled at the girl briefly, and then looked back to the class. "Okay, what does the eraser do before it starts falling?"

For a moment there was silence. Then the tall boy, the one who had smiled before, said, "I think it hesitated, sir."

"Right. Good. That's what I want you to see." And then, "Why?"

"I don't know, sir."

"Anybody? Anybody know why?"

There was silence again; but this time an interested silence. "*Good.* Nobody knows why. Today I earn my salary. I'm gonna tell you why. Anybody here know about a man name of Isaac Newton? No? Good. We got plenty to learn . . ."

A week later, Miss Dodd stopped him in the hall. He smiled to see her. A nice-looking woman, almost forty, and her hair graying, but a nice figure under her suit, and big, fine eyes, except for the stern, dominating look in them . . .

"Mr., ah, Kronsteidt," she said, pronouncing his name as though it were an offensive thing, "there's something I wanted to discuss with you."

He smiled. "Sure."

"Not out here, Mr. Kronsteidt. In the faculty room."

He shrugged. "Okay. But I got to hurry. Some equipment is to get ready for my next class." He followed her down the hall. "Maybe you like to see it. Big electromagnet. Pull the hairpins right out of your hair."

Her voice was like ice. "Some other time maybe." He rushed up and opened the door for her, and smiled inwardly at her very pleasant perfume as she walked by him into the room. Too woodsy maybe; but one couldn't expect a school principal to wear very passionate perfume. She took a seat in one of the shabby, slipcovered chairs. He lit a cigarette and sat on the couch, leaning forward to hear what she had to say. He glanced at his fingernails, glad that he had been taking pains to clean them, since the look she had given them on that first day. "Mr. Kronsteidt," she said, "I wonder if Mr. Morton has acquainted you with our system for taking the roll in the classroom."

He pretended not to notice the distaste in her voice, and answered her amiably. "Oh, sure. He told me about it."

"Well, then why don't you use it?"

"I take the roll, Miss Dodd. Every day."

"Oh?" She turned and looked at him, her eyebrows raised. "Well, then, those who told me differently must have been ... mistaken."

He leaned forward slightly, interested. "Maybe. Do you have spies in my room, Miss Dodd?" He wondered how she would look in a bathing suit. He smiled to himself. At one time, as a boy, in Budapest, he had thought that market women wore bathing suits all of the time.

She stared at him for a moment, coldly. "Students sometimes come to me with their—problems, Mr. Kronsteidt. A few of them have said some things about you."

He smiled. "That's nice."

"Yes." She examined her fingernails. "I'll have to reprimand them for deceiving me about your roll taking."

"Oh," he said, "no need. They were confused. You see I don't use the roll book. I just remember who is absent." He smiled. "I keep my grade records that way too."

Her eyes flew wide. Caught off guard, she looked very pretty. "You ... *memorize* your record? For *five* classes a day, Mr. Kronsteidt?"

He laughed gently. "I see you don't believe me. Okay." He thought for a moment. "You teach History, don't you?"

"Yes." The set of her lips, tight together now, was not flattering at all to her. And she had pretty lips.

"What is your class studying now, in your most advanced course?"

She hesitated, but then answered, as if humoring him, "Early French history."

"Ah." He smiled. "Then let me quote for you *Les Vies des Commynes*, have you read that? Name any part you wish."

She remained silent, still staring at him. "Or maybe you would like to hear the *Etat* of Froissart. I can say it for you in the original French, or Modern French, or English."

Abruptly, she stood up. "That, Mr. Kronsteidt, won't be necessary. I'm quite willing to take your word about your ... unusual memory."

"Okay," he said, watching her legs as she was leaving the room. Very pretty legs. Yes. A very fine looking woman. But, poor thing, such an additude ...!

And then, just before she had left the room, he said, "Miss Dodd?"

She turned, looking at him coolly.

For once, he did not smile. "You must be patient with me, Miss Dodd," he said. "I have been in this country only six months; and I taught in Hungary for twelve years. I have many of your ways to learn."

Her face softened slightly, and she attempted a small smile. "Of course."

He smiled again, broadly. "That's much better," he said. "A very pretty woman like you should smile every time she has the chance."

The smile vanished. "This is hardly the time, Mr. Kronsteidt."

"Of course. But as I say, you must be patient."

Miss Dodd tried—or thought she tried—to be patient with Mr. Kronsteidt. But the effect of this was merely that she ignored him as much as possible. Although this was difficult: Mr. Kronsteidt seemed to be everywhere. And the students talked about him continually. Some—the brighter ones, she had to admit—spoke his name with high praise; boys who worked their heads off for the first time in their lives, studying Math and Physics. Others, especially the appalling number that he had flunked out during the first six weeks, talked of him as if he were some kind of an ogre, or clown. And he flunked students with no concern for its effect on their personalities, their development . . .

And then it happened, towards the end of the first six weeks. Gloria Shumaker brought the news into her office between classes. Birdlike, she glanced hastily around the room before she spoke. "Anita, have you heard about Emil Kronsteidt?" Her voice was hushed, excited.

"I've heard a good many things about Emil Kronsteidt, Gloria." Gloria could be very irritating; Anita tried to keep the irritation from showing in her voice.

Gloria smiled archly. "Haven't we all? But I mean what happened this morning."

Anita smoothed her hair in place with her hand. "What happened this morning?"

Gloria took a step closer, dramatically, her mouth tight-lipped. "Well, this morning, he asked one of his girl students to stay in a minute after class—it was Laurie Williams—and then he . . . made an indecent proposal."

She had heard this kind of thing before, and she knew it was probably nothing—a lie, or an imagined insult. But if there *were* something in it . . . She smiled wryly. "Laurie Williams? Well he picked a good one. I imagine Laurie knows an indecent proposal when she hears one."

Gloria did not seem to know how to take this. "It's all over school," she said.

Anita leaned back in her chair, several thoughts running through her mind at once. If this turned out to be only some silly notion of Laurie's, it would be unfair to use it against him. On the other hand, however, if there was a grain of truth in it ... And he certainly was a weird one; he might be capable of anything. "I suppose it is 'all over school,'" she said. "What did he say to her?"

Gloria shifted her stance, nervously. "I don't actually know. But Laurie went straight home afterwards without telling anybody. She and her mother have been in Mr. Morton's office since lunchtime. There's going to be a ... meeting in his office. At four o'clock. You're to be there."

"Well," said Anita, chewing abstractedly on her pencil end, "it looks as if we've a scandal in the making." She looked up. "How do you feel about all this, Gloria?" Something was bothering her; she wasn't certain what.

Gloria attempted an arch smile. "I certainly know how *you* must feel. There's been no mistaking your additude towards that ... man."

She averted her eyes a moment. "Yes. I suppose my attitude has been clear enough. I don't think that Mr. Kronsteidt is the ... kind of teacher that Jefferson needs to have." Then she glanced up again at Gloria, at her bony, old maid's frame, her nervous, pale lips, and her little eyes, eager to see someone whom she didn't like get hurt. *In twenty years*, Anita thought, *if I don't watch it, that's me.*

"And you think Laurie's telling the truth?"

"Well," Gloria pursed her lips thoughtfully, "he must have said something ..."

After Gloria had left, she sat in her office, thinking quietly, for several minutes. The blinds were drawn, and it was dark and quiet in the office, and she tried to calm herself, to quiet the thing that was troubling her. Then she stood up. There was something she should have done weeks before; she certainly should, in conscience, do it now. She glanced at the big clock on the wall. Fifteen after two. She patted her hair in place again, straightened the tight-fitting jacket of her suit, and left the office, walking purposively down the hall.

Kronsteidt had just begun lecturing when she entered the class and tried to slip unobtrusively into a seat in the back row. When she was seated, he smiled graciously at her but said nothing. Somehow she felt shamefaced, as if she had been caught spying on him. And yet this was part of her duty. But she wasn't supposed to visit a class only before recommending that the teacher's contract be dropped.

He had begun talking again, and she began listening to him. Her first feeling was irritation; she knew he lectured the students, and she did not approve of that method of teaching. She liked to think of her methods as more progressive. But she soon forget her irritation, becoming interested in what he was doing.

He had sitting on his desk an apparatus that looked like a shoebox with two metal balls mounted on it, and a crank, which he turned as he talked. And his talk—at first it took her a moment to get in with the rhythm and the speed of it—his talk was almost hypnotic. His face was animated, alive, his eyes bright, intense; his voice beautifully modulated, yet clipped, direct, forceful. He was talking about electrical potential, about resistance and capacitance, about the way electrons built up on one side of a conductor and protons on the other, about the force that was trying to drive the electrons across the highly resistant air between the two metal balls, until she could see and feel the energy that he was talking about with some of the intensity that was in his voice, and could understand the meaning and the power of those electrical terms. Dry, once meaningless terms that she had heard in boredom in some forgotten General Science class on some forgotten day twenty years before.

Twice he turned quickly to the board to write, in fast, strong strokes, symbols and numbers. Electrical formulae; but the way he put them there made them seem to have the wisdom of incantations. And the class—miracle of miracles—the class seemed to understand them, for, looking about her now, she could see that almost all of them were with him, following him as she was, seeming to draw energy and enthusiasm— even intelligence—from his little fat, agile body and his bright, serious eyes, and his strong, thickly accented voice. His voice, that moved through a language alien to him with a charm and forcefulness unlike anything she had ever heard in English before.

He was brilliant. He was superb. She had seen nothing like him ever. And somewhere, absorbed as she was with the wonder of this fat, strange little man, her mind was analyzing, trying to realize, to discover what the wonderful thing was that he had.

And towards the end of the class it began to become clear. First, after the suspense with the electrons had become almost intolerable, he flicked a switch on his little machine and a brilliant yellow spark, four inches long, sizzled across the airspace between the metal balls. She gasped at it involuntarily with the rest of the class. And then she looked at his face. He was smiling beautifully, watching them, with a smile that was wise and kind and, somehow it struck her, angelic. And she knew instantly what that meant: he was watching people learn. The finest thing that a teacher can do, the very best of all the rewards the profession can offer, and one which she, in twelve years of being a principal, being correct, being proper in her running of a school, had almost forgotten.

And then he began talking again, softly now, telling about how, marvelously, it was possible to calculate the intensity of the electric spark and the resistance of the air that it had, flashing, cleft its way across. And this was possible because a brilliant Englishman named Faraday had once, all alone, with nothing but his intelligence and the sweat of his brow, worked out a little, simple formula—a formula that was true for all times and all places. Then he turned to the board and wrote, in huge letters: $E = V/S$. Then, swiftly, yet leading them through the process, he made the calculations. And she saw, suddenly, that, doing this, he was doing it with love. And it struck her, so forcefully that it seemed as if she must have always seen it, that here was a man who loved Physics, who loved his field, who loved knowledge and had power over knowledge, and who loved, deeply and strongly, to teach.

And suddenly she was ashamed. And she became aware of a thing she had once known but that years of "professional training" had made her forget: That all the Group Work, all the Classroom Adjustment, all the Educational Psychology and all the watered-down "Progressive" course work that made up the training of a modern teacher could not produce the one finest thing that an intelligent child can ever encounter in a school-room: a devoted teacher with a fine mind and a deep love for— and knowledge of—his subject.

His timing was perfect. When he had shown them the resistance equation and had solved a problem with it, he assigned them twenty similar problems from their textbook, and another chapter—a whoppingly huge assignment—and smiled at them. Then, as if he had it too on cue, the bell rang.

Some of the students seemed to leave almost reluctantly—as if that could be possible. She looked at them, wondering if any of them would ever forget $E = V/S$ as long as he lived. But one of the students, passing near but not noticing her, nudged another and said, jeeringly, "Boy, Kronny really eats that electrical junk up." It was Joe Banks, a stupid, lazy student, and for an instant she felt she could slap his insolent face. But she remained silent.

And then, when the students were gone, Mr. Kronsteidt came back, smiling and wiping his forehead with a huge purple hankerchief, and sat on the desk top next to her.

For a moment she was embarrassed and did not know what to say. But he grinned at her disarmingly and spoke first. "I'm glad you come to my class, Miss Dodd. An honor. I hope I didn't bore you too much with the electricity."

"No." Suddenly she felt nervous. She glanced away from him, and saw his hands. The fingernails were clean, impeccably. "No. On the contrary, it was . . . fascinating." She wondered, somehow, if the fingernails were always clean like that; if it were only something unavoidable that had made them dirty before. "You're a . . . remarkable teacher, Mr. Kronsteidt. Remarkable."

He laughed gently. She looked up at his face for a moment, closely. He wasn't greasy looking. Only dark. And fat. And his hair was oily—but only because he probably didn't know better than to grease it down, as Europeans probably never did. Somehow, ridiculously, she thought of Adolf Hitler and his patent leather hair. That kind of thing could be shampooed out. Napoleon had curly hair. So did Caesar. *My Lord*, she thought, *what's making my mind wander?*

She pursed her lips together, for strength, looked at him and said, as precisely as she could, "Mr. Kronsteidt, I think it only fair to tell you that there will be a little meeting downtown, at Superintendent Morton's office, today at four. To discuss your . . . pupil relations. I think you should be present." By the time she had finished, her voice was in control again, and she could look at him squarely.

But he only smiled. "Sure," he said, "I'll come." And then, not pausing between, but softly, gently, "But you must not be so stern, the way you tell me of it. Just a minute ago you were so soft, and confused." He laughed quietly. "Just a little confused, like a young girl. Very charming."

She tried to make her voice firm, matter-of-fact. But somehow it hesitated, nervously. "I only came on school business, Mr. Kronsteidt." She began to get up from her seat.

"My name is Emil," he said, softly.

She spun to look at him. "I know what your name is, Mr. Kronsteidt."

"That's good." He was smiling gently. "But why must we be so formal, Miss Dodd? And 'Emil' is a much nicer name than 'Kronsteidt,' don't you think?"

"I'm not an expert on names." Why was her voice trembling? Why couldn't she make this man ashamed of himself, or embarrass him? Where were all her years as a principal, a woman of authority?

"Really?" His voice was so gentle, persuasive, that she seemed unable to make herself leave the room. And there was that sense of strength in it, and of youth and vitality, yet almost hidden by the quiet gentleness. "And I think that 'Anita' is a lovely name . . . for a lovely woman." He grinned at her. "Or for a woman who is very lovely when she forgets that she is my . . . boss." He shook his head in mock sadness. "So lovely."

His—what was it? Insolence?—gave her courage. She turned towards the door. "Act your age, Mr. Kronsteidt."

"Emil. It's Emil, Anita. And I am acting my age, alas. The age of a lonely, middle-aged man who wants a lovely woman to talk to. And such a lovely one you are, and so intelligent. And such fine eyes."

It was ridiculous. It was weird and frightening. She knew he was thinking of her as a frustrated old biddy, but she could not seem to move. Something in her was fluttering, something going loose and soft. It was childish. Adolescent. But he kept talking and she stood where she was, listening. "You frightened me at first, you know, that day in the faculty room. The way you looked at me. And how grimy, how uncomfortable you made me feel. And you were such a fine woman, so neat, so sure of yourself. But I liked you, because you were intelligent and I could see in your eyes that you could laugh. Could laugh, maybe, even at yourself." And then, amazingly, he reached forward and took her hand. "I would like to hear you laugh sometime Anita."

He held her hand only an instant, while she stood transfixed, unable to think or move. And then she jumped back from him as if she had touched an insect. She had thought of Laurie Williams. *What kind of man is this?*

She turned from him suddenly, her mind a confused whirling motion, and walked quickly from the room, not turning back. She could feel her face burning; and her hand trembled where he had held it.

She hardly noticed the two students, staring at her, entering as she left the room. She walked purposively down the hall, clicking her heels firmly, as if for reassurance, on the linoleum floor. In her dark office, she closed the door, and sat down at her desk, suddenly dizzy. She shook her head to clear it, gritted her teeth together, and began staring at the clock on the wall in front of her. Ten after two.

At four o'clock there were five people in Mr. Morton's office, all of them sitting in ancient oak chairs. Anita Dodd, Mr. Morton, Laurie Williams, her mother, and Emil Kronsteidt. No one was smiling, not even Kronsteidt.

Mr. Morton, promptly at four, began talking. He started slowly and hesitantly, as long-winded men do, and continued, uninterrupted, until four-thirty. Actually, he said little; but everyone present seemed to follow his vague allusions about "the honor of the profession" and "the opinions of our school board" except Mr. Kronsteidt, whose face seemed to show nothing but polite puzzlement. And, perhaps, Laurie, who had a strangely petulant expression on her overrouged features.

And then, finishing off his speech, with a confidence and forthrightness that it had taken him a half hour to work up to, Mr. Morton looked at Kronsteidt, cleared his throat, and said, "For these reasons, Mr. Kronsteidt, the school system of this county—and Mrs. Williams, feel that you should make an account of yourself."

Anita watched Kronsteidt's face, and for the first time she had ever seen it, he seemed to have lost his poise. His face was a mask of bewilderment. He tried a smile, and then said, "How do you mean, Mr. Morton? An account?"

Morton colored slightly. Then he said, "About what you said to Laurie Williams. This morning."

Kronsteidt stared at him a moment, then at Laurie, without comprehension. Then he said, to Laurie, "But . . . but what *did* I say?"

Laurie shifted her eyes from his face and stared at the floor. Her voice was whining, trembling slightly at first. "You made me stay in after class and said things about my . . . my . . . *underthings*. In class you're always saying crazy things, Mr. Kronsteidt, and then you said all those crazy things to me about things that are . . . *private* and all . . ." Her voice ran out abruptly and she turned her face quickly up to her mother's. Mrs. Williams looked at her comfortingly and then stared at Kronsteidt, her face now a mask of disgust and hate. "She cried all morning, Mr. Kronsteidt." And then to Mr. Morton, "Everybody in town knew something like this would happen. Everybody knows how peculiar he is, with his funny way of talking and those little, smart-alecky eyes of his . . ."

Anita looked at his face. The eyes were certainly not "smart-alecky" now. They seemed very sad, as if he were about to weep. He looked at Mrs. Williams' face, and then at Morton's. Morton met his gaze as firmly as Morton could. Then Kronsteidt looked at her, Anita. She turned her eyes away from his. Then, abruptly, he shrugged his shoulders, in a way that seemed resigned and European—the way a tired, middle-aged man from Budapest, Hungary might be expected to shrug his shoulders.

"And you believe, then, that I tried to be . . . indecent . . . with this little girl?"

Mrs. Williams cleared her throat. "You tried something with her."

He smiled, sadly, looking at her—the broad, gray-haired woman with her rouged and powdered daughter now huddled close to her. "And you think that, because she goes all painted and tries to be like a movie person, I, an old lecherous man, was trying to . . ." Abruptly, he stood up. Then he turned to Mr. Morton. "And you? You think so too?"

Morton shifted his eyes, embarrassedly. "I haven't heard your . . . statement, yet, Mr. Kronsteidt. I'm willing to be fair . . ."

For a moment, Kronsteidt's eyes blazed. "Oh, sure. That's why you called all this . . ." he gestured sweepingly around the room, to the little jury in oaken chairs, "called all this before you could maybe bother to ask me, privately, what I said to this little girl. You look at Emil Kronsteidt and you say to yourself, 'Now there's a funny Hungarian fellow and I'm sure he makes indecent remarks to little high school girls' because he talks funny and he flunks out all his lazy students and he has a funny way of combing his hair and so you say, 'Well, we got to see that our little girls don't get mistreated' so, naturally, you decide to have a little trial. Only you don't tell Emil Kronsteidt what's he's accused of and you already got it figured, all to yourself, what's he done to all you good people." He was sweating profusely now, and he pulled out the huge purple handkerchief and mopped his forehead with it. "Well that's nice. You all had a nice trial, and I'm guilty. I said bad things to Laurie here. Okay, now you give the sentence, and it's all over." He looked at Morton, his eyes blazing.

"Well . . . But, Mr. Kronsteidt." Morton was beginning to sweat too. "There's no need to take it that way. Aren't you being . . . overexcited . . . ?"

Kronsteidt paused a moment. Then he said, levelly, "Overexcited? Maybe." He turned his face away. "Only, with just this kind of little trial I lost my brother once." He wiped the handkerchiefs across his forehead. "Of course I didn't know what *he* was accused of either. But in the Hungarian People's Republic they don't always waste time with that. They shot him, though. Very efficient." Suddenly, he turned. "No need to fire me, Mr. Morton. I'll leave. You been letting me know, for a long time now, I should leave." He began walking towards the door.

Before she knew it she was out of her seat. "No. Wait ... Emil."

He turned, his eyes wide. She met his look. "Sit down," she said.

"No use," he said. "I better go."

There was a trembling in her voice, but it was sure of itself, and she could feel the ring of authority in it—the authority of more than a high school principal. "Sit down. You've made me ... ashamed of myself and I want you to stay, at least for ten minutes. Please."

He looked at her for a moment. "All right." He sat down.

She looked around her, at the people in the room. Then she looked at Laurie. She knew Laurie Williams well, knew her for a silly-headed, conceited little fraud. A clinger-on, a little, vindictive, brainless thing. "Laurie," she said, a tight, ringing note in her voice, "*Laurie*."

Laurie tried to look at her, but could not. "Yes?"

"Yes *what*?"

"Yes, Miss Dodd."

Her voice was like steel. "Laurie, what, exactly, did Mr. Kronsteidt say to you this morning?"

Laurie looked nervously at her mother.

"Go ahead, Laurie," Anita said. "Whatever it is, I think we can stand it. We've all been about as thoroughly embarrassed as we can get in here already."

Laurie said nothing.

Anita looked at Mrs. Williams. "Well, Mrs. Williams, do you think you can make her repeat it?"

Mrs. Williams looked flustered for a moment. "Well . . . I don't exactly know if she . . . should . . ."

Anita felt her face reddening in anger. "You don't exactly know? *You don't know?* Let me tell you something, Mrs. Williams. Yesterday I didn't think so, not in the least, but today, just now, I'm beginning to think that this gentleman—this *gentleman*, Mrs. Williams—whom we have been trying to shame here is one of the finest people I've ever been lucky enough to know and work with. And *you* don't exactly know if we should hear the evidence against him before we send him away from our school and our town in disgrace."

She stopped, her head spinning, and looked at Laurie. Laurie was crying. Her make-up was streaking under her tears. For once, she looked her age: fourteen years.

"All right, Laurie. Tell us what he said."

Laurie sniffed once. Then again. Her voice was a weak, childish whine. "He . . . He told me I was flirting and . . . distracting part of his class." She wiped a tear away with the back of her hand. "He said that a . . . girl my age shouldn't be so . . . forward. That I shouldn't wear . . ." she looked at the floor, ". . . f-falsies."

Anita stared at her, in disbelief, for what seemed an incredibly long, silent time. Then, suddenly, she laughed. She stood, hands on her hips, and laughed a long while. "Falsies," she said, laughing, "*Falsies.* Is that what it was? All of it . . . ?"

Laurie tried to look at her, but failed. "I was never . . . so shocked in my life."

Anita stopped laughing, and straightened her face as well as she could. Then she said, "I'll bet, Laurie." And then, "Well, do you wear them?"

Laurie looked up at her desperately, silent.

Then Anita looked at Mr. Morton, who was blushing deeply. "Well," she said. "Maybe Mr. Kronsteidt is abrupt sometimes, but do you think we should call his remarks 'indecent'?" She glanced briefly at Laurie. "They might be very pertinent— although short on tact."

Mr. Morton cleared his throat. "Perhaps . . . perhaps we owe Mr. Kronsteidt . . . an apology."

She turned to look at Emil. He was looking at her strangely, but smiling. Then he said, "But I owe Mrs. Williams—and Laurie—my apologies, too. I should be more careful, more considerate. And I must learn more of American ways. So I am sorry." He smiled at them all, the old, charming, very European Kronsteidt smile . . .

After the others had left, he seemed to be staring at her, and for a moment some of the awkwardness she had felt that afternoon came back. But then, remembering what had just happened, a flicker of the anger she had felt returned—together with her own shame for what she had thought of him—and she said, not looking at him, "You know why I think we were really all after you? Because for years we've all been talking about Education and Learning, so much that when we come against a truly educated, learned man, we can't recognize him for what he is and we're afraid of him. I think that's what it really is."

Her voice was quieter, tired, now. "We were frightened of you, and jealous—snobbish-jealous—because you seemed to know so much, and to love knowing. And teaching."

His voice was the softest she had ever heard it. "You are too good to say that. I do not deserve it. I was only ... strange, to you. And you ..." he laughed softly, "I have never seen a woman like you were in here, when you were talking to us. You were ... magnificent. And beautiful."

Suddenly she looked at him and smiled, wryly, but gently. "I'm not beautiful, and you know it, Emil. And neither are you."

He laughed again, softly. "Ah," he said, "but don't say it, please. You are not young," he smiled, "but beautiful, yes. A fine, lovely woman, yes."

The thing in her was fluttering again; but she did not fight it this time. "All right," she said, "I'm beautiful."

He laughed, and then held his hands, both of them, out to her, his small, delicate, chubby hands. "And lonely? Like Emil Kronsteidt?"

She took his hands, her eyes looking in his, his little, bright, intense eyes—his amused, intelligent, gentle eyes. "Not now," she said, "not now, Emil."

GENTLE IS THE GUNMAN

The first thing I want to say about this man is that he was one of the strangest-looking people I ever saw. And you see plenty of odd-looking specimens around a town like Denbow, what with the beat-up saddle tramps and all that come through, looking for jobs on the ranches out in the country. There's always plenty of flattened-out ears and noses around, and maybe sometimes a split lip or two. But he wasn't ugly like that—only homely.

He wasn't homely in any ordinary way, I could tell that the minute he came in the store and started looking around at the hardware. My mother and I run a hardware-and-feed store, right in the middle of town. I mean there wasn't anything dirty or sloppy-looking about him; in fact, his face was clean-shaved, and his clothes, such as they were, were as clean and neat as any. But the general, overall effect of him, so to speak, was what made him stand out. Under his jacket he was wearing this black sweater that came up to his chin, and under that sweater he was as big around as a rain barrel, and his face was all tanned and rough-looking, and on the back of his head he had this little blue wool cap like the kind that kids wear; and where you could see his hair, it was all tousled.

One thing about his face that struck me right off was the way his eyes looked. They were mighty little eyes for that rough and homely face; but they were coal-black, and they had whites that were as clear as fresh snow. They had a quiet and interested look. When he looked over at where I was standing behind the firearms counter—I was probably staring like a rabbit—his eyes looked at me in a friendly and curious way and didn't blink, not one little bit, until I kind of turned my head away.

Well, he walked up to me in a peculiar kind of lumbering, rolling way, and I said, "Yes, sir, can I help you?"

When he answered, his voice was another surprise. It was all smooth and soft, and you could tell he was pronouncing his words correctly, like a schoolteacher. "I'd like to see Mrs. Caywood, please."

Well, I stammered a little and said Mrs. Caywood was my mother and she was upstairs fixing lunch right now, but it was all right to wait.

He nodded, very serious, and walked over to the corner and sat down on a pile of feed sacks, and then he did something you don't often see in Denbow. He reached into his hip pocket and pulled out a book. Then he reached into his jacket pocket with the other hand and put on a pair of steel-rimmed spectacles, and begun to read. And after a while he begun to hum, still reading. Well, I couldn't keep my eyes off of him.

For one thing, I noticed his gun, which, by itself, seemed kind of strange with the outfit he was wearing. It was a big old-style revolving pistol, and the handle looked like it had been used to drive nails with, and the back of the hammer had been broken off. The whole outfit was stuck down in a holster that looked like it had been homemade out of a sow's ear on a rainy afternoon.

He kept on reading and humming, and I kept fooling around behind the counter, oiling up guns now and the like, because there really wasn't much to do around lunchtime like that. After a while mother come downstairs bringing lunch. She had it heaped up on a tray like always. Well, when she saw the stranger, she looked right puzzled. She set the tray down on the counter, and the stranger got up and walked over and smiled very polite and said, "Mrs. Caywood?" and mother said that was who she was, also very polite, and what could she do for him?

He smiled again and said, "I'm Geoffrey Merrill, Mrs. Caywood. Mr. Arthur at Abilene told me you needed someone to work for you."

Well, when she heard that one, mother just stared at him for a minute. Then finally she let her breath out all at once, the way she does when she's peeved about something; then she said, "You're the man that Harry Arthur said he was sending?"

The stranger seemed too polite to act like he'd noticed her tone of voice. He just kept smiling and looking right at her with those black eyes of his and then he nodded his head. Now, mother's usually pretty strong on politeness, so I was a little shocked to see the way she was looking at the man, even though he was pretty much of a specimen. Mother never was so strong on good looks that she could exactly boast herself—especially with being almost forty years old and a widow for ten of them.

Like I say, mother stared at the stranger's big homely face

for quite a while, and then I saw her drop her eyes and look at that old horse pistol of his; then she said, kind of grim, "I thought I told Harry I wanted a gun fighter."

Well, you can imagine that kind of took me back a little! I hadn't heard a thing about mother's going out to hire a gun artist to work for her. And I sure hadn't suspected Mr. Fat-and-Homely there of being anybody important in that kind of way. But as soon as I got over staring at mother, I could figure out, easy enough, what she had in mind. We'd been having some trouble with Gordie Wilkenson's men from out in the country—nothing real serious; but they'd torn up the store a few times after mother broke up with Gordie several months back—and it was plain that mother was getting pretty sick and tired of it all and she'd just gone out and got herself a body-guard. But I reckoned she got something that looked a little different from what she was expecting.

Well, the man was still smiling, and the next thing he said, very soft and gentle, sounded strange—like it had come out of a storybook. "I was something of a fighter in my youth," he said.

Mother tightened her lips and said, "With guns?"

He shook his head and said, "No, Mrs. Caywood. I was a wrestler." Well, I'd never seen a wrestler before, but it made sense, considering the size of him.

All of a sudden mother laughed real loud, and when she stopped laughing she said, "There's nothing to wrestle with around here but the rats." Of course, a feed store does have its rats, but I thought mother was being pretty rude to the man. "I need a man who can fight with guns." She tried to smile at him pleasant, because I think she was a little ashamed of herself for laughing at him.

For a minute he didn't say a thing. Then he reached down to the counter where I had spread out a bunch of guns to clean, and he picked up the little target gun and looked at it a minute in the palm of his hand, and then he took one of the cartridges from the counter where I had emptied them out and he started loading the gun. Well, I knew mother didn't care much for shooting inside the store, but I figured the man was polite enough that if he was going to shoot at something, to show how good he was—like they do in the books—he'd use the least gun possible to do it with, and that's why he took the target gun.

"I can't pretend to be a professional," he said, loading up, "but I can shoot well enough." He held the loaded gun for a minute or two while he watched the back wall, over where we kept the stock of feed bags, and I knew what he was watching for.

Sure enough, after a minute this brown rat came out from behind a feed sack and began walking sassy along beside the wall as *la-ck-da* as you please. I'd seen his type before—a real nervy, cock-of-the-walk rat, taking his constitutional probably or on his way to lunch. Well, the stranger kind of held the pistol out toward the rat, aiming it like it was a toy. I don't know how he managed to wedge one of his fat fingers inside the trigger guard, but I guess he did, because the gun made a polite little bang, and that rat on the other side of the room was suddenly without a tail. You never saw a more astonished-looking animal in your life. Well, after he'd taken muster, so to speak, he just kind of slunk back where he came from, all the cockiness gone out of him, and I couldn't help wondering what he was going to tell the boys back at the nest about it.

The stranger flipped the empty cartridge out and set the gun back on the counter. I thought he'd done right well; but, of course, I couldn't help wondering if he'd really been aiming for the rat's tail or was just trying to kill him and had, in a way, missed.

But mother wasn't going to let on that she was impressed—that's mother. "Why didn't you kill him?" she said.

The stranger didn't smile, but I could see from the look in his eyes that he wanted to smile. He just said, very pious, "I didn't see the need for bloodshed." Mother couldn't help laughing at that, but in a nicer way this time. I was glad to see that now she seemed to like the way he talked too.

"Well," she said, "you'll have to do. You can clerk in the store and you can sleep on a cot down here, and the pay'll be thirty-five dollars a month."

"Fine," the man said and grinned, and I could see he had the prettiest, most even teeth I ever saw.

"And you can start out," mother said, "by digging that bullet out of my floor and smoothing out the wood where it's splintered."

"Yes, Mrs. Caywood," he said and began pushing up his sleeves. And, my gosh, what arms that man had on him! I want you to know his forearms were as big around as powder kegs and all dark brown from the sun and covered with bleached-out hair, and the muscles in them looked like wire cables. Right smack in the middle of each forearm, in a little place where the hair was kind of worn off, was a real tattoo; and each tattoo was a picture of a little blue fish with his tail sort of flipping behind him as natural as life. I never saw the like!

I began to think that if he'd been a wrestler, there must be a whole lot of other wrestlers still hurting in the backbones from tangling with him. And yet, with his sleeves rolled down, he didn't look one bit tough—only fat. Well, mother gave him a screw driver and a spokeshave, and he started to go over to where the bullet hit and get to work, but mother said, "On second thought, you can do it after lunch." He grinned at us then, and we grinned right back.

The meat and potatoes had got pretty cold by that time; but you should've seen the way that man could put away his food—and with the best table manners ever I saw!

He fixed the floor up as pretty as could be, and that wasn't all he fixed. He was about the handiest fellow I ever heard of, and during the next week he rigged up all kinds of sporty things, like a rack of shelves for storing grain sacks and a new set of iron hinges for the big tool cabinet and a new way of setting in the lamp chimneys so they wouldn't smoke up so much and a new kind of rat trap that was made out of wire and burlap and that pulled the rats in like a magnet.

He never did say much, just worked away quietly and never seemed to be working too hard—in fact, he always found himself plenty of time to read his books. But he got just about everything you could think of done. Of course, being just fifteen years old, I naturally tried to get him to talk to me about himself. And he did talk a little too. For instance, I found out he'd been a sailor for about twelve years—that's where he'd learned about rats—and he took up wrestling when he lived in Japan for a spell. Why, he'd been most every place, and if he'd been the talking kind, I reckon he could have told some stories. But he wasn't that way, and he'd mention things like seeing Queen Victoria of England at a parade just like you might say you'd run into the mayor of Abilene the other day; and would I have to sweat to get him to tell me about it! But all he'd say was that the queen looked like a nice plump lady and he'd heard she was right proper and moral. Well, that kind of talk didn't satisfy me much, but that's the way he was.

I found out a thing about that pistol he carried; it was one day when he was cleaning it, and I got a better look at it. It hadn't been used to drive nails at all, like I thought. From close up I could see what made the butt of it look so beat up was that it was all carved, in the fanciest way, with little pictures of men with what I'd have sworn were goats' feet, and of ladies wearing bed sheets, and I don't know what all. It was made out of two pieces of wood that were as black as soot. He said this wood was called ebony and he'd got it in the Barbados—wherever that is—and had carved it himself with his pocketknife and then put it on this old gun that he'd bought for junk and fixed up. Well, when you looked at that gun close, you could see it was well taken care of; but it was fixed the way that wasn't for show—even down to that fancy handle that wouldn't look fancy to anybody who was more than two feet from it.

After a while I began to think that mother was getting to like him right well although she didn't say nothing about it. Of course, mother always was pretty good-natured; but she seemed to be doing a little more humming and singing after Mr. Merrill come to work for her. Her cooking, which was never much to begin with, began to improve a little—at least her gravy was a little less lumpy, and you weren't so likely to find gravel in the beans, and I appreciated that.

Well, of course, it was bound to happen that Gordie Wilkenson's men would hear about mother's hiring herself a strong-arm man and would come by to beat him up. Although it was a natural thing for them to do, it was probably Gordie that put them up to it. Of course, he would never come by the store himself after mother laughed him out the front door that time he'd asked her to take a trip to Chicago with him, to see the stockyards—and not even mentioning they should get married first. We hadn't seen him since, but every few weeks or so afterward a bunch of his men might come in and cut open a couple of sacks of feed and shoot out the lamps and make a general mess and laugh and cuss a good bit. We couldn't do much about it except call the sheriff, which was a waste of breath if there ever was one. Gordie wasn't a bad man, but he sure didn't like being laughed at.

Now, this day I started to tell about was a Wednesday around two weeks after Mr. Merrill come to work for us, and he and I were alone in the store and these three fellows came drifting in kind of slow, and I said to myself, *Oh, oh!* One of them was a big horsy-looking fellow that they called Bow Wow Payton for some fool reason, and he was one of Gordie's foremen and pretty well known for general meanness. Mr. Merrill looked up from his book, real quiet, when they come in, and I didn't have to tell him what they were there for. He could see right away, and the first thing he did was get his spectacles off and onto the shelf behind him, and the second thing he did was set his book on the counter. Then he got up and walked out to meet them in the middle of the store and he said, "May I help you?" as smooth and polite as you please.

Well, the other two seemed to think that was right comical and they began to grin a little and they looked at Mr. Merrill like he was some kind of a freak. But Bow Wow, who was pretty straightforward, just gave him a glassy look for a minute and then he said, "Hell, I don't need no help from you, Fatty."

Mr. Merrill just stood there and shrugged like a big sleepy elephant and smiled. Now, about that time, I almost hollered out because I saw that while Bow Wow was standing his ground, the other two men were each easing around to Mr. Merrill's sides. I didn't holler because I hardly got a chance, it was all so fast. Those two just grabbed Merrill by the arms and hung on tight, and Bow Wow drew back his fist and let fly with a great big gosh-awful punch right smack in Mr. Merrill's belly.

Now, once I saw a man named Billy Mosher, who was pretty drunk at the time, get all sweated up and make a lot of bets that he could fell a bull with one kick on the side of its head. Well, naturally a bunch of men wanted to see that, so they got them a bull that was due to be slaughtered anyhow and they dragged it out in front of the saloon. After the money was up and there was a crowd around—including me, of course—Billy Mosher rolled up his sleeves and spit on his hands and drew back his right arm and came down with all the strength in him right alongside that bull's neck. And do you know what that bull did? He blinked up once at Billy Mosher and then he begun chewing his cud. He wouldn't have looked more disturbed by a fly. I don't think I'll ever forget the look on Billy Mosher's face when he saw that bull wasn't even going to bother to get mad.

And that was the way Bow Wow Payton looked when he pulled back his fist afterward and saw Mr. Merrill smiling at him over that big belly of his. I mean that punch hadn't even changed the expression of Mr. Merrill's face; he didn't even blink, like Billy Mosher's bull.

Well, everything was quiet for a couple of long seconds, and then Mr. Merrill kind of shook himself the way a grizzly bear does sometimes, and those two men let go of those arms like they really were powder kegs and had just exploded. And then

Mr. Merrill kind of drew his right arm back and didn't do a thing more than slap Bow Wow alongside the face with the back of his hand, and Bow Wow kind of rose, real graceful, and sort of flew backward and staggered back against the wall and just leaned there, looking glassy-eyed and peaked, and the blood was running down his nose onto his shirt.

One of the other men had got up from the floor and he was still standing next to Merrill and about that time he kind of quietly set his hand on the butt of his gun and started to draw it. Well, he got it just out of its holster when Mr. Merrill brought his hand down—and it was the edge of his hand, like he'd told me they did in Japan—and his hand caught that man on the wrist, and the force of it battered that gun down slam-bang to the floor like somebody had taken a twelve-pound sledge and driven it there. And that man's hand just kind of hung down from his wrist like an old dishrag.

Then Mr. Merrill was very gentle and polite about collecting the three of them and ushering them out the front door. When that was done, he picked up the broom and began cleaning up.

It wasn't more than fifteen minutes before Gordie Wilken-son was coming in the door—and I was surprised it wasn't sooner, but I guess it took those men of his a little while to get it all told. Gordie looked his usual, and I have to admit he was a handsome-looking man. It was a glory to see the clothes he wore too. He had on his fancy hat and coat and his blue brocade vest and was sporting a necktie and wearing those two big flashy pearl-handles of his, butts foremost, in the holsters just like he was a big-time gun handler—which, of course, he wasn't, even though he was the best in our county. And I began to worry about Mr. Merrill and how he was going to be able to do any good, drawing that big old ugly gun of his against Gordie, what with his really being only a sailor and all.

Well, Gordie came in looking pretty nasty and he walked up to Mr. Merrill, who was putting some feed bags up on the storage shelves, two at a time like he always did it. Gordie looked at him a minute, taking him in—it always took people extra time to take Mr. Merrill all in. Well, after a minute Gordie cleared his throat real loud and said, "I hear there's been trouble in here."

Mr. Merrill put up the last of the feed bags and then turned around and looked at him and said, "Oh, nothing very serious, sir."

It was easy to see that polite way of talk just made Gordie madder, and he said, "One thing I hate is somebody who makes trouble."

But Mr. Merrill just peered at him close a minute with those sharp, dark eyes of his and he didn't say a thing.

Gordie cleared his throat again. "Most often a troublemaker's a coward," he said.

Mr. Merrill just kept looking at him, like he didn't understand.

Well, I could see Gordie was feeling awkward now and getting hotter all the time. "I see you're wearing a gun," he said, and his voice was too loud, "and I suppose you know how to use it."

Mr. Merrill just smiled and then he said, "Excuse me," and pulled mother's little inventory book and a pencil out of his hip pocket. Then he put his glasses on and began marking down for the feed sacks he'd just put up.

Well, that did it for Gordie. I could see his fingers begin-

ning to twitch for his guns, and he was fighting to hold himself down. He started to say, "Mister, I think you and I better
go outside this store and find out—" but he never finished
it, because what happened then caused his voice to kind of
fade out.

There had been an uncommon number of rats playing around
down at the other end of the store that day, and while Gordie
was talking, Mr. Merrill set his pencil down on a shelf and did
something that seemed just as ordinary and natural as brushing a fly off his nose. He just kind of glanced over toward the
wall and saw a couple of rats strolling along, and then his right
hand made the smallest, quickest little wave downward, and
that big revolving pistol seemed to jump right up into it and
go off twice. And I want you to believe me, the noise it made
was as fierce as thunder; and before you could tell it, that pistol
was back in Mr. Merrill's holster, and he was looking a little
apologetic for interrupting, and there were two rats clear across
the store that didn't have any heads at all. And he'd done it just
like you might have swatted a mosquito with a rolled-up piece
of paper.

   Well, I mean to tell you, Gordie looked at those rats.
I believe he'd have been looking at them till closing time if
mother hadn't come over just about then and sort of brought
things back to normal. Mother is nobody's fool, and it didn't
take her a half minute to take it all in. Nobody understands
women, and I would have bet my last nickel that mother would
laugh her head off once she got the idea; but she just smiled
sweet at Gordie and she said, "Hello, Gordie Wilkenson."

   He said, "Hello, Mary," very quiet. Then he cleared his throat and said he had better be getting along, and he said good-by to me and to Mr. Merrill and walked out.

Like I think I've already said, I was fifteen years old at the time, and you can imagine who my almighty hero was from then on out. I mean I just couldn't hear enough about Geoffery Merrill, and I was even considering going to San Francisco and getting a job on a ship heading for Japan. Another thing, too—it didn't take me long to remember that I could have used a father in those days, and I managed to mention that to mother every now and then—in an offhand way, of course, and without saying anybody's name. Mother didn't make me hush about it either, although she wouldn't say anything one way or another.

Now, Mr. Merrill kept all his things in a big wooden chest of his behind the grain shelves; and one morning about a week after Gordie had been in, he went and got that chest open and took out a red box that was about the size of a dinner plate and he set it under the counter and didn't say a thing to me about it. But it was plain enough it was something important, the way he'd keep passing by there all that morning and would stop and look at it for a minute. I do believe he seemed edgy about that box—which wasn't a frame of mind I was used to for him.

Well, mother came downstairs at lunchtime like she always did, and even I had to admit that she was looking pretty, what with wearing a blue dress, and her hair combed real careful and all. When she came down, I could tell right off that he was even more nervous. I began to guess, real hopeful, what he might have on his mind, and that made me a little nervous. We had kind of a shaky lunch of it, but mother didn't seem to notice hardly at all. After lunch, Mr. Merrill got his box out from under the counter and set it down in front of mother and he gave a real polite speech, telling how he bought what was in this box in Japan and had been hoping he could find a nice lady to give it to and how nice it would be if mother would accept it.

Well, when she opened the box, her eyes just got big and round, and she pulled out this big silky thing that I reckon was about the prettiest thing I ever saw. It was a thing they call a kimono, and I mean it was fiery to look at, with blue and red dragons on it, and I don't know what all. Mother always was a plain woman and never owned a thing like that before, and I could see she was a little shaky, holding it and feeling how silky it was and looking at all those colors on it, as bright as a wood duck's neck feathers and all shiny in the light.

Everything was quiet for a minute, and you could sort of feel how pleased and nervous everybody was, and then a kind of peculiar look came on mother's face and she set the kimono on the counter and she said, her voice kind of sad, "It's the loveliest present I've ever seen, Geoffery." And her calling him "Geoffery" sounded strange, but she said it natural, just like they'd been first-naming each other for quite a while. Come to think of it, maybe they had—since I never was around the store much in the afternoons and never would have known it. Well, she hesitated a minute and then she went on. "But I don't think I should keep it."

His smile weakened, and he said, "Why not, Mary?"

She kind of smoothed out her dress with her hands and looked down and said, "Doesn't a gift like that mean—" Her voice trailed off.

"Maybe it does," he said. "But I thought—" And his voice

trailed off. It was a peculiar way of talking, but it seemed to be doing the job.

Well, then, mother kind of nerved herself up and looked him in the eye and said, "Geoffery, you're the finest man I ever knew and I ought to thank the Lord for how good you've been to me. But you're a man of violence."

Well, that threw him. "A what?" he said.

"A man of violence."

Well, you could see he just didn't know how to take that. But after a minute, he said, very slow and serious, "Mary, I've never fought except when I was forced to. Do you know what I used to work at when I was a sailor?"

"What?" she said.

"I was a cook—for twelve years I was a cook. That's not a violent profession, Mary."

Well, mother just stared at him, and I couldn't tell what the expression on her face meant. But she didn't say anything, and finally he said, "I never shot at a man in my life."

"You never shot at a man in your life?" mother said. "Then what were you doing coming here as a gunfighter?"

"I didn't say I was a gunfighter." He smiled at her, very gentle. "When I left the sea, it was to settle down and work in a store somewhere. When I heard about this position, I felt I might be able to handle the bodyguard part as well, since I'm rather big."

But she just shook her head and she said, "I don't believe it. You're too expert with your gun not to have killed a man."

Then he just laughed a little. "Only rats," he said. "That was what I bought the gun for in the first place." He smiled at her, sort of sheepish. "A ship always has a great many rats, and in twelve years a person can develop a good deal of skill at shooting them." He shook his head, smiling. "I won't tolerate a rat in my kitchen."

Well, you should have seen mother—she looked all out of breath, and her eyes were the widest I ever saw them. And then, all of a sudden, she began laughing and she laughed so long I thought I was going to have to whop her on the back to stop her, and Mr. Merrill was looking kind of upset and worried, and I was getting mad at mother for laughing like that. But she stopped finally, and there were tears all down her cheeks. Then she did the most surprising thing I ever saw her do. She just threw her arms around Mr. Merrill's big thick neck and she hugged him for all her life and then she drew back a little and kissed him, right on the mouth. I never saw the like. And she said, "Geoffery Merrill, you're too good to be true!" and I mean did he ever look flustered and happy! And I have to admit I was almost ready to split, I was beginning to feel so good.

Well, that's all been two years now, and we don't have any more rats around—although there's quite a few bullet holes in the walls, along the edge of the floor—but I do have a baby brother. And I mean to tell you he's a great one when it comes to eating and laughing and generally sitting up in his cradle and looking sassy. And mother and father are mighty silly about him, and they seem to think he's the finest-looking thing ever they heard of. Well, now, I am mighty tickled to have him and I wouldn't trade him off for the best colt in the country, but I feel I ought to be honest about it—he is the homeliest baby anybody ever saw. But maybe that's why I like him more than anything else.

THE MACHINE THAT HUSTLED POOL

What I mean, you been around the rooms as long as I been around the rooms you get so there's very little in the way of hustling that is going to force you to raise one eyebrow or maybe two. That's poolrooms, I mean. And pool hustling, which is one of the six or seven deadly arts commonly practiced in the rooms.

What I mean, I seen them all. I seen Michigan Benny, one of the finest five-ball players running, stroll into the room looking like a sharecropper—or whatever it is that wears them blue cardboard pants with the dickey—and seen him walk out with a roll you could of bought every boll weevil in Georgia with. And I seen Howie Johnson, the Arizona Mudball, wearing, so help me, Bermuda shorts and a Jungle Jim hat, win a half interest in a diamond mine from a man with a elephant gun you could of hit a elephant with if the elephant was in Africa and you was in, say, Nova Scotia, and you could see that far.

Now in our room we have got a lot of regulars and they are

some of them pretty fair and they are some of them not. But I suppose the only hustler with real class—I'm not including myself in this—is a fellow named Polk who we call The Chicago Pig, not because he is fat, which he is, but because he is a very greedy person. The Pig is greedy about money. Personally, in a poolroom you can't be choosey; but personally I have only very slight use for the Chicago Pig.

So anyway this one afternoon there is about eight of us regulars sitting around thinking dark thoughts and doing very little, since our poolroom (which is sometimes a gay, carefree and lively place at nights) is at this moment completely without a game of pool.

So we are just sitting around meditating, and I personally am meditating about a wager of fifteen large dollars which I have placed with a friend of mine named Arthur that a horse named Lo-ball will win a race tomorrow in California when in comes this kid.

He is a kid of maybe twenty years old and he comes in with some books under his arm and kind of a innocent look on his face—what there is of his face you can see under his glasses—and he asks Freddie the Squirrel, who is the proprietor since the day several years ago when he threw seven straight passes and the former owner into a cataleptic state on table number three with house dice, he asks Freddie can he practice.

Freddie looks around at his fourteen empty tables and he says, "If I can find room for you, kid."

So the kid looks at the empty tables too and then he looks at Freddie the Squirrel real close, like maybe he is near-sighted, and he says, "Say! That was pretty funny!" like he is meaning it from the bottom of his heart.

This reply shuts Freddie up, since he is not very bright anyway at anything except dice—at which it is true he shows some of the earmarks of genius—so he racks up a set of balls for the kid and the kid sets his books down and picks him a cue and chalks it up and by this time there is four hustlers standing around the table looking very friendly.

Now the Chicago Pig is amongst the crowd which is watching and I look over at him and I see that he has a familiar look in his eyes which is closely akin to the look with which a genuine pig might contemplate a bucket of slop. Although of course in this case it is only a small bucket—as this kid does not appear to be the wealthy type—it must be said of the Pig that he enjoys the challenge to his skill afforded by the better-playing class of suckers.

So after a minute the kid shoots a pretty fair shot, a kind of reverse cross-corner bank and the Pig lets out this big long whistle and he moves up and he says, "Say, kid! How did you do that?"

The kid stops cold, like maybe he had just heard the voice of a departed lover, and then he turns and looks real hard at the Pig and he says, "You mean, how did I make that shot?"

The Pig plays right along with this and he says, real earnest, "Yeah! That was really some shot! I wish I knew how to make it."

So the kid thinks about this a minute and then he says, "Okay." And he starts explaining, real careful, how the shot is made, and the Pig keeps nodding his head, serious, and agreeing; and then he tries the shot himself a couple of times and barely misses it and then he makes it once and he is real friendly about thanking the kid.

Now all of this would be very comical—since the Pig has probably invented that shot himself before the kid has even learned how to keep his pants dry—but somehow I find small reason to laugh, since I have found out there is something about this kid that appeals to me.

I'm not going to bore you with all the grisly details, because you can imagine what happens. In five minutes the kid and the Pig are playing a game for fun and the kid is winning and then the Pig is casually slipping in a small bet and the kid still continues to win. And then the bet grows and the kid begins to find himself about twenty dollars hooked and, suddenly, he is playing the Chicago Pig a game of pool for twenty dollars, which is about the same thing as if he was to take two hundred dimes and try to see if he could throw them across Lake Michigan, one at a time.

Now the Pig has never been widely known for his tactfulness, and now that he figures that this is the kid's last game he ceases to hold his fire any more and he blasts the kid from the table in a way that is genuinely tragic to behold.

But the kid preserves a dignified silence and when it is all over and he hasn't even scored a single point on the Pig during the last game he just pays over his money, racks his cue, comes over to the Pig, looks at him and says, "You're a real pool hustler, aren't you?"

The Pig is counting the money, hungrily. "How's that?" he says, and winks at us.

"I say you are a hustler. You fooled me into playing you. So you could win my money." Now there is nothing whining about the way the kid is saying this. He is just as usual making sure he gets his facts straight.

By this time the Pig has finished counting and he looks at the kid and he laughs, loud. Then he says, "Kid, if that's the way you figure—if you figure you been took—I guess that's what happened." Then he laughs again.

The kid nods, thoughtful, and then he says, "Well, goodbye." And he leaves.

This is sort of a peculiar reply and in fact I am still wondering about it next week when who should come in again but the kid. This time he has not got his books but instead he is carrying a set of bow-legged calipers and a little gadget like a hammer with wires on it and what looks like a portable radio and a steel tape and some kind of a ruler with a sliding magnifying glass on it and altogether he is quite a collection of oddities never before seen in Squirrel's room.

Fortunately for the kid the Chicago Pig is out of town on business and so he is able unmolested to go about his business, which seems to be the repairing of table number five for surgery or for an excavation or some other such piece of scientific work. Because the kid is measuring this table and he is pounding the rails with his little hammer and taking readings from the little portable radio and he is running the magnifying glass up and down that ruler like he is maybe trying to give it a hand-rubbed luster, and he is writing down numbers in a little book as he goes along, and all along he is whistling what, so help me, sounds like two tunes at once, very soft.

This performance naturally draws no small crowd and no small number of bright sayings and witticisms; but the kid is paying them no heed.

Then, suddenly, he finishes, tucks his equipment under his arm, says, "Thank you," to nobody in particular, and leaves.

Four months later it is one of those dead afternoons and the Pig is back with us and all is much as it had been that first day and, sure enough, in comes the kid. Or to be more exact in comes almost a procession. There is the kid and there is these two old guys in baggy suits and there is some kind of what looks like a big suitcase full of lead that the two guys are carrying and all three of them are sporting them sliding-type rulers with the magnifying glasses.

Anyway, the three of them set their loads down by table number five and the kid walks up to the Pig and he looks close at him and he says, "Do you want to shoot some straight pool? For five dollars a game?" and he pulls out a billfold which he reveals to be well-filled.

Now in such cases the Pig is a man of few words. "Yes," he says.

So then, instead of heading for the rack for a cue stick, the kid hustles over to his two baggy pants buddies and they begin to take the lid off of the suitcase. Only it isn't really a suitcase because when they take the lid off there is dials and knobs and little wires and even a little TV screen. And there is switches and fuses and I don't know what-all on the top of this suitcase, and on one end of it there is what looks like a nozzle sticking out maybe four inches.

Now one of the regulars, a boy named Fast Eddie who is somewhat of a comic, has been taking all of this in, and when he sees the kid running wires to a plug in the wall he looks at the kid and he says, "Say, kid, you got a license to broadcast this pool game?"

"No," says the kid, going on with his business. He starts unfolding a bunch of long metal tubes and screwing them together so as to make some kind of framework with four legs and with the suitcase sitting on top and with little rubber-tired caster wheels at the bottom of the legs.

"Well," says Eddie, looking disturbed, "you got maybe permission to set up that transmitter machine?"

"Oh," says the kid, checking some dials and switches, "this is not a transmitter."

At this point the Chicago Pig who has been standing with his cue stick ready for about five minutes says, loud and mean, "Then what in hell is it?"

The kid looks at the Pig, deadpan as ever, and he says, real slow, "This," he says, "is a pool playing machine. It's going to play you for five dollars a game."

Then the Pig comes to a little and he says, "Now wait a minute."

And the kid says, "Certainly."

"Now wait a minute," repeats the Pig. "I didn't say nothing about playing no *device*. I said I am going to play *you* for a five."

The kid doesn't blink. "You said you would *play* for five dollars."

"*Now wait a minute,*" the Pig says, an edgy sound in his voice.

"Oh," says the kid, innocent, "I believe I see." He gives the Pig his usual peer through the big glasses. "You're *afraid* to play against my machine, is that it?"

"No!" says the Pig, "I just ain't playing no device. It's against my principles." And he starts racking his cue. This incidentally is the first reference I have yet heard in this life concerning principles held by the Chicago Pig.

"I see," says the kid.

So while the kid is standing there peering at the flustered Pig, Eddie speaks up again and he says that this is all very interesting to him, since he has long been a believer in progress, and he wonders where he can buy him a pool hustling machine, himself, to put to work for him on his off days.

So the kid focuses on Eddie and he explains, real careful, how that would be difficult because this machine is unique and is also one of a kind and he has, in fact, constructed it himself with the aid of three machinists and these two baggy pants men who it seems are two of his professors from the University who are teaching him a course in what is called Creative Engineering in which each student must construct a mechanical device as part of his work, and he has had this project suggested to him by no less a personage than the Chicago Pig, and he is very thankful to the Chicago Pig for giving him this worthwhile idea.

Well now of course all of us regulars start gathering around the Pig and we start telling him about how there is no machine built that shoots pool to beat the Chicago Pig and how as this crazy kid has just dreamed up a way to lose himself some more money.

So our arguments finally prevail on the Pig and he agrees to risk a five to see what will happen.

So the kid tells the Pig that he can break the balls and the Pig gives a suspicious look out of the corner of his eye at the machine, and he steps up and breaks and he breaks pretty safe so there is only one ball, the fourteen, where it can be made; and it is no simple shot by any means.

So the kid pushes his machine on its wheels up to the edge of the table and you can see that the framework is just the right size to straddle the table the short way, and he points the nozzle at the cueball. Then he starts making little adjustments so that a little sharp pin point that sticks down from the underside of the nozzle is right above the center of the cueball and when he has got it the way he wants it he pulls a little lever that seems to lock the wheels and everything in place.

Then he throws a switch and there is a blue spark and the most God-awful percolating sounds start coming out of the machine and then he throws another switch and the little TV screen lights up and the machine ceases percolating and starts peeping like a bird and two little beams of light come out of a row of little holes right above the nozzle and the kid starts turning these dials until the beams of light are lined up—one on the middle of the fourteen ball and one smack on the middle of the far corner pocket.

Then the kid peers up over the dials at the Pig and he says, "Fourteen ball. Corner pocket." And everybody holds his breath and the kid presses a button and the lights on the machine go off and the machine goes *tick, tick, bleep,* and the nozzle swings down behind the cueball and all of a sudden a little cue stick tip jumps out of the nozzle and blasts the cueball and jumps right back in its little hole. And the cueball crashes down the table and slams into the fourteen ball and the fourteen ball flies into the middle of the corner pocket so hard you could of heard the sound if you was deaf and wearing ear plugs.

There is at the sight of this a moment of hushed and reverent silence shared by each and every one present except for the machine which has commenced cheerfully peeping again like a canary.

It is a very tense moment as the kid swings his machine on its framework up to where the cueball is now laying in the middle of a splattered-out rack of balls and goes through the same routine of lining his shot up which is this time the three ball in the side, and then he presses the button and everybody holds his breath again.

But this time the machine goes *tick, tick, tick, BLOOP* and the little four inches of cue stick comes creeping out like it has suddenly got very timid and it nudges the cueball and the cueball rolls maybe five inches and comes to a halt without hitting another ball.

So everybody lets out his breath with a soft sigh and all of a sudden I realize that I have been pulling very hard for the machine and so is everybody else, probably because most people of normal perceptions share my hostile feeling towards the Chicago Pig.

The Chicago Pig looks pleased with himself and he grunts and says, "Kid, you just step aside a minute and check the oil on your friend there while *I* shoot."

So the kid rolls the machine away and the Pig shoots. And right off you can see that the Pig is taking this contest of man versus monster pretty serious, because he starts out shooting a very sharp game of pool indeed and makes, in fact, forty-three balls before he misses and then he sits down looking for all the world like the pig he is.

So the kid steps up and he starts shining his lights and turning his knobs and watching the little lines on his screen, which jump around when he twists the dials, and he throws switches and the machine hums and burps and wiggles and it shoots too hard and it shoots too easy and it coughs and it sputters, but it makes twenty-nine balls before it finally miscues and sends the cueball flying off the table so hard it nearly knocks a hole in the back wall.

And then as the game progresses we each and every one of us start to become slowly aware that we are standing in the presence of an awe-inspiring marvel of this scientific modern world of today, for the machine is gradually getting control of its shooting and its shooting is becoming a spectacle to behold. In fact it ends the game by a magnificent run of sixty-three; and by this time it no longer rumbles and percolates as before, but has settled down to a quiet, dignified purring.

When the Pig hands his five dollars over to the kid there is a strange, wild look in his eye and instead of quitting he says, "Rack the balls, Freddie." And Freddie racks the balls and the machine breaks and they play another and this one is a fantastic spectacle for the machine grinds the Pig out of the game with unheard of precision. Maybe you never seen a modern bottling machine in a fizz-water factory. Well the thing about those machines is the way they just keep slapping them caps on them bottles, one right after the next, and they don't miss or never even put one on a little loose or wiggly or nothing. I mean it's a natural phenomenon to watch one.

Well that's the way the machine is. It drills them balls into them pockets, one at a time, just like they are fat little soldiers and know damn well where they are supposed to go and it wins the game by the astronomical score of 125 to 11. And right off the Pig says, "Rack, Freddie." And Freddie racks.

Now the Chicago Pig is not the sort of man to continue with a bad bet because of principles and when I see he is not quitting this fantastic game I am at first astonished and then I look at his face and I see that there is a lurking appearance in his pig-like eyes and that he must be fermenting a plot of some kind. But the machine continues to shoot with machine-like precision and in the middle of the game it has just made a very delicate little bank shot and the Pig looks at the kid with his old phony admiration and he says, "Gee, that machine must really be a precision device!" and the kid peers at him and says, "Yes," and the Pig says, "It must have a pretty delicate balance?"

and the kid says, "Yes," and goes ahead to let his machine beat the Pig 125 to 17.

The Pig pays up his five real peaceful and then he says, "Excuse me, kid." And he hustles up to the front counter where Freddie the Squirrel is now busy discussing probable race results with some sportsmen friends and the Pig engages Freddie in some agitated conversation and I think I see that Freddie has slipped something or other to the Pig under the counter and then the Pig comes back and looks at the kid and then he looks at the machine and then he looks at the kid again. Then he says, "Kid, I got a feeling that your mechanical friend here is the kind that chokes up a little under pressure."

The kid eyes him and says, "So?"

"So," says the Pig, "I'll back up that feeling with, say, two hundred small dollars. Because I don't think that device can play for real money." And this is quite surprising to one and all not only because we are awestruck to say the least by the machine but because the Chicago Pig is not known as a big money player himself, twenty dollars being his usual limit.

"Well," the kid says, "we'll play you for two hundred dollars, if that's what you want." And the Pig says that's what he wants and he starts racking the balls up for Freddie, who is still discussing horses up front and the kid goes over to his baggy pants friends and starts taking up a collection from them, since I imagine they are carrying the stakes; and while the kid is not looking I see the Pig do a very strange thing. I see him quickly slip the cueball into his pocket and slip out another one that looks just like it and for a minute I do not know what he means by this and then I remember that Freddie keeps one of those old fashioned white break balls up front that looks just like any other cueball except that it weighs probably half again as much, and now I know what Freddie has slipped to the Pig and I also know why the Pig was asking questions about the machine's precision.

So they start playing and just as the Pig had hoped the machine is badly shook up by the heavy cueball and it has lost much of its accuracy and in fact the Pig is able to get ahead of it in score by fifty-three points to twenty in a very few minutes and in fact, after the machine has by then missed three dead shots and only barely managed to make the twenty it has scored he becomes quite careless and misses and leaves a beautiful running shot with the balls spread all to hell over the table.

It is at this juncture that the kid calmly wheels the machine, framework and all, off the table and over into a corner, rolls up his sleeves, and says, "*I'll* finish," and the Pig looks at him dumbstruck and says, "Hey! Wait a minute ..." and the kid picks a cue out of the rack and stops and looks at him hard and says, "Remember I said that *we'll* play you?" and the Pig has no idea what to reply to this and stands there with his mouth hanging open and the kid steps up and makes a run of sixty-eight balls and plays the Pig safe and when this is done the Pig's mouth is hanging just a shade wider open than it was before—as well as mine and everybody else's. In fact the Pig's mouth is maybe open so wide it strains his eye muscles or some such because when he tries to make his next shot he miscues so bad the cueball dribbles down the table like maybe a basketball and scratches in the corner pocket. So the kid picks the cue out of the pocket, hefts it once, says, "Well!" real thoughtful, smiles faintly at the Pig, shoots, and runs fifty-seven and out.

By this time the Pig is sitting down, kind of dazed, and when the kid has made the last ball he pulls out his billfold religious like and counts out the two hundred dollars and gives it to the kid. And the kid says, "Thank you very much," and he puts the money in his pocket and goes back to his machine and starts folding it back up again into its satchel shape and as he is doing so suddenly the Pig blurts out, "What happened, kid? How did you get so good?" and the kid says, "Practice," and the Pig says, "Practice?" and the kid says, "*Somebody* had to teach the machine how to play," and he finishes up packing the machine together.

And then the kid is starting to leave and I can see that the Chicago Pig is beginning to sweat to get in the last word and he says, "Well, anyway, I didn't get hustled by no *machine.*"

And the kid stops cold and he turns around and looks at the Pig and then he looks at the table where all the balls are gone except the heavy white break ball that the Pig has put there and then he looks back at the Pig real hard and he says, "You didn't?" And then he walks out.

THE OTHER END OF THE LINE

Hungover from cheap whiskey, George Bledsoe made a simple error that many people make: he mistakenly dialed his own number on the telephone. He was attempting to call a girl he knew—a homely girl, but one with the virtues of being quick and easy—and, through his customary impatience and general fogginess, let the wrong pattern of digits govern his pudgy index finger: BE-8-5883.

He did not get the busy signal. He should have; but he did not. Instead, the phone began clicking and an operator's voice announced dimly, as if from a great distance, "That's a ship-to-shore connection, sir." George Bledsoe, just then realizing that he *had*, in fact, dialed his own number, said, "What the hell?" There was a great deal of static and then a man's voice said, "All right. Who is it?"

George blinked. The voice was loud and arrogant. It sounded somehow familiar, but he could not place it.

But George was not by nature a deferential person. "Who in hell are *you*, friend?" he said.

The voice paused a moment and then it said, "This is George Bledsoe."

"Look, friend," George Bledsoe said, "you can take that and . . ." He started to hang up and then stopped. *How could . . . ?*

"That's right," the voice said. "How could I *know*?" And then, "You let it sink in a minute, George, and then you get that tablet of paper out of the top dresser drawer and get yourself a pencil out of the box on the refrigerator and you get ready to write some things down. We don't have all day."

George was staring at the phone in disbelief. It *was* his voice, as if on a tape recorder. He blinked, and found himself sweating. But, unused to taking orders, he said, "Why should I?"

"*Don't argue, dammit.* I'm talking to you from October ninth. I'm sitting in a boat, twenty-eight miles and two months from where you are and I've got a pile of newspapers, Georgie, that haven't even been printed yet, back there in August where you're talking from. I'm going to make you rich."

It sounded like a con game. George's eyes narrowed. "Why should you?"

"Because I'm you, you stupid bastard. Get that paper and start writing. I'm going to give you the names of some racehorses and of three issues of stocks. And a baseball team. You'd better get them right the first time. There won't be another."

George was staring around the room dizzily; the hand that held the phone was sticky with sweat. "How can . . . ?"

"Dammit, shut up. *I* don't know how. It just is."

———

He got the notepad, and got them all down. Twenty-six race-horses and three stocks and the ball team that was going to win the World Series. Then the phone clicked and the line went dead. Thoroughly dead; he could not even get the dial tone.

There were three horses on his list for the next day. They were all medium-long shots, and they all won. He had started with fifty dollars; he left the track in a kind of cold, glassy-eyed frenzy, with over seven thousand dollars in cash in his pockets. In his shirt pocket, over his heart, was the sheet of notepaper, his greatest gift in the world—a gift from himself.

During the next two months the horses all won at their different tracks and the stocks all split, shot up, declared unexpected dividends. By nosing out the wealthiest bookies at home, in Miami, and in four other cities, and by careful spreading of his bets, George was able to make himself a mil-lionaire after the first five weeks. He won a quarter million on the World Series alone. It was on this last that a bookie who hadn't hedged his bets adequately against George's hundred-thousand-dollar lay-out was forced to offer him his own luxury fishing boat, anchored off Key West, as part payment. George, seeing the handwriting on the wall plainly enough, accepted with what was for him considerable graciousness. That is, he merely called the bookie a chiseling bastard, trimmed five thousand off the boat's evaluation, and took it.

He knew that it was somehow in the nature of things that he must be aboard a boat with a telephone on October ninth. He would be getting a phone call.

The ordaining of it all took no effort on his part. He was called a week later by the telephone company, who wished to know if he planned to continue the ship-to-shore service on the boat. He told them yes, and then, as if it were an afterthought, mentioned that he would like his old Miami number transferred to the boat—important friends would be calling. The number? BE-8-5883. Then, when he had bet the final horse on his list, betting the track odds down to the point of diminishing returns, phoning and nagging the nine remaining New York and Chicago bookies who would still take his bets, he hired a chauffeured limousine to take him to Key West. He did not go alone; with him were two attractive young ladies, a gambling friend, a large box of frozen prime steaks, and two cases of twenty-dollar-a-bottle whiskey. And a pile of newspapers.

It was during the ebullient stage of his drunkenness on this automobile ride, after he had tired of needling his friends, that a striking thought occurred to him: what if he decided not to go to the boat at all? His mind fogged at the thought. But how could he *not* be on that boat October ninth? He had, in a sense, already been there. That part of his future was a part of his past, and you couldn't change the past. But you could change the future, couldn't you? He could not understand it. He drank more whiskey and tried to forget about it; it wasn't important anyway. What was important was his twelve-hundred-dollar platinum wristwatch, his two-hundred-dollar shoes, his cashmere jacket, his bank accounts. He had come a long way in those two months. One of the girls, whose name was supposed to be Lili, snuggled up to him. He began playing with her and tried to forget about time paradoxes.

The boat looked to George like something out of a Man of Distinction ad; it was big, sleek, polished, and beautifully equipped. His heart swelled with something resembling pride when he surveyed its lines, standing drunkenly on the dock, with a disheveled Lili hanging on his arm. They went aboard, and Lili giggled, and whistled at the mahogany bar, the inner-spring mattresses, the hi-fi, the impeccable little stainless steel galley. George, suddenly pensive, left Lili fixing drinks at the bar for the party and went into the boat's little air-conditioned cabin, to look around.

Somehow the sight of it shook him: sitting on a small table, next to a tan leather armchair, was a bright, glossy red telephone. He walked over to it slowly and read the number on the dial. The man from the company had been there, for it read MIAMI: BE-8-5883. Outside on the deck the girls were laughing now, and there was the sound of ice clinking in glasses. Someone called out drunkenly, "Come on out, Georgie, and have a *bon voyage*." He didn't answer, still looking at the phone.

A pilot had been hired and he took them out that afternoon. They fished in a desultory way, too drunk and noisy to care. George drank continuously, bullied everyone loudly, made no attempt to fish. A restlessness, an impatience, was eating at him; in his mind telephones were ringing faintly all day. By sundown of the first day they were spent with liquor, sex, sunshine and quarreling. George passed out across the deck, near the one fish that Lili had, miraculously, caught: a small, wide-eyed bonito with a white, flabby belly. The last fleeting thought to enter his mind before he fell into smirking unconsciousness was *Why can't that lousy son of a bitch call me early? Why should I wait?* . . .

The ninth of October was overcast—cold and muggy—as was George's disposition. No one was any longer interested in fishing. The gambler slept; the girls kept to themselves on deck; and George shut himself up in the cabin, waiting for the phone to ring. He swore under his breath occasionally, but otherwise passed the morning in silence. He contemplated the luxury of his silk dressing gown, the brass and mahogany furnishings around him, the good, solid teakwood deck beneath his feet; and the thought of the virtually penniless and belligerent drunkard who was about to call him from a crumby little beach house in Miami. At his feet sat the pile of newspapers, opened to the sporting pages. He looked down at them now and swore. He was beginning to sweat.

Outside the cabin window the sky was dead white, hanging thickly over the cold green Atlantic horizon. They were ninety miles out from shore, the pilot had said. George continued drinking, angry now at himself—the other himself—for not having bothered to mention the time of day his call had been received. He had dialed the number at about two in the afternoon; but of course that didn't mean that two o'clock was the time it was received, two months later. He continued looking at his watch and at the telephone and at his watch again, drinking. Occasionally he would look out the window at the serenely violent ocean, ice green beneath the fishbelly sky, and curse.

And then, just before two o'clock, an idea struck him, a very simple idea: Why should *he* wait? He would make the call himself. He had never, in the two months since it had happened, tried dialing his own number again—why had he never thought of it? Why should he wait for that poor slob of a hungover George Bledsoe to call *him*—him with his private fishing boat and his twenty-dollar whiskey?

He picked up the phone angrily, with thick fingers, and began dialing: BE-8-5883. He was breathing heavily. After the last digit the phone began to buzz, ringing. He smiled sweatily and leaned back in his chair. Then there was a *click* and a voice answered. "Hello?"

He sat bolt upright in his chair. It was a woman's voice.

He hesitated and then said, "Hello." *Could he have dialed the wrong number?* "What number is this?"

The voice was that of an old woman, quavery but matter-of-fact. "This is BE-8-5883. Mrs. Arthur Cavanaugh talking."

"Oh." He took a quick sip from his drink. "Is . . . is George Bledsoe there?"

"No. No, he isn't." There seemed to be some hesitation in her voice. "Mr. Bledsoe hasn't lived in this house for some time."

Abruptly he felt relieved—he had probably only moved to a bigger home. About time, anyway. But why had he been frightened of this old bat on the phone?

The woman was saying querulously, "Are you a friend . . . of Mr. Bledsoe's?"

He laughed suddenly, coarsely. "That's right, lady. I'm a friend of Mr. Bledsoe's."

"Well, I don't know just how to tell you this," the woman said, "but a person would have thought you'd read about it in the papers. It was in all the papers. They found Mr. Bledsoe's body, stark naked, a hundred miles out in the Gulf. It was about two months ago they found him, and the thing is there's nobody yet knows how he got out there."

He sat silent for what seemed a very long time. There was a faint clicking in the phone, but he ignored this. The woman must be mistaken. An old fool. A bitch. Although the cabin was tightly closed, he felt the distinct sensation of a cold wind blowing on the back of his neck. Shaking himself, he gathered his voice together. The woman was a lying bitch. "How George Bledsoe got out there, lady, was in his private boat," he said, more to himself than to her. "The same way he's gonna get back to shore. In his private boat."

The wind on the back of his neck was stronger now, and he was shivering. The wind seemed to be penetrating his clothes, even, blowing through his dressing gown, through the tailored silk shirt beneath it. Dimly, as if from a great and dreadful distance, he heard the old woman's voice saying, "Why, Mr. Bledsoe never had a boat, Lord forbid. Mr. Bledsoe was a poor man . . ."

Abruptly he leaned forward, shouting, "*No.* No, you rotten bitch!" and he slammed the phone back in its cradle. It was cold in the room. He was shivering. There was a bright, grayish light in the cabin, getting brighter. He grabbed the phone again, shaking, and dialed *O*, for the operator. The dial felt soft to his finger, squashy.

The operator's voice came, faint. "Ship-to-shore service."

His voice was hoarse, strange in his ears. "This is Bledsoe. BE-8-5883. Is there a call for me?"

"No, sir. Or, yes, there was a call."

"From who?" It took an effort to keep from shouting—or screaming.

"Just a moment." And then, "That's odd, sir; it must be an error. I have the number calling listed as BE-8-5883. And that's your number, sir."

"*My God, I know. Put the call through.*"

Her voice was fainter, fading away from him. "I'm sorry, you'll have to wait until the party calls again. When he called, a few moments ago, the line was busy . . ." The last words were so faint that he could hardly hear them. He was screaming when she finished, "*Put the call through, God damn it, put the call through.*"

From the receiver her voice was the minute thread of a whisper, but he heard it plainly. "I'm sorry sir, the line was busy."

And then the phone went altogether dead.

Then, after sitting for a moment with his eyes shut against the impossible white daylight in the closed cabin, his body huddled against the cold wind that was blowing through the bulkheads of the rich man's boat that he could not possibly have been in, blowing coldly against his body through the rich man's clothes that he, George Bledsoe, could not possibly have afforded, he took a deep breath and opened his eyes, looking down.

Below him, through the fading, now translucent teakwood deck, he could see the flat, ice-green water of the Atlantic Ocean, ninety miles from shore.

THE SCHOLAR'S DISCIPLE

He appeared to be no more than twenty-five, and his eyes were bright orange. Except for these he would have looked like an ordinary, somewhat handsome young man. He stood in the center of the chalked diagram on Webley's kitchen linoleum and shifted his weight from one small foot to the other. He was dressed impeccably in an Oxford gray suit and he wore a "peace" button in his lapel.

Webley sat motionless on the kitchen stool for a moment, not knowing exactly what to say. This sort of . . . person was not at all what he had expected. His guest glanced uneasily at the two plastic mixing bowls that sat just inside the chalked lines. Finally he blinked his orange eyes and looked at Webley.

"Well?" Webley said.

"Yes, sir?" The fellow's voice was polite; it had the controlled tone of a proper young graduate student's.

Webley cleared his throat. "Aren't you going to drink the blood?" he said, "or do something with the entrails?"

The other shuddered. "No, sir."

Webley began to feel irritated; it had taken a great deal of work to gather the things. "Then why in Heaven's name are they in the . . . invocation?"

"In whose name, sir?" The young fellow blushed, averting his eyes.

"Sorry. In the name of Hell, then."

"Yes." The fellow smiled engagingly and, more at ease, withdrew a bright red cigarette case from his pocket, offering one to his host, who declined it. The cigarettes were long, and coal black. "I don't really know, sir, why some versions of the procedure call for such things as . . ." he glanced hesitatingly toward the bowls again, "those. Impure texts, possibly. It's all in the words. One has to say them right. Apparently you mastered the feat well." He pressed the end of a well-manicured forefinger against the tip of his cigarette and it lit in a tiny burst of flame. When he exhaled, the smoke had a perfumed odor.

Webley was somewhat placated by the compliment, although it had taken a year of searching to dig up those "impure texts." "Well," he said, "you *are* a demon, anyway, aren't you?"

"Oh, hell yes," the fellow said, with feeling. "By all means."

"And your name?"

"Makuka . . . It's hard to pronounce, sir . . . Makuka-buzzeeliam. In Hell our clients generally call me Robert."

"And you can serve me?"

"After a fashion, yes. Of course, I have a good many other duties."

Webley poured himself a drink, offering one to the demon, who refused. "I don't think I would overwork you, Robert. What I want you to do, primarily, is to write a dissertation for me. And, perhaps, a few scholarly articles."

The demon seemed to think this over a moment. Then he said, "What field, sir?"

"English. English literature."

The demon smiled abruptly, revealing even, white teeth. "That might be interesting, sir," he said. "We have a good many of your English writers . . . available, so to speak." His orange eyes seemed to twinkle. "And a fine bunch too, sir, I might add. But why," he said, "would you ever call up a demon to write your dissertation for you?"

"Well," Webley said, "I am one of the few people who know how; that's one consideration. I have my first Ph.D. in Folklore, you see. Done a lot of research in Folklore. After twelve years of it I began to realize that most of the lore worked out very well. I cure a little asthma here and there, with black-eyed peas, practice a little Voodoo—nothing important, just to amuse my friends."

"Voodoo never has been very effective," Robert said understandingly. "Overrated."

"I fear so. Anyway, I began to realize that I'd never get anywhere in the academic world with a Folklore degree—just isn't recognized by enough schools. The logical thing was to get into a parallel but more respected field. And, with a few good articles, I might be able to swing a professorship." Webley finished his drink and shuffled, ponderously, over to the sink, where he began fixing another. "Trouble is, Robert, I hate writing—especially scholarly writing. Consequently, I thought

I'd try invoking a demon to do it for me." He settled back in his chair, smiling, and began sipping the drink. "I think it's going to work out very well."

The demon smiled engagingly. "I hope so," he said. "I'll go check with the legal department—about a contract." He blinked his eyes and vanished. . . .

When Robert returned, after more than an hour, he had with him an estimate on the value of Webley's immortal soul. They haggled for a good while before agreeing on the terms, but Webley was quite pleased with them; he had done better than he had expected to. The young demon seemed to bluff very easily.

Webley would, of course, go to Hell upon his death; but he would have a suite there, a mistress—to be changed yearly—air conditioning—Robert tried to explain to him that Hell was not in the least bit hot; but Webley stuck to his guns on this point—weekly valet service, and ready access to his landlord should any inconvenience develop. He would be roasted over the coals for one day out of every month; but he was guaranteed that there would be no harmful aftereffects from this. "In fact," Robert said, "some of our clients look forward to that part of the life in Hell, since the possibilities for pain among the dead are so few, and the senses are so dulled by the extraordinary amount of pleasure we have to offer."

"Then why do you have this roasting business at all, if Hell is such a pleasant place?" Webley asked, pouring himself a drink.

"Well, we are under orders from the opposition. We can't make Him out to be a liar, you know. And then those coals *are* rather unpleasant."

"I see. But what, then, do they do in Heaven?"

Robert thought a moment. "It's been a long time since I was there, of course. They sing, mostly, I think. And do exercises or something."

In return for his agreeing to the damnation Webley would receive the services of Robert for one year, in which time an acceptable dissertation must be written, as well as at least ten publishable scholarly articles. Webley had with him a razor blade to open a vein for signing the contract; he was mildly piqued when the demon brought out a ball point pen, even though the ink was bright red. It dried brown, however.

Immediately after he finished signing there came the sound of a small and dry little voice, from somewhere, it seemed, in the basement. The voice said one word, which it enunciated with precision. "*Agreed.*"

"Who the devil is *that*?" Webley said.

Robert blushed again, momentarily. "Our . . . legal department, sir," he said. He folded the contract and then vanished gently. . . .

He appeared for work the next morning. Webley had already prepared an office for him in a disused upstairs bedroom, complete with typewriter, *The MLA Style Sheet*, and a small library of learned journals. He worked methodically and well, seemed to take a certain pleasure in his writing, and within three months had produced a monumental, definitive work, titled "The Lyric Cry in Colley Cibber: A Reappraisal." When this was finished, Robert suggested that he show it to Mr. Cibber, who, he said, had a small walk-up apartment in suburban Hell; but Webley would not hear of it. "Just stick to the scholarship, young man."

The dissertation, upon acceptance and publication by the University press, created a stir among a great many academic people, few of whom read it. Webley soon found himself in possession of a very congenial job, with a low salary and few duties. A month later he received a large fellowship from a foundation; and upon his first *PMLA* publication, the controversy-stirring article "Threads of Francophilism in John Webster's *The White Devil*," found himself with an associate professorship and even fewer duties.

The demon's work was inspired. His style managed to be ornate and terse at one and the same time; he was greatly sardonic about everyone and everything except a handful of third-rate poets; he displayed an astonishing prowess at ignoring the obvious and seizing upon the manifestly impossible; and his footnotes were awe-inspiring. Within a year Webley's name had become an unshakeable star in the academic firmament.

When Robert handed the tenth paper to his employer he seemed actually sad that this would be the last of his scholarly work. He had grown to love his job.

Webley, interpreting Robert's hesitancy rightly, was immediately struck by an idea. He explained it to the demon. He, Webley, would apply for a year's leave of absence with pay, so that he might write a book. He had been feeling oppressed, of late, by the restrictions of his teaching schedule, however light; and, besides, there was a graduate assistant, a certain Miss Hopkins, with whom he was much taken. Miss Hopkins had already expressed a deep-seated wish to visit Acapulco. As for himself, he enjoyed spear fishing as well as the next fellow. Now, as for the book. . . . He would be glad to sign a new contract.

Robert's face showed doubt, although Webley could tell

that he was pleased with the idea. "I don't know, sir," he said, "I do have my other duties; and my supervisor doesn't generally like to alter a contract. People are always accusing him of coercion when he does something like that. He's very scrupulous, you know."

"Well, see what you can do," Webley said. "And remember, you can write the book any way you want to."

"Well . . ."

"You can name your own subject."

The demon smiled sheepishly. "I'll see what I can do," he said, and vanished in a puff of perfumed smoke.

It was three days later that Robert returned with the new contract. The terms were fairly hard, but this time Webley was unable to talk them down. Robert said that this was the least his legal department would allow. There would now be three days per month on the coals, together with one day of boils, from sole to crown. Also he would have to share the bath in his suite, and his choice of mistresses would be limited to brunettes. But, in return, Robert promised to produce the finest, most significant and monumental work of English literary criticism ever written.

After four hours of bickering, Webley finally threw his hands in the air. "All right," he said, "I'll sign. After all, a man ought to produce one good book in a lifetime. And Miss Hopkins is growing impatient."

Robert smiled. "I'm certain you won't be disappointed in the book, sir." He blushed slightly. "Nor in Miss Hopkins either. I took the liberty of checking on her file, and found her . . . promising."

"That's interesting . . ." Webley said, smiling thoughtfully and taking the ball point pen from the demon's outstretched hand.

As before, there came the little voice, saying, "Agreed. . . ."

Miss Hopkins was not disappointing, not in the least. Nor was Acapulco, nor spear fishing, nor tequila. But especially not Miss Hopkins. When the year ended and Robert appeared, Webley was lying in bed in a small adobe hut, with a mild headache and with Miss Hopkins, who was fortunately sound asleep. The demon, appearing from Hell with a very thick book under his arm, found him there.

During the past year Webley's face had taken on a certain bloated haughtiness; and his tone now with Robert was patronizing. "What's the title, Robert?" he said, making no move to get up from the bed.

"*The English Literary Tradition: A Re-evaluation.*" There was a tiny hint of pride in Robert's voice.

Webley frowned. "That's a little general, Robert," he said. "But I suppose it'll do. How long is it?"

"Seventeen hundred pages, sir."

"Yes. Well, that ought to impress them well enough." He leaned over on one elbow. "Tell you what you do, Robert. You pack that manuscript off to my editor for me; and then I want you to take a message to the University. Tell them I'm delayed and won't be back for about three or four weeks. Tell them I'm working on the index or something." He reached a chubby hand over and gave Miss Hopkins a gentle pat on the rump. She stirred and giggled softly in her sleep. "Now do that for me, Robert, and it'll be all wrapped up between us."

There seemed to be a hurt look in the demon's eyes. "You're not going to read the book, sir?"

Webley waved a hand royally. "When it comes out in print, man," he said. "Right now I'm busy."

"Yes, sir," Robert said, vanishing.

It was six weeks later that Webley was mailed a copy of the book by his publisher. Since he was well absorbed at the time with other pursuits, it was another two weeks before he read it. Or he did not read it exactly—not entirely. He was two-thirds of the way through when, red in the face and eyes glaring, he shrieked the proper incantation and Robert appeared.

"What in the name of Hell do you mean by this—this asininity, this patent absurdity?" Webley said. "Any half-baked scholar with a quarter of a brain could demolish this, rip it to shreds! This is tripe, Robert. Fraudulent, unscholarly, unforgivable tripe. You've made an ass of yourself and of me."

Robert seemed dumbfounded; his entire face was an enormous blush. "But, Professor Webley," he said, "I . . . I thought you would like it, sir. Thought it would be . . . just the thing."

Webley seemed to explode. "Just the thing!" He slammed the book on his desk. "Good lord, Robert, if I couldn't write a more accurate work of literary criticism in six months' time I'd . . . I'd let you roast me in Hell. Seven days a week."

From somewhere beneath the floor came a little voice, saying *"Agreed."*

Webley stopped in the middle of a breath. Then he said, "Now wait a minute, Robert. You can't . . . surely you. . . ."

The demon's face showed embarrassment, and his tone was

extremely polite, apologetic. "I'm afraid we can, sir," he said. "Verbal contract, you know. Hold up in any court."

For a moment Webley's eyes searched frantically around the room. Finally they landed on the book, which lay now on the table, and immediately the glance of uncertainty was replaced with a look of triumph. "All right," he said. "All right. You think you've got me, don't you? Think you've trapped me into a bad contract. The only thing you've neglected is that I *can* write a better book than this one." He picked up the book, flipping through it again. "Look at this. More than two hundred pages of Shakespeare analysis—not to mention the rest, from The Pearl Poet to Oscar Wilde—and not one genuine, scholarly idea in the lot. Well written, possibly. But any graduate student knows that Shakespeare didn't model Cleopatra on his *mother*—the idea's absurd. And an idiot would know that the textual problem is the only clue to *Hamlet.*"

"But . . ." Robert said.

"But nothing!" Webley slammed the book back on his desk. "It's not merely your insidious way of trying to steal my soul that infuriates me—it's this fool book you're trying to do it with. Who in Hell ever gave you these stupid notions about literature?"

Robert seemed uneasy. "That's what I've been trying to tell you, Mr. Webley," he said. "It was a great many people in Hell. You see, I didn't exactly write the book myself, sir."

"Then who . . . who wrote this nonsense about Shakespeare?"

"Shakespeare, sir. I sobered him up and. . . ."

Abruptly, Webley's voice took on the tone of a small man speaking from the bottom of a well. "And Milton. Who . . . ?"

The demon managed a weak smile. "John had some revealing things to say about *Comus*, didn't he, sir?"

Webley's eyes were taking on a strange, hunted look. "And *Beowulf* . . . Surely you didn't . . ."

"I'm afraid I did, Mr. Webley. We have the author of that one too—he slipped up once on the Fourth Commandment. Fellow named Seothang the Imbiber. Drinks mead."

Webley stood in stony silence for several minutes, holding the heavy book in a limp hand. His eyes were closed.

After a few minutes he opened them. Robert had, tastefully, vanished. In his place was a small, black table. On this were arranged neatly a typewriter, a stack of white paper, and a calendar.

THE KING IS DEAD

The library had books, of course, and a lot of gray, open space and only a few people, and Will thought instantly, *This is going to be the best room to be in for that whole damned six months.* On one wall was a cheap Matisse print, an odalisque. There was a funny smell to the room.

The prisoner behind the desk was small, middle-aged, sandy-haired, with tight lines around his mouth. There were papers and books on the desk but no chessboard. Will walked over, waited for another prisoner to finish checking out a law-book, then said to the man behind the desk, "Are you Findlay Baskin?"

The man blinked. "Do you want to check out a book?" His voice was toneless.

Will cleared his throat. "I understand your F.I.D.E. rating is over two thousand."

The other man's expression did not change. "What do the letters F.I.D.E. stand for?"

Will began to feel better. He felt a touch of anger at the man's little game, and anger was always his antidote for nervousness. "It stands for *Federation Internationale des Echecs.*" He gave the enunciation his full City College, minor-in-French nasality, thinking, *If this man likes to play that kind of conversational chess.* . . .

The man looked toward the cheap Matisse print on the wall for a moment and said, "I'm Findlay Baskin. My rating is two-three-four—oh—two. Or was."

That would make him number ten or fifty in the country. And then Will said, *"Was?"*

Baskin looked back from the picture and into Will's face. "I've hardly had the opportunity to play in tournaments for three years."

"Three years? And I never heard. . . ."

Baskin smiled for the first time, and the smile was a surprisingly pleasant one. "I'm not Fischer, you know. My particular crime managed to draw a quarter column in the *Times.*"

Will started to ask him what that crime had been, but he wasn't yet sure of prison protocol about that kind of question. "I embezzled, myself," he said. And then, "My rating is eighteen eighty-five."

Baskin looked at him thoughtfully for what seemed a long time. A couple of aging cons came into the room, whispering, sat at a table and began to flip through magazines. Then Baskin reached into his pocket, took out a quarter, spun it on the desk in front of him and then, like swatting a fly, flattened it with his right hand. "Heads or tails?" he said.

Will shrugged mentally. "Tails."

Baskin lifted the hand, revealing heads. "That makes you black." And then, no longer smiling, "Pawn to king four."

Will stared at him. "Where's the board?"

"No board," Baskin said. "Pawn to king four."

Will looked around him, at the six or seven quiet cons in the room, and then he said, "Okay, but I've never done this before. Pawn to queen's bishop four."

"Don't make excuses," Baskin said. "I'd beat you on a board just as easily."

Baskin had him mated in seventeen moves, with a bishop that seemed to come from nowhere. Will had blundered away two pawns and a knight anyway by that time, just from being unable to keep the imaginary board clear in his head. He started to ask Baskin, with irritation, why they couldn't use a board; but instead he said, "Now I'm white. Pawn to king four. . . ."

It took Baskin twenty-four moves to mate him this time, and Will made no serious blunders. Once he got that picture of a nice, sharp board, with clean-cut, Staunton-pattern pieces on it, it wasn't too difficult. He was even beginning to like it, did not even mind losing, which was inevitable, anyway. He had lost to pros before, in his hustling days in college, and had learned to take it. And of course he had never played a grand master before. There was no real damage to his pride from losing, because the real game was just to see how long he could hang in there. And maybe learn something.

After the second game he said, "Another?" and Baskin pointed to the library clock. It was 9:30.

"Here," Baskin said, and he reached under the desk and

pulled out a fat book. "Read this." The book was *Modern Chess Openings*, the bible on the subject.

"I've read it." That wasn't altogether true; but he had read most of the main variations of the Sicilian defense—the Najdorf, the dragon.

"Then memorize it," Baskin said.

"*Memorize* it?"

"What else are you going to do in your cell? Dance?"

Will grinned, taking the book. "Okay. I'll try."

"And later," Baskin said, "I'll let you have the Fischer games book. And the Petrosian. And the Spassky."

"Jesus Christ!"

"Most chess is memory."

"I didn't mean that. I meant, what kind of a prison library is this?"

Baskin looked expressionless again. "Who do you think orders the books for it?" he said.

They played verbal chess every evening for a week before Will got his first draw game. And then a stalemate. And, finally, after three weeks and over fifty games, Baskin blundered and left a rook hanging. Will, his voice trembling as he called the move, snapped it off with a knight fork. And traded the grand master down until he, Will, got to say, for the first time, that lovely ancient and potent word, "Checkmate." Checkmate. *Shah mat*: The king is dead.

"Well," Baskin said, "you've been doing your homework." Then he reached beneath the librarian's desk and produced a rolled-up cloth chessboard and a box of large, Staunton-style pieces. "And for doing your homework, this is the reward."

"Beautiful," Will said, staring at the set. After over a month of playing on that board in his mind, he felt as Mozart must have felt when at last he heard the orchestra play the sounds that he had been hearing in his head. Still, it was possible that the real geniuses preferred the pure and ideal music of their games. But to him, a man who loved women and food and freedom and several other substantial things more than chess, the set, with its cylindrical rooks and its dutiful, stubby pawns and its *solidity*—right there on the table as well as in his head and his memories—was a solid, existential joy.

They set the pieces up wordlessly, in a kind of mutual reverence, and began to play. Outside the room, in the lights of brilliant lamps around which night insects fluttered, guards patrolled. Four hundred other prisoners watched Mary Tyler Moore on television. Over the chessboard in the library only a dim 60-watt bulb shone, but it made sharp shadows of the pieces: king, rook, pawn, queen, knight.

In two months Will had memorized all of the useful lines of play and counterplay in the Sicilian defense and in the queen's gambit, games that Baskin, strangely, kept playing almost exclusively. Will had learned to play in his head, and during the morning-exercise walks in the prison yard, he would go over some of the Fischer-Spassky games, the Reykjavik ones, in his mind. As a bright child in New Haven, he had lived chess for several years, but never before like this.

Once, during a game in the library, while they were playing with a double-faced chess clock, playing a fierce, twenty-minute game, and Will was wavering between setting up a bishop uncover or giving check with a knight, Baskin reached forward and stopped both clocks. Then he said, "How do you like prison life, Will?"

Will shook his head trying to break the spell the move choice had over him. "The food is terrible," he said, "and most of the men are animals. But it's not quite so bad as I'd expected." And then, almost in appeal, "But it all makes me so goddamned nervous. . . ."

"Yes," Baskin said, "it makes you nervous. And chess makes you nervous, too. You should have taken the check with the knight. It loses you nothing. Then, while I was getting out of check, you could have made up your mind about the bishop-and-rook combination."

Will smiled weakly. "Being nervous doesn't necessarily—"

"How do you think Fischer would take to prison life? Would he cower at the guards?"

He knew what Baskin meant. He didn't exactly cower at guards, but he knew he was running scared. "Well, Fischer would complain about the lighting in the cells."

"He would have confidence," Baskin said. "Which you, Will, sorely lack. Do you know what Bogolyubov said, when somebody asked him whether he preferred playing white or black?"

"No."

"He said, 'It makes utterly no difference. When I play white, I win because I am playing white; when I play black, I win because I am Bogolyubov.'"

Will laughed out loud. "Okay," he said. "I need confidence."

After three months, Will was finally able to get himself transferred to the library, where there was now time to play Baskin as many as eight games a day. He was lucky to win one out of the eight; but he was learning.

With a chess clock, they would sometimes play five- and ten-minute games, as well as the standard tournament-style two-hour ones. The short games made for more nerve-racking play, but they prevented dawdling and made for fast thinking. And with the clock, you didn't have to play touch move—where, if you so much as touch a piece with your sleeve, you have to move that piece. Instead, they used the rule where the move isn't final until you hit the button that stops your clock and starts the other player's ticking. He liked the clock: two clean faces, a teak case with brass trim and good solid German workmanlike ticking. Pawn to king four. *Click*, with the button, and the other man's clock began to tick away until he moved. Then *click* again and your clock started. It was all good and sound and rational and something to pull mind and spirit out of a brown prison where you were surrounded by ugliness, boredom, foulness, brutality. *Tick, tick, tick*, and then mate.

One afternoon during his fourth month in prison, after he had beaten Baskin on a very lovely combination that had come to him in a flash—as a whole *Gestalt*, a sudden pattern of check, interpose, uncover, and then the mate with a knight coming almost out of left field—Baskin stared at his mated king for a minute and then said, his voice flat, "I hear you're a CPA."

"That's right." The two of them had never talked about their pasts. But Baskin was the sort of man who seems to have a way of finding out everything.

"What will you do when you get out of here? Nobody'll hire a CPA with embezzlement on his record."

"I can open a tax-figuring office."

"Is that what you were planning to do with the money you embezzled?"

"Yes." And then, "What are *you* in here for?"

Baskin raised his eyebrows. "You don't know?" He picked up a bishop from the chessboard, deftly, and then twirled it between his grayish fingers. "Do you have enough money to open up a tax office?"

"I'm . . . I'm not sure."

"How much do you have left? After paying your lawyers?" He set the bishop down, neatly, on its home square. "I presume you weren't able to keep what you embezzled. Do you have any money left?"

Will wasn't certain whether to resent the question or not. But he answered it. "About five thousand dollars."

Baskin was looking at the odalisque. "That's not enough to start a business," he said. "You could play chess for money."

"Oh, come on. I could win a few hundred dollars in the chess parlors. Who plays strangers for more than five or ten?"

Baskin turned from the print and looked at Will closely. "You could play someone who plays rated players for money."

"Like who?"

"There's a man near Raleigh, North Carolina, who will play you for five thousand a game. Once you identify yourself and he's sure you are who you say you are. His name is Wharton."

Will started to say something sarcastic, then it hit him. "Is he rated?"

"About three hundred points higher than you. Than you *were*."

Will began to feel a little warm. He was still nervous, his stomach a bit tight, but he was confident. "And I've improved by about five hundred since you've been teaching me."

Baskin's face remained expressionless. "Four hundred. Perhaps." And then, "But you have another advantage." Baskin smiled slightly. "When he plays white, he generally plays queen's gambit. On black, he plays the Sicilian with the dragon variation."

"And that's what you've been playing against me all along."

Baskin smiled again. "Do you think you would have beat me at all if I had been varying my play as much as I can?"

Will was silent for a minute. Then, abruptly, he said, "What are you in prison for?"

Baskin looked genuinely surprised. "No one ever told you?"

"No."

"I was taken in *flagrante* with a sixteen-year-old boy."

Will shook his head, trying to shake off the shock, and the strangeness of it; he had never seen a trace of homosexuality in Baskin's manner. "You're *gay*?" he said.

"Not in here," Baskin said wryly. "Just queer."

Will's embarrassment became suddenly acute. Switching subjects desperately, he said, "This man . . . Wharton?"

"Yes," Baskin said. "Wharton. Thomas Jefferson Wharton." He picked up a knight between two fingers, set it gently down on a center square. "An oxymoron of a name."

Will had no idea what oxymoron meant, but did not want to ask. "Where does his money come from?"

"From his very peculiar mind," said Baskin abstractedly. "He started with nothing, made a fortune in textiles before he was thirty-five. In the fifties, the Republicans gave him a fairly high appointive job in the Department of Defense—as a kind of appeasement to Joe McCarthy, it was rumored. Wharton was pretty well known for strong views on what he called the 'nigger-Red-faggot complex' in Washington. Anyway, getting into the Cold War suited him just right. You remember that game theory was starting to be very fashionable in those days? Wharton got seriously involved in chess as 'a way of reading the Soviet mind.'"

Will laughed cautiously. Everything Baskin said had such a tone of irony that Will couldn't be sure. "'A way of reading the Soviet mind'? But that's a stupid—"

Baskin looked at him sharply. "There's nothing stupid about T. J. Wharton," he said. "And don't forget it. Political mania, yes. Irrationality—maybe even paranoia. But nothing dumb. There are more of his kind around than you may think, too." He picked up the knight again but this time held it in his fist, firmly. "On the outside, Mr. Wharton looks like a big, dumb Southern fat cat. And, in some ways, he has all the culture as well as the social views of Archie Bunker. But his intellect is frightening." Baskin smiled grimly. "That intellect isn't easy to see, at first, because men like him know it pays to hide an I.Q. of a hundred eighty. But the man can absorb almost *anything*. Anything that his manias tell him is necessary. He became a chess player of near-master strength in about four months. Which may have been his undoing."

"How could that be?" Will said.

Baskin looked at him quietly. "For you and me, Schneider, chess is an opposition of two intellects. Pure mind; no potent emotions. But to Wharton it got to be a life-and-death struggle. He got to feeling he was playing against the Politburo, or the Kremlin, instead of people like me." He paused, still clutching the knight firmly in his hand.

"And what happened?"

"I beat him, for one thing. He had got to be a damn good player, but I could beat him three times out of four. I think that may have had something to do with it. Or maybe the department chucked him when Joe McCarthy began to skid. Anyway, he seemed to have been checkmated in some vital way. One day he was just gone. The papers said he had resigned for 'family reasons.' I never saw him again. But I suppose he'll hate me as long as he lives."

Will took in a deep breath. "Is *that* why you've been . . . training me? To . . . carry on for you?"

Baskin set the knight back on the board very carefully, with a kind of reverence for the cleanly and handsomely carved piece of wood. "I'll tell you how to get in touch with him," he said. "Just don't let him find out that you know me."

Will looked for a moment at the knight on the center of the board, at its equine, impassive, glistening presence. "Thanks," he said. "Thanks, Mr. Baskin."

It was a brilliant August day when they let Will out. With a prison suit, fifty dollars and the address of a halfway house. He spent the fifty dollars on a whore. She was worth every penny of it.

And there he was, walking on Broad Street in the sun in Columbus, Ohio, and then getting his money out of his Columbus bank. Five thousand in traveler's checks and $780 in cash. He had clothes in an uncle's house in Cleveland but hadn't bothered sending for them before leaving the state prison. Instead, he went to Dunhill's and bought a navy-blue double-knit blazer, light-gray, flared slacks, a pale-blue, buttondown shirt and a wide, bright silk Givenchy tie.

Getting through to Wharton on the hotel phone took four hours; in desperation, he decided, *What the hell?* and used Baskin's name. It couldn't really hurt. The name finally got him through secretaries and excuses to the man himself. "Wharton speaking." Deep Southern voice; tone of command—almost exactly what Baskin had made him expect.

"My name is Schneider, Mr. Wharton. Findlay Baskin told me you might like to play some chess." And then he thought again, *What the hell?* and said, "For money."

"You're not a player of Baskin's strength?"

Even in those few words, the tone of arrogance came through—but the words were also those of a man who never let a challenge go by. He could have said "Screw off" and hung up. So Will tried to sound as affable as he could.

"God, no. My rating is eighteen eighty-five."

"How do you know Baskin, then? He's an international master."

Will had thought one move ahead for that question. He said, "Postal chess."

Wharton snorted. "Baskin must be hard up there in the Ohio State Pen." Will had guessed the man would have that detail.

"Probably. Do you want to play me?"

"For how much?"

He tried not to let his sucking in of breath be heard on the telephone. "Five thousand dollars."

"How do I know you're not a hustler? A master in disguise."

"You can look my rating up in *Chess Life and Review*. And I have identification." And then, "Do you want to play, Mr. Wharton?"

"By house rules. Two hours each on the clock. And the president of the Raleigh chess club will referee."

They would play then. The relief—with just a tinge of fear—was exquisite. "Good. When?" And then, "What are 'house rules'?"

"We'll play Saturday afternoon at one. House rules around here mean things like touch move."

Will hesitated. "I hate touch move, Mr. Wharton. Why don't we let the clock punch make the moves final?"

Wharton didn't even snort. "Touch move," he said.

"Okay, touch move." And then, "You have a Staunton set, don't you?"

The voice was plainly scornful. "Of course I have a Staunton set."

"Good. I'll be there Saturday afternoon."

"Flying?"

Actually, he had planned to save money by taking a Greyhound bus; his car was in Cleveland. But he said, "Yes."

"When you arrive, call me. I'll have a car sent."

"Fine," Will said, "fine." But it wasn't fine.

It was Thursday and he had one more night in Columbus. Instead of a whore this time, he found himself a girl. A student. At the art museum. But they drank some kind of foul college student wine and with the dumbness it gave his head—his first liquor in six months—and with the thought of the game coming up, he found making love to her a problem. But he managed, and afterward, naked in the hotel bed, he found himself staring at her good, sound, milk-fed body and abruptly he thought: *What's all this foolishness about hustling chess? A girl, a good, smooth girl like this, is worth the whole goddamn fugue of a game.* But the next day he caught the plane to Raleigh.

The car was, as he had halfway expected, a chauffeured Cadillac, but the chauffeur was white. They did not talk on the drive.

Wharton's house was big but not enormous. Not particularly Southern, just a rich man's house. Maybe $250,000 worth of Permastone and garage and redwood and deck and fishpond at the side. And a putting green; and a swimming pool.

Wharton met him at the door. He looked exactly to be the "fat cat" that Baskin had called him. Big, tall, heavy, with bushy eyebrows, a potbelly. Ban-Lon golf shirt and white slacks. And a tanned, enameled wife in a flowered hostess dress. The wife muttered something about "you men and your games" and whisked off in a cloud of heavy perfume. Wharton took him through several rooms, one of which had a fountain with sentimental, fake-Bernini angels spitting water into a pool. And then into what Wharton called his game room, with—of course—animal heads and rifles and a trophy case and real walnut paneling and real leather chairs, as though it had all leaped off the front page of a 1953 Abercrombie & Fitch catalog. Including the giant chess set that stood between two black-leather chairs on one of those tables that come from Calcutta or Bombay and have inlays crawling up their curved legs and around their edges. The set was huge, with rooks the shape of elephants bearing round howdahs on their backs, soldier pawns with spears, a queen in a sari and a king with a mustache. It was all ivory and filigreed gold—the kind of thing designed to arouse profound contempt in any serious chess player. The kind a rich *patzer*—a wood pusher—would buy while on tour in the Orient. Except Wharton was no *patzer*; he was a rated player.

Wharton's voice boomed at Will. He must have been staring at the set for some time. "How do you like it?" he said. "It cost me over two thousand. Eighteen-carat gold and heart ivory. It's one of a kind—and there'll never be another one like it, because the maker is dead now."

Will smiled grimly. "I thought you said you had a Staunton set?"

There was just a hint of a sneer in Wharton's voice. "Of course I have a Staunton set, Mr. Schneider. I have three of them. But this is the one I feel most at home with, and it seems appropriate to a five-thousand-dollar game. House rules—we use *this* set."

Will almost said that it seemed appropriate for a whorehouse, but he was beginning already to feel put down by the man: by his size, the edge of irony in his voice, that goddamned *look* of being a born winner. For a moment he thought: *I should get out of this, I'm going to do something dumb and lose my ass.*

Wharton then shouted abruptly, "Arthur," and there were footsteps and then a mild insurance-salesman type in a brown suit came into the room. "This is Mr. Schneider, Arthur," Wharton said. "Arthur is president of our Raleigh chess club and will serve us as referee." Then Wharton walked to a sideboard that was made of what looked like elephant leather stretched over some kind of bamboo frame. On it were glasses and about eight bottles of Jack Daniel's. "Whiskey, Mr. Schneider?" he said.

"No, thanks," he answered. He loved Jack Daniel's and could rarely afford it, but it would be stupid of him to risk any chance of fogging his mind now. Besides, he disliked Wharton's arrogance in having nothing else to offer his guests, however good the whiskey might be.

"Oh?" Wharton said, and he poured himself a generous shot into a brandy snifter. He did not offer a drink to Arthur. Then Wharton went over to the board and picked up a white and a black pawn and held them behind his back, switching them back and forth for a moment. "Take your pick, Mr. Schneider."

Suddenly Will felt his stomach muscles tighten. *Here we go.* "Your left hand," he said.

Wharton showed the piece. It was black. "Tough ..." he said, and then he replaced the pieces on the board. They sat down. "Okay," Wharton said. "Now it's touch move, two hours on the clock and five thousand dollars a game. Which reminds me. Schneider, do you have the money? I want to see it."

He had thought that might happen, but he still resented it. He took the book of traveler's checks from his breast pocket and handed it across the table, almost knocking over a seven-inch-high bishop. He cursed himself silently for the awkwardness and for the visible tremor in his hands.

Wharton flipped through the book cursorily and then leaned over the board and handed it back to him, smiling; his hand was as steady as a rock. "Fine," he said. "Do you want to start my clock now?"

Will had hardly noticed the clock before, so overwhelming were the chess pieces, but he looked at it now. It was an oddly effete little thing, in contrast to all the phony *machismo* of the room: porcelain, with pink cherubs and gold buttons to push. He felt rather fond of it. He pushed the button on his side. *Click.* There was a faint ticking.

Wharton moved pawn to queen four. Beginning the queen's gambit, almost for sure. Then he pressed the button that stopped his side of the clock and started Will's.

"Pawn to queen four," Arthur said in an overloud voice.

My God! Will thought. *Must we have this nonsense, too?* But he said nothing and reached out gingerly—nervous of the touch-move aspect of the thing, with these enormous and confusing pieces—and picked up his queen's pawn and set it on the fourth rank. The piece was as heavy as a billiard ball, but he found the weight satisfying.

"Pawn to queen four," Arthur said.

Will pushed the button on the clock and began thinking, trying to see through all those filigree-and-ivory ornaments and imagine the clean pattern of a classic board.

It turned out to be the queen's gambit, all right, and Will accepted it, taking the big weighty white pawn and setting it on the side of the table. They played the opening routinely, by the book, for about forty-five minutes, very carefully, setting up patterns and positions, neither of them trying anything unorthodox.

Then Wharton finished his snifter of whiskey and, coolly ignoring the fact that his own clock was running, got up from the table, went to the sideboard, picked up the bottle and said, "Still afraid to drink, Mr. Schneider?"

It was a cheap ploy, but he could not help himself. "Pour me a double, Mr. Wharton." He said it aloud, and thought *Yes, pour the goddamn fool a double.*

Wharton brought him the drink, sat down, abruptly picked up his white bishop and took Will's bishop's pawn from over Will's castled king.

"Bishop takes pawn," Arthur said.

Will stared at it. It had come as a total shock. It did not look like an ordinary bishop sacrifice, he could not see the follow-up. He stared at it for five minutes, while his clock ticked and he held his snifter of whiskey, untasted, in his hand. And then he saw it. If he took the bishop, there would be the routine check by Wharton's queen. Nothing to worry about there. But he would have to interpose a knight and then Wharton could move—and this was it—his goddamned *rook* that looked like an elephant. Will somehow had been taking it for a knight, probably because it was an animal figure, because in a serious chess set the only animal figure on a chessboard is a knight. When Wharton moved his rook over three squares, Will would be under direct threat of checkmate unless he began sacrificing pieces like crazy. And even if Wharton didn't get the mate, after it was over he would have such an advantage in material that he could muscle Will out for the rest of the game.

But, astonishingly, maybe because of the anger he felt at these idiotic, ostentatious pieces, he did not panic. Instead, he sipped his drink and then looked at his clock. He had an hour and a half. He would find some way out; the right move had to be there.

And he found it. It took him twenty-five minutes, while Wharton did several cheap tricks, drumming his fingers on the table, clearing his throat, getting another drink, offering him one and clinking glasses. But he found it: First, of course, he would not take the bishop. That would give him a move to put his king's knight in the space the bishop had vacated, and avoid the check for two moves. Then, if Wharton began to try his combination, Will would be able to threaten a king-queen fork with the knight. Wharton would have to drop the attack and start scrambling.

Before reaching for the king's knight, he sipped the drink again, savoring the idea of the move more than the whiskey itself. His hand was trembling only slightly.

Then he reached forward over several tall pieces to move the knight and his finger brushed against the big, ungainly black queen with her absurd Indian sari. The piece trembled heavily on the board. Wharton's voice came instantaneously, as if the finger had activated an alarm, "Touch move."

Will stared at the referee. "Sorry, Mr. Schneider. You must move the queen."

Jesus Christ, he thought, *Jesus Christ*.

It took him ten minutes to find a move for his queen that wasn't a total disaster. But Will's game was going to be lost in about four moves if Wharton followed the checkmate threat out. Will looked at the man's face, now flushed. Wharton was smiling, pleased completely with himself to be about to take a game on a technicality even after a strong move of his own. For a moment Will wanted to scream, and then he thought, *Goddamn it, Schneider, be like Baskin. Be cool.*

Then, he had an idea. During the past ten minutes, Wharton had been moving around restlessly, making himself a drink or finding a cigar—but always keeping an eye out for Will's queen move. Now, when he came back to the table, Will was squinting intently at Wharton's bishop, a strange Hindu figure of some sort.

"What are you looking at?" Wharton demanded.

"Oh, nothing," Will said. Then he moved his queen as calmly as he could, Arthur announced the move, and then Will said, "I didn't care much for these pieces at first, but now I rather admire them. Wonderful workmanship. But it's a shame about your bishop. I suppose it got cracked in shipping?"

"What crack?" Wharton roared. He reached for the bishop, seized it, stopped cold with realization and remained bent over the table. Arthur, from his chair, made a couple of gasping sounds.

Will said gently, "Touch move."

He had embezzled once, from a crooked and mean-spirited employer, but he had never played a dirty trick in a game before in his life. And the feeling it gave him, looking at Wharton trapped, was simple elation. Because there was no place the son of a bitch could put that bishop where it would not both get in the way of his attack and give Will an extra move.

Wharton looked at Arthur, but there was nothing for Arthur to say. His hand was still on the piece. Then he looked at Will and said, "You goddamned cheap crook," and moved the bishop.

Will made the knight move and then began a slow trading game until he had a pawn advantage at the end game and had the tempo, too, to be able to be the first to queen a pawn and suddenly Wharton reached his big meaty hand out and laid his king on its side and said, "I resign."

Will stood up and stretched. He felt wonderful. Still nervous, but wonderful. Enjoying, for once, the nervousness itself. It might have been better to have won the game on the pure, fuguelike strategy of chess instead of by a trick. But Wharton had asked for that kind of trickery, and Will had beat him at that game, too.

Then Wharton said, "Another game, Mr. Schneider? For ten thousand?"

That caught him off guard, like an unexpected gambit.

"I hadn't planned. . . ."

"Come on, Mr. Schneider," Wharton said. "You're not going to walk out after winning by a trick."

And he thought, *Damn it, I am better than he is: I think I am. And with twenty thousand dollars. . . .*

"Okay," he said. Then he smiled. "Since I play white this time."

Wharton smiled back, "But I play like Bogolyubov."

So he knew that one, too. So what? But it bothered him.

Will began setting up his white pieces, but Wharton said, as if he were talking to a maid, "Arthur, set mine up," and walked over toward the trophy case on the wall. "Perhaps I shouldn't have called you a crook a minute ago, Mr. Schneider. But the term does fit an embezzler, doesn't it?"

Will blinked at him.

"Didn't you think I'd have you checked out?" Wharton said. "I had my lawyer call the warden at the penitentiary. The one where I had Baskin put away."

"Where *you* had him put away?"

Wharton was unlocking the door of the trophy case. "The boy was a paid prostitute. I helped the police set the whole thing up, including the witnesses."

Will stared at him. "But *why*?"

Wharton smiled. "I despise faggots. And Baskin beat me out of some money at chess once." He took a big trophy out of the cabinet; it looked like something one got for hunting or for golf. "I imagine that's why Baskin put you up to all these shenanigans." Then he went over and set the trophy on the middle of the table, as though it were a King Kong of a chess piece. "But Baskin has been out of circulation for three years. So there are a few things even he doesn't know. Like this, for instance." He pushed the trophy toward Will.

Will looked at it. The figure on top was a large horse's head—a knight from a Staunton set. And the brass plate below read, CHICAGO OPEN, NOVEMBER 1972. FIRST PLACE—T. J. WHARTON.

Will said nothing, but his guts had tightened as though Wharton's hammy fists had taken his duodenum and squeezed it physically.

"I've been studying under Zoravsky for two years," Wharton said. "Every now and then I beat him. Of course, I pay him well."

Jesus Christ, Will thought, *Zoravsky is at least 300 points bet-ter than Baskin. My God, he beat Fischer once, in Vienna.* But then he thought, *What the hell,* almost feeling, astonishingly, good about it. *So it'll be one goddamned tough chess game.* And he said, "Let's play chess, Mr. Wharton."

Arthur had finished setting up the black pieces and had reset the clock faces for two hours each.

Will opened with pawn to king four. . . .

Wharton started with a classic Sicilian defense, but then after a few pawn exchanges in the center, he made two unex-pected moves with his queen's knight and, abruptly, Will found himself a pawn down and with his major pieces constricted. He had never seen that one before and it frightened him. It was brilliant. He remembered what Baskin had said about Wharton's intelligence. And when he reached to make his next move, he abruptly caught himself. He had almost touched that goddamn rook-elephant again, thinking it was a knight. It would have been disaster. And he shouldn't have let Wharton con him into drinking whiskey. Not after those dry six months in prison. And, of course, Wharton, knowing about his prison term, had planned to get him high. The Jack Daniel's gambit.

Suddenly he folded his hands in his lap, as if not to contam-inate them with these pseudo Oriental-baroque chessmen. *But Wharton hasn't won this chess game.* Then, his clock ticking, he looked at Wharton and said, evenly, "Do your . . . house rules allow the referee to move my pieces for me?"

Wharton stared at him. "What kind of chickenshit . . . ?"

"*Do* they?" Will looked at the big man steadily. *Go ahead, you bastard,* he thought. *Refuse.*

"You're scared of touching the wrong piece?" But Wharton's voice was unconvinced.

Will smiled. "Is that the kind of advantage you want, Mr. Wharton?"

Wharton reddened slightly. Then he looked at Arthur.

"It's all quite legal, Mr. Wharton," Arthur said, lamely.

"I know it's legal," Wharton said, "and I know it's chicken-shit. And I know I'll beat his cheap ass, even if he brings in Raquel goddamn Welch to move his pieces for him."

"Thank you," Will said. Then he stood up, took hold of his big leather chair and began turning it around.

"What in God's good goddamn hell are you doing?" Wharton said.

Will had the chair turned facing completely away from the board. "I'm turning my back on you, Mr. Wharton. And on your chess set." Then he thought for a moment, composing himself, and said, "Knight to queen's bishop five."

He hardly heard Arthur making the move for him, or the click of the punched clock. For the pure Staunton set of the brain, that beautiful abstraction as clean as the axioms of Euclid, had leaped before him in all its grace and sharpness. And that was where the game was at. Not in this cheap and tawdry business of tricks and one-upmanship and money and bluster. That was the whole beauty of chess: a lovely abstraction. A game. A trivial, exquisite game.

Wharton played dazzlingly. He whittled Will down by a second pawn—his king's pawn, a bad one to lose. And he had got an open rook file. But Will kept his mind there in that interior space and waited—watched it, the diagonals and lines, and patterns and configurations—and waited.

He managed, by playing with great care, to free up his pieces. But it cost him another pawn. And Wharton—whom he now did not even picture in his mind—had his king safely castled.

But something was beginning to show finally in the pattern. Will was getting only the edges of it into his perception, because it was so overwhelmingly hard to see that far ahead. But it was there. He could feel the potential of it. It would have to start with opening the bishop's file, and then maybe a check. But a check with what? The queen? But that would cost the queen, and you can't afford that. He shook his head, trying to penetrate it. *First I trade knights, and that puts his pawn over on the other file. Then I threaten his rook with my queen. . . .* He shook his head again and tried it the other way. *I don't trade knights, I bring out the queen first, and he'll threaten it with the rook, because he'll be going for the position, and there are at least seven alternatives from there, and I have to know where each one leads. . . .*

And then Arthur said, "You have ten more minutes on your clock, Mr. Schneider. Mr. Wharton has fifty-three." And his whole body seemed to shake in one tremor, as if the ground had quaked. *Had it been that long?* Then his mind pushed itself up and over the hump and it was like the Red Sea opening at his feet and he saw the whole thing. As Isaac Newton must have seen it on that day he wept when he saw how things really worked. *You check with the knight,* his mind told him, *and he must take with the pawn. And then you bring out the queen. And if he doesn't interpose the rook, he loses a piece. And that's as far as he'll see it.* He could almost taste it.

"Knight to king's bishop six, check," he said, quietly. He hardly heard Arthur repeat it.

Wharton took the knight with the pawn. He was forced to.

Then Will said, "Queen to bishop three." And then he waited. He knew it would be a long wait, while Wharton studied, and it was. But it was Wharton's clock that was ticking now—not his. Once he became frightened that Wharton would see what was coming, but he stopped his mind from that thought. Fischer maybe would see it, or Petrosian. He stared at the far wall, at the head of a hapless lion, stuffed, mounted, wasted.

Then Wharton moved and when Arthur called out his own move, Will knew that he had won the game. "Queen takes pawn, check," he said. He heard Wharton draw in his breath.

The wait was almost intolerable. For a moment Will felt, with panic, he had gone insane, like Paul Morphy—that mad New Orleans chess genius—and it was only his delusion that this combination of moves would work.

But then he heard the pieces move and Arthur's voice said, "Rook takes queen."

Instantly, Will said, "Rook to rook eight, check."

Wharton, just as quickly, said, "It's not going to work, Schneider. You've lost your queen for nothing," and the cold sharp ring in his voice, an edge in it that Will had not heard before, abruptly brought back Baskin's words about the man— about his "frightening intellect."

But his own mind told him, *It's a won game, Schneider. It's a won game.* So he said, aloud, "Mr. Wharton, I'll bet you two thousand dollars against your chess set that it works."

And Wharton's voice shot back, with a contempt that was palpable in the air of the room, "It's a bet, Schneider. It won't work."

His heart was trembling, but there was relief in hearing the other man's words—because Will knew what that move was going to be.

Not waiting for Arthur to announce it, Wharton said, "Rook to bishop one." Loudly. And then, "I *interposed*, you dumb motherfucker."

And then Will's words came out steady and soft. "Bishop to knight three, check," and he stood up and turned around and looked straight into Wharton's face.

Wharton's face, red now with whiskey and emotion, was fierce and confident. For about five seconds. And then it crumbled. Because, finally, he saw what was coming. There was only one legal move and Wharton, not resigning, made it. King to rook one. And for a moment, weariness hit Will's entire body. He pressed his right hand to his forehead. Then he said, "Rook takes rook." He looked at Wharton, dizzily, strangely. "Checkmate."

Wharton said nothing. He merely sat there, staring at the board, his red, fleshy face sagging. Finally he said, "Son of a bitch." The tone of his voice was flat, cold, hardly human. "Son of a bitch."

Something about that tone took some of the weariness out of Will. He looked toward a window and was surprised to see that it had grown dark outdoors. Then he looked back at the chessboard, at those ivory pieces that he hated. *His* pieces now. Then he reached over and picked up the white king and held it in his two fists, while Wharton stared at him, and, twisting with all his strength, he cracked the ivory and filigreed gold into fragments. Then he put the fragments into his coat pocket and said, "You can keep the rest of the set, Mr. Wharton. And after you pay me the money, you can have your man take me back to the airport."

Wharton looked at the chessboard, with its white king gone, as if in profound disbelief. His face was blank.

Then he reached into the drawer, took out the checkbook and a pen and began to write.

RENT CONTROL

"My God," Edith said, "that was the most *real* experience of my life." She put her arms around him, put her cheek against his naked chest, and pulled him tightly to her. She was crying.

He was crying too. "Me too, darling," he said, and held his arms around her. They were in the loft bed of her studio apartment on the East Side. They had just had orgasms together. Now they were sweaty, relaxed, blissful. It had been a perfect day.

Their orgasms had been foreshadowed by their therapy. That evening, after supper, they had gone to Harry's group as always on Wednesdays and somehow everything had focused for them. He had at last shouted the heartfelt anger he bore against his incompetent parents; she had screamed her hatred of her sadistic mother, her gutless father. And their relief had come together there on the floor of a New York psychiatrist's office. After the screaming and pounding of fists, after the real and potent old rage in both of them was spent, their smiles at one another had been radiant. They had gone afterward to her apartment, where they had lived together half a year, climbed up the ladder into her bed, and begun to make love slowly, carefully. Then frenetically. They had been picked up bodily by it and carried to a place they had never been before.

Now, afterward, they were settling down in that place, huddled together. They lay silently for a long time. Idly she looked toward the ledge by the mattress where she kept cigarettes, a mason jar with miniature roses, a Japanese ashtray, and an alarm clock.

"The clock must have stopped," she said.

He mumbled something inarticulate. His eyes were closed.

"It says nine twenty," she said, "and we left Harry's at nine."

"Hmmm," he said, without interest.

She was silent for a while, musing. Then she said, "Terry? What time does your watch say?"

"Time, time," he said. "Watch, watch." He shifted his arm and looked. "Nine twenty," he said.

"Is the second hand moving?" she said. His watch was an Accutron, not given to being wrong or stopping.

He looked again. "Nope. Not moving." He let his hand fall on her naked behind, now cool to his touch. Then he said, "That *is* funny. Both stopping at once." He leaned over her body toward the window, pried open a space in her Levolor blinds, looked out. It was dark out, with an odd shimmer to the air. Nothing was moving. There was a pile of plastic garbage bags on the sidewalk opposite. "It can't be eleven yet. They haven't taken the garbage from the Toreador." The Toreador was a Spanish restaurant across the street; they kept promising they would eat there sometime but never had.

"It's probably about ten thirty," she said. "Why don't you make us an omelet and turn the TV on?"

"Sure, honey," he said. He slipped on his bikini shorts and eased himself down the ladder. Barefoot and undressed, he went to the tiny Sony by the fireplace, turned it on, and padded over to the stove and sink at the other end of the room. He heard the TV come on while finding the omelet pan that he had bought her, under the sink, nestling between the Bon Ami and the Windex. He got eggs out, cracked one, looked at his watch. It was running. It said nine twenty-six. "Hey, honey," he called out. "My watch is running."

After a pause she said, her voice slightly hushed, "So is the clock up here."

He shrugged and put butter in the pan and finished cracking the eggs, throwing the shells into the sink. He whipped them with a fork, then turned on the fire under the pan and walked back to the TV for a moment. A voice was saying, ". . . nine thirty." He looked at his watch. Nine thirty. *Jesus Christ!* he said.

But he had forgotten about it by the time he cooked the omelets. His omelets had been from the beginning one of the things that made them close. He had learned to cook them before leaving his wife and it meant independence to him. He made omelets beautifully—tender and moist—and Edith was impressed. They had fallen in love over omelets. He cooked lamb chops too, and bought things like frozen capelletti from expensive shops; but omelets were central.

They were both thirty-five years old, both youthful, good-looking, smart. They were both Pisces, with birthdays three days apart. Both had good complexions, healthy dark hair, clear eyes. They both bought clothes at Bergdorf-Goodman and Bonwit's and Bloomingdale's; they both spoke fair French, watched *Nova* on TV, read *The Stories of John Cheever* and the Sunday *Times*. He was a magazine illustrator, she a lawyer; they could have afforded a bigger place, but hers was rent-controlled and at a terrific midtown address. It was too much of a bargain to give up. "*Nobody* ever leaves a rent-controlled apartment," she told him. So they lived in one and a half rooms together and money piled up in their bank accounts.

They were terribly nervous lovers at first, too unsure of everything to enjoy it, full of explanations and self-recriminations. He had trouble staying hard; she would not lubricate. She was afraid of him and made love dutifully, often with resentment. He was embarrassed at his unreliable member, sensed her withdrawal from his ardor, was afraid to tell her so. Often they were miserable.

But she had the good sense to take him to her therapist and he had the good sense to go. Finally, after six months of private sessions and of group, it had worked. They had the perfect orgasm, the perfect release from tension, the perfect intimacy.

Now they ate their omelets in bed from Spode plates, using his mother's silver forks. Sea salt and Java pepper. Their legs were twined as they ate.

They lay silent for a while afterward. He looked out the window. The garbage was still there; there was no movement in the street; no one was on the sidewalk. There was a flatness to the way the light shone on the buildings across from them, as though they were painted—some kind of a backdrop.

He looked at his watch. It said nine forty-one. The second hand wasn't moving. "Shit!" he said, puzzled.

"What's that, honey?" Edith said. "Did I do something wrong?"

"No, sweetie," he said. "You're the best thing that ever happened. I'm crazy about you." He patted her ass with one hand, gave her his empty plate with the other.

She set the two plates on the ledge, which was barely wide enough for them. She glanced at the clock. "Jesus," she said. "That sure is strange . . ."

"Let's go to sleep," he said. "I'll explain the Theory of Relativity in the morning."

But when he woke up it wasn't morning. He felt refreshed, thoroughly rested; he had the sense of a long and absolutely silent sleep, with no noises intruding from the world outside, no dreams, no complications. He had never felt better.

But when he looked out the window the light from the streetlamp was the same and the garbage bags were still piled in front of the Toreador and—he saw now—what appeared to be the same taxi was motionless in front of the same green station wagon in the middle of Fifty-first Street. He looked at his watch. It said nine forty-one.

Edith was still asleep, on her stomach, with her arm across his waist, her hip against his. Not waking her, he pulled away and started to climb down from the bed. On an impulse he looked again at his watch. It was nine forty-one still, but now the second hand was moving.

He reached out and turned the electric clock on the ledge to where he could see its face. It said nine forty-one also, and when he held it to his ear he could hear its gears turning quietly inside. His heart began to beat more strongly, and he found himself catching his breath.

He climbed down and went to the television set, turned it

on again. The same face appeared as before he had slept, wearing the same oversized glasses, the same bland smile.

Terry turned the sound up, seated himself on the sofa, lit a cigarette, and waited.

It seemed a long time before the news program ended and a voice said, "It's ten o'clock."

He looked at his watch. It said ten o'clock. He looked out the window; it was dark—evening. There was no way it could be ten in the morning. But he knew he had slept a whole night. He knew it. His hand holding the second cigarette was trembling.

Slowly and carefully he put out his cigarette, climbed back up the ladder to the loft bed. Edith was still asleep. Somehow he knew what to do. He laid his hand on her leg and looked at his watch. As he touched her the second hand stopped. For a long moment he did not breathe.

Still holding her leg, he looked out the window. This time there were a group of people outside; they had just left the restaurant. None of them moved. The taxi had gone and with it the station wagon; but the garbage was still there. One of the people from the Toreador was in the process of putting on his raincoat. One arm was in a sleeve and the other wasn't. There was a frown on his face visible from the third-story apartment where Terry lay looking at him. Everything was frozen. The light was peculiar, unreal. The man's frown did not change.

Terry let go of Edith and the man finished putting on his coat. Two cars drove by in the street. The light became normal.

Terry touched Edith again, this time laying his hand gently on her bare back. Outside the window everything stopped, as when a switch is thrown on a projector to arrest the movement.

Terry let out his breath audibly. Then he said, "Wake up, Edith. I've got something to show you."

They never understood it, and they told nobody. It was relativity, they decided. They had found, indeed, a perfect place together, where subjective time raced and the world did not.

It did not work anywhere but in her loft bed and only when they touched. They could stay together there for hours or days, although there was no way they could tell how long the "time" had really been; they could make love, sleep, read, talk, and no time passed whatever.

They discovered, after a while, that only if they quarreled did it fail and the clock and watch would run even though they were touching. It required intimacy—even of a slight kind, the intimacy of casual touching—for it to work.

They adapted their lives to it quickly and at first it extended their sense of life's possibilities enormously. It bathed them in a perfection of the lovers' sense of being apart from the rest of the world and better than it.

Their careers improved; they had more time for work and for play than anyone else. If one of them was ever under serious pressure—of job competition, of the need to make a quick decision—they could get in bed together and have all the time necessary to decide, to think up the speech, to plan the magazine cover or the case in court.

Sometimes they took what they called "weekends," buying and cooking enough food for five or six meals, and just staying in the loft bed, touching, while reading and meditating and making love and working. He had his art supplies in shelves over the bed now, and she had reference books and note pads on the ledge. He had put mirrors on two of the walls and on the ceiling, partly for sex, partly to make the small place seem bigger, less confining.

The food was always hot, unspoiled; no time had passed for it between their meals. They could not watch television or listen to records while in suspended time; no machinery worked while they touched.

Sometimes for fun they would watch people out the window and stop and start them up again comically; but that soon grew tiresome.

They both got richer and richer, with promotions and higher pay and the low rent. And of course there was now truly no question of leaving the apartment; there was no other bed in which they could stop time, no other place. Besides, this one was rent-controlled.

For a year or so they would always stay later at parties than anyone else, would taunt acquaintances and colleagues when they were too tired to accompany them to all-night places for scrambled eggs or a final drink. Sometimes they annoyed colleagues by showing up bright-eyed and rested in the morning, no matter how late the party had gone on, no matter how many drinks had been drunk, no matter how loud and fatiguing the revelry. They were always buoyant, healthy, awake, and just a bit smug.

But after the first year they tired of partying, grew bored with friends, and went out less. Somehow they had come to a place where they were never bored with, as Edith called it, "our little loft bed." The center of their lives had become a king-sized foam mattress with a foot-wide ledge and a few inches of head and foot room at each end. They were never bored when in that small space.

What they had to learn was not to quarrel, not to lose the modicum of intimacy that their relativity phenomenon required. But that came easily too; without discussing it each learned to give only a small part of himself to intimacy with the other, to cultivate a state of mind remote enough to be safe from conflict, yet with a controlled closeness. They did yoga for body and spirit and Transcendental Meditation. Neither told the other his mantra. Often they found themselves staring at different mirrors. Now they seldom looked out the window.

It was Edith who made the second major intuition. One day when he was in the bathroom shaving, and his watch was running, he heard her shout to him, in a kind of cool playfulness, "Quit dawdling in there, Terry. I'm getting older for nothing." There was some kind of urgency in her voice, and he caught it. He rinsed his face off in a hurry, dried, walked to the bedroom and looked up at her. "What do you mean?" he said.

She didn't look at him. "Get on up here, Dum-dum," she said, still in that controlled-playful voice. "I want you to touch me."

He climbed up, laid a hand on her shoulder. Outside the window a walking man froze in mid-stride and the sunlight darkened as though a shutter had been placed over it.

"What do you mean, 'older for nothing'?" he said.

She looked at him thoughtfully. "It's been about five years now, in the real world," she said. "The real world" for them meant the time lived by other people. "But we must have spent five years in suspended time here in bed. More than that. And we haven't been aged by it."

He looked at her. "How could . . . ?"

"I don't know," she said. "But I know we're not any older than anybody else."

He turned toward the mirror at her feet, stared at himself in it. He was still youthful, firm, clear complexioned. Suddenly he smiled at himself. "Jesus," he said. "Maybe I can fix it so I can shave in bed."

Their "weekends" became longer. Although they could not measure their special time, the number of times they slept and the times they made love could be counted; and both those numbers increased once they realized the time in bed together was "free"—that they did not age while touching, in the loft bed, while the world outside was motionless and the sun neither rose nor set.

Sometimes they would pick a time of day and a quality of light they both liked and stop their time there. At twilight, with empty streets and a soft ambience of light, they would allow for the slight darkening effect, and then touch and stay touching for eight or ten sleeping periods, six or eight orgasms, fifteen meals.

They had stopped the omelets because of the real time it took to prepare them. Now they bought pizzas and prepared chickens and ready-made desserts and quarts of milk and coffee and bottles of good wine and cartons of cigarettes and cases of Perrier water and filled shelves at each side of the window with them. The hot food would never cool as long as Edith and

Terry were touching each other in the controlled intimacy they now had learned as second nature. Each could look at himself in his own mirror and not even think about the other in a conscious way, but if their fingertips were so much as touching and if the remote sense of the other was unruffled by anger or anxiety then the pizzas on the shelf would remain hot, the Perrier cold, the cars in the street motionless, and the sky and weather without change forever. No love was needed now, no feeling whatever—only the lack of unpleasantness and the slightest of physical contact.

The world outside became less interesting for them. They both had large bank accounts and both had good yet undemanding jobs; her legal briefs were prepared by assistants; three young men in his studio made the illustrations that he designed, on drawing pads, in the loft bed. Often the nights were a terrible bore to them when they had to let go of each other if they wanted morning to come, just so they could go to work, have a change of pace.

But less and less did either of them want the pace to change. Each had learned to spend "hours" motionless, staring at the mirror or out the window, preserving his youth against the ravages of real time and real movement. Each became obsessed, without sharing the obsession, with a single idea: immortality. They could live forever, young and healthy and fully awake, in this loft bed. There was no question of interestingness or of boredom; they had moved, deeply in their separate souls, far beyond that distinction, that rhythm of life. Deep in themselves they had become a Pharaoh's dream of endless time; they had found the pyramid that kept the flow of the world away.

On one autumn morning that had been like two weeks for them he looked at her, after waking, and said, "I don't want to leave this place. I don't want to get old."

She looked at him before she spoke. Then she said, "There's nothing I want to do outside."

He looked away from her, smiling. "We'll need a lot of food," he said.

They had already had the apartment filled with shelves and a bathroom was installed beneath the bed. Using the bathroom was the only concession to real time; to make the water flow it was necessary for them not to touch.

They filled the shelves, that autumn afternoon, with hundreds of pounds of food—cheeses and hot chickens and sausage and milk and butter and big loaves of bread and precooked steaks and pork chops and hams and bowls of cooked vegetables, all prepared and delivered by a wondering caterer and five assistants. They had cases of wine and beer and cigarettes. It was like an efficient, miniature warehouse.

When they got into bed and touched she said, "What if we quarrel? The food will all spoil."

"I know," he said. And then, taking a deep breath, "What if we just don't talk?"

She looked at him for a long moment. Then she said, "I've been thinking that too."

So they stopped talking. And each turned toward his own mirror and thought of living forever. They were back to back, touching.

———

No friend found them, for they had no friends. But when the landlord came in through the empty shelves on what was for him the next day he found them in the loft bed, back to back, each staring into a different mirror. They were perfectly beautiful, with healthy, clear complexions, youthful figures, dark and glistening hair; but they had no minds at all. They were not even like beautiful children; there was nothing there but prettiness.

The landlord was shocked at what he saw. But he recognized soon afterward that they would be sent somewhere and that he would be able to charge a profitable rent, at last, with someone new.

THE APOTHEOSIS OF MYRA

Out beyond the French windows during the day's second sunset the grass began singing. It had begun as a hum and as it gained in strength quickly became song. Edward pushed the French windows farther open and stepped out onto the terrace. Lovely there now, with a sky dark blue like an Earth sky. And, frightening though it was, the singing too was lovely—melodic, slow-tempoed, a sort of insistent lullaby. In three years here he had heard about it; this was the first time he had ever heard it. He sipped from the glass of gin in his hand. He was half drunk and that made it easier to take than it might have been. An enormous plain of dark grass lay before him in twilight, motionless, singing. No one knew the language. But it was clearly a language.

After a few minutes Myra came out from the living room, moving stiffly and rubbing her eyes. She had been asleep on the couch. "Goodness!" she said. "Is that the *grass*?"

"What else?" he said, turning away from her. He finished his drink.

Myra's voice was excited. "You know, Edward, I heard a recording of this . . . this grass. Back in college, years ago. It was before anybody had even heard of Endolin." She was trying to make her voice sound lively, but she could not override the self-pity in it. Myra, Edward felt, swam in self-pity as a goldfish swam in water. It was her own transparent medium. "It was in a course called 'The Exploration of our Galaxy,' I think. Dull as dishwater. But the professor played some records of life forms, and I still remember Belsin grass." Belsin was the name of the planet. "There was a question about it on the midterm. What are you drinking there, Edward?"

He did not look at her. "Gin and tonic. I'll get you one."

He walked along the moonwood deck past her and into the house. The liquor was in the kitchen. During the last year he had taken to bringing a case at a time out of the storage room, where supplies from Earth were kept. There was the half-empty last case of Gordon's gin and a nearly empty one of Johnnie Walker side by side on the kitchen counter next to a stack of unwashed dishes. The dishwasher had broken down again and he hadn't felt like trying to fix it. He grinned wryly, looking at the pile of dirty Haviland that Myra had insisted on bringing with her out to this godforsaken part of the galaxy. If he could get her to do the dishwashing he might not kill her. Fat chance.

The idea of killing her was fairly recent. Originally he had thought the arthritis and the self-pity and the booze would do it for him. But Belsin had worked for her far better than he had expected, with the fresh Endolin that had made her demand to come here in the first place. Endolin was a scraggly little plant and the finest pain-killer and anti-inflammation drug ever known. It grew only on Belsin and did not travel well even in total vacuum. Myra was rich and her family was powerful; she had provided the money and her grandfather the power to get him the job here. She was thirty-four and had had violently painful arthritis since the age of six.

He made her drink, as usual, stronger than his own. There was no ice, since that wasn't working either.

She had seated herself on the moonwood bench when he got back out on the terrace and was looking at the stars, her head slightly inclined toward the singing of the grass. For a moment he paused; she was really very beautiful. And the look of self-pity had gone from her face. He had loved her, once, when she was like this. He hadn't married her only for her money. The singing had become softer. It would end soon, if what he had heard about it was true. It happened so rarely, though, that everything about it was uncertain and no one had the foggiest notion of how the grass did it in the first place, let alone why.

Myra smiled at him, not even reaching for the drink. "It sings so . . . *intelligently*," she said, smiling. "And feeling-fully." She took the drink finally and set it on the moonwood bench beside her. Moonwood was not really wood; it was sliced from quarries and outcroppings near Belsin's north pole. You could drive nails into it and even build houses from it. Their house, though, was a prefab, cut from steel and glass in a factory in Cleveland and shipped out here, for a king's ransom.

"And nobody knows why it sings?" she said.

"Correct," Edward said. "How are your hands?"

She smiled dreamily toward him. "Very good." She flexed

them. "Hardly any pain at all. And my neck is easy tonight. Supple."

"Congratulations," he said, without feeling. He walked over to one of the deck chairs and seated himself. The problem with killing her was not the killing itself. That would be very easy out here, on a planet with only a few hundred settlers. The problem was in making it totally unambiguous, clear and simple and with himself blameless, so he could inherit. The laws concerning extraterrestrial death were a mess. One little snag could keep it in court for thirty years.

"You know what I'd like to do, Edward?" she said.

He took a swallow from his drink. "What's that?"

"I'd like to get out the EnJay and take a ride to the orchids."

"Christ!" he said. "Isn't it pretty late?" She had not ridden in the EnJay for a year or more. "And doesn't the bouncing hurt your legs? And back?"

"Edward," she said, "I'm better. Really."

"Okay," he said. "I'll get a bottle. And some Endolin."

"Forget the Endolin for now," she said brightly. "I'll be all right."

The Nuclear Jeep was in a moonwood shed at the back of the house, next to the dark-green Mercedes and the two never-used bicycles. He backed the jeep out, shifted gears, and scratched off around the house. In the low gravity of Belsin scratching off was difficult to do but he had learned the trick. He pulled up to the turnaround in front of the house where Myra's elevator normally let her out and was astonished to see her walking down the stairs, one hand on the banister, smiling toward him.

"Well!" he said as she got into the jeep.

"Pretty good, huh?" she said, smiling. She squeezed his arm.

He drove off with a jerk and across the obsidian surface of their front yard. Much of Belsin was obsidian; it was in fissures in that glasslike surface that the Endolin grew. At the end of the yard a winding path, barely wide enough for the jeep, went through the Belsin grass, which was still singing, but much more softly. He liked driving the path, with its glassy low traction and its narrow and often wrongly banked curves. There was hardly any way to build a real road on Belsin. You could not cut Belsin grass—which wasn't grass at all and seemed to grow out of the granitic rock beneath it like hair—and if you drove on it it screamed and bled. Bringing from Earth the equipment to grade and level the obsidian would have been almost enough to bankrupt even Myra's family. So when you drove on Belsin you used a car with a narrow axle, and you followed the natural, vein-like pathways on the planet's surface. There weren't many places to drive *to*, anyway.

The singing, now that they were driving with the grass on either side of them, was remarkable. It was like a great chorus of small voices, or a choir chanting at the edge of understanding, alto and soprano. It was vaguely spiritual, vaguely erotic, and the truly remarkable thing about it was that it touched the human feelings so genuinely. As with Endolin, which magically dovetailed so well with the products of terrestrial evolution, producing a molecule that fit a multichambered niche in the human nervous system as if made for it, the grass seemed to have been ready for humanity when humanity first landed on Belsin sixty years before. Captain Belsin himself had heard it during the first explorations. The grass had sung for that old marauding tycoon and he had written in his journal the now famous words, "This planet speaks my language." When Endolin had been found, years later, it had seemed fitting that the planet, able somehow to touch human feeling with its astonishing music, could also provide one of the great anodynes. Endolin was hard to come by, even in the richest obsidian fields, but it was nearly perfect when fresh. It could all but obliterate physical pain without affecting the reason or the perceptions. And there was no hangover from it. Myra's life on Earth had been hell. Here, it was passable.

"Boy, do I feel good!" Myra said. "I think I could dance till dawn."

He kept his eyes on the road, following it with the wheel. "In an hour you'd be screaming from the pain. You're forgetting how Endolin burns out." That was its great drawback, and he was glad to remind her of it. That, and the fact that you couldn't take it constantly. If you did it paralyzed you.

For a moment she sounded crushed. "Honey," she said, "I haven't forgotten." Then she brightened. "But lately my bad hours between pills have been easier."

"That's good," he said. He tried to put conviction in it.

After a while they were driving along a ridge from which they could see, far off to the right, the lights of the Endolin packing plant and the little spaceport beside it.

"I didn't know they worked at *night*," Myra said.

"For the last six months they have."

"Six months Earth time?" There was Belsin time, with its seventeen-hour day and short year, and there was Earth time. Edward had a way of shifting from one to the other without warning.

"Earth time," he said, as if talking to a child.

"You almost never tell me about your work, Edward," she said. "Have orders gone up?"

"Yes," he said. "Business is booming. We're sending out a shipload every month now." He hesitated and then said, "Earth time."

"That's terrific, Edward. It must make you feel . . . useful to be so successful."

He said nothing. It made no difference to him how well the business did, except that more shippings meant more supplies of gin and of television tapes and things like peanut butter and coffee and caviar from Earth. Nothing on Belsin could be eaten. And the only business—the only real reason for humanity to be there at all—was Endolin.

"Will you have to increase the number of workers?" Myra said. "To keep up with bigger harvests?"

He shook his head. "No. The equipment has been improved. Each man brings in two or three pounds a day now. Faster vehicles and better detectors."

"That's *fascinating*!" Myra said, sitting upright with a slight wince of pain. "I had no idea what was going on."

"You never asked," he said.

"No," she said, "I suppose I didn't."

They drove on northward in silence for a long time, listening to the grass. Edward himself, despite his hidden anger and his frustrations, became calmed by it. Finally Myra spoke. "Listening to that singing is . . . is amazing," she said softly. "It seems to go very deep. You know"—she turned abruptly in her seat to face him—"the more I take Endolin the more . . . mystical my feelings are. Or spiritual." She looked a little self-conscious saying it, probably because she knew how impatient he was with her interests in poetry and in music. And in reincarnation.

"It's bound to affect your mind . . ." he said.

"No," she said. "I know that's not it. It's something I've had since I was a child. Sometimes after the arthritic pain I'd have a ... a burned-out feeling in my nerves and a certain clarity in my head. I would lie in my bed in the hospital or whatever and I felt I knew things just the other side of the edge of knowing."

He started to speak and glanced over at her. He saw that she had not finished the drink she was carrying. That was unusual, since Myra was close to being an alcoholic—something he encouraged in her. He decided to say nothing.

"I lost those feelings when I got older," she went on. "But lately I've been getting them back. Stronger. And the grass, singing like that, seems to encourage it." She stopped for a minute. "You know," she said, "the grass is giving me the same feeling. That something on the other side of knowledge can really be known. If we could only ... only relax somehow and clear our minds and grasp it."

Edward's voice was cool. "You can get the same effect from two martinis on an empty stomach."

She was unperturbed. "No, you can't, Edward," she said. "You cannot."

They were silent again for several miles. Past the plant the road broadened for a while and became straighter. Edward speeded up. It was late and he was getting bored. The grass's singing had become quieter. He was focusing on the road when he heard a sharp intake of breath from Myra and then he saw that somehow there was more light on the road. And Myra said softly, "The *rings,* Edward," and he looked up and there they were: the lavender and pale blue rings of Belsin. Normally invisible but now glowing in a great arc from east to west above them. Fairy rings. Rings of heaven.

The grass seemed to crescendo for a moment, in some kind of coda, and then became silent. The rings brightened. The effect was stunning.

"Stop the jeep," Myra said. "Let's look."

"Haven't time," Edward said, and drove on.

And Myra did something she had never done before because of the pain her unlucky body could cause her: she pushed the lever on her seat and leaned in it all the way back and looked up at the beautiful rings in the sky. She did it with care and lay back and relaxed, still holding her unfinished drink, now in her lap. Her dark hair blew behind her in the jeep's wind. Edward could see by the light of the rings that her face was glowing. Her body looked light, supple, youthful in the light. Her smile was beatific.

He noticed the unfinished drink. "God," he thought, "she may be getting well."

The orchids grew down the sides of the only cliffs on Belsin. Belsin was a nearly flat planet with almost nothing to fall from. That, and the low gravity, made it a very safe place, as Edward had noted early in his life there.

The orchids were not orchids, were not even plants, but they looked somewhat like orchids. They were the outward flowerings of some obscure life form that, like the grass, seemed to go down to the center of the planet. You could not uproot an orchid any more than you could pull a blade of the grass loose from the surface; a thin but incredibly tenuous filament at the base of each of them went through solid obsidian down to a depth far below possible exploration or investigation. They were stunningly beautiful to see.

They glowed in shades of green and yellow with waving plumes and leaves shaped like enormous Japanese fans. They were both luminous and illuminated and they shifted as they moved from transparent to translucent to opaque.

When he stopped the jeep near the orchid cliffs, he heard a small cry from Myra and looked over to see her features in the familiar grimace of pain; riding that way had almost certainly been too much for her, even with Endolin.

Yet she sat up easily enough, though very slowly, and got out of the jeep. He did not offer to help; she had told him years before that she preferred doing things by herself when she could. By the time she was standing she was smiling again. As he came around to her side of the jeep he saw her casually emptying her drink on the ground at her feet, where it made several pools in the obsidian. She set the glass in the jeep.

They walked forward slowly. Both wore gum-rubber soles on their shoes, but the surface could be treacherous. She appeared to have recovered from the pain in the jeep; her walking was as certain as his own. Possibly steadier. "Myra," he said, "I think you're getting better." His voice was flat.

"It would be really something, Edward, not to be just a sick rich girl. To be able to do something besides lie around and take pills and try to get around the pain. It would be great to *work.*"

"Work?" he said. "At what?"

"I don't know," she said. "At anything. I could learn to be a pilot, or a librarian. You know, Edward, I'm not terribly smart. I think I could be very happy doing housework. Having children. Just being *busy* for the rest of my life, instead of living in my mind all the time."

"It's good to see you thinking about it," he said. But it wasn't.

He hated the whole idea. A sick Myra was bad enough; he did not want this chipper, nearly well one around to clutter up his life.

And the more well she became the harder it would be to kill her and to blame her death on the arthritis.

He looked toward the orchid observation platform. There was another couple standing there, and as they came closer Edward could see that the man was an engineer named Strang—one of the steadier, more reliable people from the plant. The girl was somebody from Accounting.

And it began to shape up for him then. The situation was really good. He had long suspected that the orchid cliffs were the best place for it. And here were the perfect witnesses. It was dark and everyone knew the orchid cliffs were dangerous at night. Myra had been drinking; the autopsy would show that.

It began to click off for him the way things did sometimes. He embellished it. As they approached the other couple enough to be overheard he said, "Myra, it's really strange of you to want to come out here like this. Maybe we shouldn't go to the cliffs. We can come back in daylight tomorrow . . ."

She laughed in a way that he hoped would sound drunken and said, "Oh, come on, Edward. I feel marvelous."

"Okay, darling. Anything you say." He spoke to her lovingly and then looked up to greet the other couple.

"Nice seeing you, Mr. MacDonnell," the engineer said. "The orchids are really fine by ringlight."

"I'd still rather be in bed," Edward said amiably. "But Mrs. MacDonnell wanted to come out here. She says she could dance till dawn."

Myra beamed at Strang and Strang and his girl nodded politely at her. Myra never saw people on Belsin. Arthritis had made her life sedentary, and even though Belsin had relieved the pain greatly she had never learned to be sociable. Most of her time was spent reading, listening to music, or puttering around the house.

"More power to you, Mrs. MacDonnell," Strang said. And then, as they went out on the ledge toward the staircase, "Careful out there, you two!"

There was a meandering walkway, partly carved from obsidian, partly constructed from moonwood, that ran along the cliff face toward a high waterfall. The steps were lighted by hidden electric lights and there was still ringlight from above. There was a safety rail, too, of heavy moonwood, waist high. But it was only a handrail and a person could slip under it. The thing could have been done better, but there was only so much human labor available on the planet for projects of that kind.

The two of them went slowly along the staircase, still in view of Strang and his girl. The light on the orchids was gorgeous. They could hear the sound of the waterfall. It was very cool. Myra was becoming excited. "My God," she said, "Belsin is really a lovely place. With the grass that sings, and the orchids." She looked up at the sky. "And those rings."

"Watch your step," he said. He looked back at Strang and waved. Then they went around the edge of a cliff, and along a wet obsidian wall where the light glared off the wetness and was for a moment almost blinding. For an instant he thought of pushing her off there, but they were too close to Strang: if there were a struggle it might be heard. They walked along a level place for a while. Myra would look across at the orchids on the other side, with their fans gently changing color in the night air and would gasp at the beauty of them. Sometimes she squeezed his arm strongly or hugged him in her excitement. He knew it was all beautiful, but it had never really touched him and it certainly wasn't touching him now. He was thinking coolly of the best way to kill Myra. And some part of him was second-guessing, thinking that it might not be bad to go on living with Myra if she got well, that it was cruel to think of killing her just when she was beginning to enjoy her life. But then he thought of her dumbness, of her innocence. He thought of her money.

Suddenly they came around a turn in the walkway and there was the waterfall. Part of it reflected the colors of the rings above. There was spray on his face. He looked down. Just ahead of them was a place where the obsidian was wet. The moonwood railing had been doubled at that point but there was still a distance of at least two feet from the bottom where a person could easily slip under. He looked farther down—straight down. The chasm was half a mile—the highest drop on Belsin.

He looked behind him. They could not be seen. *Okay,* he thought. *Best to be quick about it.*

He took her firmly by the arm, put his free arm around her waist.

She turned and looked at his face. Hers was calm, open. "You're going to kill me. Aren't you, Edward?" she said.

"That's right," he said. "I didn't think you knew."

"Oh, I knew all right," she said.

For a moment he was frightened. "Have you told anyone? Written anyone?"

"No."

"That's stupid of you. To tell me that. You could have lied."

"Maybe," she said. "But Edward, a part of me has always wanted to die. My kind of life is hardly worth the effort. I'm not sure that getting well would change that either."

They stood there like that by the waterfall for a full several minutes. He had her gripped firmly. It would only be a matter of putting one of his feet behind hers, tripping her and pushing her under the railing. She looked very calm and yet not passive. His heart was beating furiously. His skin seemed extraordinarily sensitive; he felt each drop of spray as it hit. The waterfall sounded very loud.

He stared down at her. She looked pathetic. "Aren't you frightened?" he said.

She did not speak for a moment. Then she said, "Yes, I'm frightened, Edward. But I'm not terrified."

He had to admit that she was taking it very well. "Would you rather jump?" he said. He could let go of her. There was no way she could outrun him. And he wanted no bruises from his hands on her arms, no shoe mark of his on her legs. Her body—what was left of her body—would be studied by the best criminologists from Earth; he could be sure her family would see to that. She'd be kept frozen in orbit until the experts got there.

Thinking of that, he looked up toward the sky. The rings had begun to fade. "No," Myra said. "I can't jump. It's too frightening. You'll have to push me."

"All right," he said, looking back to her.

"Edward," she said. "Please don't hurt me. I've always hated pain."

Those were her last words. She did not fight back. When he pushed her off she fell silently, in the low gravity, for a long,

long time before smashing herself on the obsidian at the bottom of the chasm.

As he looked up the rings appeared again, but only for a moment.

Getting her out with a helicopter and then making the statement and getting Strang and his girl to make their statements took all night. There was no police force and no "law" as such on Belsin, but the factory manager was Acting Magistrate and took testimony. Everyone appeared to believe Edward's story—that Myra was drunk and slipped—and condolences were given. Her body was put in a plastic capsule from a supply that had sat idle for years; she was the first person ever to die on Belsin.

Edward drove back at daybreak. His fatigue was enormous but his mind was calm. He had almost begun to believe the story himself.

As he approached the now empty house across the broad plain a remarkable thing began to happen: the grass began to sing again. Belsin grass was only known to sing in the evening. Never at dawn. But there it was singing as the first of the planet's two suns was coming up. And somehow—perhaps because of the clarity in the fatigue he felt—it seemed to him that the grass's song was almost comprehensible. It seemed to be singing to him alone.

He spent half the next day sleeping and the other half of it sitting in various rooms of the house, drinking gin. He did not miss Myra, nor did he feel guilty, nor apprehensive. He thought for a while, half-drunkenly, about what he would do, back on Earth as a rich, single man. He was still under forty; if he was lucky he would begin to inherit some of Myra's millions within a year.

There were still a few things to decide upon now and as he drank he thought about them from time to time: Should he continue running the Endolin plant while waiting for the inquest into Myra's death and for the ship that would take him back to Earth? If not, there was very little else to do on Belsin. He could spend some time exploring down south, where the obsidian was a light gray and where no Endolin had been found. He could sit around the house drinking, listen to some of Myra's records, watch TV from the tape library, work out in the basement gym. None of it really appealed to him and he began to fear the dullness of the wait. He wanted to be on Earth right now, at the heart of things, with bright lights, and variety and speed and money. He wanted his life to start moving fast. He wanted travel: loose and easy nights on gamier planets with well-dressed women, guitars playing. He wanted to buy new clothes on Earth, take an apartment in Venice, go to the races in the Bois de Boulogne. Then see the galaxy in style.

And then, as twilight came, he moved out onto the terrace to watch the setting of the second of Belsin's two small suns, and realized that the grass was singing again. Its sound was very faint; at first he thought it was only a ringing in his ears. He walked, drink in hand, to the railing at the end of the big moonwood terrace, walking softly in bare feet across the silvery surface, cool as always to the touch. Belsin, bare and nearly devoid of life as it was, could be—as Myra would say—lovely. He remembered Myra's falling, then, as in a dream. At one-half Earth gravity her body had fallen away from him slowly, slowly decreasing its size as it had lazily spun. She had not screamed. Her dress had fluttered upward in his direction as he stood there with his hands lightly on the wet railing of the Orchid Chasm.

Suddenly and surprisingly he began to see it from her falling-away point of view; looking up at himself standing there diminishing in size, seeing his own set features, his tan cotton shirt, blue jeans, his rumpled brown hair. His cold unblinking eyes looking down on himself, falling.

The grass was not really singing. It was talking. Whispering. For a shocked moment it seemed to him that it whispered, "Edward. Edward." And then, as he turned to go back into the house for another drink, "Myra is here. Edward, Myra is here."

Another very strong drink put him to sleep. He dreamed of himself in lines of people, waiting. Long, confusing lines at a cafeteria or a theater, with silent people and he among them also silent, impatient, trapped in an endless waiting. And he awoke sweating, wide awake in the middle of the Belsin night. Before his open eyes Myra fell, at a great distance from him now, slowly spinning. He could hear the sound of the waterfall. He sat up. He was still wearing his blue jeans.

It was not the waterfall; what he heard was the grass, whispering to him.

He pushed open the bedroom window. The grass was clearer now. Its voice was clearly speaking his name: "Edward," it said. "Edward. Edward."

Into his mind leaped the words from the old poem, studied in college:

> Why does your sword so drip wi' blood
> Edward, Edward?

The fuzziness of liquor had left him. His head was preternaturally clear. "What do you want?" he said.

"I want to talk," the grass said. Its voice was lazy, sleepy.

"Can't you be heard everywhere?"

"Do you fear overhearing?" The voice was fairly clear, although soft.

"Yes."

"I'm only speaking near the house." That was what he thought it said. The words were a bit blurred toward the end of the sentence.

"Near the house?" He pulled the window open wider. Moved closer. Then he sat on the edge of the bed by the window and leaned out into the night. Two small moons were up and he could see the grass. It seemed to be rippling, as though a slight, thin-aired wind were stroking it. The grass grew about two feet high and was normally a pale brown. The moonlight was like Earth moonlight; it made it look silver, the color of moonwood. He sat with his hands on his upper thighs, his bare feet on the floor carpeting, listening to the grass.

"Near the house, Edward," the grass said.

"And you're Myra?"

"Oh, yes, I'm Myra." There was a tone of gaiety in this, a hushed joyfulness in the whispering. "I'm Myra and I'm Belsin. I've become this planet, Edward."

"Jesus Christ!" he said. "I need a drink. And a cigarette."

"The cigarettes are in the kitchen cabinet," the grass said. "Come out on the terrace when you get them. I want to see you."

"See me?" he said.

"I can see with my rings," the voice said. Myra said.

He got up and padded into the kitchen. Strangely he did

not feel agitated. He was on some ledge somewhere in the middle of the quiet night, hung over and a wife-murderer, yet his soul was calm. He found the cigarettes easily, opened them, took one out and lit it. He poured a small amount of gin into a glass, filled it the rest of the way with orange juice, thinking as he did so of how far a distance from California that juice had come, to be drunk by him here in this steel kitchen in the middle of the night on a planet where the grass had become his wife. The whole planet was his wife. His ex-wife. He drank a swallow from the glass, after swishing it around to mix the gin in. The glow from it in his stomach was warm and mystical. He walked slowly, carrying his glass and his cigarette, out to the terrace.

"Ooooh!" the grass said. "I can see you now."

He looked up to the sky. "I don't see the rings," he said. "Your rings."

And then they appeared. Glowing pink and lavender, clearly outlined against the dim-lit sky. They disappeared.

"I'm only learning to show my rings," Myra said. "I have to thicken the air in the right place, so the light bends downward toward you." There was silence for a while. The grass had become clearer when it last spoke. It spoke again finally and was clearer still, so that it almost seemed as if Myra were sitting on the terrace next to him, her soft voice perfectly audible in the silent night. "There's a lot to learn, Edward."

He drank again. "How did it happen?" And then, almost blurting it out, "Are you going to tell people about what I did?"

"Goodness, Edward, I hadn't thought about that." The voice paused. "Right now I don't know."

He felt relieved. Myra had always been good-hearted, despite the self-pity. She usually gave the benefit of the doubt.

He sat silent for a while, looking at the vast plain in front of his eyes, concentrating on his drink. Then he said, "You didn't answer me, Myra. About how it happened."

"I know," the grass said. "I know I didn't. Edward, I'm not only Myra, I'm Belsin too. I am this planet and I'm learning to be what I have become." There was no self-pity in that, no complaint. She was speaking to him clearly, trying to tell him something.

"What I know is that Belsin wanted an ego. Belsin wanted someone to die here. Before I died and was . . . was taken in, Belsin could not speak in English. My grass could only speak to the feelings of people but not to their minds."

"The singing?" he said.

"Yes. I learned singing when Captain Belsin first landed. He carried a little tape player with him as he explored and played music on it. The grass learned . . . I learned to sing. He had headaches and took aspirin for them and I learned to make Endolin for him. But he never used it. Never discovered it." The voice was wistful, remembering something unpleasant. "I couldn't talk then. I could only feel some of the things that people felt. I could feel what happened to Captain Belsin's headache when he took aspirin and I knew how to improve on it. But I couldn't tell him to use it. That was found out later." The grass rippled and was still. It was darker now; one of the moons had set while they were talking.

"Can you bring up some more moons? So I can see you better? See the grass?" There were four moons.

"I'll try," Myra said. There was silence. Nothing happened. Finally Myra said, "No, I can't. I can't change their orbits."

"Thanks for trying," he said dryly. "The first person to die here would become the planet? Or merge with its mind? Is that it?"

"I think so," Myra said. He thought he could see a faint ripple on the word "think." "I became reincarnated as Belsin. Remember the rings lighting after you pushed me over?"

"Yes."

"I was waking up then. It was really splendid for me. To wake into this body. Edward," she said, "I'm so alive now, and vigorous. *And nothing about me hurts.*"

He looked away, back toward the silent house. Then he finished his drink. Myra's voice had been strong, cheerful. He had been calm—or had been *acting* calm—but something in his deep self was disturbed. He was becoming uneasy about all this. Talking with the grass did not disturb him. He was a realist, and if grass could talk to him in the voice of his dead wife he would hold conversation with grass. And Myra, clearly, wasn't dead—although her old, arthritic body certainly was. He had seen it as they brought it in from the helicopter; even in low gravity, falling onto jagged obsidian could lacerate and spatter.

"Do you hate me for what I did?" he said, fishing.

"No, Edward. Not at all. I feel . . . removed from you. But then I really always did. I always knew that you only allowed a small part of yourself to touch my life. And now," she said, "my life is bigger and more exciting. And I only need a small part of you."

That troubled him, sent a little line of fear across a ridge somewhere in his stomach. It took him a moment to realize that it was her word "need" that had frightened him.

"Why do you need me, Myra?" he said, carefully.

"To read to me."

He stared. "To read to you?"

"Yes, Edward. I want you to read from our library." They had brought several thousand books on microfilm with them. "And I'll want you to play records for me."

"My God!" he said. "Doesn't a whole planet have better things to do?"

The grass seemed to laugh. "Of course. Of course I have things to do. Just getting to know this body of mine. And I can sense that I am in touch with others—others like the Belsin part of me. Now that I have an ego—Myra's ego—I can converse with them. Feel their feelings."

"Well then," he said, somewhat relieved.

"Yes," she said. "But I'm still Myra, too. And I want to read. And I want music—honest, old-fashioned Earth music. I have this wonderful new body, Edward, but I don't have hands. I can't turn pages or change records. And I'll need you to talk to, from time to time. As long as I remain human. Or half human."

Jesus Christ! he thought silently. But then he began to think that if she had no hands, even needed him to run microfilm, that she could not stop him from leaving. She was only a voice, and rings, and ripples in the grass. What could she do? She couldn't alter the orbits of her moons.

"What about the other people here on Belsin?" he said, still careful with his words. "One of them might want to read to you. A younger man, maybe . . ."

This time her laughter was clearly laughter. "Oh no, Edward," she said. "I don't want them. It's you I want." There was silence for several long moments. Then she continued, "They'll be going back to Earth in a few months anyway. I've stopped making Endolin."

"Stopped . . . ?"

"When you were asleep. I was planning things then. I realized that if I stopped Endolin they would all go away."

"What about all those people on Earth who need it?" he said, trying to play on her sympathies. He did not give a damn, himself, for the pains of other people. That was why living with Myra had not really been difficult for him.

"They'll be making it synthetically before the supplies run out," she said. "It's difficult, but they'll learn. It would make people rich to find out how. Money motivates some people strongly."

He said nothing to that except "Excuse me" and got up and went into the kitchen for another drink. The sky was lightening; the first little sun would be up soon. He had never known Myra to think as clearly as she could think now. He shuddered and poured himself a bigger drink. Then, through the terrace doors, he heard her voice. "Come on back out, Edward."

"Oh, shut up!" he said and went over and slammed the doors shut and locked them. It was triply thick glass and the room became silent. He walked into the living room, with its brown-enameled steel walls and brown carpet and the oil paintings and Shaker furniture. He could hear the grass from the windows in there, so he closed them and pulled the thick curtains over them. It was silent. "Christ!" he said aloud and sat down with his drink to think about it.

Myra kept several antique plates on little shelves over the

television set. They were beginning to vibrate. And then, shockingly, he heard a deep bass rumbling and the plates fell to the floor and broke. The rumbling continued for a moment before he realized that it had been an earthquake. He was suddenly furious and he hung on to the fury, covering up the fear that had come with it. He got up and went through the kitchen to the terrace doors, flung them open into the still night. "For Christ's sake, Myra," he said, "what are you trying to do?"

"That was a selective tremor," the grass said. There was a hint of coyness in its tone. "I pushed magma toward the house and let a fissure fall. Just a tiny bit, Edward. Hardly any at all."

"It could have fallen farther?" he said, trying to keep the anger and the sternness in his voice.

"Lord, yes," Myra said. "That was only about a half on the Richter scale." He suddenly remembered that Myra had studied geology at Ohio State; she was well prepared to become a planet. "I'm pretty sure I could go past ten. With hardly any practice."

"Are you threatening to earthquake me into submission?"

She didn't answer for a minute. Then she said, pleasantly, "I want to keep you here with me, Edward. We're married. And I need you."

The earthquake had been frightening. But he thought of the supply ships and of the ship that would be bringing the people for the inquest. All he would have to do would be to lie to her, act submissive, and then somehow get on board the ship and away from Belsin before she earthquaked.

"And you want me to read aloud? Or run the microfilm for you?"

"Aloud, Edward," she said. "I'll let the others leave, but I want you to stay here. Here in the house."

"I'll have to get out every now and then."

"No, you won't," Myra said.

"I'll need food."

"I'm already growing it for you. The trees will be up in a few days. And the vegetables: carrots and potatoes and beans and lettuce. Even tobacco, Edward. But no liquor. You'll have to do without liquor once the supply is gone. But this place will be *lovely*. I'll have a lake for you and groves of fruit trees. I can grow anything—the way I grew Endolin before. This will be a beautiful place for you, Edward. A real Eden. And you'll have it all to yourself."

He thought crazily of Venice, of women, guitar music. Venice and Rome. Panicked suddenly, he said, "I can run away with the others. You can't earthquake us all to death. That would be cruel . . ."

"That's true enough," Myra said. "But if you leave this house I'll open a fissure under you and down you'll go." She paused a long moment. "Just like I did, Edward. Down and down."

He began to talk faster, louder. "What if they come to take me away, to force me to go back to Earth?"

"Oh, come on, Edward. Quit it. I won't let them ever get to the house. They'll go away eventually. And I'll never let anyone land again. Just swallow them up if they try it."

He felt terribly weary. He walked out onto the terrace and slumped onto the moonwood bench. Myra remained silent. He had nothing to say. He sipped his drink, letting his mind go blank. He sat there alone for a half hour. Or not really alone. It was beginning to dawn on him that he might never be alone again.

Then Myra spoke again, softly. "I know you're tired, Edward. But I don't sleep. Not anymore. I wonder if you would read to me a while. I was in the middle of *The King's Mistress*. If you'll switch the microfilm machine on you'll find my page."

"Christ!" he said, startled. "You can't *make* me read." There was something petulant in his voice. He could hear it and it disturbed him. Something of the sound of a small boy trying to defy his mother. "I want to have another drink and go back to bed."

"You know I don't like insisting," Myra said. "And you're perfectly right, Edward. I can't make you read. But I can shake the house and keep you awake." Abruptly the house shook from another tremor, probably a quarter of a point on the Richter scale. "And," Myra said, "I can grow food for you or not grow food for you. And I can give you what you want to eat or not give you what you want. I could feed you nothing but persimmons for a few months. And make the water taste terrible."

"Jesus Christ!" he said. "I'm *tired*."

"It'll only be a couple of chapters," Myra said. "And then maybe a couple of old songs on the player, and I'll go back to contemplating my interior and the other planets around here."

He didn't move.

"You'll be wanting me to grow tobacco for you. There are only a few cartons of cigarettes left." Edward smoked three packs a day. Three packs in a short Belsin day.

He still didn't move.

"Well," Myra said, conciliatory now. "I think I could synthesize a little ethyl alcohol. If I could do Endolin, I suppose I could do that too. Maybe a quart or so every now and then. A hundred ninety proof."

He stood up. He was terribly weary. "*The King's Mistress?*" he said.

"That's right!" the grass said, sweetly, joyfully. "I've always liked your voice, Edward. It'll be good to hear you read."

And then, before he turned to go into the house, to the big console that held thousands of books—thousands of dumb Gothic novels and books on gardening and cooking and self-improvement and a few technical books on geology—he saw everything get suddenly much lighter and looked up to see that the great rings of Belsin were now fully visible, bright as bands of sunlight in the abruptly brightened sky above his head. They glowed in full realization of themselves, illuminating the whole, nearly empty planet.

And Myra's voice came sighing joyfully in a great, horizon-wide ripple of grass. "Ooooooh!" it said happily. "Ooooooh!"

ECHO

"How many electrodes are there in that thing?" Arthur said.

Mel gave him an irritated look. "More than anyone could count, old buddy." He was checking some of the connections of the coils that went from the big tape recorder to the helmet; they were as profuse on the helmet as Medusa's snakes. Arthur and Mel had left the party upstairs to come down to Mel's basement laboratory. Mel taught paraphysics at the University.

"You mean you don't *know* how many there are? You put the fucker together and you don't know yourself?"

"*I* didn't put the fucker together, old buddy." Mel gave a jerk to the coil between his hands and somewhere deep in the recording device there was a *click*. "A Hewlett-Packard computer did. I only told it what to make, and it made it."

Arthur just stared at him. Then he took an annoyed swallow from the glass of whiskey in his hand. *These goddamn paraphysi-*

cists. It would be just like the sons of bitches not to want to know how many connections you had to make to record an entire human mind. But he said nothing. When Denise had talked him into doing this thing he had made enough objections. Such as, "Why me? Why should I be the guinea pig for some crazy attempt to make a recording of a whole personality?" Denise's answer had merely been, "Because Mel is your *friend*." And so on.

So he sat and drank his drink and watched Mel finish checking out the helmet and submitted quietly when Mel placed the heavy thing on his head. He could just barely see beneath and around dangling wires and he was wondering how long he would have to put up with it to please his wife and Mel when he heard and slightly saw Mel walk over to the recorder and heard him say, "Here we go, old buddy." Then he threw a switch. . . .

And Arthur awoke to a world askew and furred. Something was madly wrong with his vision, even though the wires were gone. His eyes could not encapsulate the scene for him; all he really saw were pale colors, pale lights, some slight movements. There were smells somewhere, too, but they made no sense: roses, maybe, and vinegar. Somebody somewhere was singing in Chinese, or Anglo-Saxon. He closed his eyes. Only one thing was certain. He had an erection. He went to sleep.

Even the dreams were not right. They seemed to be someone else's dreams.

Days passed. He woke from time to time, and was fed. Sometimes there were tall, slim people in the room with him. They spoke Chinese. Or Anglo-Saxon. Once a long-haired person spoke to him in strange English, "How are *you*, sir or madam?" He had no answer for that.

Finally he woke up and was able to focus his eyes and brain well enough to see that he was not in his own body. He learned that from his arms, which were hairless and chocolate. Was he a Black? A Polynesian? He did not feel as shocked as it seemed he should have felt. *Drugged? Very likely. Whom by? God knows.* He felt of his face. It was all wrong: the nose was too broad, the chin too soft, the ears were too big. *Why is it I'm not upset at this? Drugs?* But then he had been wanting to be dead for over a year, had been thinking of suicide with the intensity that some of his colleagues had when they thought of a promotion. So maybe whatever had happened to him didn't make any difference. If he didn't like it he could always kill himself. And there was no pain in whatever was going on. He felt all right.

A person in a sort of well-tailored red bathrobe came into the room. He was tall and thin and pale, and his face was smiling shyly. His hair was blond and straight and came down nearly to his waist. Or maybe it was a she. But then the person spoke and the voice was male. "How are *you* nowadays?" The man was smiling at him more broadly now.

"I'm okay," Arthur said. "But where am I? And who?" He held up his dark brown arm. "In this . . . body?"

The other man looked pleased. "It's artful," he said.

Arthur stared at him. "*Artful?*"

The man looked embarrassed. Then he said, "Artificial."

"Artificial?"

"Your body," the man said, with more confidence. "It is artificial now."

"For Christ's sake," Arthur said. And then, "I liked the other one well enough."

The man smiled sweetly. "Long dead," he said. "And rotten."

"Jesus Christ," Arthur said. "Jesus Christ."

He slept after that and the next day the long-haired man was there when he awoke. Arthur assumed that a day had passed because the man's bathrobe was yellow this time. Arthur had a question ready. "Where did this body come from?"

The man smiled at him with encouragement. "Cleveland."

He hadn't been ready for that. He felt he might never be ready for whatever this childlike and epicene person might tell him. "Did you grow this body in Cleveland, or something?"

"Or something is correct. We made you first in Cleveland in bodily form before we grew you big in here. The mind was poured into you. Poured into your pretty and always body." The man looked at him quizzically. "Bodies not made in Cleveland in your time?"

"In my time?"

"In your time of the world. When you was alive and well and running around."

Arthur continued to stare. "Is this the *future*?" he said.

The man shook his head. "It's only nowadays," he said. "Like always." Then he smiled. "And you was born in the twenty-second century anno domini, in crowded times and places?"

Arthur let out a heavy sigh. Then he said, "Can you get me a drink? With whiskey or gin? Ethyl alcohol?"

The man did not seem to understand.

"An intoxicating drink."

The man smiled again. "I understand that thing. And yes, I will." He turned to leave the room. "Not the twenty-second century anno domini?"

"The twentieth," Arthur said in a voice near a whisper. Finally it was all coming down on him. "What century is this?"

The man turned and smiled at him before he left the room. "The forty-seventh," he said. "Anno domini."

The drink turned out to be a sort of screwdriver—spiked orange juice. It was in a simple glass that did not look at all futuristic. After Arthur drank it, he said, "How did I get here? In this body from . . . from Cleveland?"

"Refrigerator," the man said. "We found a refrigerator, all wrapped and sealed underground where a city was. With a tape of you inside. Under rubble. From time so far and distant long agone so hard to tell."

From time so far and distant long agone. . . . "Have you a name?" Arthur asked.

"Yes. I am always Ben."

"Ben?"

"Yes. Always Ben."

Arthur began to sit up for the first time. It was not as difficult as he had feared it might be. He felt fairly strong. "What kind of tape, Ben?"

"Oh, machine tape. Ancient computer tape," Ben said. "They had all of you all over on the tape. Except a body."

Arthur had already figured that one out. Some time or other, even years after that night with the thing on his head, Mel had stuck that tape in a refrigerator for some reason. And twenty-seven centuries later somebody had dug it out, freakishly preserved, and figured out what it was: a record of the memory, mind, imagination, personality, lusts, ambitions, neuroses and everything else of Arthur Franks. Then somebody had gotten some kind of artificial body from a factory in Cleveland and had played the tape into it. And here he was, reconstructed from some point before his life's end. Somewhere out in this strange world the dust of his first life lay; he was now being given a chance to live out the last part of that life again. If he wanted to.

How long had he lived, a near-suicide, back in the twentieth century? Had he killed himself?

"You found me as a recording," he said. "Without a body."

"Yes," Ben said. "And as a student of the ancient tongue of English and of old times long agone I had you made especially a body. To have a thing to put the tape into so then to talk with me. As we indeed are doing now."

"Do you know anything more about me? Like when I . . . died? Or about my wife?"

Ben looked sad, his normally smooth forehead wrinkling. "Sorry always." Then he smiled. "All I know for sure and always is America was home for you."

"Okay," Arthur said. Maybe it was better not to know what had become of himself—of that other himself. "Is there still an America?"

Ben continued smiling. "Two. One north and one is always south."

"That's good to know," Arthur said. "Could I have another drink?"

The bathroom was much like a twentieth-century one except that the water from the taps was scented and the light coming from the ceiling was like daylight—yellowish and very pleasant to his eyes. Over the sink was a mirror.

He stood and stared at himself for several minutes, shocked.

He was very Negroid and very handsome, with a short Afro of glossy black hair, a broad nose, generous ears, thick lips and clear eyes. His shoulders were broad and the chest beneath them was smooth, hairless, and powerful. His stomach was flat, his arms well muscled but soft-looking, like a woman's.

He stood back to see himself full length. His body was perfect; there wasn't a blemish on it. He looked at his face again—his new face—and smiled. *What the hell*, he thought, *this beats suicide.*

Later, when Arthur was able to walk a little each day, Ben brought others. Some were apparently women—very calm, straightforward types, like Ben. But none of them spoke English. They smiled a lot. They were all nice-looking, but a bit forceless, passive; and they all seemed young. He wondered if they had some way of staying young-looking whatever their ages. Probably so. Or maybe their bodies came from another factory in Cleveland.

He liked the sounds of the women's voices, more like Chinese than Anglo-Saxon, soft and slurred in speech and with musical pitch. Sometimes they sang. He liked the way they moved around and looked over at him, in his bed, from time to time, with curiosity but with no hint of flirtatiousness.

Outside the room's only window, where the view was of an empty field and, beyond that, a dark row of trees, it was raining heavily under an iron-colored sky. There was no work of human building to be seen from that window, only grass and sky and the line of trees.

Ben left the room for a while and returned with another

woman, different from the others, and stood with her near the door and talked for a moment. Arthur looked at her. She was dressed like the others in some kind of a tan robe. But her hair was cut short and her face had a puzzled animation about it and a sense of some quality—urgency maybe—that was missing in the others. She had very pale skin and auburn hair; she was tall and her figure was splendid.

Ben brought her over and introduced her to him as Annabel. Surprisingly, she spoke English. He was astonished at this at first, until she smiled and said, "Ben tells me I'm from the same century you're from. We thought it was the twenty-second at first."

"Don't you remember?" Arthur said.

"No," she said, "I don't remember. Something about the way the tapes were played into this body, Ben says. I know how to speak, but I don't remember a thing . . ." She looked toward Ben.

"It is always amnesia," Ben said. "She was the first to be made from ancient tapes a year ago. But the tapes were not right for her brain so she forgot it all. She forgot all the time long agone when she lived before. Then we made you and did always better with your tape."

"Maybe it's best not to remember," Arthur said.

She smiled at him wistfully. "Still I'd like to know. I don't even know what my name was. I'd like you to tell me about our time—the twentieth century—and maybe it'll help me remember."

"Sure," Arthur said. "What do you want to know?"

For several weeks she came to his room at breakfast and asked questions. He told her about cities and government and clothing and animals and the way things looked and how people lived. But none of it touched her memory. Arthur liked her, and there seemed at times something familiar about her. It made sense that there would be, since she had probably been taped by Mel—possibly after the same dinner party, after he himself had been "copied" onto the tapes. She could be Denise. Except she wasn't, and he knew that. Maybe she was the wife of someone he knew, some woman he had talked to briefly once and then forgot about. She was clearly as intelligent as he, and as quick; her vocabulary was excellent. And her personality— something about her personality sometimes haunted him. He would be drinking coffee with her and would happen to look at her hand holding the cup or at the way she brought the cup to her lips and there would be something terribly familiar about it. But he could not place it. It was like *déjà vu*.

On his first day outside, with Ben gently helping him walk on wobbly legs, the thing he felt most was the clarity and cleanness of the outside air. It was a spring morning, with small leaves on the trees by the door of the building; on the grass near the door a thick robin stood attentive, its ear cocked toward the ground. A small white dog scampered as such dogs always had toward a hill and then disappeared from view. There was a warm breeze, riffling his kinky hair.

Arthur walked a few yards, then turned to look at the building he had just left for the first time. It seemed to be made of green stone, with a slightly peaked green roof, and large

windows. Except for the green color it could have been a
large bank from downtown St. Louis or Denver. There were
five other buildings, more or less like it, making a complex,
with gray rubbery walkways between them. At a distance two
long-haired men walked hand in hand in quiet conversation
from one building to another, one of them smoking a cigarette.
Arthur's heart was light, his stomach fluttery with the warmth
of the day and the sense of the new. They walked around the
building and Arthur stood and looked toward the dark green
line of woods in the distance and then they went back inside;
he was still too weak to walk anymore. But he could tell that
the body he inhabited was healthy and youthful and would
soon be strong. There were firm muscles under the brown skin;
his arms and legs were straight, well formed; and there were
good, springy arches in his feet. His hands were capacious and
wise; he could sense the power, the aptitude and heft, of them.

The next day he and Annabel went for a walk, going about a
third of the way down the gray path toward the woods before
he became too tired to go further.

They said little. For a few moments he took her hand, but he
sensed something in her that stiffened when he did so. Somehow, he felt no desire for her, even though she was clearly a
lovely woman, and he could not understand why. There was
nothing wrong with his sexuality in this new and young body;
even in his old, haggard and soft one there had been no problems there. He had always been a strong lover; that alone had
kept him going for years against the tide of his old life that had
pulled so strongly in other ways toward death. Toward drink,
and guilt, and alienation and despair.

But Annabel with her fine breasts and firm round ass did
not turn him on. He could not understand it.

Later, in his room, when she was in a chrome-and-leather chair and he was lying against the pillows in bed, he tried talking about it. "If this were a movie," he said, "we would be falling in love by now."

She looked toward him thoughtfully. "I suppose so. I think I may be homosexual. A lesbian."

He looked at her. What she said seemed true. Maybe that explained his lack of feeling toward her. "Do you find the women here attractive?"

"No," she said, and then smiled at him. "I bet you don't either."

He smiled back. "No, I don't," he said. And then, "Why don't you come over here and kiss me on the mouth? It couldn't hurt anything."

"Okay," she said and got up. She walked over toward him, seated herself on the edge of the bed, bent over slowly, and kissed him, with her mouth open and soft. At first he felt almost nothing, as though he were kissing the smooth palm of his own hand. But they held the kiss and, gradually, he felt an excitement begin in his stomach. It was a different feeling from what he was used to; there was some kind of very strong and frightening power to it. He continued kissing her, working his lips a bit now but not using his tongue and not reaching his hands toward her breasts that hung down over his chest. There *was* some great power there; but something in him would not let him yield to it. There was something he was afraid of. He pulled away from her, and looked up. Her face was very serious and just a bit frightened.

"Something is scaring me," he said quietly.

"Me too," she said. "I think I'd better go."

She got up from the bed and left the room without saying good-bye. He lay there silently for a long while, thinking of her. Somewhere in his stomach there was still a ribbon of unpleasantness—of fear. But the fear was being buried by the excitement of desire, becoming indistinguishable from it.

In the middle of that night he was awakened by her wet mouth kissing his breasts, under the sheet. He could smell the faint smell of sweat from her warm body—had been smelling it even while asleep. It aroused him immediately. Then without saying a word she moved her head down to him and took him in her mouth. Still in his stomach was the ribbon of fear, but the excitement, the movement toward ecstasy, buried it. And he exploded into her mouth, beneath the sheet. She stayed with him, holding his hips, for only a minute afterward and then left, padding slowly—somehow, it seemed, thoughtfully—out of the room in bare feet, leaving him alone in bed. Neither of them had said a word.

He did not see her the next morning at breakfast; for several days she had been joining him for the farrago of oats and wheat and honey that a silent male nurse brought him every morning together with a yellow cup full of powerful, astringent coffee. Nor did she join him for his lunch of odd-looking vegetables and what he thought of as "Mystery Soup."

Ben dropped in on him after lunch for a conversation about twentieth-century America; Arthur told him about movies and cars. His heart wasn't in it; he could not get Annabel off his mind.

"Are there still cars?" he asked Ben.

"Oh, no. Very little mechanical nowadays."

"How do you travel?"

"Walking. Always walking," Ben said. "Sometimes we use a flyer, for traveling long."

"Is a flyer an airplane?"

"Somewhat," Ben said. "But no motor and no jets."

"How does it work?"

"Nobody knows," Ben said. "No need to know."

"Who does the cooking around here?"

"Cooking?" Ben said.

"Yes. Preparing food to eat." He almost said "always" before "eat."

"Food is always assembled," Ben said. "Assembled from little atoms by the cooker. Like clothes and buildings."

"Oh," Arthur said, and thought *Jesus.* "Then nobody does any work?"

"I study things. Always ancient America. Others study things. And we talk a lot."

"And that's all you do?"

Ben smiled at him benignly. "Always."

"I've never seen any children around, Ben. Do you have children in other places?"

"No. No children. And there are only very few and small other places and no children there. Only big ones like you and me."

"Then what . . . ? Then how do you reproduce?"

Ben smiled and shook his head. "Oh, we never reproduce. We always live ourselves. Always."

"You're *immortal*?"

"Oh, of course," Ben said. "We live forever. And you indeed will live forever too in that strong body."

"Jesus," he said aloud and lay back against the pillows. And then, "Don't you get *bored*?"

"Oh, sure," Ben said. "But it goes away. And we forget a lot and always learn things over."

"How old are you, Ben?"

Ben shook his head. "I never know at all how old. Centuries. Someday I'll die myself by fire as others do and that will be an end."

"Then someday you'll tire of it and kill yourself. And that's been happening for some time now and there aren't many left."

Ben smiled dolefully, his youthful and bland face registering a kind of pleasant painfulness. "That's all there is to know," he said.

Ben turned to leave, walking out of the room with his loose-jointed gait, his long hair covering his narrow shoulders and back. At the door he stopped and turned back toward Arthur. "Long life is good enough for most," he said, "and death is not so bad."

Arthur said nothing. When Ben was gone he began working at the room's little table on the chess set he was making from a soft material like Styrofoam. He was using a knife that Ben had gotten him, and he began working on the most difficult pieces, the knights, carving them with a great deal of care.

When he had finished the first one and had begun to copy it for the second, Annabel came in. She was wearing a green robe and she looked beautiful to him.

At first he did not know what to say. Then he looked at her and said, "Thanks. Thanks for last night."

"Sure," she said. "It was strange. But I liked it."

"Then you aren't a lesbian," he said, trying to make his voice light but feeling some kind of embarrassment in it. He set the unfinished piece and the knife on the desk in front of him and swiveled in the chair to see her better. She was tall and fair-skinned—a beautiful woman. "Would you like to take a walk?" he said. "I think I could make it to the woods."

She was silent for a minute. Then she said, "Sure." She walked over to the table and carefully, thoughtfully, picked up the finished piece and held it between thumb and forefinger. "This is a knight," she said.

He stared at her. "How did you know that?" Chess did not exist, as far as he had been able to find out, in this world. Ben's people did not play games. "It's a twentieth-century thing."

"I don't know," she said. "I really don't. I just know it's called a knight."

"Do you know what 'chess' means?" he said.

"'Chess'?" She said the word carefully. "No. No, I don't."

He shook his head and then took the piece from her and set it down by the finished pawns. "Let's take that walk."

While they were walking and he had his hands in the pockets of his robe and his eyes down on the strange plastic shoes he had been given, he said, "Ben tells me I'll be very strong when my body has a chance to . . . to ripen or whatever it is."

"Do you look the way you looked before? In your other life?" she said.

"No," he said. "God, no. I was white, and middle-aged. A professor of chemistry and getting pot-bellied."

"Yes," she said. "I have no idea what I looked like, but I know it wasn't like this." She extended her long and pale arms from her sides, palms upward, and looked earnestly at him. "I know I'm entirely different now from what I once was."

"It's a strange feeling," he said. "Still, the way you look now is fine by me." But that wasn't exactly true; there was a touch of idle and self-assuring flattery in it. She was beautiful enough, but he still was not at ease with her beauty. Something about it haunted him as though at times there were superimposed upon her face and body another face and body, from his past, very faint but disquieting.

He did make it to the woods, although he was tired when he got there. Ben had told him it would take months to get the full strength of his new body. The body had been cloned from synthetic, composite genes, but it had never been exercised and its muscles were soft and new.

In the woods they sat on a fallen log and smoked the odd-tasting cigarettes that Ben supplied them with. Then they began to make love, slowly and cautiously, first with their hands and then with their mouths. He brought her to a light orgasm in the spotted daylight that filtered through old trees, while she sat on the log dreamily and he kneeled in front of her. After that they found a grassy clearing with dry ground and lay together. Somehow they were perfectly matched, and knew exactly what to do for each other.

But then, as he was beginning to feel the oncoming orgasm, she looked down on him from her position above him and said, "Jesus, do I love this." The words fell somehow like lead on his spirit and he became suddenly afraid, frozen in his movements. The same fear came in her face. They stared at each other while his soul shrank from her. He did not know what had happened; he only knew that her words—words that were somehow terribly familiar to him—had frightened him. Forest light flecked her beautiful and glowing skin; her fine breasts were warm

in his upward-reaching hands; somewhere a bird was singing jubilantly, and wind rustled the leaves of the trees. Inside
himself he was cold, trembling. He rolled out from under her
and lay on the grass in turmoil—frightened and angry. "What
happened?" he said.

"I don't know. I said that, and something went wrong. I don't
know."

He shook his head. "Maybe it's these new bodies," he said.
"Maybe we'll have to just get used to them."

She shook her head and said nothing.

He did not see her for several days and was relieved not to. He
spent the time easily enough—when he was not troubled by
thinking about her—finishing his chess set, exercising lightly,
and wandering through the building where he lived.

On the third day Ben and another man whose only English
was the word "Hello" took him to the far end of the building to
a laboratory. There were four large tanks, coffin-like and bright
green, lined up along one wall. Ben walked over to the second
of these from the left, set his long-fingered hand on its lid, and
said, "This is where we grew your self for years."

Arthur walked over to it and Ben lifted the hinged lid for
him. Inside it was like a large, green bathtub, with about half a
dozen little metal pipes entering it on one side. "How long was
I in this thing?" he asked.

"Three years," Ben said. "No way to go faster."

"Was it difficult to play the tape into . . . into me?"

Ben smiled and shook his head. "Oh, yes," he said. "We did
it wrong two times. First we had the body wrong and next the
tape. But then we got you always right and here you stand."

Then he looked at the other man with him, who was apparently some kind of technician, and the other nodded toward Ben with a faint smile.

Arthur started to pursue this but Ben, abruptly for him, turned and walked over to one of the consoles and took from an otherwise empty shelf a box about the size of a candy box, walked back to Arthur and handed it to him. "Here is your soul," he said, softly.

Arthur took the box in both hands. "My tape?" he said.

"Of course," Ben said. "Your ancient tape. Your soul."

Arthur opened the box with care. Inside was a full plastic reel with a label that read "Advent Corporation. Boston, Mass." And under that someone had written with a ballpoint pen, "Arthur Franks."

That evening he finished his chess set and then made a board by ruling the sixty-four squares on a sheet of white, flexible plastic and darkening half of them with what seemed to be a Magic Marker. It was late and he was tired, but he set the pieces up, the white ones on his side of the board, and began to play King's Gambit against the black, using Morphy's way of sacrificing the king's knight for a heavy attack on black's kingside. It was strange to see his brown arm and hand moving chess pieces around on a board; he thought he had become used to his new color—even liked it—but it was a shock to see himself in this old context; he had been captain of his chess club in high school and when other kids had been out shooting basketball or stealing hubcaps or whatever, he had sat in his room at home working out variations of chess attacks. But with a thin white arm, a pale hand on the pieces—not this smooth and chocolate arm with the big and nimble hand at the end of it.

Outside the window was a nearly full moon in a jet-black sky. The window was open, and warm air, hinting of summer nights, filled the room. He could hear the shrill sounds of tree frogs and somewhere a cricket.

Then the door opened quietly and Annabel walked in. He turned to look at her. She was barefoot, dressed in a white robe. Her hair had been pulled back and was tied behind her head, framing her face. She was lovely. He felt tense, frightened. "What do you want?" he said.

"I wanted to make love the way I did before. I thought you would be asleep." Each word came to him as if it had been spoken for him before, as if he had thought it just before she said it. *Déjà vu.* He shook his head, trying to shake it off.

"No," he said, "I don't want that right now."

"I know," she said. She took off her robe and sat on the edge of the bed. "I think we ought to start where we left off yesterday."

He stared at her as she lay back, naked, against a pillow. "I don't know if I can . . ."

"Yes, you can," she said. "That was only a barrier for us. We've crossed it now."

"I was thinking something like that myself," he said. He came over and sat beside her on the bed.

"Sure you were," she said. "We're really very much alike. We think the same things."

He slipped off his sandals. "You're really something," he said.

"So are you," she said.

She was right. The barrier or whatever it was had fallen. The fear had subsided. The pleasure of lovemaking was different from what it had been before for him, with other women he had had. It was very inward, very intense. He hardly looked at her.

When he climaxed something seemed to open up inside him. There was a sense of release in a secret part of himself, at the center of his aching and suicidal life. His eyes were shut and he heard himself laughing, immersing himself in himself.

He lay back afterward, spent and blissful. They did not speak, nor did they look at one another. He stared at the moon outside the window, the early summer moon, as cold and luminous and clear in the black sky as was his soul within himself.

They slept together that night for the first time. Not touching, but naked together in the same bed, each turned to the right in a nearly fetal position, like a pair of twins.

In the morning they awoke silently together and silently drank coffee, sitting side by side in bed. There seemed to be no need to speak.

And then, as they were drinking their second cup of coffee, she began looking at something on the other side of him and he saw that it was the chessboard, still set up from the night before. She was looking at it intently and her eyes began to widen.

"What is it?" he said. "Is something wrong?"

"That's the King's Gambit," she said. "Morphy's Attack."

Something prickled at the back of his neck and he heard a tremor in his own voice. *"Yes, it is,"* he said.

"And the next move is bishop takes bishop's pawn." She turned and stared at him, her eyes wide and her lips trembling.

"Yes," he said. "Bishop takes bishop's pawn. . . . Not many people know that."

"I've known it since high school," she said. "Grover Cleveland High School. Where I was . . ."

"Captain of the chess team." His voice was like gravel in his throat. His heart was pounding and his mouth was dry. "Ben's mistake," he said, whispering because his dry mouth made him whisper it. "You're Ben's wrong body."

And she whispered too. "I'm Arthur Franks," she said.

"Oh Jesus," he said. "Oh sweet Jesus." He lay back in bed and stared at the ceiling for a long while. And then, later, when a calmness had come into him and he let his hand reach out slowly and gently and let it fall sensuously upon her smooth and cool thigh he felt, at exactly the same instant, her hand soft and sexual upon his own thigh. "Oh, yes," he said aloud, softly. "Oh, yes."

And he heard her say it too. "Oh, yes. Oh, yes."

OUT OF LUCK

It was only three months after he had left his wife and children and moved in with Janet that Janet decided she had to go to Washington for a week. Harold was devastated. He tried not to let her see it. The fiction between them was that he had left Gwen so he could grow up, change his life and learn to paint again. But all he was certain of was that he had left Gwen to have Janet as his mistress. There were other reasons: his recovery from alcoholism, the years he had wasted his talent as an art professor, and Gwen's refusal to move to New York with him. But none of these would have been sufficient to uproot him and cause him to take a year's leave from his job if Janet had not worn peach-colored bikini panties that stretched tightly across her lovely ass.

He spent the morning after she left cleaning up the kitchen and washing the big pot with burned zucchini in it. Janet had made him three quarts of zucchini soup before leaving on the shuttle, along with two jars of chutney, veal stew in a blue casserole dish, and two loaves of Irish soda bread. It was very international. The mess in the tiny kitchen of her apartment took him two hours to clean up. Then he cooked himself a breakfast of scrambled eggs and last night's mashed potatoes, fried with onions. He drank two cups of coffee from Janet's Chemex. Drinking the coffee, he walked several times into the living room where his easel stood and looked at the quarter-done painting. Each time he looked at it his heart sank. He did not want to finish the painting—not that painting, that dumb, academic abstraction. But there was no other painting for him to paint right now. What he wanted was Janet.

Janet was a very successful folk art dealer. They had met at a museum party. She was in Washington now as a consultant to the National Gallery. She had said to him, "No, I don't think you should come to Washington with me. We need to be apart from each other for a while. I'm beginning to feel suffocated." He had nodded sagely while his heart sank.

One problem was that he distrusted folk art and Janet's interest in it, the way he distrusted Janet's fondness for her cats. Janet talked to her cats a lot. He was neutral about cats themselves, but he felt people who talked to them were trivial. And being interested in badly painted nineteenth-century portraits also seemed trivial to him now.

He looked at the two gold-framed American primitives above Janet's sofa, said, "Horseshit!" and drew back his mug in a fantasy of throwing coffee on them both.

Across from the apartment, on Sixty-third Street, work-men were renovating an old mansion; they had been at it three months before, when Harold had moved in. He watched them for a minute now, mixing cement in a wheelbarrow, and bringing sacks of it from a truck at the corner of Madison Avenue. Three workmen in white undershirts held sunlit discourse on the plywood ramp that had replaced the building's front steps. Behind windows devoid of glass he could see men moving back and forth. But nothing happened; nothing seemed to change in the building. It was the same mess it had been before, like his own spiritual growth: lots of noise and movement and no change.

He looked at his watch, relieved. It was ten-thirty. The morning was half over and he needed to go to the bank. He put on a light jacket and left.

As he was waiting in a crowd at the Third Avenue light he heard a voice shout "Taxi!" and a man pushed roughly past him, right arm high and waving, onto the avenue. The man was about thirty, in faded blue jeans and a sleeveless sweater. A taxi squealed to a stop at the corner and the man conferred with the driver for a moment before getting in. He seemed to be quietly arrogant, preoccupied with something. Harold could have kicked him in the ass. He did not like the man's look of confidence. He did not like his sandy, uncombed hair.

The light changed and the cab took off fast, up Third Avenue.

Harold crossed and went into the bank. He went to a table, quickly made out a check to cash for a hundred, then walked over toward the line. Halfway across the lobby, he stopped cold. The man in the sleeveless sweater was standing in line, holding a checkbook. His lips were pursed in silent whistling. He was wearing the same faded blue jeans and—Harold now noticed—Adidas.

He was looking idly in Harold's direction. Harold averted his eyes. There were at least ten other people waiting behind the man. He had to have been here awhile. An identical twin?

A mild hallucination, making two similar people look exactly alike? Harold got in line. After a while the man did his business and left. Harold cashed his check and left, stuffing five twenties into his billfold. Another drain on the seven thousand he had left Michigan with. He had seven thousand to live on for a year in New York, with Janet, while he learned to paint again, to be the self-supporting artist his whiskey dreams had been filled with. Whiskey had left him unable to answer the telephone or open the door, in Michigan. That had been two years ago. Whiskey had left him sitting behind closed suburban blinds at two in the afternoon, reading the J. C. Penney catalog and waiting for Gwen to come home from work. Well. He had been free of whiskey for a year and a half now. First the hospital, then A.A.; now New York and Janet.

He walked back toward her apartment, thinking of how his entire bankroll of seven thousand could not pay Janet's rent for three months. And she had taken this big New York place after two years of living in an even larger apartment in Paris. On a marble-topped lingerie chest in one of the bathrooms was a snapshot of her, astride a gleaming Honda, on the Boulevard des Capucines by the ironwork doorway of that apartment. When that photograph was taken Harold had been living in a ranch house in Michigan and was driving a Chevrolet.

He glanced down Park Avenue while crossing it and saw a sleeveless sweater and faded jeans, from the back, disappearing into one of the tall apartment buildings. He shuddered and quickened his pace. He shifted his billfold from a rear to a front pocket, picturing those pickpockets who bump you from behind and rob you while apologizing, on the streets of New York. His mother—his very protective mother—had told him about that twenty years before. Part of him loved New York, loved its action and its anonymity, along with the food and clothes and bookstores. Another part of him feared it. The sight of triple locks on apartment doors could frighten him, or of surly Puerto Ricans with well-muscled arms, carrying their big, noisy, arrogant radios. Their kill-the-Anglo radios. The slim-hipped black men frightened him, with long, tight-assed trousers in pale colors, half covering expensive shoes—Italian killer shoes. And there were drunks everywhere. In doorways. Poking studiously through garbage bins for the odd half-eaten pizza slice, the usable worn shirt. Possibly for emeralds and diamonds. Part of him wanted to scrub up a drunk or two, with a Brillo pad, like the zucchini pan. Something satisfying in that.

The man in the sweater had been white, clean, non-menacing. Possibly European. Yet Harold now, crossing Madison, felt chilled by the thought of him. Under the chill was anger. That spoiled, arrogant face, that sandy hair! He hurried back to Janet's apartment building, walked briskly up the stairs to the third floor, let himself in. There in the living room stood the painting. He suddenly saw that it could use a sort of rectangle of pale green, like a distant field of grass, right there. He picked up a brush, very happy to do so. Outside the window, the sun was shining brightly. The workmen on the building were busy. Harold was busy.

He worked for three solid hours and felt wonderful. It was good work too, and the painting was coming along. At last.

For lunch he made himself a bacon and tomato sandwich on toast. It was simple midwestern fare and he loved it.

When he had finished eating, he went back into the living room, sat in the black director's chair in front of the window and looked at the painting by afternoon light. It looked good—just a tad spooky, the way he wanted it to be. It would be a good painting after all. It was really working. He decided to go to a movie.

The movie he wanted to see was called *Out of Luck*. It was a comedy from France, advertised as "an hilarious sex farce," with subtitles. It sounded fine for a sunny fall afternoon. He walked down Madison toward the theater.

There were an awful lot of youthful, well-dressed people on Madison Avenue. They probably all spoke French. He looked in the windows of places with names like Le Relais, La Bagagerie, Le Bijou. He would have given ten dollars to see a J. C. Penney's or a plain barber shop with a red and white barber's pole.

As he was crossing Fifty-seventh Street, traffic-snarled as usual, there was suddenly the loud *harrumphing* of a pair of outrageously noisy motorcycles and with a rush of hot air two black Hondas zoomed past him. From the back the riders appeared to be a man and a woman, although the sexual difference was hard to detect. Each wore a spherical helmet that reflected the sun; the man's helmet was red, the other green. Science fiction helmets, they hurt the eyes with reflected and dazzling sunlight. There was a smell of exhaust. Each of the riders, man and woman, was wearing a brown sleeveless sweater and blue jeans. Each wore Adidas over white socks. Their shirts were short-sleeved, blue. So had been the shirts of the man in the taxi and the man in line at Chemical Bank. Harold's stomach twisted. He wanted to scream.

The cyclists disappeared in traffic, darting into it with insouciance, tilting their black bikes first this way and then that, as though merely leaning their way through the congestion of taxis and limousines and sanitation trucks.

Maybe it was a fad in dress. Maybe coincidence. He had never noticed before how many people wore brown sleeveless sweaters. Who counted such things? And everyone wore jeans. He was wearing jeans himself.

The movie was at Fifty-seventh and Third. The theater had only a scattering of people in it, since it was the middle of the afternoon. The story was about a woman who was haunted by the gravelly voice of her dead lover—a younger man who had been killed in a motorcycle accident. She was a gorgeous woman and went through a sequence of affairs, breaking up with each new lover after the voice of her old, dead one pointed out their flaws to her, or distracted her while making love. It really was funny. Sometimes, though, it made Harold edgy, when he thought of the young lover Janet had had before him, who had disappeared from her life in some way he, Harold, did not know about. But several times he laughed loudly.

And then, toward the end of the movie, her lover reappeared, apparently not dead at all. It was on a quiet Paris street. She was out walking with an older man she had just slept with, going to buy some coffee, when a black Honda pulled up to the curb beside her. She stopped. The driver pulled off his helmet. Harold's heart almost stopped beating and he stared crazily. There in front of him, on the CinemaScope movie screen, was the huge image of a youngish man with sandy hair, a brown sleeveless sweater, blue shirt, Adidas. The man smiled at the woman. She collapsed in a faint.

When the man on the motorcycle spoke, his voice was as it had been when it was haunting her: gravelly and bland. Harold wanted to throw something at the screen, wanted to scream at the image, "Get out of here, you arrogant fucker!" But he did nothing and said nothing. He stayed in his seat, waiting for the movie to end. It ended with the woman getting on the dead lover's motorcycle and riding off with him. He wouldn't tell her where he lived now. He was going to show her.

Harold watched the credits closely, wanting to find the actor who had played the old lover. His name in the film had been Paul. But no actor was listed for the name of Paul. The others were there, but not Paul. *What in God's name is happening?* Harold thought. He left the theater and, hardly daring to look around himself on the bright street, flagged down a cab and went home. Could a person hallucinate a character into a movie? Was the man at the bank in fact a French movie actor? Twelve years of drinking could fuck up your brain chemistry pretty badly. But he hadn't even had the D.T.s. His New York psychiatrist had told him he was badly regressed at times, but his sanity had never been in question.

In the apartment he was able, astonishingly, to get back into the painting for a few hours. He made a few changes, making it spookier. *He* felt spookier now and it came out onto the canvas. The painting was nearly done. When he stopped, it was eight o'clock in the evening. The workmen across the street had finished their day hours before. They had packed up their tools and had gone home to Queens or wherever. The building, as always, was unchanged; its doorways and windows gaped blankly. There was a pile of rubble by the plywood entry platform where there had always been a pile of rubble.

He went into the kitchen, ignored the veal stew Janet had made for him and lit the oven. Then he took a Hungry Man chicken pie out of the freezer, ripped off the cardboard box, stabbed the frozen top crust a few times with her Sabatier, slipped it into the oven and set the timer for forty-five minutes.

He went back into the living room, looked again at the painting. "Maybe I needed the shit scared out of me," he said aloud. But the thought of the man in the sweater chilled him. He went over to the hutch in the corner, opened its left door, flipped on the little Sony TV inside. Then he crossed the big room to the dry sink and began rummaging for candy. He kept candy in various places.

He found a couple of pieces of butterscotch and began sucking on one of them. Back in the kitchen he opened the oven door a moment, enjoying the feel of the hot air. His little Hungry Man pie sat inside, waiting for him.

There had been a man's voice on television for a minute or so, reciting some kind of disaster news. A California brush fire or something. There in the kitchen Harold began to realize that the voice was familiar, gravelly. It had a slight French accent. He rushed into the living room, still holding a potholder. On the TV screen was the sandy-haired man in the sweater, saying ". . . from Pasadena, California, for NBC news." Then John Chancellor came on.

Harold threw the potholder at the TV screen. "You son of a bitch!" he shouted. "You ubiquitous son of a bitch!" Then he sank into the director's chair, on the edge of tears. His eyes burned.

It was dark outside when his pie was ready. He ate it as if it were cardboard, forcing himself to eat every bite. To keep his strength up, as his mother would have said, for the oncoming storm. For the oncoming storm.

He kept the TV off that evening and did not go out. He finished the painting by artificial light at three in the morning, took two Sominex tablets and went to bed, frightened. He had wanted to call Janet but hadn't. That would have been chicken. He slept without dreaming for nine hours.

It was noon when he got up from the big platform bed and stumbled into the kitchen for breakfast. He drank a cup of cold zucchini soup while waiting for the coffee from yesterday to heat up. He felt okay, ready for the man in the sweater whenever he might strike. The coffee boiled over, spattering the white wall with brown tears. He reached to pull the big Chemex off the burner and scalded himself. "Shit!" he said, and held his burned hand under cold tapwater for a half minute. He walked into the living room and began looking at the painting in daylight. It was really very good. Just the right feeling, the right arrangement. Scary, too. He took it from the easel, set it against a wall. Then he thought better of that. The cats might get at it. He hadn't seen the cats for a while. He looked around him. No cats. He put the painting on top of the dry sink, out of harm's way. He would put out some cat food.

From outside came the sound of a motorcycle. Or of two motorcycles. He turned, looked out the window. There was dust where the motorcycles had just been, a light cloud of it settling. On the plywood platform at the entryway to the building being renovated stood two men in brown sleeveless sweaters, blue shirts, jeans. One was holding a clipboard, and they were talking. He could not hear their voices even though the window was open. He walked slowly to the window, placed his hands on the ledge, stared down at them. He stared at the same sandy hair, the same face. Two schoolgirls in plaid skirts walked by, on their way to lunch. Behind them was a woman in a brown sleeveless sweater and blue jeans, with sandy hair. She had the same face as the man, only slightly feminized in the way the head sat on the shoulders. And she walked like a woman. She walked by the two men, her twins, ignoring them.

Harold looked at his watch. Twelve-fifteen. His heart was pounding painfully. He went to the telephone and called his psychiatrist. It was lunch hour and he might be able to reach him. He did, for a minute or two. Quickly he told him that he was beginning to see the same person everywhere. Even in the movies and on TV. Sometimes two or three at a time.

"What do you think, Harold?" he said to the doctor. The psychiatrist's name was Harold, too.

"It would have to be hallucination. Maybe coincidence."

"It's not coincidence. There've been seven of them and they are identical, doctor. *Identical.*" His voice, he realized, was not hysterical. It might become that way, he thought, if the doctor should say "Interesting," as they do in the movies.

"I'm sorry that you have an hallucination," Harold the psychiatrist said. "I wish I could see you this afternoon, but I can't. In fact, I have to go now. I have a patient."

"Harold!" Harold said. "I've had a dozen sessions with you. Am I the type who hallucinates?"

"No, you aren't, Harold," the psychiatrist said. "You really don't seem to me to be like that at all. It's puzzling. Just don't drink."

"I won't, Harold," he said, and hung up.

What to do? he thought. *I can stay inside until Janet comes back. I don't have to go out for anything. Maybe it will stop on its own.*

And then he thought, *But so what? They can't hurt me. What if I see a whole bunch of them today? So what? I can ignore them.*

He would get dressed and go out. What the hell. Confront the thing.

When he got outdoors, the two of them were gone from in front of the building. He looked to his right, over toward Madison. One of them was just crossing the street, walking lightly on the Adidas. There were ordinary men and women around him. Hell, *he* was ordinary enough. There were just too many of him. Like a clone. Two more crossed, a man and a woman. They were holding hands. Harold decided to walk over to Fifth Avenue.

Just before the corner of Fifth was a wastebasket with a bum poking around in it. Harold had seen this bum before, had given him a quarter once. Fellow alcoholic. There but for the grace of God, et cetera. He fished a quarter from his pocket and gave it to the bum without solicitation. "Say," Harold said, on a wild impulse, "have you noticed something funny? People in brown sweaters and jeans?" He felt foolish, asking. The bum was fragrant in the afternoon sun.

"Hell, yes, buddy," the bum said. "Kind of light brown hair? And tennis shoes? Hell yes, they're all over the place." He shook his head dazedly. "Can't get no money out of 'em. Tried 'em six, eight times. You got another one of those quarters?"

Harold gave him a dollar. "Get yourself a drink," he said.

The bum widened his eyes and took the money silently. He turned to go.

"Hey!" Harold said, calling him back. "Have a drink for me, will you? I don't drink, myself." He held out another dollar.

"That's the ticket," the bum said, carefully, as if addressing a madman. He took the bill quickly, then turned toward Fifth Avenue. "Hey!" he said. "There's one of 'em," and pointed. The man in the brown sleeveless sweater went by, jogging slowly on his Adidas. The bum jammed his two dollars into a pocket and moved on.

Well, the bum had been right. Don't let them interfere with business. But it wasn't hallucination—not unless he had hallucinated the bum and the conversation with the bum. He checked his billfold and found the two dollars were indeed gone. Where would they have gone if he had made up the bum in his unconscious? He hadn't eaten them. If he had, the whole game was over anyway and he was really in a straitjacket somewhere, being fed intravenously, while somebody took notes. Well.

He turned at Fifth Avenue, toward the spire of the Empire State Building, and stopped cold. Most of the foot traffic on the avenue was moving uptown toward him, and every third or fourth one of them was the person in the brown sweater and the blue short-sleeved shirt. It was like an invasion from Mars. And he saw that some of the normal people—the people like himself—were staring at them from time to time. The brown-sweatered person was always calm, whistling softly sometimes, cool. The others looked flustered. Harold jammed his hands into his pockets. He felt suddenly cold.

He began walking down Fifth Avenue. He kept going for several blocks, then on an impulse ran across the street to the Central Park side and climbed up on a park bench that faced the avenue and then from the bench onto the stone railing near the Sixtieth Street subway station. He looked downtown, up high now so that he could see. And the farther downtown he looked, the more he saw of an array of brown sweaters, light brown in the afternoon sunlight, with pale, sandy-haired heads above them. On a crazy impulse, he looked down at his own clothes and was relieved to see that he was not himself wearing a brown sleeveless sweater and that his jeans were not the pale and faded kind that the person—that the multitude—was wearing.

He got down from the bench and headed across Grand Army Plaza, past people who were now about one-half sandy-haired and sweatered and the other half just random people. He realized that the repeated person hadn't seemed to crowd the city any more than usual. They weren't *new*, then. If anything, they were replacing the others.

Abruptly, he decided to go into the Plaza Hotel. There were two of them in the lobby, talking quietly with one another, in French. He walked past them toward the Oak Bar; he would get a Perrier in there.

In the bar, three of them sat at the bar itself and two of them were at a table near the front. He seated himself at the bar. A man in a brown sweater turned from where he was washing glasses, wiped his hands on his jeans, came over and said, "Yes, sir?" The voice was gravelly with a slight French accent, the face blank.

"Perrier with lime," Harold said. When the man brought it, Harold said, "How long have you been tending bar here?"

"About twenty minutes," the man said and smiled.

"Where were you before?"

"Oh, here and there," the man said. "You know how it is."

Harold stared at him, feeling his own face getting red. *"No I don't know how it is!"* he said.

The man started to whistle softly. He turned away.

Harold leaned over the bar and took him by the shoulder. The sweater was soft—probably cashmere. "Where do you come from? What are you doing?"

The man smiled coldly at him. "I come from the street. I'm

tending bar here." He stood completely still, waiting for Harold to let go of him.

"Why are there so many of you?" Harold said.

"There's only one of me," the man said.

"Only one?"

"Just one." He waited a moment. "I have to wait on that couple." He nodded his head slightly toward the end of the bar. A couple of them had come in, a male and a female as far as Harold could see in the somewhat dim light.

Harold let go of the man, got up and went to a pay telephone on the wall. He dialed his psychiatrist. The phone rang twice and then a male voice said, "Doctor Morse is not in this afternoon. May I take a message?" The voice was the gravelly voice. Harold hung up. He spun around and faced the bar. The man had just returned from serving drinks to the identical couple at the far end. "What in hell is your name?" he said, wildly.

The man smiled. "That's for me to know and you to find out," he said.

Harold began to cry. "What's your goddamned *name*?" he said, sobbing. "My name's Harold. For Christ's sake, what's yours?"

Now that he was crying, the man looked sympathetic. He turned for a moment to the mirrored shelves behind him, took two unopened bottles of whiskey and then set them on the bar in front of Harold. "Why don't you just take these, Harold?" he said pleasantly. "Take them home with you. It's only a few blocks from here."

"I'm an alcoholic," Harold said, shocked.

"Who cares?" the man said. He got a bright orange shopping bag from somewhere under the bar and put the bottles in it. "On the house," he said. Harold stared at him. "What is your goddamned, fucking *name?*"

"For me to know," the man said softly. "For you to find out."

Harold took the shopping bag, pushed open the door and went into the lobby. There was no doorman at the big doorway of the hotel, but the man in the sleeveless sweater stood there like a doorman. "Have a good day now, Harold," the man said as Harold left.

Now there was no one else on the street but the man. Everywhere. And now they all looked at him in recognition, since he had given his name. Their smiles were cool, distant, patronizing. Some nodded at him slightly as he made his way slowly up the avenue toward Sixty-third, some ignored him. Several passed on motorcycles, wearing red helmets. A few waved coolly to him. One slowed his motorcycle down near the curb and said, "Hi, Harold," and then sped off. Harold closed his eyes.

He got home all right, and up the stairs. When he walked into the living room he saw that the cats had knocked his new painting to the floor and had badly smeared a corner of it. Apparently one of them had rolled on it. The cats were nowhere in sight. He had not seen them since Janet had gone.

He did not care about the painting now. Not really. He knew what he was going to do. He could see in his mind the French movie, the man on the motorcycle.

In the closet where she kept her vacuum cleaner, Janet also kept a motorcycle helmet. A red one, way up on the top shelf, behind some boxes of candles and light bulbs. She had never spoken to him of motorcycles; he had never asked her about the helmet. He had forgotten it, having noticed it when he was unpacking months before and looking for a place to put his Samsonite suitcase. He set the bag of bottles on the ledge by the window overlooking the building where men in brown sleeveless sweaters were now working. He opened one bottle with a practiced fingernail, steadily. The cork came out with a *pop*. He took a glass from the sideboard and poured it half full of whiskey. For a moment he stood there motionless, looking down at the building. The work, he saw without surprise, was getting done. There was glass in the window frames now; there had been none that morning. The plywood ramp had been replaced with marble steps. Abruptly he turned and called, "Kitty! Kitty!" toward the bedroom. There was silence. "Kitty! Kitty!" he called again. No cat appeared.

In the kitchen there was a red-legged stool by the telephone. Carrying his untasted glass of whiskey in one hand, he picked up the stool with the other and headed toward the closet at the back of the apartment. He set the whiskey on a shelf, set the stool in the closet doorway. He climbed up carefully. There was the motorcycle helmet, red, with a layer of dust on top. He pulled it down. There was something inside it. He reached in, still standing on the stool, and pulled out a brown sleeveless sweater. There were stains on the sweater. They looked like bloodstains. He looked inside the helmet. There were stains there, too. And there was a little blue plastic band with letters on it. It read Paul Bendel—Paris. Once, in bed, Janet had called him Paul. *Oh, you son of a bitch!* he said.

Getting down from the stool he thought, *For him to know. For me to find out.* He stopped only to pick up the drink and take it to the bathroom, where he poured it down the toilet. Then he went into the living room and looked out the window. The light was dimming; there was no one on Sixty-third Street. He pushed the window higher, leaned out. Looking to his right he could see the intersection with Madison. He saw several of them crossing it. One looked his way and waved. He did not wave back. What he did was take the two bottles and drop them down to the street where they shattered. He thought of a man's body, shattering, in a motorcycle wreck. In France? Certainly in France.

A group of four of them had turned the corner at Madison and were walking toward him. All of them had their hands in their pockets. Their heads were all inclined together and they appeared to be having an intimate, whispered conversation. *Why whisper?* Harold thought. *I can't hear you anyway.*

He pulled himself up and sat on the window ledge, letting his legs hang over. He stared down at them and forced himself to say aloud, "Paul." They were directly below him now, huddled and whispering. They seemed not to have heard him.

He took a breath and said it louder: *"Paul."* And then he found somewhere the strength to shout it, in a loud, clear, steady voice. "Paul," he shouted. *"Paul Bendel."*

Then the four faces looked up, shocked. "You're Paul Bendel," he said. "Go back to your grave in France, Paul."

They stood transfixed. Harold looked over toward Madison. Two of them there had stopped in their tracks in the middle of the intersection.

The four faces below were now staring up at him in mute appeal, begging for his silence. His voice spoke to this appeal with strength and clarity: "Paul Bendel," he said, *"you must go back to France."*

Abruptly all four of them averted their eyes from his and from one another's. Their bodies seemed to become slack. Then they began drifting apart, walking dispiritedly away from one another and from him.

———

He was redoing a smeared place on the painting when the telephone rang. It was Janet. She was clearly in a good mood and she asked if the zucchini soup had been all right.

"Fine," he said. "I had it cold."

She laughed. "I'm glad it wasn't too burned. How was the *jarret de veau?*"

Immediately, at the French, his stomach tightened. Despite the present clarity of his mind, he felt the familiar pain of the old petulance and jealousy. For a moment, he hugged the pain to himself, then dismissed it with a sigh.

"It's in the oven right now," he said. "I'm having it for dinner."

A VISIT FROM MOTHER

(for Herry O. Teltscher)

By the marble fireplace in the main bedroom a discreet television set was playing. It sat on a Regency stool with inlaid legs. The program was a videotape of a ballet.

"My God," Mother said, as he brought her and Daddy in. "It's in *color!*"

Barney was flustered. They had been dead a dozen years and for a moment he had forgotten. "Sure, Mom," he said. "Color TV's been around for years . . ."

Mother's face, bright for a moment, became wistful. "It's a pity," she said. "Your father would have enjoyed it so . . ."

Barney glanced at his father shyly, then glanced away. His father's face was impassive; as always, he neither confirmed nor denied what Mother had said about him.

"Would you like something to drink?" Barney said to her. "Coffee maybe?" It was eleven in the morning.

"You go ahead, Barney," Mother said, pronouncing his name with a kind of sigh. "I don't want anything for myself."

She was wearing the same J. C. Penney dress she had worn to Daddy's funeral, the same black patent shoes. Daddy was wearing a blue serge Nixon suit and brown shoes. His hair was pale gray; his face was pained, as though his false teeth were hurting.

They were both Midwesterners and they looked out of place in this New York apartment. Somehow, Barney remembered, they had even looked out of place in their own Ohio ranch house, however much Mother had tried to possess the space of it by endless dusting of furniture, by the covering of its cheap parquet floors with her own hooked rugs. Daddy alone had filled and held one corner of the living room of that air-less house with its pastel walls, its Currier and Ives prints, the hooked rugs everywhere, Grandmother's sofa, Aunt Millie Dean's cherry table, the coat of arms on the kitchen wall by the never-used copper molds—the curved fish, the decorated ring, the gingerbread man that might have formed mousses or cakes but never had. Daddy had made that dark corner his, sitting grimly in the overstuffed armchair with his *Time* or his crosswords or staring out beyond the pale curtained window at the nothing at all that surrounded them. As a child, Barney's heart had moved toward that silent and frightened man with inarticulate love, unable to look him in the eyes.

Later, after his coronary, Daddy's place had become the painted brass bed in the corner bedroom, where he lay and smoked Viceroys in a holder and continued his grim solutions to crossword puzzles in magazines and almost never spoke.

Mother had completely become his voice: "Your father doesn't think much of the fall programs, Barney," or "Your father believes the economy is headed for a slump." But he never heard Daddy say anything.

Barney led the ghosts out onto the terrace. Mother gave a polite gasp at the view of the Hotel Pierre, rising to the right of the General Motors building. Two pigeons flew up from the floor of the cedar decking. The terrace was splendid on this June morning; the ivy on its fence glistened in the bright sun; its scarlet geraniums glowed.

"You certainly have a lovely apartment, Barney," Mother said. As usual her voice held back somehow in the praise. There was a "Yes, but . . ." in it, if only by inflection.

For years he had ignored the way Mother gave with her words and took away with her voice. But now he said, "What's wrong with it, Mother?"

Daddy was seating himself carefully in one of the lava gray deck chairs, as though, even dead, he had to protect himself from exertion.

Mother looked shocked, then reproachful. "I didn't say there was anything *wrong*, Barney . . ."

Anger hit him suddenly and unexpectedly. "Damn it, Mother!" he said, astonished at the strength in his voice. "I *heard* the way you said it."

She looked powerless but she came back instantly. "I wish you wouldn't use that kind of language, Barney. I know that times have changed since we passed on, but your father . . ."

"Fuck my father," Barney said. "It's you I'm talking to, Mother."

At the word "fuck" his mother gasped and fluttered her hand

over her heart. For a moment she became Blanche DuBois, raped by Stanley Kowalski.

Barney glanced toward Daddy and saw his face frozen in pain. "I'm sorry, Mother," he said. "I shouldn't have said that."

Mother's relief was immediate. She became Lady Bountiful at once. "Oh, I suppose people talk that way all the time now," she said, as if her absence from the living had produced the degeneration in standards she had always expected it would. "It's just that we're not used to it is all."

He was wondering how she could know how people talked nowadays when she said, "Some things do come through to us, you know. Not a whole lot."

"Where are you when you're not here?" he asked. "Is it Purgatory?"

"Oh, no," she said. "It's not Purgatory. Your father and I don't even know if there *is* a Purgatory. We're in a quiet place," she said, with the old hint of a whine in her voice, as if she were trying to tell him something too painful for words. That he didn't write to her often enough?

He had shown them the whole apartment now, in the ten minutes since he had prayed to see them and they had, surprisingly, stepped out of the elevator. He had had no idea such things were possible, yet accepted it easily enough. There had been a lot of new and surprising things in his life lately and this was another of them.

He had only lived in the apartment six weeks, here on the Upper East Side between Fifth and Madison, with skylights and high ceilings and marble fireplaces. A year before he had been living in an old house near a small Ohio town, wishing he were dead. Now he had an $1,800-a-month apartment, was a slim fifty-one years old, had grown a beard. The folk art paintings on his walls alone had cost more than his annual salary as a professor. The apartment was the top floor of what had once been a millionaire's mansion. Barney had made the money by writing a book about viruses that had, wildly, become a best seller for thirty-seven months. Two Nobel laureates had pronounced it the best work on the subject ever written.

"It certainly is nice to have a terrace," Mother was saying. "If only Gwen were here to enjoy it. Gwen always liked being outdoors."

So that had been it. The "but." "Gwen can go outdoors in Ohio any time she wants to, Mother," he said. "She has three acres all to herself."

Mother looked hurt. "You know what I mean, Barney."

Immediately he felt the stab of guilt that Mother had clearly wanted him to feel. He buried it. "Gwen is well rid of me," he said. "And I'm happy with Isabel."

"It's too bad we can't meet Isabel. I suppose that when a woman goes out to a job . . . ."

He could have brained her with a two-by-four. "Can you stay for an hour?" he said.

That caught her by surprise and she turned to Daddy. "I don't really know. What do you think, Allston?"

Daddy grunted some sort of assent, his first vocalization since arriving. Mother turned back to Barney and said, "Well, I suppose it'll be all right. No more than an hour."

"Good," Barney said, with triumph. "I'll call Isabel and tell her to jump in a cab. We can all have lunch together."

"Barney!" Mother said. "You're such a child. We don't need lunch. We're dead."

————

Isabel arrived breathless but poised. In her tight Sasson jeans and T-shirt her figure was stunning; her face, without makeup, framed by curly gray hair that matched her gray eyes, was luminous. Gwen's waist was thick, her face solid and plain; she had a comforting look to her, domestic and tranquil. Isabel looked like a movie star on a day off. Gwen dyed her hair; Isabel glowed in gray.

"Mother and Daddy," Barney said, "I'd like you to meet Isabel." Isabel looked at their faces wonderingly. She had seen photographs of them. "Jesus!" she said. She held out a hand to Mother.

Mother was cool. "I'm sorry, dear, but there's no touching."

Isabel looked up to his face. "What's going on, love?"

"It's real, honey," he said. "Hard to believe. But you get used to it."

"I'd like a glass of wine," Isabel said.

The four of them sat on the terrace. A blue jay perched itself on one corner of the fence, facing itself toward Central Park. The sky was a perfect blue. There was no breeze. Mother's hands were folded in her lap, over the pleats of the blue rayon dress. Daddy stared at the middle distance. Isabel sipped her wine, Barney his coffee. The black cat, Amagansett, came to the open French doors and crouched himself toward the jay, motionless.

"Is your accent British?" Mother said at last to Isabel. It was a fencing question; if Isabel's accent were *not* British de Gaulle had been Japanese.

Isabel nodded over her wine. "Scottish."

"Such a civilized country," Mother said. "With the lochs." She pronounced it *lox*.

"Mmmm," Isabel said and set her wineglass down on the deck.

"Yes," Mother said, somehow satisfied by the exchange. She had managed to remove for herself any threats that Scotland might have for her and was ready to get down to business. "Are the two of you married? I don't want to be rude."

"No, Mother," Barney said. "We have no plans to be married."

Mother pursed her lips. "You're very . . . liberated," she said.

"Oh, come on, Mother. It's no big deal and you know it."

"*Barney,*" Mother said. "I'm not thinking about what other people do. And God knows you're *old* enough to do as you like."

He looked at her. She was Mother all right, with the dewlaps at her neck—or wattles, or whatever they were—and the pink-painted and wrinkled lips in a kind of pout. He had seen that pout a hundred times on the streets of New York. She sat now in the deck chair with her knees a foot apart and the hem of her rayon dress pulled back. He could see the sagging white flesh of her inner thighs above her rolled-down beige nylons. He turned his head away, pretending to look at the blue jay. "Then what are you thinking of, Mother?" he said.

"Of your health, Barney," she said, and he looked back at her own rampant unhealthiness. "Of the doctors who told me you should take it easy, should not excite yourself . . ."

My God, he thought. *That again.* "Mother," he said aloud, "I've had cardiograms yearly for thirty years. I don't have rheumatic heart anymore." Yet in her presence he hardly believed it. "I'm not a sick child." But the words lacked conviction.

Isabel stood up and stretched. "I've got to get back to work at the museum," she said. Isabel was a director of the American

Museum of Folk Art; Barney had been in love with her for nearly a year. She was forty-three, twice divorced, with a Ph.D. in Art History from Glasgow and a perfect bottom. "Goodbye, Mrs. Witt and Mr. Witt," she said. "Your son's a terrific lover." She finished off her wine at a gulp and left. No one had eaten lunch.

"Well," Mother said, "she certainly is up-to-date. I see she feels comfortable without a bra."

"Come off it, Mother," he said. "Are you trying to tell me she's a whore?"

Mother looked away with a grimace. "Times change, Barney," she said, as though they didn't. "I just hope you're sure she's what you really want."

"I hear you, Mother," he said. "You said that about my first bicycle, the red one."

"It's just that your father and I want you to make up your own mind about what's right for you . . ."

"My father hasn't said anything about Isabel," he said. It was something new for him to speak like that and he felt a sense of exceeding proper limits. But he did not look at his father, the pathetic and silent figure in the chair.

"I know how your father feels about you," she said. "We've been married a long time."

"How are your . . . your existences, now?" he said, changing the subject.

She brightened a bit. "Your father rests well," she said. "I still seem to have my old difficulty sleeping." As far as he could remember, his mother slept all right. She only liked complaining about not sleeping, about "tossing and turning." "You know, Barney," she went on, "where we stay now sometimes our forms change and we become different ages of our lives. Sometimes

I'm the age I was before you were born. And sometimes your father and I become babies, just little fat things with diapers on. When that happens I just sleep and sleep."

"Wow!" he said, genuinely astonished. "Do you have any control over it?"

"Well, yes. It's more or less a matter of willing it."

"But, my God," he said, "then how can you have a sleeping problem? You can make yourself an infant whenever you want to and just sleep." He shook his head in exasperation. "Like a baby."

She pursed her lips. "It just doesn't seem *right,* Barney. For a grown-up person ..." Her voice trailed off in a way he recognized, a way that meant, *Don't pry into my sorrows, Barney. I have sensitivities you wouldn't understand.*

When she was living he wouldn't have persisted, but things were different now. "Come on, Mother," he said. "If you really wanted to sleep it certainly wouldn't strain your dignity to be a baby." Then the stupidity, the narrowness of her struck him and he said, "Jesus, there's something terrific about being a baby for a while."

She shook her head adamantly, giving the look that meant, "I knew you wouldn't understand." Finally she said, in a confidential and pained voice, "Barney. There's no one to change the diaper. It's ... humiliating."

He stared at her in disbelief. *Of course. All those matches in the bathroom, those bottles of Air Wick.* The way she made him run the lavatory tap when he peed, and aim for the edge of the toilet, so she couldn't hear it. The horror on her face if he farted.

And then something else struck him. "You're both the same ages you were when you died. Why don't you make yourselves younger? Why be *old*?"

She looked at him wonderingly and for a moment her ever-lasting guard seemed to be down. "Why not be old?" she said.

It rushed upon him, overwhelmed him. There they sat, on his New York terrace, both in their physical sixties, with pale, sagging bodies, false teeth, bags under their eyes. And by choice. They could be whatever age they wanted to be in whatever Limbo they had their existence.

He stared at her. "Make yourself young for me, Mother," he said.

She seemed not to hear him. She had fallen into some kind of guarded reverie.

Throughout his adult life Barney had suffered a frustrating disparity between sexual desire and sexual performance. Years before, a psychiatrist had uncovered memories of Barney's mother undressing in front of him, when Barney himself had been three and four years old and had slept in a cot in Mother's room. "Now don't peek, Barney," she would say, and pull her dress over her head. He always did peek, at the peach-colored slips, the flared rayon panties, the dark triangle of hair between her legs.

When, in the psychiatrist's office, he tried to remember his mother's face at those times, tried to remember more than her hips and breasts and underwear, he was never able to. He could not remember his mother with a face other than the sagging old woman's face her ghost now wore.

"What was that, Barney?" Mother said, smiling faintly.

"Could you make yourself young for me?" He tried to keep his voice casual, but he could hear the strain in it.

Mother looked at him sharply. Then she smiled. "How young?"

He was flustered. "I don't know. Young."

"Well, it's sort of silly. But I'll try." Her face made a little pout of concentration. She put her knees together, sat up straight in the chair, squinted her eyes shut.

For a moment her body and clothes, in the still sunlight of the terrace, became murky and dark, shrinking. And then before him sat, in a middy blouse and pleated cotton skirt, a little girl of about twelve. She had a blue ribbon in her hair and her face was bright, pretty, well-scrubbed, pink-cheeked. She wore black shoes with buckles and little white socks.

The blue jay flew away. The cat, startled, turned back toward the kitchen.

"Jesus!" Barney said, and turned toward Daddy. Daddy remained unchanged, not even looking at his child-wife.

"Well," Mother said, "how do you like me?"

He stared at her. She was a very pretty little girl, very proper, but with a flirtiness in her eyes. She had the same pout that she would wear as an old woman with false teeth and sagging jowls—a woman who never exercised, never walked except to shop for dresses in drab department stores. The flirtiness in her now was frank and not hidden. And the astonishing thing about her was the look of health.

"Jesus, Mother," he said, "I've never seen you look better."

"Don't try to be funny, Barney," she said. And then, astonishingly, she winked at him. "Let me show you how I looked when I married your father."

She shut her eyes again and her form melted and darkened and grew. And she sat in front of him then, his mother, as a beautiful flapper of twenty-five. She wore a cream-colored cloche hat over dark, shiny bangs and a low-cut, scoop-neck jersey dress with a short skirt, also cream-colored. Her hose were pale beige silk and her shoes silken. She had a long rope of white beads. Her face shone with health, with sex. She was the most beautiful woman he had ever seen in his life.

He stared at her. She was clearly his mother, yet so different. So beautiful—more beautiful than Isabel—with her long white throat, her high breasts.

She leaned forward toward him, confidentially. "Barney," she said, in a youthful, trilling voice—a theatrical, coquettish voice, "I think I'd like a cigarette."

"Sure," he said weakly, and fumbled in his shirt pocket for a pack of Trues. He held the pack out to her and she reached out with scarlet fingernails and took one delicately. "These dumb filter tips," she said. "I always smoked Sobranies, or Cubebs." She laughed—a trilling, light, airy laugh.

Daddy was staring toward Central Park, his liver-spotted hands folded in his lap, his face set. Below his pants cuffs his clocked maroon socks were wrinkled over bony ankles.

Barney lit her True with his Cricket, then lit one himself. When she bent toward him he could see the edge of fine lace at the top of the beige chemise beneath her neckline and below that the hint of cleavage. He was becoming aroused. It did not frighten him. Somehow his spirit had moved imperceptibly to a place of no rules, here on this cedar deck in Manhattan with the spring sun heating the back of his neck.

Mother exhaled smoke open-mouthed; smoke curled in the sunlight around her face. She blinked her long lashes slowly. "I think I'd like a drink, Barney," she said. "Let's go in the kitchen."

Sometimes, as a child, he had heard that tone of voice; it had thrilled him then as it thrilled him now. It was a voice she could use on a picnic or when suddenly deciding that they should all forget about dinner at home and go to a movie and just eat candy and popcorn. Sometimes she would just drop the whole middle-class pretense, the whole anxious, fretful Motherhood role, and become for a while a lively, bouncy, sly person. And seeing it now, there with an erection pressing in his jeans, he knew that was the thing he had searched for in women, for years: the voice that said, "What the hell, Barney, anything goes."

He looked nervously for a moment toward his father, opened his mouth to speak.

And Mother said, "Why don't you just stay here and rest for a while, Allston? It'll do you good."

His father did not turn to face them. "Whatever you want, Anna," he said.

"Well then," she said and stood, smoothing her dress along her behind, checking her stocking seams. "Do you have any gin, Barney?" she said. "I'd like a Gibson."

"Sure," he said. Leaving the terrace, he reached for her arm, to help her across the threshold, to touch her.

She pulled away. "No touching, Barney," she said. "You mustn't touch the dead."

The reminder was a shock, knotting his stomach. The whole Oedipus fantasy dissolved: getting his young mother drunk, running his hand up under her dress, along those pale silk stockings, lolling his tongue gently into her crimson mouth . . .

As he closed the French doors to the terrace she said, "Your father was always a good man, Barney. But there were some things he never wanted to understand."

He looked through the glass at Daddy, sadly. There the man sat, alone as ever.

————

He fixed her a big, dry Gibson with trembling hands, and another for himself. She leaned against the refrigerator, cupped the drink in both hands, giggled. Then she drank greedily and he fixed her another.

"My father was rich, you know," she said.

"I know." Her father had been a banker in Cleveland. There had been pictures of him everywhere at home. He had died before Mother married, had left his money to a young mistress.

"This dress was made by Coco Chanel. Daddy would take me to New York in the summers, and we'd stay right there at the Pierre."

He was astonished at that. He did not remember her talking about New York. But he had never imagined his mother, his anxious, cheaply dressed mother, as this gorgeous flapper.

Abruptly she took off her hat with one hand and set it on the dishwasher. Then she shook her head and the shiny black hair, short, beautifully cut, framed her face. His penis began to harden again, but hopelessly. She was dead, untouchable, now that the word "incest" was as meaningless to him, a virologist, as an obscure tribal taboo.

"It's warm in here," she said, smiling. "Fix me another drink and I'll take my clothes off for you."

His hands shook so much that he spilled gin in the sink, on the floor. But he mixed the drink somehow, not looking at her. He could hear the sound of silken clothes, of stockinged legs rubbing together. He looked up at the Kliban Cat Calendar over the stainless steel sink: "June, 1980" it read. In the morning he would have an appointment with his dentist. Isabel would be home from the museum in three hours. His penis ached. His whole body trembled.

When he turned, holding the drink out to her, he almost

dropped it. She was still leaning back against the refrigerator but now her dress lay on the floor. She was wearing a beige silk chemise over her breasts—the breasts that had nursed him—and a matching silk half-slip, so short that the place where her garters stretched her stockings above her thighs was visible. She had kicked off her shoes and her legs and feet were beautiful.

She looped her thumbs under the waist of the slip as he stood there holding out the Gibson. Then she paused. "Set the drink on the counter, Barney," she said. She looked him over thoughtfully. "You know, Barney," she said. "My father was a tall man like you. And rich, like you are now."

"I know," he said, in almost a whisper.

"He always bought my clothes for me. Never Mother. Always Daddy."

"And you bought mine," he said.

She smiled. "That's right."

"Take your slip off, Mother," he said.

"Do you know, Barney?" she said. "You're old enough, right now, to be my father."

He thought about that a moment, here in this nice kitchen with its European fittings, its gray slate floor, its flawless white dishes. His trembling subsided, but not his penis. He began to take off his belt, unbuttoned the top button of his jeans. "Well, Mother," he said, as something in his chest seemed to open to the bright light in the kitchen, into the splendid vision of Eros in front of his gaze, "love always finds a way."

"Oh, yes," she said, her voice trembling, bending her young body to pull down her slip with slim fingers. "Oh, yes."

DADDY

Barney came back out on the terrace. After their half hour together, Mother was asleep on the living room couch, regressed to an infant.

"Daddy," Barney said. "Why didn't you come and see me in the hospital?"

Daddy shifted his weight uneasily in the deck chair. "Which hospital?" he said gruffly, not looking toward his son. He had never, when alive, looked toward his son while speaking to him.

"Oh, come on, Daddy," Barney said. There was bravado in this familiarity; Daddy's edge was not easily overcome.

Daddy said nothing. He was looking in the direction of Central Park.

"It was the Children's Hospital, Daddy. Where they gave me the heat treatment for rheumatic fever. Where they almost killed me."

"I remember," Daddy said.

"Well, why didn't you come and see me?" Barney said. "Why didn't you send me a postcard in that fine handwriting of yours? Or call me on the phone?"

There was silence for a while. Daddy's figure, for a moment, seemed to shimmer as Mother's had done when she had begun to change her form. But Daddy did not change. "Nothing to say," he said, finally.

Barney stared at him. To his surprise, he found himself crying. "Anything," he said. "You could have said *anything*."

Daddy shimmered again. "Silly," he said. "Childish."

"Daddy!" Barney cried. *"I needed you."*

Daddy shimmered more seriously. Then he turned and looked at Barney. He was younger than before, slightly less gray. "You were a mama's boy," he said. "There was nothing for me to say to you."

It took an effort for Barney to speak. "You could have said 'Hi.' You could have mailed me a card that said 'Get Well Soon.'" Saying this, he felt a pain in his stomach, like a stitch. It grew and became a hot wire beneath his diaphragm. He began to sob, silently. He had been standing at the French doors; now, he seated himself in one of the director's chairs, arms around his middle, and squinted his eyes shut until the sobbing ended.

"You always were a crybaby, too," Daddy said, as if stating the weather report.

Barney opened his eyes but could not speak. He stared at his father, who was younger now—definitely younger. Daddy was no longer wearing his serge suit. He wore a white sport shirt with an open collar and white flannel pants. He looked like Don Budge, ready for a set. His hair had lost almost all its gray. His socks were white; his shoes, black and white.

It was early afternoon and hot; there was sweat at the back

of Barney's neck. He was wearing Levi's; they were too heavy for this June afternoon. He began taking his shoes off to cool his feet. "I had a lot to cry about," he said.

Daddy looked at him a moment. "Who doesn't?" There was contempt in his voice. His eyes were pale blue. His face had lost twenty years while they were talking but the expression on the face had not changed: Daddy was angry, as he had always been. "My father beat me with his walking stick and I didn't cry."

"I'm sorry, Daddy," Barney said. "I'm sorry the son of a bitch beat you." He sighed. There had been no relief in saying it. Maybe he wasn't sorry at all.

"I never finished high school," Daddy was saying, looking toward Central Park again. There was a hint of suntan on his normally pale face, and the flesh of his jaw was tight, strong-looking. His hair was black and slick. "My first job was unloading sacks of Portland cement for eighty cents a day. I saved money and bought the Encyclopedia Americana so I could know where the Suez Canal was and what the names of the chemical elements were. I lived on cheap food and slept on the floor. After five years I bought my first car, a black Model A, and I was cheated on it; the differential was bent and when I drove it fast the axle broke and broke my left leg with it. When I married Anna—your mother—in nineteen twenty-four, I still walked with a limp and was still paying for that goddamned wrecked Ford." He grimaced. "I never even told anybody this before."

"I'm glad you're telling me," Barney said.

His father abruptly turned a hard, cruel face to him and looked directly at his eyes. "Are you?" he said. "Are you glad?"

Barney stared back at him, abashed. "I don't know."

"Good," Daddy said, with relief. "You can drop that psycho-therapy horseshit. What you always wanted was to have Anna to yourself. Put your goddamned face against her tits."

Barney set his shoes on the deck, then took a cigarette out of his pocket. He had never, in his lifetime, heard his father say words like "tits." Daddy had never once discussed sex with him—not in any way at all. From the time he was five his father had hardly spoken to him. He lit a cigarette. This conversation was overdue. The pain in his stomach had changed to rawness. His hands had stopped shaking. "Daddy," he said levelly, "you didn't know how to keep her. I wanted her for myself."

"What do you mean I didn't know how?" Daddy said. "She never loved anybody."

"Maybe her father," Barney said.

Daddy looked at him a minute. "Maybe you aren't so stupid after all."

"I don't think she really wanted me either. I think she just liked teasing me. She never could let anything alone."

Daddy was more relaxed now. "I'll take one of your smokes," he said.

"Sure." Barney offered him the pack. There was an ease now in his stomach.

When Daddy lit up his whole body seemed to relax. It was wonderful to see—something Barney had waited to see for a long, long time.

"That goddamned woman could not make a sandwich without turning it into soap opera. She could not stop chattering and pissing and moaning. We would make love on Sunday mornings when you were at church with those crazy evangelists and she would have to get out of bed and put in her suppositories. Then when I got hard she had to get up and pull

down the shades or take the phone off the hook. She said I was
too animal for her spirit. I would tell her I loved her soul. It
was all bullshit. Just bullshit."

"Were you scared?" Barney was watching him. He began
to shimmer again. Now he looked to be twenty years old, was
wearing a white sweater and navy blue pants.

"I never knew what I felt when we were in bed," Daddy said.
"She kept everything so goddamned *confused* . . ."

"I know."

"The hell you know." Daddy stood up, springy on his young
legs, looked around the terrace. "Get me a drink, you dumb son
of a bitch," he said. "Get me a glass of gin."

"You stopped drinking when I was eleven. You wouldn't
even eat Aunt Sallie's fruitcake, because of the little shot of
whiskey she used."

"And I didn't cry about it, either. Get me that gin. It won't
hurt now. I'm dead. God damn it to hell, I'm *dead*."

When Barney gave him the gin, he asked, "Are you in
Limbo?"

Daddy took a long swallow before answering. His throat
trembled with the gin going down. "I suppose it is Limbo.
There's nobody to tell you anything. You're free to come and go
and to change around, but it doesn't mean anything anymore.
Nothing means anything at all. It just goes on."

"That's how you *lived*," Barney said.

"Yes," Daddy said. "Maybe it's Hell. I don't know and I don't
care."

Barney sat down and cried a moment. The tears came sim-
ply and easily; he mourned for his father's lost life and for his
own, unable now to tell them apart. "You blew it, Daddy," he

said. "Why did you have to blow it? Why didn't you shut her up? Why didn't you hit her in the face?"

"I wasn't a brute," Daddy said. "And she was too much for me." He finished off the glass and handed it back. "Barney," he said, "to tell the truth, *you* were too much for me. I'm no father. Nobody taught me to be a father. They talked about responsibility and I didn't know anything about a noisy kid with a diaper full of shit. They told me about the love of a man for a woman but I didn't know what to do with that neurotic bitch. *She talked all the time.* It was like she walked around rubbing herself. Twitching. And she aroused me so much. At the movies she would put her hand in my pocket and squeeze me and then we'd go home and she wouldn't let me touch her."

There were tears coming down his father's cheeks and his face was bright red. He seemed only fifteen years old now, and was wearing a frayed white shirt with no collar, and knickers. "I would go to the bathroom and . . . abuse myself."

Barney had never talked to anyone in his life this way. He was covered with goosebumps. "I jacked off in that bathroom, too," he said, with the words coming easily, relievingly. "Afterward I'd look in the bathroom mirror and I would hate myself. I was disgusted. I thought if you ever found out you would never speak to me again."

His father's voice was very youthful now. It was the voice of a boy at puberty, cracking into high pitch from time to time. "I could never get that part of myself *clean* enough." For a moment he looked as though he were going to vomit. He was about ten years old now, and smaller. "And I never wanted any of that . . . disturbance."

"I know," Barney said. "I know how that feels."

Daddy held out his short arms and looked at them. He was wearing a middy blouse and short pants. There was no hair on his arms and the hair on his head was neatly combed, jet black. Then he looked toward Barney shyly. "This is the way I like to be. This way or old. I don't want the things in between."

Daddy stood there in front of him as a child, scrubbed and slightly pretty. He looked up at Barney, shook his head. "I don't want to be a baby. Not yet."

He shimmered and then began to darken, to melt and flow in the bright afternoon light. After a moment he was an old man again in blue serge and with liver-spotted wrists. His face was deeply lined, weak, both hurt and angry. He seated himself cautiously. "Get me another drink. But mix it with something this time."

Barney got him gin and orange juice and stirred it with one of the silver spoons he had inherited from Mother. He went into the living room to check her out. She was still a three-month-old infant, chubby and scowling, with a wet thumb in her mouth and her body on its side in the fetal position. Both her small fists were clenched.

She slept on the black Chesterfield couch; he had pushed two dining chairs against it to keep her from falling off. Above her the huge living room windows looked out on two mansions with dark mansard roofs—older, most likely, than she. He reached down and felt her diaper; it was still dry.

On the terrace Daddy said, "My father was a state senator; he was an old man when I was born. My mother was his third wife and was far beneath him socially. She took in wash when she was a girl."

"I know." Barney had heard this before, but never from Daddy.

Daddy flashed a look at him—the same silent look he had always given Barney as a child. "What in hell do *you* know?" he said.

Barney sighed; his father had never *said* that before—had only burdened him with the silent weight of his contempt. "Right now," Barney said levelly, "I know more than you ever did know. More than you ever will. Your life was sheltered, and you hardly lived it."

His father's face darkened even more and he clenched a fist. "Don't threaten me," Barney said. "I can take her away from you."

Daddy turned his head away, forced a grim laugh. "Take her," he said. "You're what she wanted anyway. A mama's boy with poetry in his soul. An oversexed crybaby."

Barney looked at his set face, his lined face, and saw clearly the weakness in it. "You self-serving son of a bitch," he said.

"You're a weak sister and you know it, Barney," his father said. "You never had the guts to make your own way."

"You used to wet the *bed* when you took us on trips in the car. You'd get drunk on wine in tourist courts and sleep with your clothes on and wet your *pants*. You acted tough with me when I was eight but you cringed with every mailman or shoe clerk when you were in the real world . . ."

Daddy lurched forward and shouted, "*You* cringed when I came home from work and caught you sitting in the kitchen with her. You'd be drying the silver or telling her about yourself—and she'd be smiling at you like a goddamned vamp. And you'd see me come in and you'd fidget because I caught you in your goddamned gigolo act." He paused, and then said, "You can *have* her."

Barney stared at him. "You don't mean that. You can't live

in Limbo alone. And you never had anybody else but her. You could have had me . . ." His throat constricted without warning, and his eyes began to burn. ". . . But you didn't want me. You put me in that hospital and hoped you'd never see me again."

Daddy seemed now to be somehow subdued—nearly at peace. He said nothing to Barney's accusation. He finished his drink. When he handed him the empty glass there was a note of resignation in the gesture, but he said nothing.

Barney took the glass and stood up. "Do you want another?" His father nodded. "The same."

"Daddy," Barney said. "I love you. I loved you more than I ever loved her . . ."

His father nodded silently.

Mother was awake now, her eyes staring upward, unfocused. She lay on her back, grasping; her small hands greedily opened and shut. He did not speak to her. She remained silent, wrapped up in her own thoughts, or plans . . .

He fixed gin and orange juice and made himself a cup of instant coffee. The pain was in his stomach. He had always loved that man out there. He had loved him when they flew kites together at the Embarcadero, had loved him when the man took him to see Eddie Cantor at the Fox Theatre on Market Street. He had ridden on Daddy's back in the living room, rejoicing at Daddy's warmth, Daddy's strength. And then, about the time of kindergarten, Daddy had started drinking every night. Once Barney had tried to climb on his back and Daddy had shoved him across the room. Barney had sat down and bawled and his father, huge and now terrifying, had thundered over to him and slapped his face twice and said, "Cry for your Mama; don't cry in front of me. Or I'll give you something to cry about." His breath stank. The rage in his voice was an earthquake.

Standing in the kitchen under the skylight, now, facing the Cat Calendar with 1980 written on it, Barney began crying again. He set the gin and orange juice down on the dishwasher and wept.

And then he heard a sound like the sound of his own crying and turned around, facing the pass-through into the living room. Mother, his greedy infant mother, her face red and twisted, was crying with him. She cried a baby's cry, furious at a world that did not continuously serve her wishes.

When he came out onto the terrace again it was a half hour later. He had decided to make himself a drink, and then another. His mother stopped crying, fell asleep again; her compact, narcissistic self was turned away from him, toward the black back of the couch. He carried two glasses with him: both were rich in gin.

The terrace was very hot. It was midafternoon and the sun was ferocious. Daddy had taken off his coat and sat in rolled-up white shirt-sleeves, still wearing his dark blue tie.

Barney did not feel drunk so much as he felt ready for anything. Anything at all. "Here's your drink." He held the glass out and Daddy took it with a curt nod. He seated himself and stared for a while at the green roof of the Hotel Pierre above the terrace fence. Isabel's black cat came through the French doors and began to explore some ivy leaves near the deck; he would look up hopefully from time to time as birds flew overhead and then would seem sad that none flew down to him. He must feel, Barney thought, that the world owes him a bird now and then. And maybe it does, since the world made him a cat.

"Daddy," he said, "I want to tell you about the pyrotherapy they gave me when I was ten."

"Why bring that up now?" his father said wearily.

"Because you wouldn't let me tell you before. When you picked me up at the train station."

"You were chattering away like your mother. And I had to drive. It was rush hour."

"It always was."

"What good would it do to tell me?"

"I'll decide that."

His father scowled, began to shimmer. Quickly Barney got up, reached out, took the glass from Daddy's iridescent hand. "I'll pour your drink out if you don't stop that."

The shimmering stopped. Barney gave him back the drink.

"You need me to want you here in the world, don't you? Or back you go to Limbo where there aren't any drinks."

Daddy scowled and did not answer.

"They put me into a kind of homemade machine of brown-painted steel. It was half a cylinder and it covered my body from neck to ankles. I was flat on a hospital bed. They had already wrapped me tightly in a gray wool Army blanket and I was stifling with the heat of that before they even threw the switch on.

"There were about forty light bulbs screwed into sockets under the curved top of that brown thing, Daddy, and when they turned them on and the heat came pouring into that blanket it was unbearable. My hands were strapped to my sides under the blanket, so I wouldn't hurt myself when I had convulsions, or break the light bulbs ..." He realized that he was sweating profusely. He set his drink on the deck and took off his shirt, wiped his wet chest with it, dabbed at his neck.

"Daddy," he said, "I've been afraid of heat all my adult life. They kept me in that thing fourteen hours a day for two weeks. Each day they brought my internal temperature up to a hundred seven. There was no clock in the room and when I'd ask the attendant what time it was she'd be cross with me. So I lay there and tried to count off the time in my head, a second at a time. Each minute was longer than I could imagine. I prayed to die, tried to will myself dead."

Daddy shifted his weight in the chair, sipped his drink. He rolled up his sleeves another notch, showing pale bony arms, with fine gray hairs on them and brown spots, like big freckles. The cat sniffed at an ivy leaf.

"The doctor had supervised my first day in the machine; the treatment was a project of hers—later abandoned, as too dangerous. She was like a Nazi, Daddy—a Nazi doctor who had me given to her. She said you had signed the authorization for the treatment." He looked at his father, sweat pouring down his forehead into his eyes. The afternoon sun was murderous.

His father did not look at him. He raised his drink slowly to his old, pale lips. Then Barney, moving very quickly, reached out and, with the edge of his right hand, knocked the drink from his father's weak grip. The glass flew across the terrace and smashed into the side of the fence. The cat spun around and fled into the house.

"The doctor said you'd come and see me on the weekend, Daddy. For the first five days I held in my mind a picture of you holding a glass of water for me while I lay under that torture box. But you didn't come."

His father turned, shocked by the lost drink, and looked at him open-mouthed. He looked hopelessly old, frail, vulnerable. "You worthless bastard," Barney said. "You didn't come. I want you to rot in hell for it."

"I was sick," his father said.

"You were not sick, Daddy. You were drunk. You were sitting in your moss-green overstuffed chair in the living room on that Saturday, drinking gin. That was June 17, 1938. It was the worst day I've ever lived, and it soiled my life."

"You're making a soap opera out of it, like your mother. Doctor Morton did charity work with poor children. She was no Nazi. You've built it up in your mind."

"That's horseshit, Daddy. The next kid they tried it on died, the poor bastard. After five days of it. I told you that in the car, in Dayton, when I got there on the train after the year in the hospital."

"I don't remember . . ."

"You remember moving out of the goddamned *state* after you and that flirt in there put me in the hospital, don't you? And you never . . ." Barney leaned forward, saying each word carefully. ". . . And you never wrote me a single word. When I tried to tell you about how I had gone through that treatment and *hadn't cried once,* the way you would have wanted me to, you told me to be quiet because you had to drive the fucking *car.* Daddy," he said, *"I didn't cry."*

"Those were tough times. It was the Depression . . ."

"The Jews in Auschwitz treated their children with more concern, Daddy. Most of them did." He turned his face away from his father's and looked toward the Pierre. "Some of them might have been looking, like you were, for somebody to blame."

"Blame for what?" Daddy's voice sounded weaker.

"For the way your life fell apart. For marrying that god-damned woman in there. For the way she stole your balls from you right in front of your eyes. So you could call me a mama's boy . . ."

"You *were* a mama's boy. Still are." There was a tremor now in the voice. "I know what the two of you were doing an hour ago in the kitchen."

Barney turned toward him. "That's right, Daddy. We climaxed together. It was wonderful."

"Bullshit," Daddy said. His voice shook. His face was gray.

Barney suddenly began to laugh. "Maybe you can't believe it."

"She was frigid. It was the way she was brought up . . ."

"Bullshit," Barney said, laughing. "She wasn't frigid for *me*, you cowardly son of a bitch."

Suddenly his father's face twisted in pain and his pale hand went to his chest, squeezing at the shirt pocket. His lips were blue.

Barney stared at him. "You can't have a heart attack when you're dead," he said.

Daddy choked and fell off the chair onto the deck. He lay there, silently writhing, for several minutes. His hands were white; they clenched into fists and unclenched rhythmically. After a while a kind of foam began to appear on Daddy's lips; his face was ghastly. His eyes stared upward toward the sky. He made no sound. Then, abruptly, he twitched over on one side, toward where Barney sat. Barney stared at him. His age had not changed but his position was now fetal. Barney remembered a time forty years before when as a small child he had seen his father lying like that in the bed of a cheap California motor court; his body had been pressed into a wet stain on the rumpled sheet. Barney remembered the smell.

"Oh, my God, Daddy," he said aloud, looking down at his father, "you're just like she is. You're a goddamned infant. You always were."

A blue jay was chattering somewhere beyond the terrace fence. The black cat came softly back outside into the sun and walked toward Daddy. There came a soft, hissing sound from Daddy's throat and then a hoarse, convulsive shuddering, and then silence. The cat nudged Daddy with his nose and then began to purr. Daddy was clearly dead.

Barney heard footsteps from the French doors and turned to look. Mother was there, as a middle-aged woman in a cheap dress. She spoke through loose false teeth. "It looks as if Allston's died again," she said, matter-of-factly.

"How can that be . . . ?" Barney said.

Mother shook her head worriedly. "I don't know, Barney, but it happens to both of us all the time where we are. The same deaths."

Barney stared at her. "Then you have to go through lung cancer?"

Mother pursed her lips. "Often," she said.

"Jesus!" Barney said. "Then maybe it isn't Limbo at all. Maybe it's Hell."

"Best not to know," Mother said, briskly. "I've got to get him back now, and get back myself. Strict rules." She looked away from him toward the Hotel Pierre and began to shimmer. "My Daddy always stayed at the Pierre," she said, wistfully. "And there were always flowers in his room." As her body began to fade, Barney glanced down and saw that Daddy's dead body was fading too. There was shattered glass on the deck. He felt tears again, just beginning.

He looked back to Mother, who was now translucent. "I loved him, Mother," he said. "I still love him."

She smiled at him flirtatiously. "What we did in the kitchen was naughty," she said. She winked at him.

"*Damn you,*" he said. "It's him I love. It's *Daddy*."

She was hardly visible now, and her voice was faint, far away. "It's not for you to have him, Barney," she said. "Daddy's *mine*." And they were both gone.

After twenty minutes, Barney stopped crying. Something had ended for him. He stayed in his chair for the rest of the afternoon, tremulously, testing his new life. Toward suppertime, when Isabel would be coming home from work, he began to whistle.

From time to time he looked up at the Hotel Pierre, which rose with great clarity into the New York sky.

SITTING IN LIMBO

Sitting here in Limbo, I have found I can return to and make corrections in the life I once lived. I calculate that seventeen years have passed since I died in Columbus, Ohio; it was about two years ago that I learned to return to various parts of my life and change them for the better. The work is difficult but rewarding. And what else has a dead person to do with his time?

There are no physical discomforts here under this pale and sunless sky; the boredom and emptiness that make up my existence are not intolerable. In many ways it is not as bad as being alive was. There is no one to talk to here and nothing, really, to think about except that life of fifty-one years that I was permitted to have. From my present perspective I see it as a unity, like a complex circuit diagram or an abstract-expressionist painting. I see that a part here or there may be altered—a diode or a blob of color—and the pattern will be forever changed.

From my birth in the Good Samaritan Hospital in Lexington, Kentucky, to my death from a coronary in Columbus, it is all a single, sometimes baffling, entity. And I can change it now, a small part at a time. I have the distance.

It was quite by accident that I discovered I could go back there. I have seven chairs here on which I can sit; they have been here since I arrived. Each is different from the others. One of them is a hard wooden chair of varnished oak. I sit in it when I wish to be wakeful. Sometimes I let myself drowse in a reverie for days; at other times I sit upright, my body expectant, waiting. There is, of course, nothing to wait *for* here, but I take comfort in adopting the posture. The wooden chair is exactly right for this. It is high-backed and sturdy; it squeaks when I shift my weight from one buttock to the other. There are very few noises here in Limbo and I appreciate the contribution this chair makes.

I was sitting in it some time ago when I became reminded of a desk at Morton Junior High School, in Lexington. It, too, was made of varnished oak and it, too, squeaked. It had an arm on it for writing and my Limbo chair does not, but otherwise they are much alike. I was sitting in the chair and staring at the fuzzy horizon of Limbo and squeaking every minute or so in a kind of slow dirge. And suddenly my memory came alive with myself in the eighth grade, in Miss Ralston's Social Science class. That class met for an hour every day after lunch, and it was one of the most tedious things in my life. Remembering it here was like *déjà vu*; perhaps I had been in a kind of Limbo then and had not known it. I remembered the gravelly sound of Miss Ralston's voice. I remembered the way she would adjust her teeth in her mouth with a kind of sucking between paragraphs. I remembered her dark flowered dresses, her grayish hair in a bun, her heavy brown shoes. I remembered the fight to stay awake.

And then I remembered a whimsical promise I had made myself as a teen-aged boy in that classroom: I promised I would return to that room at that time if I ever learned the secret of time travel when I grew up. I imagined myself astonishing everyone by my sudden appearance. I would be a grown and vigorous time-traveler stepping with confidence from a glass-and-chromium machine that would materialize just to the right of Miss Ralston's desk. She would stop in midsentence and her jaw would drop. Everyone would stare. In that fantasy I was both observer and observed, both adult and boy, and the imagined pleasure was exquisite.

Then, in Limbo, I remembered the date I had made myself that promise: September 23, 1942. I was born in 1928, so I must have been fourteen. I had repeated the date over and over in that classroom so I would remember it years later. And clearly it had worked. I was joyful, pleased with the continuity.

Then something inside me told me to cross my ankles in a certain way and to slump in my oak chair in a certain way and to breathe in slowly and I did all this without really thinking about it and there I was. I was in Miss Ralston's classroom in September of 1942. But I did not materialize as a grown man to see myself sitting as a young student. I found myself as that student again—ankles crossed, slumped in my chair, breathing in slowly. I heard Miss Ralston's voice droning about the primary exports of Latin America. Fawn Harrington was on my left in a green tartan skirt and green sweater; Toby Kavanaugh sat on my right. I was wearing my Thom McAn shoes, the brown ones. They were too tight and my feet hurt. I had a headache; Mother and Daddy had been fighting in the kitchen the night before and I had barely slept. I hadn't done my homework. Fawn had tried flirting with me before class but I had ignored her. I did not like flirts; I always felt they were up to something.

It was all completely familiar and all clear and real. It was no dream. I tried to stand, to get up and leave that awful room; but I could not. I found that I had no control over my body. It was doing whatever it had done on that day the first time I had lived it. I was only there, it seemed, as an observer. I felt that I could return to Limbo whenever I willed it. I calmed myself and watched.

Miss Ralston finished her reading and then called on Jack Mowbray to read. He stood—a sly, freckled boy whom I distrusted—and read a paragraph about Simon Bolivar. Miss Ralston corrected his pronunciation of Bolivar, pronouncing it poorly herself. She called on Marylinne Saunders to read. And on it went. I watched and listened, fascinated, waiting for it to come to me. I had no awareness of what I was thinking—that other, fourteen-year-old I—but I began to be aware that this was a time when something bad had happened. It was about to happen again. It was going to happen when I was called on to read. I sat in the second row; it would be soon.

When it came to me I found myself standing up awkwardly and looking down at the text. I knew that a humiliation was coming but I could not remember what it was. I heard myself begin to read. My voice was tired and a bit resentful.

Suddenly I was shocked by Miss Ralston's voice, harshly interrupting me. "Billy!" she said. "Billy Whaley. Will you please consider your appearance?"

I looked at her stupidly.

She stared at me with an ironic, prissy frown. "Please go

to the boy's room and button yourself." There was something triumphantly cruel in her voice, and it withered me. I looked down. My corduroys were open at the fly, unbuttoned. I heard a snicker from somewhere behind me, the snicker of a female voice . . .

Immediately I was back in Limbo. I was alone, standing in front of my oak chair, looking down. I am always in faded jeans here. They never wear out, never become dirty. Their fly was properly zipped, as always. I sighed aloud with relief and sat down. I was still shaking. I felt, in some obscure way, a victim.

There is a progression of time here. There are nights and days even though there is no visible sun, and I count them and remember the count. That is how I know it is seventeen years since I died. I do not know if I will be here for eternity or not. There has been no judgment of me, no communication from any god, devil or angel. Nothing has been promised, nothing explained, and I do not care. Yet I have come to believe that there may be a way out of Limbo. I have begun to feel that if I properly edit and rectify my former life that I will be able to pass on from here and be reborn. I sense that I await reincarnation and another life. I feel hopeful. Change is frightening to me and yet I feel hopeful of change.

After my first experience of return I marked off ten days while I thought of various things in my former life, as I often do, or merely counted numbers in my mind as I also often do here, and then I decided to try going back to Miss Ralston's class on that same day. It would be interesting to find myself alive again, even in that dreary schoolroom, and to be among people again. Yet I am not really bored with being dead. I could stay in Limbo for eternity. There is no pain here, no fatigue; there are no appetites. There is no danger. There are no misunderstandings.

I seated myself in the wooden chair and thought of the classroom. I visualized Miss Ralston and her false teeth and the blackboard behind her that was gray with chalk dust. I found myself crossing my ankles again and there I was again at precisely the moment I had reentered the first time. Miss Ralston was reading the same things about Latin America. She called on Jack Mowbray to read, corrected his pronunciation of Bolivar. Knowing now what was going to happen to me and knowing, too, how trivial it really was, I felt calmer this time. I decided to try something. I tried to move my hand down to my lap and button my fly. Nothing happened. My hand remained gently resting on my desk. Jack went on reading. I concentrated on moving the hand. It moved about an inch and then lay still again. Jack finished reading and Miss Ralston called on Fawn Harrington to read. Fawn stood up—a beautiful, soft-voiced girl with long lashes—and read quietly. Concentrating, I made my mind picture my right hand lifting from the desk and settling into my lap and after a moment I realized with surprise that it now *was* in my lap. I began picturing my fingers fastening the buttons. It was slow and difficult, but I could feel it happening. I got them buttoned.

When the reading came to me I stood up and read a passage about the principal fuels of Latin America and then sat down. Miss Ralston had not spoken to me! She called on Toby Kavanaugh. Toby stood up, his open book close to his weak eyes, and began to read. And then I found myself back here in Limbo, sitting in my wooden chair. I was exultant, almost awed. I had changed the past!

Immediately I wondered if that change would provoke others further along. Would I be less shy and difficult with girls when I began to date them at seventeen? Would I make a better grade in Social Science, do better in college, get a better job when I graduated, and so on? Such changes might well prevent my death at fifty-one. Yet clearly I was still dead and nothing in Limbo had changed. It was the same as ever, such as it was.

I remembered my first job interview, in my twenties, when I had become frightened and couldn't even remember my telephone number when the interviewer asked for it. Would erasing the incident of the unbuttoned fly have made me more confident in my twenties? I had invented a phone number for that man and he had ended the interview later, saying, "I'll call you."

I had sat in an armchair in that office, somewhat like the one I have in Limbo. I got up from the oak chair and seated myself in the armchair. I gripped its arms with my hands as I remembered doing. My body fell into that old tense position as though I were an actor who had played the scene a thousand times.

And there I was living it again in a small room with Currier and Ives prints on the wall and the interviewer, a florid man in a brown suit, smiling blandly at me. I knew instantly that it was all as it had been and that it would not end differently. Buttoning my fly in the classroom had changed nothing.

I remained through the inventing of the phone number and then I returned to Limbo. It was clear that I could only change things one at a time; I could not start new chains of circumstance.

Eventually I was to find out that my intuition was correct. I could change particular scenes in my life, erasing mistakes as it were and adding corrections, but I could not seriously change the substantive details. I was a high school teacher for my adult life and I could not change that. I was married twice and divorced twice; I could not alter that either, although I could edit my more unfortunate scenes with my wives. Honesty compels me to say there were many of these scenes. By judicious editing over a period of Limbo-years and hundreds of trips back I was able to improve my behavior in arguments, make myself kinder and more understanding, and the like. But I still divorced them and I could not change that. And truly I did not want to.

I could only make the transition to the past while sitting in the appropriate chair. I found that with some effort it was always possible to associate a chair with every part of my past I wished to explore and then, when needed, change. I have come to believe that the chairs were put here as vehicles for me to render my former life less painful to remember—less embarrassing and wrong. Perhaps other inhabitants of Limbo have more or fewer chairs. Perhaps not. I have never seen another inhabitant.

My first wife was Jane; I was married to her five years. It took me all of two years in Limbo to edit the relationship, yet with all the changes the divorce took place on the same date it had the first time around.

After three years of marriage to Jane I had lost interest in her and had stopped having sex with her. I had found—and I shudder to mention this—ways to blame her for my lack of interest. I told her that her clothes were all wrong—especially her underwear. I told her her education was lacking, that I felt she was afraid of sex. I had married her in the first place because she was a kind of boyish, no-nonsense woman, and now I blamed her for being that way, told her I wanted her to be more feminine. Yet the truth was that I mistrusted women who were very feminine. I told Jane in anger that I thought she was a repressed lesbian because of the way she wore blue jeans all the time. It was horrible of me to say such things. I had winced over them more than once, here in Limbo, before I discovered that I could change them. I am not a cruel person; I really wanted to erase those cruelties.

And I did. I went through the five years with Jane, making myself into a pleasant and honest person. I told her of the tapering off of my desire for her. I was kind to her in every way. She was understanding, and grateful for my straightforwardness. There were no fights.

I did not have sex with her any more than I had had originally. Living in Limbo all these years had obliterated any interest in sex for me. I made no changes in that department.

My second wife was named Millie. She was a librarian for a chemical company and very serious. Millie was a *very* serious person. It was eventually that seriousness that I learned to hate. Whenever I spoke to her, even about unimportant matters like the grade of hamburger we were using or the best kinds of plant food, she was always incredibly attentive. Millie had a good figure and an earnest sexual style, but she wore drab clothes. She looked like the librarian she was to the core.

Within a year of our marriage I had stopped making love with her. I was drinking a good deal by then and I would sometimes find a seductive woman at one of the bars I went to and take her to a motel for the night. Millie would look even more serious the next day but she would never ask where I had been. I knew she felt lucky to have gotten me in the first place. I was a respected biology teacher at a large high school and my salary was far above the average. I had clean habits and was generally polite. My indiscretions were always careful. I had no interest in provoking scandal. Besides I had no real liking for any of the women I took to bed in motels. It was just something I did. Sometimes, in fact, there would be no real sex involved. I would just watch the woman undress herself, feel satisfied enough, and fall drunkenly asleep.

Yet I felt guilty. And from Limbo I was greatly relieved to make the necessary changes, to spend those motel nights at home with Millie, reading or watching television.

In something like four and a half years of Limbo-time I have managed to edit my relationships with my wives in such a way that I now feel guiltless and at ease about what happened. I have altered some other aspects of my life—as a student, a teacher and a church member. I am satisfied. I hope to be reborn, to have another life. So far it has not happened, but it may not take place immediately. Limbo is slow, and I understand that. I would like to be reborn as a woman—as a vivacious and sexy woman. Why not?

Days pass and nothing happens. I sit and wait, moving from chair to chair. Must I go back and reedit? Was I wrong in expecting a second life after rectifying the first? I think not. I feel certain that good editing will propel me toward a new existence. I no longer feel content with Limbo. I am ready to move on. I want to be a girl. I want my name to be Beth. I want to be white, middle-class, pretty, and I want to be given a good education and be well dressed.

———

One of my chairs is smaller than the others. It is clear to me now that it is a child's chair. I have never sat on it. I am beginning to feel that I must, however uncomfortable it may be, if I am to finish my first life properly. I must sit in the child's chair. I am afraid to.

Eventually I sat in the small chair. I folded my hands in my lap, because that seemed the thing to do, and inclined my head. The chair was not uncomfortable at all. I felt quite natural and comfortable in it. I closed my eyes.

When I opened them after a bit I found that I was looking at my own small knees. They were bare below short pants and were scraped and rough-looking the way boys' knees sometimes are. I looked up. I was sitting facing the corner of a small bedroom papered in pink wallpaper. To my right was an open closet and to my left a bed. It was Mother's bedroom. I had been sent there to sit in the corner for an hour because of something bad I had done. I was not to speak or squirm or wriggle. I felt terribly uncomfortable and for a moment I panicked and almost willed myself back here to Limbo, but I decided to hold off for a while to see what would happen. My heart was beating fast. I was about six years old and I knew I had been here in this chair in the corner many times and I knew that something important was going to take place. Something would happen that always happened when I was sent to sit in the corner. I began to have a dim sense that I had *wanted* to be sent there, had done something deliberately bad so that it would happen.

Time passed. I sat and tried to remember how my mother had looked when I was a small child, but I could not. My father—that weak, almost absent man—had told me that she was an "extraordinarily beautiful" woman when he had married her. All I could remember was the way she had looked in the few years before she had died, when I was in my late thirties. Both of my wives had hated her and said I was too good to her, had resented the closeness of the two of us. Well. That had been their problem, not mine. I only saw my mother when she came to visit. She was thick-waisted and had gray hair then and she wore cheap print dresses. But she was fun to talk to and she laughed a lot when we would sit and drink sherry together in the living room. Mother could be really funny when she was a little tipsy, and she was devastating in the way she could point out the pretensions of others. I have always admired her mind.

I sat there for about twenty minutes and thought of Mother and her false teeth and her wit and the big gestures she would use when talking and how she would say things like "to my utter astonishment" and "That, my dear, will be the day." Whatever my wives had said, she was a pleasure to be with.

And then in my chair there in the past I heard footsteps behind me and heard a voice saying, "Billy, it's getting too warm in the living room. I'm going to change into something cooler. You mustn't look."

She had stopped talking before I recognized with a distinct shock that it had been Mother's voice. It was the same cadence that I had remembered, but so much more youthful, so much . . . so much *richer*, than when I was grown up. I heard more footsteps. I heard her opening a drawer somewhere in back of me.

On the inside of the closet door to my right was a full-length, framed mirror. The frame was enameled in a creamy yellowish-white. A few men's jackets hung in the closet—gray and brown ones—and I knew they were Daddy's and that Daddy was away. Daddy was almost always away. Somehow I was glad he was.

I could see the mirror without moving my head. All I had
to do was open my eyes slightly and look to the right. The mirror reflected the bed and part of a white-painted dresser, with
silver-backed brushes on it and two photographs. One photograph was of me as a baby, the other was of Mother herself;
they were both in yellowed ivory frames.

And then someone came into view in the mirror and something deep in me thrilled to see. It was Mother; I could tell
even though her back was toward the mirror because she was
walking toward the bed. Her waist was slim and her step was
light and youthful. She turned and looked past me toward the
mirror and smiled. She must have been smiling at her reflec-
tion, seen across the room. She was so beautiful, so shockingly,
overwhelmingly beautiful, that my heart almost stopped. Her
hair was jet black and bobbed; her skin was creamy white. Her
lips were scarlet, her eyelashes long, her neck and jaw smooth
and perfect and the scarlet of her fingernails matched the scarlet of her lips. Her eyes were big, dark and mischievous. She
was wearing a blue dress with a short pleated skirt and shiny
silk stockings with no shoes. She sat on the bed, still smiling.

I saw her with the eyes of a grown man who knows a beautiful woman when he sees one, and I saw her also with the eyes
of a six-year-old child—an only child to whom his mother is
the most wonderful thing in the world. The combined effect
was devastating. I was hypnotized. I did not move a muscle.

Then she pulled up her dress lazily and began to unfasten
her garters. When I saw the cream white of the insides of her
thighs I felt for a moment as though I would faint. I had never
seen anything so exciting in my life. I remained frozen in my
little chair. She took her silk stockings off, laid them beside her
on the bed's pink coverlet. The room was silent; from some-

where outside I could hear the chattering of a squirrel. For a moment I tried to turn my eyes away from the mirror, but I could not do it.

She stood up and, facing the window now so that she was reflected in profile, she began taking the dress off, pulling it over her head. She was wearing a short pink slip underneath.

Sometimes in my life I have wondered how it must feel to inject pure heroin into a vein. I think the pleasure would be electric in its intensity. I felt that now, looking at Mother through the eyes of both youth and age. There was, too, the sense of danger and of power that comes with seeing another intimately without being seen. There was the erotic joy of seeing a woman so beautiful, so self-absorbed, take off her clothes. And it was such a *forbidden* thing to see my mother expose her body. I could not take my eyes away—not while this heroin was in my blood.

She continued, as I knew by now she would. She pulled the slip slowly over her head, shook her lovely black hair back into order, and laid the slip on the bed by her hose. She was wearing pink silk step-ins and a lacy pink brassiere. Her figure was perfect and her skin perfectly white. I sat transfixed. The feelings in me were like a hurricane, and my soul was in the eye of it. I felt frozen in the moment. I wanted to stay in it forever.

And then I heard her voice again as from a distance. It was softer now and a bit throaty. What she said was, "Now be sure you don't peek, dear." Then as I watched she bent and took off her panties. I saw the jet black of her pubic hair, so flawlessly seated in that charismatic V. I could see the tiny lips of her vagina, as pink as the coverlet on the bed, as pink as the wallpaper, as her slip, her panties. My heart pounded like a mallet in my chest and then as she removed her brassiere and stood there naked by the bed, still smiling, smiling now toward where I sat upright in my little chair, I felt a swooning inside myself. The heroin had me. My vision blurred and I was back in Limbo.

I sat stunned for several moments. And then I felt a brief flash of anger shake my body. I felt *had*, in some fundamental way, felt pinned down and tormented by the tableau I had just lived through.

But the anger left me soon. I was washed out, vaguely guilty, empty. I slept. I dreamed of Mother in her black wool coat in autumn when I was in the first grade. She would walk me carefully to school, helping me with the intersections. I dreamed of the way she would hold my right hand tightly in her left and I could feel the firm, metallic pressure of her engagement ring and her wedding ring. She would talk to me aimlessly of this and that—the weather, the new dresses she was going to buy—and I would hang on every word. I loved her terribly.

That was a long time ago in Limbo-time since I first went back to Mother's pink bedroom. I have stopped counting days and years here but I know that a great deal of time has passed.

Sometimes I feel restless and I yearn to finish the editing of my past so that I can be reborn to continue in whatever plan whatever god there is has made, and I feel that I know what needs to be done. I need to go back to Mother's bedroom and merely close my eyes and keep them closed. *I must not look in that mirror.*

And God knows I have tried. I have gone back there a hundred times and more, have sat in that chair and heard that soft and throaty voice saying, "Now be sure you don't peek, dear," and have stared at that face, those hips, those breasts, that lovely flesh. I have swooned, over and over. Her movements exist now in frozen choreography in my brain; they seem to have erased everything afterward in my one life so that the ten minutes in the bedroom when I was six years old are what that life was *for*. My swoon is like the hub around which the rest of my life revolves; should I change it the rest of my life might scatter into empty and frightening disorder.

Yet it would seem simple to close my eyes or turn them downward, only once, to render those ten minutes of my past null and void, so that I may move on to whatever other destiny waits for me—to that pleasant Beth I have wanted to be, in my warm home with dolls and a pet cat and children's books. I can feel at times the yearning of Beth within me wanting to become real and alive in the world. And so I go back to the pink bedroom from time to time, but I cannot change a thing.

It is always the same: Mother, the bed, the small chair, the long mirror on the closet door. And I never close my eyes.

I pray sometimes to God that Beth, who will never live, will forgive me, for I cannot erase those ten minutes from my life no matter how many times I try. I truly cannot.

THE COLOR OF MONEY

Twenty years have passed since "Fast" Eddie Felson conquered the underground pool circuit. During that time he married and opened his own pool hall. But he's left that all behind and is now badly in need of money, and pool is all he knows. On the beautiful aquamarine waters of the Florida Keys, he ropes his former rival Minnesota Fats into a series of exhibition matches in the hopes of picking up a cable TV deal. But playing the old master, a terrible feeling nags at him—that he's sat on his talent and the best part of him is now gone. And when he vows to get back in the game— seriously this time—he finds a challenging road ahead, and the only thing standing in his way is himself.

Fiction

THE STEPS OF THE SUN

The year is 2063. Earth's energy resources are dangerously close to being depleted, a new world superpower has upset America's global dominance, and the threat of another ice age looms large. Fortunately, there is one man brave enough—and perhaps foolish enough—to venture beyond the planet to find the mineral resources that will secure the country's future: Ben Belson. One of the richest men in the world, Belson is haunted by personal demons and wanted for his unlawful space travel, but he will stop at nothing to fulfill his crucial mission—and discover a future greater than he could ever have imagined.

Fiction